THE EXILED HEIR

AUTUMN'S FALL SAGA

Jonathan French

OPEN ROAD
INTEGRATED MEDIA
NEW YORK

For Mom, who told me in no uncertain terms
that I had to finish this.

All rights reserved, including without limitation the right to reproduce this book or any portion thereof in any form or by any means, whether electronic or mechanical, now known or hereinafter invented, without the express written permission of the publisher.

This is a work of fiction. Names, characters, places, events, and incidents either are the product of the author's imagination or are used fictitiously. Any resemblance to actual persons, living or dead, businesses, companies, events, or locales is entirely coincidental.

Copyright © 2010 by Jonathan French

ISBN: 978-1-5040-9519-8

This edition published in 2024 by Open Road Integrated Media, Inc.
180 Maiden Lane
New York, NY 10038
www.openroadmedia.com

PROLOGUE

The darkness was larger than his cell. He could feel it waiting beyond the four walls for fathoms in every direction.

Above, below, all around, it loomed and it hungered. Squatting within its onerous center, the prisoner slept away his confinement.

Eyes open or closed made no matter in that perfect blackness. He slept, passing the time on the knife-edge of death.

Time!

No longer was it measured in suns and moons and the passage of stars. It was marked with the sound of an unseen hatch in an unseen door, sliding back, the cold iron scraping. Next, the barest disturbance in the stale air as bread hit the stone floor.

Quickly, the scraping would come again, the hatch closing, fastened with latches and spells. These noises were his only measure. Three hundred and two thousand, two hundred and twenty hunks of dry bread.

His prison was underground, deep in the Earth. Beyond the cell, beyond the endless darkness, he could hear the threatening song of Water, its heavy, hollow echoes waiting to crush him. Oh, but his cousins had fashioned him a dreadful hole in their sacred burial grounds! How they feared him, to place him alive in this place, far below the kingdom he once helped conquer, far above the kingdom that was once home.

Yet, he was no stranger to the embrace of the world. Long ago, he was born beneath its surface, but not in some cold gullet like the one which now caged him. No, he had matured within the world's fiery heart, nursed from its molten blood, bathed and basked in its heat until it was bound within his flesh. Long had he dwelt within the kingdom of Ghob, the seat of his people won from dragon-kind. It was a realm of sweat and steam, a realm of Fire!

When the command came, he had arisen with his brothers, back to the green, back to the blue, where even the noon-day sun was a pitiable candle to the flames of home. There, upon the surface, they had placed a crown upon a mortal's brow and known centuries of rule.

Those had been days of light and lust and war, and the only darkness was night. Night!

He wanted to laugh, but dared not, lest the darkness claim his tongue. This true darkness where they kept him, deeper than black, where the eyes see nothing and cease to matter, cease to exist.

There was no sight. What was night compared to that? A bad mimic, a poor mockery, a whore playing at being a lady.

Since his captivity began, the darkness gnawed at him, piece by piece. It took his eyes first, popped them into its blacker than black maw like sweetmeats. They were gone the instant they tossed him into the cell. It took his ears next, but not quickly. The blackness leaked in slowly, filling the cavities, dissolving his eardrums with cautious cruelty. He did not realize he was deaf until it was too late. He could dispel it if he spoke. Shouted. Laughed.

Cursed. Screamed. Screamed. Screamed. He never did, always waiting for the scraping of the hatch to remind him he still lived.

When he was first a prisoner, they did not keep him so deep underground, so deep in the dark. The gnomes, his cousins and captors, were forever ruled by the elves. Their soft ways insisted upon courtesy, even for an enemy. Mocking their mercy, he escaped. Once. Twice. Thrice. More. He escaped and they caught him. Once. Twice. Thrice. More and more. They caught him. And, at last, they put him in the dark.

Down in the deep, down in the dark, beyond where his sweet cousins laid their dead, that was where they chose to inter him. The gnomes banished him to the suffocating Earth, the undine sealing his cell with Water. The sylphs were kept away, for fear he would use the Wind to rekindle his powers. They kept him smothered, miles of ancient rock and dirt pushed in around him, dampening his power. His gaolers were venerable, blind gnomes, each a potent Earth Shaper and warded against him. Their sight had been stolen by the slow crawl of centuries or their eyeballs savaged in war by smoke and iron. They came blind to the darkness and would never see again.

But he did.

Unbeknownst to his captors, he could still call forth the flame to fight the darkness. But Fire burned, consumed, demanded sacrifice of its own and hungered for fuel. It was all he could do to summon a spark, barely an ember, a pitiful gnat of flame. He fed its craving heat and starved himself. Three hundred and two thousand, two hundred and twenty hunks of dry bread. He gave them all to the Fire.

They burned, and the burning sated him more than a hundred feasts. He transformed every meager meal into a single star in an endless sky. Ash in the eye of the blackness. An ulcer in the gut of his prison.

During those fleeting moments, he lived. He awoke. His eyes were restored and his ears returned to the sizzle of burning bread. It was tortuously fleeting. Quick. Painful. Ecstasy. Enough time to feel, to be whole, to breathe, to mark the wall, to count the days. Three hundred and two thousand, two hundred and twenty days. Each time, when the flame died and the darkness returned, he slept again to avoid following the Fire into nothingness.

When his hair grew long enough, he would cut it, gnawing through the filthy strands with his teeth. He mixed it with the contents of his slop bucket and summoned a true Fire. The blaze illuminated his cell, fed by his leavings, the waste from a wasted body. He danced and cavorted, cursed the darkness and counted the marks on the wall. Tallying the cost. Totaling his captivity.

Three hundred and two thousand, two hundred and twenty days.

Yet today, the meal had not come. No bread. No Fire. No count. No life. He was blind. He was deaf. He was asleep. He was dead. And he would not live again.

Panic seized him. This stomach of Earth would claim him at last. The Water would rush through the stones, the bile of the world, eager to digest him. He would be shit out into oblivion.

The walls of his cell imploded, punching his ears with concussive force, showering him with grit. Any moment, he would begin to drown.

Then, he smelled it. Burning dirt. The Earth was on Fire.

Burning. Smoking. The charred air filled his nostrils, arousing him.

Straightening, he stood.

Where once stood a rarely seen wall scarred with tally marks, there was now a great, gaping hole. Figures stood in the fissure. Squat of body, wiry of limb, flat of head, pointed of ear.

Not his cousins. His brothers! Saviors silhouetted in the magnificent glow of violent firelight.

Light!

Constant, steady and painfully bright.

He was free and a new day could begin! Another chance for conquest and vengeance. Another chance to burn, to burn it all and never stop until the scions of his King sat the throne.

As his brother goblins stepped into the shattered cell, he smiled and his atrophied voice was a croak.

"One."

ONE

Padric let his knuckles bleed and cursed his small hands. He dipped his injured hand back into the frigid creek and tried to watch his blood mix with the water, but the current was too fast.

Even this small creek cared nothing for his tiny contribution.

Padric spat in spite and gave a snort of self-mockery when the flowing water also overcame his foamy expulsion. His hand started to go numb, but he did not remove it, hoping the water would cool his anger as well as his pain. He knew it would do neither.

The betrayal of his hands was an old hurt. Familiar and constant, even predictable. Today, it was a welcome distraction from the rage that had been building for some days, threatening to boil over and tempting in its promise of relief. So far, Padric had resisted. He feared what would happen if he lanced the poison within and exposed it to the village. Mostly, he feared himself.

There was murder in his heart. He did not want to kill Eirwen, but even his small hands could complete that grisly work with confidence if fueled by the torment in his head.

Eirwen's callous disregard did not deserve such a punishment and Padric could think of what others would say if they knew his feelings, but the dark thoughts in his head were ungoverned by the opinions of others. In truth, Padric could think of no crime of either the law or the heart that would merit the killing of a woman. He remembered the widow who had given her daughters over to the gruagach last year. Even she was spared by the village council. Sent to the Knucklebones, of course, but still alive. Padric was not vicious or violent by nature, but the fire of passion burned the brighter when lust turned suddenly to hate. At least, that is what he told himself.

He took his hand from the water, closing the cold, swollen fingers into a fist. He watched as the blood welled up once more on his ragged knuckles, then shook his hand, ridding it of droplets both clear and crimson. He thought of returning to the border ditch, but tarried by the creek instead. The prospect of going back to the company of his father and the other men was not a welcome one. No matter that he was a man grown, Padric always felt the fool child around his father. There was no task Padric could perform for the benefit of the clan that his father could not do with greater ease and greater haste.

He had been sent to gather more spades and was happy to get away, for the tedious labor did nothing to distract his mind from Eirwen. His thin fingers and narrow palms had lost their grip on the hafts of the tools as he was backing out of the small stack stone shed. Foolishly, he had tried to carry four in each hand; to avoid the embarrassment of a second trip. His father could have handled five, maybe even six in each of his meaty clutches. Three was pushing it for Padric. His overzealous efforts were rewarded with nothing but an awkward juggle for control of the heavy tools which Padric quickly lost, but not before he had managed to rake the back of his left hand against the rough stone of the shed wall.

He made two trips after all.

After giving over the second bundle of tools with as much pride as he could muster, he mumbled some excuse and headed for the creek. He felt the eyes of the men on his back as he stalked away. He could almost hear the shake of his father's head.

He was such a failure. And it did not matter if his father or the other men thought it. Padric thought it of himself. His only real accomplishment was winning the affections of Eirwen, but even that prize had vanished in the time he had been away.

Two-months!

The thought of how quickly her feelings fled set his teeth to grind and sent his mind skulking into its darkest corners where schemes of blood and vengeance squatted in wait. He could escape in the mundane tasks of his daily life for only so long before some unexpected thought of her sent him seeking out those black fantasies in order to calm his anger and comfort his pain. But the more he thought on them, the more difficult it became not to act upon them, to bring them forth from his wounded heart and cast them in her face.

The sound of the creek dwindled behind him, and it was some moments before Padric realized he had set off toward the village. His jaw was sore from clenching. He tried to relax it before he ground his teeth to dust. He was vaguely aware of the maul riding in his injured fist and made his way along through familiar habit. His vision was clouded with the image of Eirwen's tear-streaked and pleading face, the body of her new and unknown lover wrecked upon the ground. He had never seen the man, but he knew Eirwen and her tastes. He would be fair of head, broad of shoulder and deep of chest, with a soft, simple face and not an ounce of cleverness behind his eyes. He would be the opposite of everything Padric was.

A growl of frustration echoed behind Padric's clenched teeth and his pace quickened. He did not know for certain where she was, but his anger told him he could sniff her out wherever she dallied. And if he found them together, so much the easier. There would be no choice then.

He reached the upper outskirts of the village, where his father's house lay. Instinctively, he gave it a wide berth, knowing that giving his mother even the briefest glance of him would alert her to his intention. Mothers knew that kind of thing. He would try Eirwen's rooms first, hoping to find her there, otherwise he would have to go up to the fort and search the ciderhouse. The thought of that familiar task only increased the burning behind his eyeballs.

By the bones, that girl could drink! And dance. Those were her true loves. Public displays of frivolity that only increased her appeal with the men of the village and the fort. That and the fact that she was slim, with a round bosom and backside, with long, red tresses, creamy skin and a flashing smile. But Padric knew the truth was in her eyes. Frigid and distant and overly large, so like a fish, and when they knew fear, they turned to puddles of panic. The shapely woman fled and the lost child was left behind. He had seen it many times. Despite all appearances she was not a lusty wench.

Padric often thought she had inherited the madness of her mother, for fear was her driving factor in all things. She gave her body readily enough and that could be forgiven had she found true joy in it, but she did not. It was simply that she feared to be alone. Two-months and she had replaced him!

The old widow that lodged Eirwen had not seen her that day. She looked up at Padric with an expression both lost and full of pity. Padric was not sure she recognized him and he began to wonder, not for the first time, how many men had come calling at this woman's door, seeking her itinerant lodger. Eirwen did not sleep here often, that he did know. He could not count the nights they had spent together, hidden away in some turf shed or root crib.

She would always drop off to sleep directly after and leave him lying awake, pondering the lack of true affection between them. He did not love her, then or now. That knowledge, however, did not ease the sting of her betrayal.

The widow slowly closed the door. Padric stood a moment and glared at the house. He wondered if Eirwen was doing the cooking or the washing for the widow as she was supposed to.

Shame settled over him with the thought that he had been one of the numerous distractions that kept Eirwen from tending to her duties and caring for this poor woman who had taken her in. Not again, he promised himself. He had wasted enough time with her and no matter what course this day would take, he would see himself free of that worthless wench.

He felt sick to his stomach as he made his way up the hill.

The familiar sight of the fort at the summit curdled his anger into a swimming nausea. He hated this place with its ciderhouse and barracks. The drunken warriors with their big talk and idle ways made Padric glad he was a farmer's son. The labors of the land were thankless, boring, and hard on the bones, but at least the result kept the children's bellies full. These louts did nothing but create more hungry mouths. Their killing made orphans, their carousing made bastards. Padric was glad his seax was still under his bed. He was like to use the large knife given his mood and he could ill afford a fight with one of these sword-wearing swine. He was not a fighter by any means. Had he the bulk, which he did not, he would still be a farmer's son. Farmer's sons were not fighters, they were strugglers.

He did not even glance at the sentries by the gate. Padric discovered long ago that simply appearing direct in action was enough to remain unchallenged by these fools. They perceived he had business in the fort, some menial labor to perform and were not interested enough to bother with him. Or they could have just been afraid of him. He deepened his frown and pushed on, leading with his shoulders as he passed through the gate.

It was a risk coming here. Always was for Padric. The warriors might try to goad him into a fight. They had before, sometimes with success. The drunken ones were the most likely to try or the ones that liked to mask their fear with bullying. Just another reason to hate this place, hate the fearful and simple-minded people who branded him.

Raven-touched. Death Cap.

Ill luck was in his blood or so the midwives said. Those ugly crones should be sent away too, like the child-selling widow and Eirwen's mother. He should have stayed away. Fafnir had asked him to journey farther and it had been tempting, but Padric felt obligated to return. His father needed him.

Padric's face twisted.

It was a lie he told himself then, as now. He was a burden to his father, a mouth to feed that was rarely useful except to draw the ire of the other farmers when a sheep died or the milk turned sour. For true, his uselessness was the reason he had been given leave to travel with Fafnir and he left with a high heart. This place could contain his revulsion no longer. The distrust of the village had poisoned him, he was full up with it and it leaked out of him.

He had idled here over tedious years, the sour frustrations of his own short-comings seeping out of him, soaking into every house and every person that surrounded him until he had poisoned them in kind. Leaving it all behind was like coming out of a long illness, a sudden breaking fever and then nothing but easy breaths, clear and deep. It was not a long journey, but how he had enjoyed it. He had been free of this place. Free of Eirwen, free of the endless work, free of a people who judged and feared one of their own simply because his hair was the color of coal. Padric hated them for believing such a thing. He hated them for making him believe it.

Eirwen always admitted to believing the things that were said about him. Rather than shunning him, she seemed to take pleasure in his reputation. It excited her and made folk talk of her also, which she relished. She had no family to speak out against their coupling, so their romance kindled. To her, he was a dangerous novelty and she was a child playing with fire. When she was in good spirits she delighted in reminding him what the villagers called him, as if he would take equal pleasure in hearing the unwanted titles. When angered she would spit them in his face and proclaim how cruel he truly was, how she feared for herself when he was near. He was rarely the cause of her sorrows, in truth, but it was easier for her to place the blame upon his dark brow.

The fort stank as it always did. Wet, freshly cut timbers, rotten apples, sweat, urine and Eirwen. All of these smells hit his nostrils, moist and unpleasant. He slogged through the thick, dark muck of the yard, not bothering to avoid the puddles. He was filthy enough from the labor at the ditch and was likely to be far more soiled before he was done here. It was possible he would be completely covered in mud before the day was out, buried in a rank grave.

He paused. Padric was not afraid to die. It would certainly put an end to his shame, his anger, his hurt. He was more afraid to simply do nothing, to walk away and continue to carry the crushing weight of his failures. He could brain Eirwen's new lover, his maul scattering pieces of the fool's skull into sticky, broken pottery. It was a sweet thought, but the balm of his enacted vengeance would be fleeting. Afterwards he would have to make a choice. Flee and be hunted, bringing worry and shame to his family or stay to face the knives of those seeking a blood debt and the fines that would ruin his kin. Warriors rarely had family, but they always had friends.

Either path brought sorrow and hardship to those he cared for; the people who cared nothing for the color of his hair and who endured the same gossip it created.

Fae-friend. Piskie kissed.

Padric did not care for himself, but he did care for his family. He would not let his selfish fury destroy them as well. But more than that, he would not make the villagers right. He would not be remembered as a killer, a madman, and the doom marked son that brought ill luck to his kin just as everyone said he would from the day he was born. Dead or alive, Padric could not bear their hearthside prophesies to come true by his own hand.

Padric emerged from his brooding and found his eyes staring straight at a discarded coin lying in the mud. He stooped and pinched it from the mire, careful to keep his skinned knuckles from touching the muck. It was one of the tin pieces used to pay the garrison of the fort. All but worthless to them, but a welcome find for Padric. He had seen only a few coins in his life and held fewer still. He gave it a halfhearted rub on his jerkin to clean it and held it up to his nostrils, breathing deeply. Padric knew the scent of tin from the village foundry and from his father's tools. It was strange that this small piece of the same metal would smell so differently. It was repulsive and comforting, alluring and venomous.

Just like her.

He made for the ciderhouse.

The pungent heat of the turf fire packed around his head as he pushed through the door, making his nose run. All the clinging smells of the fort gathered closely together in the gloom of the wretched place. Padric coughed once and swallowed hard. A drunken minstrel performed for a few apathetic wastrels, his voice high and scraping. No one paid Padric any mind. He was just a dirt covered farm boy and they were well into their cups. The ciderwife was tapping a keg in the corner, her strokes clumsy, her hair free and lank. Padric approached, the maul now propped on his shoulder, his head slightly bent in the low room. The woman did not look up.

"The girl Eirwen. Do you know her?" he asked the top of her greasy head.

The ciderwife stopped, tossing the bung mallet contemptuously on top of the barrel. She looked up with swimming eyes, took a sneering breath to answer and stopped short.

Fear. It was always first.

Her moist face hardened into a sickening scowl and she retrieved her mallet, resumed her labor, did not answer.

Hate. It always followed.

Padric flicked the coin onto the barrel just as the mallet was coming down. The ciderwife jerked and the mallet head smashed into the wood, caving in the top of the barrel. The sweet, cloying scent of fresh cider cooled the air around them.

"That is for her. When she comes in tonight. As many cups as it is worth. See that she gets them."

She always delighted in calling him names, feigning her affection as if he was some sorcerer king of legend, to be feared and worshiped. Mocking him, in truth. He remembered her favorite. He smiled then. Smiled at their memory. Smiled at her foolishness. At his own.

"Tell her to drink deeply. Compliments of Padric the Black."

The bees were angry and that made Rosheen laugh. *Little buzzing bastards.* They chased her as far as their tiny minds allowed, then dutifully turned back to the hive as soon as they forgot why they had left. Rosheen took her prize to the lowest branch of an old alder and settled in to wait. *Still all orange and gold, friend.* She missed the green.

Her arms were sticky to the elbow, as was her breast, where she had been clutching the honeycomb, which now called to her.

She broke off a fistful of the dripping comb and began munching while she waited, licking her fingers once the morsel was gone. The rest of the comb lay in her lap and the honey oozed its way over one knee, snaking its way down to her toes. Rosheen watched it drip down to the dense golden carpet below and listened for the soft tap of each droplet as it struck the fallen leaves. She thought about eating some more, but decided to save it for Padric. *He won't want any.* But she saved it anyway.

The honey trail on her leg had hardened by the time he came tromping into the grove, his every step dashing yellow leaves out in front of him. She giggled. *He thinks he's changed.* He looked up at the sound of her laughter and frowned.

"You have *not* changed," she said to his amusing face.

"Quiet, you," Padric said half-heartedly.

Rosheen considered that a moment. "Are we leaving now?" she asked.

Padric did not answer. He stood looking across the grove, his eyes focused on nothing. Brooding. *Like always.* Rosheen wondered if Padric was happiest when tormented. His moods had grown so dark of late, so different from the gleeful child he had been an eye blink ago. She had laughed when he took his first steps, for he was already taller than she. Now, she barely reached his knee.

And even at twenty he is still such a child. Try as she might, she never saw him as anything else and probably never would. He knew it, too. He was clever. *For a mortal.* It bothered him that she saw him thus and he was forever out to prove otherwise. Mostly it just made her smile.

She scooted off the branch and let herself glide down onto his shoulder. She sat there for a minute staring at his temple, silently daring him to turn her way. *This always works.* The tension built up quickly as he continued to stubbornly keep his head averted. Rosheen had to bite her lip to keep from laughing when she saw his jaw muscles begin clenching. She fluttered her wings so that they brushed ever so slightly against the back of his ear. *He hates this.* A frustrated inhalation of the mouth was immediately followed by a defeated exhalation of the nostrils. He turned his head and looked at her, still frowning.

Rosheen held the honeycomb out in both hands. "Want some?"

"No," he said, followed by an off-put growl. "You are all sticky!" He gave a small leap to the side, forcing her to take flight.

She let her laughter escape as he made his way over to the base of the alder and sat down.

"Stickier down there," she told him, still hovering. He looked up and gave her a confused twitch of the mouth. "It dripped," she finished and pointed above him at the branch she had been sitting on.

"Aaawwwwhh!" issued from Padric as he rolled back to standing. "Hhhhrrr!" followed the discovery of the leaves sticking to his rear end. Rosheen tried to contain herself, but failed when Padric proceeded to try and dust the leaves off his backside, only to have them stick to his hands instead. Her laughter drowned his curses as he scrubbed his palms on the bark of the tree.

"I hate this place," he mumbled, stooping to fetch some damp leaves from the ground to clean his hands further.

"Then leave," she said. "And this time, do not return." She threw a little force behind the last word, knowing it would aggravate him further, but unwilling to let the point go by unmentioned.

"It is not that simple," he said, tossing the leaves back to the earth.

Yes it is. "Why?" *If I must play this game.*

"I am needed here." He attempted some conviction, but failed.

"That has never been true."

He turned swiftly towards her, his eyes burning. "You know nothing of it!"

"I know what you have told me and what I have observed and that is all. That is enough."

Padric's eyes went dead, his shoulders slumped slightly and his skin went ashy grey. *Do not give up, damn you!* Rosheen knew that his anger was the only thing with enough momentum to send him from this place. *He needs to go.*

"People hate me because of you," he said. There was no malice in his voice, just resignation. "Eirwen hates me because of you."

She loves you. Hates me. And herself. "She is foolish. A feckless cow. And nothing but a child."

"We're all children to you, Rosheen." He walked wearily a few paces away and slumped to the ground, his back against a rotting log. She flew over slowly and landed a few feet away from his outstretched legs. His head rested on the water swollen wood, his eyes staring up into the branches overhead, but not to the sky beyond. He looked beaten, petulant and ill. Lost in his own miserable little life. Worthless to the world. Worth even less to himself. *They waste so much on this foolishness.*

She went over and hopped up onto his knee, began walking up his leg, then his stomach until she reached his chest. Here she sat, munching her honeycomb, and looked him full in the face.

"What do you want from here?" she asked.

His eyes flicked down towards her. Rosheen rode the rise and fall of his chest as he breathed deeply.

She pressed on. "To jump the jug with that strumpet? To remain here, a farmer of little skill? Distrusted by your neighbors? Your father and mother . . ."

"Enough," Padric snapped. "I know all of this."

"Then catch up with that metal-peddling dwarf before it is too late. Get back on the road where you were at least content."

"I was never content. I have no gift as a peddler."

"And you are a capable smith? A fine warrior? Skilled minstrel?" She shook her head. "Stop looking for what you are best at and start living with what you are capable. Out there traveling, at the very least, you have not the time to whinge about. And you are never in one place long enough for your simple-minded people to cast their suspicions at your feet. Go to the places where being dubbed a Fae-friend is not a slight nor a cause to fear."

"I made my choice to return," Padric said. "To leave again would seem like weakness."

"Returning was weakness. Fafnir asked you to stay and help him." She watched his jaw clench again. "Who here asked you to return?"

A smirk cracked his frown. "Certainly not you, you flippant piskie."

"I did not need to. I knew you would be back." She leaned forward. "Now eat this. I am tired of holding it," she said, stuffing the honeycomb past his lips.

Padric tested the edge of the seax with his thumb and frowned. It could use some attention from a whetstone, but there was no time. He wanted to be gone before the sun set. It was dangerous sleeping out in the wilds, but Padric feared finding himself still in the village come the dawn more than he did anything that may wait out in the dark. He had made up his mind to leave and somehow it was easier to depart with the dying light. Mornings were too stark, too real and tempting with false promises of fresh intentions. It was better to leave now. Let the night swallow this place as he turned his back on it forever.

He had slept out before on herd watches and sometimes with Rosheen for no reason at all. It was not a comfortable way to spend a night, for certain, and the prospect filled Padric with a healthy dose of caution. He turned the big knife over in his hand, relieved that it would be with him. Padric had worked with tools all his life, but the seax was the first he had ever possessed that was not meant to turn soil, cut turf, or break stone. It was a stout fighting knife, wide bladed and well-balanced. From blade tip to pommel, the weapon was longer than his forearm and hand combined. And it was steel. Not the crude, heavy, black iron that the warriors from the fort wielded, no, this metal was smoke colored and light, seeming to shine with an inner fire.

Padric had worn the blade for close to a month so that he might better protect Fafnir's goods and grown used to the weight of it on his belt. Secretly he had nursed the hope that he could one day barter it from Fafnir. Padric remembered his surprise when the dwarf had insisted he keep the knife after their journey had ended.

After all, he had refused the peddler's offer to journey further and such generosity made Padric feel shameful. Fafnir simply told him he would need it if he was to journey home alone and went back to tightening the bags on Ingot's back. It had only made Padric feel worse about his choice.

He pushed the seax back in its sheath. He was going to reverse that choice and prove his worthiness of the gift. He pulled his heavy woolen coat over his head and belted it at the waist, the weight of the knife close and reassuring across the small of his back.

He checked his pouch for the fourth time to ensure his flint, hook, and line were still there, then rolled a candle in his blanket and tied it into a bundle. He grabbed his mantle and hood from the peg on the wall, wrapped them about his body and secured them with a brooch. He stopped and squinted hard at the floor, willing it to tell him if he had forgotten anything.

"If you are looking for your axe, I put it in here."

Padric blinked out of his mental inventory to find his mother standing in the doorway holding a large, round object.

There was a smile on her face that did not reach her eyes and a hesitance in the way she held the object out to him.

"I covered one of our apple baskets in goat hide and then with otter pelts. It should keep most of the wet out. These straps . . . so you can carry it across your back."

He took the pack from her and looked it over. Solid.

Elegantly simple. Brilliant. Just like she was. He took his time inspecting it, afraid to look up again. She was the one thing he would miss from this suffocating place and he felt sick that he had to turn his back on her along with the rest. The last time he left was not difficult for him. Maybe he knew he would come back. Maybe he did not know what he was leaving. He did now.

He was her son and a walking curse. A shadow she bore from her own body. He was given names that tainted them all. The ridicule had turned him sour at an early age and often he turned his spite on those who fed him, clothed him, held him when the loneliness was too much to bear. He feared she blamed herself for his lot in life. Her own life would improve with him gone. In a short time, the hamlet would no longer be able to lay their sorrows at her door; the door behind which slept the black head of her ill-luck offspring. He would go for good this time and things would be better. And it would almost break her, again. It did not matter what others said of him. He was her son. And it would pain her to see him go, but she would bear that just as she bore the disdain of her community, for him.

"This is grand, mother. Thank you." His voice was thick, the words choked out. He glanced up briefly and had to immediately look down again when he saw her face.

Her voice quavered. "There is food in there. Some eggs and bread. A flask of milk. You eat, hear me."

"Yes, mum," was all he could get out and they embraced to save each other from their own selfish tears. She seemed so little.

Over her shoulder, Padric saw his father. Waiting, awkward and strong. Padric felt embarrassed, but he did not let his mother go. He would wait for her to be ready. She deserved that. At last, her arms relaxed slightly, but she hooked her hand in his arm and stood by him, wiping her tears with her free hand while his father approached. Padric set his jaw and swallowed hard.

"Take this," his father said, handing over a sizable coil of thick rope. "Many things can be solved if you have good rope."

And then he held out his hand. Padric clasped it and could not help but smile as his thin fingers and narrow palms were enveloped by the strong grip of his father's large hand.

***

Sun is already down. Late leaving. Rosheen sat on the roof of the house and watched as Padric shouldered his pack and began walking away from his parents. *Three times. He will stop and wave three times.* She sniggered when he turned and raised his arm for the fourth time. Padric's father had turned and headed off behind the house to tend the goats at the second wave. His mother stood for all of them. She continued to stand there watching once he disappeared into the woodlands.

"Take care of one another," she said, without turning.

"We will," Rosheen told her and flew off after him.

TWO

". . . no business, behind a wretched plow. Swing a sword, push a plow, oh it is all the same! Phfaw! Follow some dumb beast across a field when you have no more sense than the animal! Have the same horns, might as well have the same brain! Which is to say none at all! Why listen to me, though? Oh no, would never think to do that! What for? Stubborn fool! Have to be noble and bull headed, help wherever there is need. People need to fend for themselves, only way they will learn. Go around pulling them out of trouble and look what happens! By my oath, if I can get him to . . . Damn you, Bulge-Eye! Stop crushing the flowers!"

Deglan pitched a clod of dirt at the great toad, which fell quite short. Bulge-Eye did not so much as twitch. Other than the constant swelling and deflating of his throat sack and the occasional blink, he had not moved for hours. And he was nowhere near the flowers. Deglan continued to glare at him for a moment, but it was impossible to win a staring contest with a toad.

Deglan sat back on his heels with a frustrated blow from the nostrils and returned to the plant in front of him.

It had taken him most of the morning to find this patch of vervain and it was almost too late. Deglan cast a calculating eye at the sun and then turned his scowl back to the dense purple blooms.

This was the best of the lot, he was sure, but he needed to wait a few more moments until the sun was at its most high. He hated waiting, but patience was always needed when time was of the essence. He slung his herb satchel off his shoulder and threw the flap back, removing a roll of fine linen and his water skin. He reached for his small trowel, but paused before his hand grasped the handle.

"Better to do this by hand."

Deglan leaned carefully forward until his forearms rested on the ground, surrounding the vervain protectively and then slowly stretched his legs out behind him. He lay belly down on the cool ground, his nose almost touching the petals.

The sun warmed the bald spot on the back of his head, but he paid it no mind. His eyes were fixed, the right one narrowing and opening convulsively.

His nostrils flared as the aroma of the vervain grew with the ascending sun. Deglan's stubby middle fingers pressed gently into the soil and traced a shallow furrow around the base of the plant.

Slowly, he settled the heels of his hands into the furrow and began kneading the dirt. His eyes closed as the deft movements worked his hands deeper into the Earth and he opened his mind to its embrace. There was a moment's resistance, but Deglan pressed his need, bluntly and humbly. The roots loosened, straightened and slid out of the soil as he cradled the vervain in his cupped hands.

He rose as smoothly as he could manage back up onto his knees and gave a winced curse as his hips popped. He turned the uprooted plant carefully and inspected it for injury. Satisfied, he held it one-handed and reached for the linen, wrapping it loosely around the roots. Pulling the plug out of the skin with his teeth, he took a mouthful of water and spit in gently over the bundle. Deglan let the air out of his lungs, then jerked his head skyward and looked again at the sun.

High noon.

"Ha!" Deglan shook his fist at the bright orb. Then again at Bulge-Eye. "Ha-ha! Teach you to tell me my business, it will!"

Bulge-Eye blinked lazily.

He gathered up his things and walked briskly over to the toad. His short legs ached and he was grateful he decided to bring Bulge-Eye along. A hike back to the village was not a welcome prospect.

"Wish I had left you behind, you great warty beast! More than likely you will make me crush this plant with all your lurching hops."

He grit his teeth and pulled himself up onto the saddle, all the while cradling the vervain to his chest with his free hand. They would not be able to cut through the woods. The toad's bulbous body made navigating between the trees too tedious, so Deglan urged his mount back across the low fens where his long, powerful hops could eat the miles away. After a while, he settled into the cascading rhythm of the ride and let the wind cool the sweat on his neck and around his ears. The sun was bright and the sky clear, for now, but Deglan took note of the grey clouds looming in the west.

He had been lucky to find the vervain when he did, but his brow refused to relax. Retrieving the herb, while a happy step in the right direction, did not end his task. He still had a good deal of work ahead of him. The type of work he did not relish.

They left the fens behind within an hour and came to the lush, rolling, boulder-strewn fields that hugged the River Trough.

Deglan came to one of the stone walls the humans built to denote the boundaries of their fields and keep their sheep contained. Had he been afoot, the wall would have been almost as tall as he was and a nuisance to climb. Bulge-Eye leapt effortlessly over, allowing toad and rider to continue on their way unimpeded. Many of the enclosed fields were vacant this far from the village proper, but Deglan saw a small flock of sheep in the distance and directly in his path. He swore softly to himself but did not halt Bulge-Eye. There was no time to go around.

They closed the distance swiftly and jumped the wall into the occupied field, scattering the sheep as the giant toad's heavy body landed beside them with a soft thud. Within seconds the dog was upon them, placing itself firmly between flock and toad, barking fiercely. Bulge-Eye regarded the growling creature with as much interest as he did most things and sat back on his hind legs, waiting for Deglan to direct him. The herdsmen followed swiftly, his long tunic flapping at his legs, staff firmly in hand. He skidded to a halt at the sight of Bulge-Eye. Deglan snorted quietly. Time was, humans never would have balked at the presence of a riding toad, but that was long ago. These later generations never did get used to seeing Bulge-Eye, who was twice the size of their sheep.

"Call that damn animal off, Laoire, before I have Bulge-Eye eat him!" Deglan yelled at the herdsmen.

The man snapped out of his stupor and calmed the dog down with a few simple commands and it ran off to gather the fleeing sheep. "My apologies, Faery Doctor!" Laoire stammered. "I did not know it was you!"

Deglan had to fight the urge to roll his eyes. He loathed that name. "Peace, Laoire. The fault was mine, but you must excuse me, I need . . ."

"Is that the herb?" Laoire cut in. "You have found it! Will it make him whole?" The herdsmen face was slack with hopeful wonder.

"Not stood here it won't!" And with that, Deglan kicked the toad into motion, leaping the man in a bound. They struck the muddy herd road soon after and Deglan punched the sides of his feet into Bulge-Eye's flanks, urging him to greater speed as the road climbed a small hill. The conical roofs of the round, wicker-work and stone houses of the human farmers came into view over the rise. Above-ground dwellings still seemed strange and impractical to Deglan, even after centuries of living among them.

"Never do keep all the rain out."

Bulge-Eye flew over the crest of the hill and down into the center of the village, his feet barely touching the road before he was in the air once more. The few women and children in the square saw him coming and made way hastily, knowing the urgency of his errand. They shot past the mill and made for the opposite side of town. Movement caught Deglan's eye as they passed the alehouse and his mouth twitched downward at the sight of the laden mule tied in front of the building, but he did not slow Bulge-Eye's pace.

On the village outskirts, Deglan nudged Bulge-Eye away from the river and set off down a narrow goat track where the land turned hilly once more.

Faabar's hut came into view and Deglan was relieved to see smoke coming from the chimney. Forgetting his cramping legs, he hopped down from the saddle and pushed through the door. It was gloomy inside and hotter than a forge, which only intensified the stink.

"I told you to keep it warm in here," Deglan said, going to the fireplace and kicking the turf apart. "Smells like you're trying to cook yourself!"

He grabbed a stool and dragged it under the window.

Mounting it quickly he reached up and threw the skins aside, allowing light and fresh air into the hut. He set the vervain carefully on the sill, before it wilted in the stifling heat, then stepped down and turned to face the room.

Faabar's massive bulk lay propped up on his pallet, his feet facing the fire—exactly the way Deglan had left him. He shook his head.

"Girl did not show up to tend the fire," Deglan declared with certainty. "I knew it! Foolish child! I will have a word with her father. If she thinks . . ."

"Do not," Faabar's voice quavered deeply. "Please. Do not. She is afraid. It is cruel to make her come here."

"Nonsense," Deglan said, approaching the pallet. "She has known you her whole life. No need to be afraid now. Someone should simply tell her that all fomori are so gruesomely hideous. In fact, you are one of the comelier ones."

Faabar attempted a chuckle, but managed only a weak grunt.

"It is the leg. Uglier than me. Children should not have to see such things."

Deglan sighed and looked into Faabar's face. "You sent her away." Faabar's eyes were cloudy and feverish, but they did not look away. "How am I going to get you up on your feet if you keep mollycoddling the help?"

He pulled the linen roll from his satchel and tore off a long strip with his teeth. He soaked the strip with a pour from the water skin and placed it on Faabar's brow. An almost useless gesture in the grand scope of healing, but Deglan learned long ago that mending bodies had a great deal to do with the mind. A wet cloth is comforting and calming; a pleasant distraction from the true, more stressful methods of healing still to come.

The fever was causing Faabar's horns to soften and split.

He would need a salve of yarrow root and lard, but that could wait.

Deglan took his gibne from the satchel and placed the wide end on Faabar's chest, cupping his hands tightly around it to create a strong seal. He bent his head and inserted the narrow end of the instrument in his own ear. Faabar's heart pumped strongly.

"Well, let's take a look at the cause of the dear child's distress then," Deglan said as he removed the gibne. He fixed Faabar with an exasperated stare. "We would not want to upset her any further now would we?"

Deglan moved down the pallet to Faabar's right leg. The wrapping plaster of wood anemone had yellowed considerably since Deglan last changed it, causing his frown to deepen. Faabar's eyes stayed fixed on the ceiling as they always did when Deglan tended him. Women will most always look at what is wrong, men rarely, and warriors never. He broke the plaster free from the leg with practiced squeezes of his fingers. Deglan let the used plaster drop to the floor.

"Damn," he muttered and bent to retrieve it, using the motion to get a good sniff of the wound. The sour odor of long damp flesh drifted up from the wrinkled edges of the wide, ragged wound in Faabar's thigh. No reek of rot. Not yet.

Deglan squinted at the split flesh, hoping to see some change for the better. More of a rend than a cut, the plow blade had done some vicious work, to the muscles most of all. They were not only torn and slashed, but pulled mercilessly out of place. It had taken the farmers too long to stop the spooked ox and Faabar had been dragged over several fields. Deglan had arrived quickly thanks to Bulge-Eye. He had the blood stopped and the wound bound within moments. It had taken six of the strongest men to lift Faabar, but they managed him into an ox cart and transported him to his hut within an hour where Deglan began cleaning the manure-filled soil out of the cavity. He had done everything he knew to do and more, using all the knowledge of his craft learned over centuries of study and practice. It should have been enough. But the plow blade had been iron. Deglan wanted to spit.

The wound refused to close, despite all his efforts. It remained gaping, taunting him like some horrible smile with skin for lips, muscles for gums and bones for teeth. Had Faabar been pure Fae, he would have died in the field, but the fomori were mortal once before receiving Magic's blessing and that kept him alive. Alive and suffering. Blessing, indeed. This was not the deserved fate of a warrior, of one who had seen Summer. Humans and their iron. Their soft minds and hard metals.

"That dwarf is back in the village," Deglan said casually, returning his mind to his work. Faabar continued staring at the ceiling, but Deglan felt his body tense.

"With the mule?"

Deglan snorted. "No, with a herd of field mice! Yes, with the mule!"

"And my sword?"

"Well, we *were* having a dozen pints of ale and I planned on asking him. But then . . . I don't know if it was the drink that got to me or the injury I had to look in on. . . ." He shook his head in mock bewilderment then threw up his arms. "Something made me forget to ask him!"

"Ask him. When you see him, ask him. I would like to see it." "Toad shit! Ask him yourself." Deglan threw the discarded plaster into the fire.

"You cannot . . ." Faabar began.

"Listen to me!" Deglan whirled on him. "I will take no deathbed requests from you! Not today! Not tomorrow! You are under my care and under that care you *will* recover! No one tells me my business! Especially not simple-minded fomori who care more for swords and the tears of little girls then they do about their own lives! And if you cannot find the will to get well on your own, then find the strength in the knowledge that this village needs you! The very people whose foolish labors saw you hurt are now defenseless because you had to play at farming!" He stopped. The last was too hard and he knew it. Thankfully, Faabar had stopped listening after—

"Defenseless?" he managed to pull himself up to a sitting position.

Deglan went over to the window and stepped up on the stool again to retrieve the vervain. This was as good a distraction as any, intended or not.

"Kederic's warriors . . ." he said, pulling the vervain apart carefully into two equal halves, ". . . rode out this morning. I saw Acwellen and his bunch headed back to the fort while I was in the forest, looking for this." He held up the split plant, then proceeded to the hearth and retrieved the bronze kettle. Thankfully, the girl must have seen it was filled before Faabar absolved her of her duties.

"Does Brogan know?" Faabar asked, some of the old force returning to his voice.

Deglan put half of the herb in the kettle and hung it over the fire. "It was barely dawn when I saw them and I was already miles from here. Must have skulked out in the wee hours." He began gently plucking the blooms off the remaining half of the vervain. "That early, I doubt anyone saw them. Maybe Slouch Hat did, I cannot say. He surely would have told. At any rate, I am sure Brogan knows now." He walked over to the head of the pallet and retrieved his satchel from the floor. He removed his bowl and muddler, then turned his back to Faabar as he went back to the stool by the window. He sat down, and placing the vervain blooms in the bowl, began grinding them down.

"He will want to go and speak with Kederic," Faabar said.

"And I cannot go with him."

"Brogan would do well to stay far and gone from that man. They have said enough to one another, for all the good it's done."

Deglan finished the grinding and hopped off the stool. He walked over to his satchel and pulled forth a sizable clay jar sealed with a thin piece of linen tied around the mouth. This he set on the pallet next to Faabar's leg. "Now hold still." Deglan scooped a portion of the ground petals out of the bowl and began massaging them into Faabar's wound. The fomori's powerful hand gripped at the bedclothes, but he did not make a sound of protest. Deglan repeated the application until the bowl was empty, paying particular attention to the exposed bone. Faabar let out a shuddering breath when Deglan removed his fingers for the final time.

"Tell me about this sword," he said lightly as he reached for the clay jar.

"You have no care for that," Faabar said.

"If I am to ask the dwarf about it, I should know of what I speak." Deglan untied the linen from around the mouth of the jar.

"Go on now. Tell me of it."

"I requested it to be fashioned in the old style. A great two-hander. 'Twil be almost three times the height of you, Deglan Loamtoes!"

"Fearsome," Deglan said and peered carefully into the clay jar. "You traded dearly for it, I know. Will it be ornate?" He reached slowly into the jar.

"Nay!" Faabar snorted. "It will be made for war. Simple and well-balanced. With a grip of tough leather."

Deglan pulled a large, blue-black beetle from the jar.

Holding it gently by its bloated body, the insect filled Deglan's palm. It kicked at the air, its long pincers biting at nothing. Slowly, Deglan lowered the beetle onto Faabar's leg so that it straddled the open wound. "Anything else?"

"It will be steel," Faabar said reverently. "Dwarf-forged, it will hold an edge like no bronze blade can."

Deglan forced the beetle's head down and it bit deep into Faabar's flesh on either side of the gash, causing a hiss to escape from between Faabar's clenched teeth. The powerful pincers came together, pulling the skin closed. With a quick jerk, Deglan twisted the beetle's body from its head, leaving the pincers embedded in the flesh, closed tightly in death. Deglan quickly reached into the jar and produced another beetle. "And what shall you do with this grand weapon?"

Faabar snarled. "Damn you, you leeching gnome! Enough of this prattle. Do it and have done!"

Deglan nodded and proceeded. The heads of six beetles lay embedded in Faabar's flesh before the wound was sufficiently closed. "I'm sorry, friend," he said when he was done at last.

"Will it work?" Faabar asked between breaths.

"I need to stitch it closed now, to be sure." Deglan produced a large, slightly hooked needle from his satchel and a roll of gut string. He began stitching the spaces between the beetles' heads. "Leeching gnome?" he asked, casting a sideling glance up at his patient.

"I ask your pardon," Faabar replied. "It was an unworthy thing to say."

Deglan laughed. "I have heard much worse. Mostly from delivering mothers." He finished another stitch. "And anything is better than Faery Doctor."

"You will always be something of a wonder to them, my friend."

"As are you," Deglan said, "when you are actually walking."

Faabar pushed a long breath at the ceiling. "We know them from children. And just as they become accustomed to our . . . gifts, they are gone and we start over with the children of yesterday's children. I have heard there are human settlements where Fae-folk are no longer welcomed."

Deglan gave a gurgle of contempt. "That is the dwarf talking. Gossip is all he is good for."

"This business has gone on too long," Faabar muttered to the ceiling after a few minutes.

"Sewing up your tough hide is hard on the fingers," Deglan said without looking up. "And stubborn patients heal slower."

"No," Faabar said. "Between Brogan and Kederic."

Deglan continued his work. "*That* business was never any of ours. Bunch of moon brained nonsense as ever there was. Freemen. Bondsmen. Human stupidity, always have said. Never live long enough to learn from their mistakes. Memories are too short."

"It was simpler when the gnomes lived here," Faabar grunted.

Deglan expelled an airy chuckle. "Oh yes, because *we* never stirred the pot!" He shook his head at the wound. "Ah well. Let folk live where they may."

"Even goblins?"

Deglan stopped his sewing, his head jerking up to see Faabar staring at him with his stupid bestial face, laid up and helpless, challenging Deglan on a question he did not have the sense to answer for himself. He held the stare for a long moment and felt his pull on the needle tighten. He had half a mind to leave, let the brutish bastard lay there and die.

The kettle sang out shrilly in the fireplace. Deglan blinked hard, looking back down at the injured leg. He finished the sutures, knotted them and bit through the excess string. He went over to the hearth and plucked the kettle from the flames. He grabbed one of Faabar's enormous tin cups from the shelf and filled it with the boiling tea, the strong smell of vervain escaping in the steam. He marched across and handed the cup over.

"Drink this down," he ordered, then fetched his tools, stuffing them into his satchel. "I will return tonight." He stalked out the door without a backward glance.

He struck off down the goat track on foot and heard Bulge-Eye fall in behind him, his slow pace forcing the toad to adopt the lumbering waddle he used when hopping was unnecessary. Deglan cut a path cross-country, wishing to avoid the village entirely. He was in no mood for questions regarding Faabar's condition from slack-jawed humans, and if he saw that dwarf peddler, he was of a mind to poison him.

"Use my own words against me, will he? Fever or no, that is not the act of a friend! Goblins, he says! Bunch of rutting, grey-skinned, gap-toothed, vicious, lying, lecherous, piss-smelling vermin! Live where they may, ha! Hob's a daft bugger, always have said. Faabar, too!" He turned on his heel, causing Bulge-Eye to come to an unexpected halt. Deglan thrust a finger in the toad's large face. "And I will tell you something about that damn fomori.

Slaughtered countless of them bandy-legged rodents, Faabar did!

During the Rebellion and decades before besides! He's killed more goblins than I have ever said a bad word about."

Bulge-Eye did not argue.

Deglan turned and resumed his trek, angrily swatting at bugs that were not there. He had a mind to go straight home.

There was work to be done, other more minor maladies to treat among the villagers. But he kept walking, regardless. The thought of trying to concentrate on proper dosage and the correct moisture content of poultices made the back of his ears itch. He hiked on into the hills, justifying his dalliance in his own mind as an excuse to search out rare herbs to replenish his stock. It was still early afternoon, plenty of time before sunset to deal with the complaints of the good people of Hog's Wallow.

Deglan came across a patch of turnips and stopped to dig out a few. Not much good for medicinal use, except to alleviate his grumbling gut. He took his meager lunch up a rocky knoll that afforded a good view of the surrounding countryside. Here he sat with his back against a moss-covered boulder and eased the tension in his back. Bulge-Eye squatted close by, seemingly uninterested in the view. The wind was stronger at this height and Deglan took a moment to button his vest up under his chin. He brushed the soil from the turnips as best he could, while looking out on the horizon.

"She's still green, our dear old isle. Give her that. Trees've been red for too long now, but the rest of her, she's still green." He bit into the largest turnip and crunched, chewing thoughtfully at the verdant fields below. Without looking, he hooked the remainder over his head at Bulge-Eye, who opened his wide mouth to catch the flung vegetable and swallow it whole.

Deglan could see Bwenyth Tor in the distance, maybe a day's walk from where he sat. The hill was as high and brooding as it ever was, the blackened ruins of stonework still visible on its crest. The green had not yet managed to reclaim the entire Tor, Deglan noted bitterly. Some things will not allow themselves to be forgotten. He squinted hard at the rocky debris which he knew to be the remnants of walls, battlements and towers, wishing he could wipe his thumb across the vista and clear them away for good.

There had been so few folk left in those days. Not enough able bodies to bury the dead, much less the broken reminders of war.

Kederic and Brogan should meet in the shadows of that place and allow those with longer memories to talk some sense into them. Or beat their soft, mortal heads against the stones.

He should not have gotten angry, Deglan knew, but Faabar knew better than to bait him so. He would make the salve for Faabar's horns when he got back to his burrow and look in on him tonight as he said he would. Everything would be fine, and neither of them would need to discuss the matter further. They had seen Summer together and fought the coming of Autumn side by side.

Some friends need no apologies.

Deglan pushed his hands back against the boulder and shoved himself upright. The day was getting on and there was nothing like a good view to get a person looking inward for longer than was healthy.

"You are just wasting time, you fat sack," he told Bulge-Eye.

He took one final look off the rise and was turning to climb into the saddle when something caught his eye in the fields below.

Movement, at first, was all he saw. He peered harder and shaded his eyes from the glare. It was a good ways off, Deglan estimated.

Possibly halfway between his perch and the Tor, but he was certain it was headed in his direction and maybe a little more to the east. It was big, too. Deglan would have had difficulty seeing even Faabar at this distance and the fomori was taller than the largest man in the village by a full head. There was something unsettling about the way it crossed the fields. Its movements were too regular, too steady. Tireless. Wrong.

Coming from the Tor. Towards him . . . and a bit to the east.

"Buggery and spit!"

Deglan heeled hard into Bulge-Eye's sides, turning him down the hill. The toad made the descent in half a dozen long hops, switch-backing down the slope. Deglan decided to forgo the road and cut back across the fields, alerting any herdsmen or farmers he found along the way. Word would spread quicker that way.

They came out of the highlands and Deglan could see the regular square partitions of land separated by stacked stone. He could make out small clumps of sheep dotted among the flat green and steered his mount towards the nearest herd. The sheep brayed and scattered as he came leaping over the wall. Deglan called out for the herdsmen. He stood in the saddle and cast about, but could see no one and there was no answer to his call. Not a dog, not a whistle. He moved on to the next flock, cursing when he found it unattended also. Maybe, with luck, someone had already seen and raised the cry. Why else would they leave their animals unguarded?

He cut hard across the fields and found the Trough within moments. Keeping the river to his left, he kicked his toad harder, pushing him south. He could still alert the men of the village and have them prepare to flee. With Faabar crippled and Kederic's warriors off and gone it would be fruitless to stand and fight. They would run. They must. Or they would stand and protect what was dear to the last. Fools. Human fools. Either way, Deglan would give them time.

The town lay before him and Deglan thanked the Earth and Stone for the speed of the great toad. The villagers had already gathered behind the ale house, but they were making no preparations to leave, nor was there a single weapon among the men. Why were they just standing there? Deglan knew he was not too late! There was no chance it could have gotten here before him!

He reined Bulge-Eye up on the edge of the gathering and jumped from the saddle. The people were simply standing around talking softly to one another, whispering behind hands and steering children away. This was not the hurried panic of a forewarned attack. This was something else. They were tense, still and awkward, standing around what Deglan supposed was the eel pond, but he was too short to see what was so remarkable about that. He pushed his way through the cluster, mutterings of relief passing through the crowd at his presence. He broke through the press and stopped short. Deglan hung his head at what he saw in the pond. Death was not coming to Hog's Wallow. It had arrived.

THREE

This is taking too long. Rosheen peered up at the darkening sky without removing her chin from her hand. The moon was already visible and it would not be the turn of an hour before they were overtaken by the night.

"Want me to do it?" she asked hopefully.

"No." Padric did not look up and continued to fret with the feeble pile of twigs and wood shavings. Rosheen blew air noisily between her lips and began drumming her fingers against her face. She had been sitting atop Padric's pack for some time now and had worked several new braids into her hair. One of them was now woven with a squirrel bone she found on the first day of their travels. She toyed with it idly and tried to fight her boredom.

There was nothing to do but watch Padric struggle to get the fire started, his flint in one hand and the absurdly large knife in the other.

Damn thing.

The knife was almost bigger then she was and Padric doted on it more than he ever did that girl-child from the fort. Still, it was not iron and that was something. Rosheen shifted uncomfortably on the pack at the thought of Padric's axe tucked away inside. It was more tool than weapon, the scourge of firewood, but his mother had wanted to leave it out for Rosheen's sake, which was a kindness. Rosheen had insisted it be brought along. There were beings in the wilds other than piskies with an aversion to the cursed metal.

A tautly whispered curse issued from Padric as he struck tiny showers of sparks from his flint with the steel knife, desperately trying to ignite the tinder. *The wood is too wet.* It had rained lightly but steadily all day as they made their way down the narrow herd paths and game trails that cut through the woodlands.

Padric was in high spirits for most of the day despite the weather and he was as fresh four days into their journey as he had been the first night out. Today, Rosheen was forced to ride along on his shoulders after her wings failed to keep up with his aggressive pace.

Their journey would take well over a fortnight, but Padric seemed determined to do it in mere days. Of course, his easy mood had fled when they stopped for the night and could find no dry wood.

There was a bark of triumph from Padric as the tinder caught fire and he hunkered down to carefully feed the flame with bits of kindling. Rosheen pushed her eyebrows as far up her skull as they would go and watched without movement or comment.

Padric nurtured it with care and then with increasing force as his frustration grew in opposition to the wilting flame. The tiny fire weakened and withdrew from the wood. A pitiful stream of mocking smoke leaked upward from the pile as the hope of light and heat died. Padric stared at it scornfully as it drifted away into the treetops, where dusk lay dying behind the leaves.

"The wood is too wet," Padric told the ground. Rosheen lowered her eyebrows and grimaced in his direction. Padric sat back on his heels and hunched his shoulders, staring off into the darkening trees. *Mustering his pride.*

"Ask me nicely," she said.

Padric looked up at her, his mouth tightening and then looked off into the trees again. He looked at her. Then the trees.

Her. The trees. Rosheen waited patiently.

To the trees he said, "Would you kindly aid me in this task . . . O wise and benevolent child of the wood?"

Rosheen jumped up dramatically on top of the pack.

"Weak-minded and foolish mortal! Your feeble entreaties have swayed us and we will now ensure that you do not perish from foe or cold here in the terrible wilds! Such is the generosity of the Fae-folk!"

She hopped down and made her way over to the fire, affecting an alluring sway of the hips. *After all, Faery saviors must appear wanton and mysterious.* She over-exaggerated her sultry swagger as she approached and by the time she reached the woodpile, she and Padric were both laughing at her ridiculous gait. She attempted to recapture her provocative air as she knelt by the failed fire, but when she looked at Padric, his hand clutched tightly over his grinning mouth, she gave up the charade.

"Hush," she told him and took a deep breath, her eyes closing.

She could still smell the smoke in the air and the charred tinder, but mostly her nostrils took in the damp, cloying smell of wet Earth and moist wood. She pushed the Earth away and focused on the wood. It was dead, lying in the pile, soaked through from the rain, bloated with water that no longer gave it life. She opened her eyes and gazed at the pile, penetrating the twigs and logs until she found their core. Her breath quickened and she pulled at the water, rhythmic, coaxing. She invited it out into the air in misty waves, allowing it to settle on her skin and dampen her naked flesh. It beaded in her tangled hair and hung on her eyelashes, coalescing and sliding in rivulets down her bare back.

She shivered hard and her eyes regained focus. She looked up at Padric who sat staring at her, his head shaking slightly from side to side.

"Now hurry up and get it lit," she told him, still dripping. "I am getting cold."

Padric was able to ignite the tinder on his first strike of the flint and within minutes he had a crackling fire going, the flames licking merrily at the bone dry wood. He had managed to hook a fish during their brief stop along the River Trough earlier in the day, so they shared some hazelnuts Rosheen harvested from the forest while the catch cooked slowly over the fire.

I wish we had some cider. "You know what would be lovely?" Rosheen said.

"Cider," Padric returned bluntly.

"No," Rosheen tossed back, aware of her pouting lip.

"We will be in Hog's Wallow soon," Padric said, popping a hazelnut into his mouth. "Fafnir said they have good ale there."

"Bwlech!" Rosheen mimed a gag. Padric sat back against a large fallen tree limb, chewing absently. Rosheen let the silence go on as long as she was able. "They usually drink mead."

"Who?" he asked, barely coming out of his trance.

"Dwarves." She made a face that suggested she found the word more disgusting than the prospect of drinking ale.

Padric shrugged. "Fafnir is well-traveled. This is not the first time he has traded in Airlann, I know. And by what I could gather, he has been all across the Tin Isles. Albain. Sasana. Maybe even beyond to Outborders."

Rosheen scoffed hard through her nose. *Tin Isles. Metal-minded dwarves.* She looked at Padric and saw he was casually tossing hazelnut shells into the fire, deep in his own head. *Again.* Probably thinking of dark, dangerous places, wishing he was traveling through them. *Or wondering if he has the courage to do so?*

Rosheen had feared Padric would turn back and go home during their first night in the wild, but he surprised her with his determination to rejoin the dwarf. His long, inward silences were still prevalent, but they seemed more contemplative and purposeful.

He was thinking through to solutions instead of swimming through the murkiness of self-doubt and private fears. He was even asking for her help in good faith, which was a rare and treasured pleasure.

She knew he was annoyed when she flew around the bend in the trail and joined him that first night. He wanted to do this alone, as if that gave the endeavor more importance. Still, he did not run her off or make much of a fuss at all. He simply fixed her with his hard eyes for a long moment, then nodded his head toward the trail and pressed on. Maybe he was truly growing wiser, as humans seemed to do so suddenly in their short lives.

"What will you do if you do not find him in Hog's Wallow?" she asked. In truth, she did not much care, but she wanted something to talk about. The night was too young for silence.

Padric stood and placed more twigs in the fire. *He has no answer.* "There is a human warlord from Sasana. Kederic Winetongue, they call him. He resides close to the village and has men in need of steel weapons. Fafnir will likely go there next."

"And if he is not there?"

"Someone will have seen him."

"And if they have not?"

"Rosheen!" Padric's voice snapped against the trees.

Too far. She went back to playing with her braids.

Padric awoke to a chill, cloud filled sky. The same bleak morning that always seemed to follow a night spent outdoors. He never really slept at night in the rough. Too many strange sounds and even stranger silences when there were no walls or people around. There was something primitive and alert that awoke in his brain when his body tried to rest in the woods. The nights became something to endure and survive, offering no comfort. Padric always found sleep with the coming dawn, when the primitive side crawled back into the cave of his skull, relinquishing its vigil to the sun. His slumber was fleeting and cruel, tempting him with relief as the sky called him to rise and get moving. Padric felt a shiver in his ribs at the thought of crawling out from under his blanket. He lay for several long minutes, staring up at the cold, new day, watching his breath escape in a vapor. He tried to will the trapped warmth of the blanket into his bones and store it there for the day ahead.

Gritting his teeth, he flung the blanket aside and rolled to his feet. The cold squeezed down on his bladder mercilessly, forcing him to hurry stiff-limbed away from the smoldering fire and relieve himself. A twisting spasm ran up his spine when he released his water and he felt instantly warmer. He stood and scanned the surrounding forest, his piss spattering sharply on the fallen leaves, the trees as grey as the sky in the morning mist. The relief in his bladder spread and he felt his body relaxing, grateful to find himself whole after the long night and looking forward to another day of traveling that would bring him closer to warm food and the illusory solace of shelter.

He ambled back to the campsite and stoked the embers of the fire with a stick. Rosheen was nowhere to be seen, but that was nothing to be alarmed about. She was rarely around when he woke and he never could reason out where she went at night. Fae-folk had curious ways and mysterious knowledge about the wilds. Padric had never seen a piskie village and was not entirely sure they ever slept indoors. He knew Rosheen's wood lore was vast, despite her casual attitude towards all things. He was grateful and more than a little relieved she had come along, not that he would admit to it.

When he left Fafnir, the trip home was an adventure.

Padric was filled with confidence from his new experiences and the seax at his belt. He saw it as a test of his resolve and his abilities, eager to be home and show Eirwen his competence, prove to his father that he was a capable man. Worthless sentiments in the end, Padric saw that clearly now. The choice of returning to Fafnir was sound, but the prospect of passing the journey alone was not a welcome one. He knew this path now and while it was not wholly familiar to him, it had certainly lost the allure of adventure his childish fancies placed upon it some weeks ago.

He did not know why Rosheen had come with him and did not ask, for fear that she would see him as ungrateful and leave. He knew he was foolish in the ways of women and Rosheen puzzled him far more than Eirwen ever did. When Padric was a child, she was a fascinating and delightful playmate. She showed him the plants and animals that thrived in the lands around his village, often seeing him home well after dark. He grew and matured, while she remained unchanged, yet new things about her became captivating.

Her wild hair, all tangled with braids and beads, shells and bones.

Her lean, strong body, unclothed save for the intricate patterns of blue tribal markings that adorned her perfect skin. Ever-young and untamed, she became the focus of the lusty stirrings of early manhood. But she was his only friend, more like a sibling and the attraction towards her felt forbidden and shameful. He came to understand that she was immortal, a piskie, and that he did not truly want her, but yearned to find her among his own kind in the girls of the village. At last, after long years of loneliness, he found just that. Or so he thought. Now that was well and done, and Padric was on to a fresh life, far away from anything painful or familiar, except Rosheen . . .

"Are you finally awake?"

. . . who was always with him.

The sparse trails that led through the forest were choked with stones and exposed roots, making the footing difficult, but Padric and Rosheen traveled hard through the early morning. The sun could not penetrate the dense clouds, leaving the forest a dim, mist-laden place. Padric became drowsy listening to his muffled footfalls and the stuffy sound of his own breathing. He yawned deeply, forcing his eyes closed, his ears filling with a hot roar. A rock turned under his foot, throwing his weight harshly backward.

He fell hard, his right elbow and hip slamming into the unforgiving trail. Rosheen hissed sympathetically, as he rose gingerly to his feet.

The pain settled into his bones as a dull, pulsing ache, but he was more concerned about the damage to his pack than he was his own injuries. Slinging the basket off his back, he checked it over carefully, ensuring the wicker had not been irreparably crushed.

Thankfully, his mother's sturdy handiwork held true. Padric glanced up at Rosheen, feeling quite the fool.

"Want me to lead for a while?" she asked.

Padric glared at her hovering an arm's length from the ground. "I doubt that would help."

"Well then . . ." She made a sweeping gesture towards him with both hands.

Padric chuckled darkly, rubbing his sore elbow. "Forgive me for holding you up."

"Oh, you're fine!" she exclaimed.

Padric gave her an indignant scrunch of his face. "I never said I was hurt!"

"I know," Rosheen said lightly. "So . . ." The sweeping gesture came again.

Padric gave a defeated groan and headed off down the trail, slinging the pack over his shoulders as he went. The trail narrowed and deepened until it was little more than a ditch, with barely enough room for Padric's feet. The trees crowded close on either side, making it impossible to climb up and travel outside of the tight furrow. The trail meandered in irregular turns, forcing them to follow an indirect path. Eventually, it led them gradually downhill, and then turned into a knee busting descent over natural steps of stone and earth. Padric chose his footing carefully, gripping the trunks of trees and low branches where he could to steady himself and slow his momentum. A break in the trees gave them a view of a grassy clearing below, nestled in the saddle of the hills. Padric took a moment to catch his breath and pointed down at the clearing.

"From there, the path is unknown to me. When I last came through here, I entered the clearing from the northeast and turned south for home. We will need to go west to reach Hog's Wallow."

From this vantage it appeared their chosen path flattened out into rolling fields for a fair distance as it left the dell, before entering the forest once more. Thankfully, it did not appear to turn uphill again.

When at last they reached the valley, Padric's legs were quivering and it felt odd to be walking again on flat ground. He tossed a glance skyward. It could not be much past midday, but the continued absence of the sun made it difficult to determine. The clearing seemed a reasonable spot to rest, but the prospect of easier terrain encouraged Padric to push on. The darkening clouds gathering to the east solidified his decision.

A breeze filled the dell, bringing the smell of approaching rain. Padric did not want to be caught out in the open during a storm, and if his sleep was to be fretful, he would rather it was at least dry. He set off to the west at a brisk pace, allowing the flat ground and long strides to stretch the tension out of his legs. The open terrain allowed Rosheen to travel alongside him, her wings propelling her leisurely along. The pair made good time and covered a fair distance, but the clouds continued to follow, rolling steadily up their heels. The land grew increasingly scrubby to their left before becoming overtaken by the edge of the forest. To their right, the fields grew steep and rocky, so they stayed in the flat lands between, keeping course until they would have no choice but to enter the woodlands once again.

Padric turned and faced the approaching clouds, continuing to walk backwards. The storm head was the color of black wool and moved threateningly towards them.

"Grand," he muttered dryly and turned back around. "I doubt we can stay ahead of it for long."

"Then we get wet," Rosheen said dismissively.

They pushed on, the edge of the forest pressing ever closer to their left and dominating the view ahead. Padric hoped there would be a trail, but he was now traveling blind. He did not know this country, but trusted that Fafnir would not embark on an overly dangerous route. Ingot was a sure-footed mule, but laden with steel tools and weapons he was likely to step wrong without a decent trail and Padric doubted the peddler would take such a risk. There would be a trail. There must be. Unless Padric had already made an error and taken them in the wrong direction.

The ground to their right leveled off slightly and Padric saw something resting on one of the lower hills. He stopped for a moment. It was stonework, the ruins of what looked to have once been a tower of some kind.

"Rosheen," he said and nodded toward the structure.

"Ruins," Rosheen said with little interest. "Quite common in Airlann, Padric."

"They might be," he replied. "But with a storm coming, common just became a happy chance." He struck off toward the higher ground, the slopes of the surrounding hillsides leading naturally toward the tower, making the going much easier than he anticipated. Occasionally, he saw square cut stones poking through the grass under his feet, giving evidence that there was once a proper road leading to the crest of the hill.

As he drew closer, Padric saw there were actually remnants of two towers, the shorter one closest to him had been obscured from a distance by the larger tower behind. Both were round, squat drums, the rear tower at least four times the height and girth of the forward, which still held a gate of two large bronze doors, green with age. Two long, curving walls swept back from the front tower and joined with the larger tower, which loomed some distance directly behind, forming a yard between the fortifications. Moss covered the stonework in thick patches and many of the blocks had loosened and separated, some had fallen from the structure entirely, leaving sizable holes.

Padric approached the gate, the doors as tall as he, and looked up to the crest of the gatehouse. He guessed he would have to stand on his own shoulders twice to be able to reach the top.

The doors had no handle or chain to pull and Padric did not bother to try and budge them. He circled the base of the tower to the left and walked along the crumbling wall until he found a place where the failing stonework left a sizable gap just above his head.

Springing up, he caught the edge of the gap and began hauling himself up. He found easy footholds in the loose blocks and was able to climb with ease until he gained the hole. There he squatted and surveyed the yard within which was overgrown and dotted with fallen stonework. It was almost as big as one of his father's fields and lay protected behind the embrace of the walls, with the towers shielding it at both ends. From where Padric sat, he noticed that the roof of the smaller gatehouse tower had fallen in, destroying the entrance to the yard and choking the interior with rubble. The large tower at the rear had no visible gate accessible to the yard. Puzzled, Padric climbed down inside the walls.

Rosheen flew through the same hole. "Why are we in here?" she asked impatiently.

"Good shelter," Padric replied. "If . . . we can find a way inside there." He pointed at the rear tower and headed towards it across the yard. He scanned the interior of the walls as he walked.

Despite their dilapidated condition, it was clear that the top of the walls held sizable walkways, with crenelations facing out as well as in, which was odd, and no remnants of stairs remained in the yard, leaving Padric wondering how anyone reached them. Even the fort back home had stairs and also . . .

"Ladders," he said aloud.

"Sorry?" Rosheen looked at him quizzically.

"They must have used ladders," he said. "To gain the walls."

They made it to the base of the rear tower and Padric craned his neck upwards. "Traveling with Fafnir . . . I saw a watermill. In Seanach's Ford. I thought that was tall, but this. This is . . . four, maybe five times the height." He shook his head while it was still turned skyward. The mill had been mostly wood and narrow at the top. This was pure stone and as wide from top to bottom.

"Wonder who built it," he said, looking over at Rosheen. She was turned away from the tower, facing the yard. "Do you know?" he asked the back of her head.

"How would I?" she said flippantly, turning to him.

Padric shrugged. "Dunno. It's been around a while, same as you. Thought you might have an idea."

"No," she said, smiling. "It's a ruin, Padric. There are hundreds of these across the isle. Once here, now gone."

"Not gone," Padric said, spreading and turning his arms to encompass the yard. "Old, but not gone. And they were once new. If there were . . . are hundreds of them, you must remember something."

"What for?" she asked with a look of genuine confusion.

"To look back on the past."

"I was there then. No need to look back."

"But what about this place?" Padric felt himself growing frustrated. "It had a purpose. It was built by someone and then was destroyed or abandoned. Do you want that to be lost?"

Rosheen flew over and placed her tiny hands on the sides of his face. She looked directly at him. "If I spend time remembering the past of some broken tower, then what I will lose is this moment, when I was here with you, now. And if I return in a hundred years . . . you will be gone. Of course, I will be able to sit and ponder the origins of this place, but I will be unable to recall our time here together, because I missed the day it happened."

Padric nodded, but was not satisfied. "The only thing I will remember is getting soaked if we do not find a way in." He detached from Rosheen and sidled closer to the right wall, which was in better condition than its mate. "There must be access to the tower from the walls," he said, shrugging out of his pack. He opened the top flap and removed the coiled rope his father had given him. "Do you think you can fly one end up and tie it off up there? Think I can climb it."

Rosheen looked as if she would refuse, but flew over and took the end of the rope from him, then was up and disappeared over the battlements, the trail of rope dangling. Padric grabbed the pack up again and put it on his back while he waited.

Rosheen popped back over the wall. "Done," she said. "Try not to break that anvil of a head."

Ignoring her, Padric took the rope in his left hand, found solid purchase in the wall with his right foot and began hauling himself up. He was able to climb the pitted wall quite easily, but kept the rope in his left hand to be safe. Within moments, he crawled up and over the crenelations, slightly winded but none the worse for wear. As he suspected there was a doorway built into the side of the larger tower where it met the wall. Whatever was used to seal the entrance was long gone and the portal yawned back at Padric, black and open. He started making his way down the wall toward the tower.

"Padric . . ." Rosheen chided him.

He looked back at her. "Just going to take a look." He stopped short of the entrance and looked inside. The dreary day cast little light into the structure and Padric could make out only the dim shadows of a refuse filled chamber. An unpleasant odor of stale air, animal droppings, damp and rot wafted from within.

Padric leaned slowly into the chamber.

He jumped back, his heart slamming into his throat at the hideous, grinning face crouching just inside the door. He went for his knife, but his brain sped past his reflexes, forcing him to stop. It was a dead badger, eyes hollowed and teeth exposed by decay.

Padric laughed aloud to dispel the lingering fear and looked back at Rosheen. "Just an animal. Crawled in here to die."

"Good place for it," she said.

"Good place to wait out an afternoon rain, too," Padric said. He plucked the stiff corpse up from the floor and flung it over the wall. Taking his pack off he propped it just inside the chamber and hunkered down next to it, removing the last of the cheese his mother had packed. Rosheen came in and settled on the pack.

"How can you eat that?" she said her nose turned up.

"You love cheese," he replied.

"I meant after seeing that badger."

"Well, he was a little too far along to cook." Padric gave her his slyest smile and bit off a hunk of cheese.

"Lovely," Rosheen responded with an eye roll and a slight chuckle.

The rain started to come down outside, sparingly at first and then the skies opened up to a full downpour, soaking the stones of the wall outside. Padric watched it fall, hoping it would pass before long. He wanted to get a few more miles behind them before nightfall. It occurred to him that Fafnir had never mentioned this ruin and Padric began to worry that he truly had led them astray. It was too prominent a landmark not to mention and Fafnir had provided detailed descriptions of his trade routes before Padric departed. He sifted through his memory, trying to pull something out that would tell him one way or another if he had made a mistake. He was certain when they reached the clearing that he had chosen the correct path, but in his hurry to outpace the storm it was possible he missed something. He clenched down on his jaw, angry at himself for not knowing, wishing the rain would stop so he could double back to be sure. It would cost precious hours, but he could not take them through the woods again without checking. There were very few settlements in the rough country and they could wander around the wilds and never find one, running out of food until . . .

"It was a Boot Rest," Rosheen said.

Padric squinted at her.

"This place. They called it a Boot Rest," she continued.

"The Goblin Kings built them all over the isle after they usurped the Seelie Court as a way to keep the Fae-folk under control. Humans, too."

Padric was confused, but he did not dare interrupt for fear that she would stop talking. There was a resolve to her face he had never seen before. She looked directly into his eyes as she spoke, knowing he did not understand. There was pain in her face. Not pain for herself, but pain for him, as if she were stealing something from him that she knew would never be returned.

"Goblin soldiers . . . the Red Caps, were everywhere in those days, terrorizing the villages, stealing where they wished. They used these to regroup, to sleep, to divide the spoils." She took a deep breath. "And when any tried to oppose them, they were brought here. Herded in, whole villages, through the gatehouse and into the killing field between the walls." Padric looked out at the wall. The wall with battlements facing in as well as out. The wall with no stairs.

"Why are you telling me this?" he asked when he was sure she had finished.

"Because you were doubting yourself," she said. "It was in your face. He would not have spoken of this place, Padric. Not even a dwarf would do that."

Padric nodded slowly and looked away. Then something occurred to him. He feared to ask, but needed to know. "Rosheen?" he ventured at last. "In the legends, the Goblin Kings were mortals. Men like me, who ruled the goblins through sorcery. Was that the way of it?"

Rosheen nodded. "Yes. It was."

Padric thought a moment. "Why do you not hate us?"

"Humans suffered as much as Fae in those times. Maybe more. Your people fought alongside us to restore the throne." She smiled sadly. "The Goblin Kings were terrible, but few. Mankind should not be blamed for the actions of Oathbreakers. The Court understood that."

"Why did you not want to tell me? We would not have come here."

Rosheen did not hesitate. "Because this is as I said it was, a ruin. Broken stone cannot preserve the evil deeds of long ago. It cannot give power back to those that did the slaughter, any more than it can return the lives of the good people who died here."

Rosheen smiled to herself as Padric fell asleep. He had reclined against his pack, stretching his legs out in front of him, to wait out the rain. She sat behind, lightly stroking his hair. It was not long before his eyes closed and his breathing grew even. *Walls and daylight. He feels safe here.* Rosheen wished she shared his ease.

The rain fell just outside to her right, while the shadowy outline of the doorway into the tower proper beckoned her with blackness. She felt pulled from both sides, tempted to flee out into the wetness and freedom, at the same time being morbidly seduced by the abandoned interior of the ruin. She told Padric there was no power in these stones, but she felt a sudden urge to worship them as a monument to the victory of her kin. She wanted to gloat inside the tower, dance inside the wreckage and laugh at its demise.

She leaned forward and kissed Padric lightly on the forehead, willing him gently into a deeper slumber. She flew off the top of the pack and wove a quick charm above the door leading outside, while behind her, the tower continued to call. Rosheen turned toward the gaping darkness, took one look down at Padric and flew into the embrace of the long dead past.

When Padric opened his eyes, he found the rain had stopped and there appeared to be a couple more hours of scant daylight remaining. He had not meant to fall asleep and rose with a mild curse. Grabbing his pack, he walked out onto the wall.

Rosheen sat on one of the crenelations facing the countryside, her feet dangling over the side.

"How long?" he asked.

"Barely an hour," she assured him.

Padric nodded in relief. Rosheen had been right, the rain passed quickly and after descending the outside of the wall, Padric led them away from the awful towers without a backward glance.

The hills were slick with the wet grass, but they quickly came down to the fields and entered the forest. The air was heavy and chill from the rain, the carpet of fallen leaves shiny. Padric found the trail immediately and they struck off between the trees.

He could not stop thinking about the terrible things Rosheen had told him. In twenty years, she had said little about herself and now Padric questioned how well he truly knew her. He knew she was immortal, like all Fae, but he could not picture her living outside of his awareness. It always felt as if they had grown up together, and while she was wise in the ways of the world, she often acted the flighty child. If the fireside tales were true, the Goblin Kings were overthrown almost a thousand years ago at the Battle of Nine Crowns, an event that had become little more than myth to the few people who remembered to recount it.

Padric's mother used to tell him the story of wicked Jerrod the Second, last of the Goblin Kings and his iniquitous son, the Gaunt Prince. Both father and son met their downfall at the hands of the Fae-folk rebels and their allies, intent on restoring their immortal Elf King to his rightful seat. Jerrod himself was thrown from the balcony of his castle by one of his slaves. A little girl, if the story could be believed. The Gaunt Prince was in the field when his father died, making war on the Fae rebels with his unstoppable metal killers, the Forge Born. The legend said the Fae crafted a powerful spell, creating a magical heart within the Forge Born. In grief over their bloody deeds, they cast down their weapons, leaving the Gaunt Prince to face the Fae armies with only his fanatically devoted goblin soldiers. In the end of the story, it always came down to three: King Goban Blackmud of the gnomes, Aillila Ulvyeh, daughter of the Elf King and the Gaunt Prince himself, a merciless warrior and wielder of dread powers. Goban Blackmud was the only survivor of that terrible conflict, the victory restoring the Elf King to the throne of the Seelie Court, at the cost of his only child.

Padric delighted in hearing the tale when he was small.

Goban Blackmud was his favorite character. Once, he even spent an eve spinning the tale for Rosheen, who sat listening intently, making engaged noises of shock and fear at all the best parts. Fool child that he was. It came to him now that not only had Rosheen lived through the events that to him were nothing but bedtime rhymes, she may have witnessed them firsthand.

The forest grew close around them, thick with bramble, and what little light remained of the day barely penetrated the dense cluster of black limbs and crimson leaves. Even with night approaching quickly, Padric was glad they had not stayed in the tower. The folk of his village were a fearful lot, despite the fort and its warriors. Their ways were bred into him. The irony that he was one of the things they feared was not lost on Padric, but every beast fears the larger predator, and the wilds were nothing if not a great, hungry hunter waiting to swallow the foolish or the unwary.

As the night pressed in around them, Padric found that he was both. In avoiding the phantom peril of the tower, he had led them straight into the very palpable dangers of the forest without enough time to even build a fire, the most basic illusion of shelter and safety. Padric fought the panic rising from his stomach and barred it from reaching his head. He stopped and looked around at the thick black columns that had once been tree trunks, strangely elusive in the feeble moonlight. Beyond the trail, the forest was too wild, too dense and overgrown to find a proper camp. They would have to fight through thick bracken, boulders and marauding hedge to move just a few feet. If they waited out the night on the trail with no fire, they risked freezing, but making a fire while so exposed was a beacon for anything that might cause them harm.

There was no choice, they had to press on.

"Rosheen," he said calmly. "We will need some light."

A hollow intake of air issued from Rosheen's silhouette. A faint glow appeared, illuminating her cupped hands. Padric could now see Rosheen's face, her mouth pressed tightly into her hands.

With each breath, she seemed to suck more light into the hollow behind her fingers, until she and Padric were bathed in a soft blue glow. Rosheen gently unfolded her fingers, revealing a shimmering blue blaze of cold fire that danced just above her left palm. The forest around them was now visible for several yards in every direction, the trees casting eerily dancing shadows across the path.

"Better stay close," Padric said and jerked a thumb towards his shoulders. Rosheen flew over and sat atop his pack, her legs straddling the back of Padric's neck. From here she could see over his head and direct the light to fall along the path. Padric drew the seax, a comforting weight in his grip. Armed now with knife and light, he set off down the trail at a cautious pace, keeping his eyes as much on the trail as on the forest to either side. It grew cold quickly and Padric felt Rosheen shiver against the back of his neck.

He stopped and carefully drew his hood up over his head and her body. He mused at the thought of the villagers seeing him now, stalking forward in the dark, long knife in hand, Faery-fire glowing from the deepness of his hood. They would need a new name for him then. He smiled. Fancies of tormenting his clan gave Padric a sinister courage and kept his mind from envisioning what could be lurking just outside the nimbus of Rosheen's conjured fire.

He was not entirely certain what to do, so he kept moving in hopes that some solace would present itself before long or discover that his steps had brought them to the sunrise. His feet were getting numb from the cold and the hard trail, but he kept walking, knowing that to halt would only invite the fear at the edge of his mind, at the edge of the light, to sweep in and feast upon them. His world shrank to the small patch of lit path in front of him, flanked by the ever-present trees, cold, suffocating sentinels, guarding against the return of hope.

Padric stopped abruptly on the trail. He held his breath, taut and rigid. He felt it creep in. After the long, stark silence of the forest, it was not difficult to detect. Life. Somewhere in the woods, off the trail, to the left. Some strange sense between hearing and touch told him it was out there, skulking in the dark. But it was not dark. He saw it now, a warm glow, pulsing through the slits between the horrible trees. Firelight.

"Rosh," he hissed and the blue glow of Faery-fire died.

Padric stood for a moment, fearing the firelight had been a cruel trick of the eye, but as Rosheen's light died, the distant glow remained.

"A camp?" Rosheen asked from inside the hood.

Padric nodded and continued down the trail, keeping the mysterious fire in sight. Within a few minutes the light was almost directly to their left, some distance into the forest where the trees grew less dense. A voice issued from the woods, causing Padric to duck down instinctively. It was faint and low and Padric realized it was not directed at him. Someone was out there, with a fire, speaking in the dead of night among the trees. It was a man's voice, Padric was certain.

"Find a good high branch and stay there," he whispered to Rosheen.

"I can look easier than you."

"No. Folk in the wilds can be suspicious of Fae. Best I go."

Padric felt Rosheen wriggle out from under the hood and fly upwards. "Tread softly."

It was difficult to make his way, despite the ambient light from his destination. He picked carefully through the trees, wincing at the loud crushing of leaves under each step. Low, unseen branches scraped and tickled unpleasantly at his face as he slid along, half-blind. The thick, pleasant smell of something cooking flitted into Padric's nostrils, pulling him closer, knife still in hand.

The voice grew nearer, easier to discern. Padric caught the intonation of a question, but not the words. If there was a response, Padric could not hear it. He could see the fire clearly now, bright between the trees. A tall figure moved around the flames, tending a stewpot hung in the center.

Padric doubted he could get any closer without being heard and trying to sneak up on someone in the dark was not likely to further their hospitality. He had to make a choice and he had to make it quickly. Rosheen was out there, alone in the cold. Gripping his knife tighter, Padric knelt down close beside the nearest tree.

"Ho the camp!" he yelled. The tall figure quickly rose and fetched something close to hand, turning sharply to face Padric's direction.

"Who calls?" the figure barked back steadily.

"A traveler seeking only warmth! Not to give or receive harm!"

A moment's pause. "Come ahead, then!" the figure called.

Padric rose slowly and reluctantly sheathed the seax. He made his way noisily over to the fire, noting the figure kept his back to the blaze so as not to blind himself. As Padric entered the clearing he saw the figure was indeed a man, tall and lean of body and face. He wore the rough clothes of a woodsman, skullcap pulled tight, his long, hooked nose and sunken cheeks cut sharply in the shadows created by the firelight. A grizzled vulture, the man appeared older than Padric's father. A great chopping axe rested easily in his large, knotty hands.

"A kindness," Padric said. "I thank you." He made his way over to the fire, to give credence to his claim and allowed the man a chance to look him over.

"Foolish to wander these woods at night," the man said, pulling a horseshoe from his belt and holding it out to Padric.

"It is that," Padric agreed, taking it. Their eyes locked for a moment and then the woodsman nodded, taking back the horseshoe. Padric's heart sank. Rosheen would not be welcome here.

The man put his axe aside, but not too far, and went back to tending the stewpot. At a glance it was clear that this was no camp, but the man's home. A small, wickerwork hut sat atop a small rise in the land, several dozen paces from the fire. A woodshed and charcoal billet were near to the hut, also well out of the small depression where the fire was built. No doubt the man kept a small herd of pigs close by, left to forage in the surrounding woods.

"Don't you go begging now. We eat shortly," the man said.

Padric turned to answer this blunt offer of food only to find that the man was facing away, not speaking to him at all. Padric was surprised to see a small child, a girl, hunkered down on the other side of the fire. Her knees were drawn up to her chin, the soot blackened toes of her grubby bare feet stuck out beneath the hem of her ragged dress. So tight was she rolled into herself that all Padric could see of her face were the wide eyes, terribly beautiful in their vulnerability, framed by shiny tresses of near-white blond hair.

After so many hours in the dark woods, the harsh light of the flames must have caused Padric to miss her when he entered the clearing.

"Good evening, little miss. My name is Padric." He smiled at her. The girl stared at him briefly then looked back into the flames.

"Not get a word from that one," the man said gruffly.

"Nary a squeak since she took ill."

Padric kept his face friendly. "She seems fit now."

The man turned his lips down and shook his head. "She's not spoke nor barely eaten in close on a week."

"She will, now the sickness is out of her," Padric replied.

"Aye," the woodsman nodded. "Close thing. Thought to lose her."

"She yours?" Padric asked.

A nod. "My woman and I had her late. Born at night, she was. Breath left the wife before sunrise. Named her Maeve, after her mother."

"She is beautiful," Padric said.

"And she will stay here, when you go," said the man pointedly.

Padric said nothing and turned back to the warmth of the fire. He did not sit or remove his pack and was careful to keep his hood well in place, this man seemed just the sort to believe in the curses that had plagued Padric his whole life. He could not afford to linger, for Rosheen's sake, but departing so soon after arriving would only arouse further suspicion in the woodsman, a sort already slow to trust. He was a rustic and lived by a certain code, made necessary by the harsh dangers of the wild woods. A spot of food and a place to sleep by the fire would certainly be offered with the understanding that Padric leave at first light, unless some chore was asked of him, wood chopping or the like. To accept these things and steal away in the night was knavery at its most pure. No, Padric needed to leave before he took from these people.

Padric began slowly. "I hope you will forgive me, good man, but for my sister's safety I came to you alone. Now that I see all is well, might I fetch her from the forest to share your hospitality?"

The woodsman leapt up and flung Padric to the ground before he could react. He hit the dirt face down, his pack bunching heavily behind his head, blinding him in the depths of his hood.

His hands were jerked behind him and pinned heavily at the base of his spine with a sharp knee.

"Look here!" the woodsman's voice was full of discovery and anger.

Padric felt the seax being drawn out of its sheath between his lower back and his helpless hands.

"Think to fetch your boys!?" the woodsman demanded.

"More cutthroats to have done with me and mine?!"

"No," was all Padric could manage, his face pressed awkwardly into the sooty earth.

"You lie to me, you bastard . . ." came the calm promise, ". . . and I'll do for you what your skulking lads had in mind for me."

"I am not false." Padric struggled for air in the gritty pocket around his mouth. "My sister . . . out there. She is small. I feared for her . . . came in alone. Swear it!"

There was a sudden, short thud next to Padric's head and the pressure came off his hands. He pushed himself up several inches from the ground and breathed deeply. He turned his head and moved the hood aside to find his seax stuck blade first into the ground, inches from his face. He left it there and stood quickly, spinning around to find the woodsman facing him, empty-handed, with a look of calm menace on his face.

"Best go get her then," the woodsman said.

Padric tried to keep the murder from his eyes and swallowed the bitter mixture of shame and fear that brewed after being overpowered by another. His clothes were dirty, uncomfortably pulling at his body in haphazard places. He felt weak, violated and useless, wanting nothing more than to pull the seax from the ground and bury it in the woodsman's guts. Looking over the fire, he saw the girl, her huge fear-filled eyes darting between her father and him. Their eyes met over the flames and Padric detected a plea behind the watery orbs that all but dominated her small, pale face. A plea that came from someone more helpless than he. Leaving the knife in the dirt, Padric turned his back on the pair and went back into the dark of the woods.

Fire-blind, Padric cursed aloud as he clumsily stumbled through the undergrowth. He was free of the wretched woodsman and his waif, alive and on his way, but leaving the knife behind was a cruel twist. Returning to Fafnir without the weapon was unthinkable, but Padric could think of no clever way to retrieve it that did not involve violence between himself and the woodsman.

Violence from which Padric was unlikely to emerge the victor. He cursed again, furious at himself for allowing things to turn so wrong. Rosheen would tell him to forget the knife, she did not understand the importance of such things, but Padric had no choice, he must get it back.

His foot came down and there was no ground to meet it.

He stumbled hard in the dark, grabbing blindly at the trees to steady himself, but he could not stop his slide down the unseen embankment. There was a splash as his misstep landed at last, hip deep in the icy embrace of a leaf covered pool. The darkness of the forest and his own black thoughts had gotten him off track. Padric almost let out a scream at the ill-luck of it all.

Raven-touched.

He slogged his way a short distance to the edge of the pool and found two thin trees growing only a few feet apart. Grasping the trunks, he prepared to haul himself out of the water when a pale face emerged from the darkness between the trees. Startled, Padric slipped back into the water.

Maeve put a small, pallid finger to her lips and cast a look back over her shoulder, her white hair slinging wispily around. She turned back again, just as quickly and fixed Padric with her voluminous eyes.

"Do you go to your sister now?" Her voice pierced the dark in a whisper.

Padric gaped. He was cold in the water and despite the girl-child in front of him, felt very alone in the forest.

"Take me," Maeve hissed, not waiting for his response.

"Maeve?" Padric managed. "Your father . . ." He began shivering.

"He is not my father," she said. "He stole me. Killed my parents. We must be away!" Her voice grew desperate, frightened.

She threw frightful looks all about them, her eyes, hair, never still.

Her face twisted into a pitiable spasm of despair. "He will not let me eat! He . . . he . . . I am so hungry!" She was almost sobbing.

"He . . . uses me."

Padric's chill body went cold. So cold he stopped shivering.

He wanted to kill the woodsman before. Out of rage. He wanted to hurt him now. Slow and grievous.

"Please. Can we go to your sister now?" she pleaded. "He will know I am gone."

Padric shushed her gently. "It will be all right, Maeve. You are safe. Come. We will go."

She nodded feebly, holding out her hand to help him from the pool.

"Padric, get away from her!" Rosheen's voice snapped through the darkness.

The strange glow of blue fire settled around them as Rosheen glided down from the treetops. She hovered above them, the Faery-fire dancing in her hand, the other outstretched. "Walk to me," she told Padric.

"Don't let her take me," Maeve whispered.

"Enough of your mummery, gruagach-bitch," Rosheen said.

"I know you. Padric . . . to me."

Padric looked from Rosheen to the girl. His childhood friend's once cheery face was etched in shimmering light, cast in a baleful mask that never left the quavering, frightened form of skinny little Maeve, cowering behind the trees.

"Rosh . . ." he started.

"She is no little girl, Padric. She is gruagach. And I name her. Be off, skin-changer! There is no child here for you!"

Maeve hid her face behind her arm and wept loudly, quaking with fear. Padric turned back to Rosheen, confused and angry, ready to force her to end this torment. He took a step toward her and froze. The girl's sobs had changed; quicker, higher, rasping. She was laughing. Her voice came out from behind her arm in a reedy creak.

"Wretched piskie. This for your mortal pet!"

Maeve's head snapped up and Padric recoiled at the wrinkled, sallow, slack-skinned face of an old woman. She lunged at him, wide eyes full of yellow hatred. In a blink she was on him, hands grabbing for his neck, knocking him backward. The water rushed in around his head, the sudden, numbing cold stealing the breath from him. He was under and she clung to him, squeezing his throat, white hair floating in a dreadful cloud around her, the surface of the water, so far above, lit by blue fire.

Too damn fast! The gruagach had Padric under the water before Rosheen could react. The water churned as they struggled, Padric's feet kicking up from beneath in a panic, but his head did not surface. The crone had him tight. Rosheen was barely a match for a skinchanger on land and they were stronger in the water.

Rosheen seethed, cursing the cruelty of gruagach and the stupidity of humans.

She focused on the pool, filling it with her anger, pouring her rage into the Water, polluting it with her wrath. She bundled her fury, allowing it to grow heavy and sink to the bottom.

Rosheen let loose a frenzied cry of release, violently jerking her ire back into herself. The water erupted from the pool, spitting forth with wet concussion, showering the woods with muddy Earth. The gruagach was thrown backwards into the air, striking a tree with snapping force and landing face down on the forest floor. *Throttling old sow.*

Padric choked, coughed, gagged up sticky water and spat it out. His ears were stuffy and throbbing, his body numb and shivering, but there was air and he drank it in gasps. He was lying in thick mud at the bottom of a depression, the horrible creature and the drowning water having been ripped away from him. He turned his head and came face to face with a pale, bloated thing. A cry gurgled in his throat and he jerked away from the corpse, rolling to his feet. The eyes were large, clouded over in milky death, the pale blond hair tangled with debris, rank with mud. The small, bare feet stuck out from under a log, where the body was jammed. Maeve.

The real Maeve, left to rot at the bottom of a forest pond.

Padric looked up and saw Rosheen still hovering above, her gaze fixed on a crumpled heap lying just out of the bowl that was once the awful pond. The heap twitched unnaturally and the crone's head jerked up, hair hanging wet and lank beside the sunken, grinning face. The pretender's face. She cackled wetly in her throat and lurched upright, her features twisting, elongating.

The skin split, tore and peeled back, falling with the child's dress to the ground. An emaciated black goat stood in the pile of ruined flesh and rags, its dead eyes burning with otherworldly malice.

It turned and sprang away into the woods. With a snarl, Padric rushed after it, leaping up and scrambling out of the muddy hole. He heard Rosheen call his name, but he paid no heed and continued his pursuit. The goat was blacker than the night and Padric could see it darting between the trees ahead of him. He ran on, leaping shadowy logs, ducking the phantoms of low-hanging limbs. He slung his pack off on the move, plucked his axe from inside and discarded the rest, never breaking stride. The wooden haft felt good in his hand, the iron head jumping into view with every pump of his arm, pulling him forward. Faster he ran, the black of his quarry a smudge on the natural dark of the night forest.

Blood pumped in swelling waves upon his eardrums, his wet clothes heavy, cold and clinging, but still he ran on. The goat darted into a dried creek bed, but Padric stuck to the higher ground above, seeing his chance. With a burst of anger fueled speed, Padric pulled even with the fleeing creature and leapt sidelong into the creek bed, raising the axe high. He brought the blade down hard, catching the beast in the flank. The force of the swing and the weight of Padric's fall buried the blade deep, spinning the goat, kicking as it fell. The axe haft left Padric's fingers as he plunged hard into the rocky creek bed, his palms skinned raw, his shoulder bashed by the stones. He rolled and slammed into the root-choked embankment, scrambling to his feet. Something, white and naked, was crawling away, down the creek bed. Padric found his axe among the mud, plucked it from the ground and stalked over to stand above the thin, wretched, bleeding thing attempting to escape.

It rolled over to face him, a little girl's grime-covered cheeks and pleading eyes staring up.

"Padric . . ." she said, her voice hopeful and innocent.

He raised the axe, brought it down, destroying Maeve's stolen face.

Padric found his way back to the woodsman's camp, dragging his feet wearily into the firelight. The woodsman lay sprawled face down in the soot, the seax hilt-deep in his back.

Padric did not have the will to pull it out and slunk down next to the fire. His clothes were sodden and cold, his nose ran, his throat was sore, his hands scraped and bleeding, his shoulder stiff and aching, every discomfort making itself known in the pleasant warmth of the cook fire.

"I found your pack," Rosheen said behind him. "Back in the woods a ways . . . drug it as far as I could."

"Thank you," Padric muttered.

Rosheen sat down next to him, said nothing.

Padric tried to keep his eyes from the woodsman's body, but his gaze kept flitting back to the pitiable sight. A man stabbed in the back by one he thought to love.

He had wanted to kill the man himself, not an hour ago and now he lay there, next to an uneaten supper, boiling over to sizzle in the flames.

"He was careful," Padric said wearily. "Had me touch iron when I came." He snorted bitterly. "Never thought to test his own daughter."

"It is the gruagach way," Rosheen said sadly. "Force men to distrust strangers while wearing the face of a friend."

Padric nodded, suddenly very drowsy. "Not all Fae have forgotten their hatred, I suppose."

"None have forgotten," Rosheen replied. "But most have forgiven. The gruagach never will."

FOUR

Pocket sneezed again. The ladder began to shake and teeter as his stomach lurched. He gripped the top rung tightly, wrestling with it to remain upright. His legs quivered from hours of climbing up and down again, over and over, always starting from the top, working steadily downward. There was a moment of blissful triumph each time his feet finally hit the stone floor, only to be dashed by the presence of yet another tapestry sitting patiently beside its brethren, waiting to be dusted. Up again to the very top, where the next long, heavy, acrid smelling beast was tethered, to start anew, beating the dust of years from the fibers.

Pocket's nose was runny and raw, his nostrils clogged with a sharp, gritty crust. His eyes were horribly irritated, the lids sandy and dry. His whole body itched where the mites had fled the tapestries only to find a new home in his hair and clothes. He tried assuming a feathered form, to help resist the scratchy particles, but his body only sprouted a few pitiful downy tufts that instantly molted and fell away to drift slowly down to the castle floor, sixty feet below.

He had worked in the Great Hall most of the afternoon and into the night. The Mumbler said he needed to have the tapestries dusted and the floor swept by the fourth crow of the morning. At least, that is what Pocket thought he said. It was always difficult to tell with the Mumbler. Whatever the specific instructions, Pocket wanted to be done before dawn. By tradition, only the knights were allowed to attend the funeral, but Pocket trusted in his ability to remain unnoticed. So he labored steadily on, starting on the left wall and working his way across. Up, slowly down, and across.

He had not eaten since supper and took only a small respite when he completed the eight hangings on the left wall. He had dragged the ladder around to the right side, taking a moment to survey his handiwork. While cleaning them, nose deep and personal, the weaves were nothing but multicolored blobs, but from a respectful distance the tapestries were a majestic menagerie of champions, battles, sorcerers and kings. Pocket had seen them all many times, but never so clean and never from his own hand. He loved the large, heroic images, depicting the greatest moments of the Order's history. From the Barbarous Times through to the Founding, that was the left wall. On the right, the Battle of the Unsounded Horn to the Building of the Roost still waited for Pocket's attention.

Now, hours later, he was almost done; halfway through the Reclamation of the Seelie Court, next to last. There were knots in his shoulders and a bad crick in his neck, but Pocket knew he would finish in time for the ceremony and that was well worth the discomfort. Coalspur was gone, and while he had not lived during the times captured in the threads of the tapestries, he was surely one of the greatest knights ever to grace the ranks of the Order.

Grand Master Lackcomb trusted none other with so much and Pocket wondered how the old war bird would get on without him.

Not that Pocket would ever ask. Lackcomb frightened him.

Pocket craned his neck around to the completed wall and gazed at the tapestry depicting the renowned charge that broke the Red Cap army of King Sweyn the Third during the opening years of the rebellion. Leading the knights, beak spread wide in a silent war call, was Mulrooster, first Grand Master, his glaive held high, embroidered goblins fleeing before him. Pocket had tried for years to adopt the features of a coburn. Sometimes he managed to produce the beak and the wattle. Once he even got a comb to sprout atop his newly feathered head. The feet were the most challenging and there were days Pocket dreamed of strutting around on talons, spurs clicking proudly, but try as he might, he could never get the form to hold. It would not matter if he did, Pocket would never be able to attain the height and powerful build.

All in the Order were coburn, daunting and proud. Even the burly human clansmen that lived near the Roost were shorter than the knights by a head and less deep in the chest. Pocket would forever be small, barely reaching the waist of the shortest knight.

He finished the final tapestry quickly and fetched his broom. The Mumbler had not said anything about laying fresh rushes, or so Pocket thought, so he swept the stones as fast as he could, finally completing the tedious chore. He wanted to nab something from the kitchens before the funeral and maybe get a little sleep.

Off he went, using one of the small servant's doors, and scampered down the narrow spiral stair. He emerged in the Under Hall, where several of the castle's human servants were busy setting up tables; rallying points for the many platters of food that would be taken up for the feast in the Great Hall later in the morning. It was still quite dark outside, the windows of the Under Hall revealing nothing but lonely blackness. Pocket could not help but grin excitedly, thinking how strange and wonderful it was that the Roost was so busy at an hour when every inhabitant would normally be slumbering.

The servants were groggily going about their work with only a few muttering communications, ignoring Pocket completely as he ambled across. Of course, there was nothing strange about that. The humans rarely spoke or looked at him.

Years ago, Sir Corc had explained the reasons for their negligence during one of his brief stays at the castle, and Pocket had come to accept his place . . . eventually. He spent a long time trying to look like a human child, hoping to fit in, but he never got it quite right. His ears were over large, sticking out from the sides of his shaggy head, the hair even creeping onto his cheeks. His eyes were too round, his nose too wide. His mouth, ever smiling, dominated the lower half of his face, with thick teeth, slightly bucked, which may have been a result of Pocket's two-month obsession with becoming a rabbit. The rest of him did not fare much better. His fingers were heavy and blunt, his limbs squat and strong, far different from the thin, fair, near-hairless human children who liked to play with him until their scowling parents came to lead them away. By the time Pocket gave up trying to look like one of them, his clumsy attempt at humanity had settled, becoming his permanent form. Now he had to concentrate greatly to hold the slightest change. In the end, he was no more a human than he was a coburn. If he had it to do over again, Pocket would have much rather been a rabbit.

At the far side of the Under Hall was yet another winding stair, which Pocket took down to his second favorite place in the castle. The warm, fluffy smell of baking bread, mixed with the salty sweet aroma of pine nuts, was carried on the heat from the ovens, pulsing off the stone walls. Large archways served as open-ings into the massive kitchens that hunkered beneath the castle, well-appointed and filled with sweating cooks. Pocket trotted along, watching the chaotic preparations and went straight for the last archway at the far end. He turned and entered the kitchens, confident that he would find one of the few people in the castle to ever pay him any mind.

"Moragh!" he near shouted over the din of chopping knives, boiling pots and moving bodies. "I am finished!"

The old woman turned her large form and fixed him with a single bright eye, a knowing smile curving the lip underneath. The other half of her face was slack, the eyelid drooping, the lip turned down in a permanent frown, a result of the seizure she had suffered years before Pocket was brought to the castle. He loved that face, a constant reminder that not every human that scowled at him would rather he were elsewhere. Or dead.

"Did you spread fresh rushes?" she asked, her voice high and airy.

Pocket made a point of not looking away. "The Mumb—" the frown spread to the other half of her face. "*Master* Bannoch, did not say I was to." The thumb and index finger of his left hand toyed idly with the opposite finger. "They only bring in more bugs to eat at the hangings anyways."

Moragh turned back to one of her colossal ovens, taking up a long, flat, wooden paddle and retrieved several loaves of swollen bread. "He is yours to deal with, then. I'll not step in for you again."

"Yes, Moragh," Pocket said, knowing the Mumbler would be too busy today to catch the oversight. Pocket's finger drifted up to dig some of the sharp grit from his nose.

"Here now!" Moragh's reproach was quickly followed by a well-placed snap of a rag, whipping the offending digit. "None of that!" She handed the rag over so that he could blow his nose and went back to her loaves.

With a long practiced jerk, Moragh slid the bread neatly off the paddle onto the cooling rack and turned back to him, her cheeks ruddy from the fire. "Have you eaten?" she asked, a meaty fist punching into her sizable hip. She pushed air out from between her lips causing them to flap rapidly and shook her head before Pocket could answer. "Child, child."

Pocket smiled. She always called him that, even though she had named him not long after he learned to walk, claiming he was always in her apron pocket. Reaching up, she snatched a sausage hanging from the rafters of the low ceiling. She then took out a long knife and cut a thick hunk from one of the loaves she had just removed from the oven, buttering it thickly with a single swipe.

"This for now, while it is still warm," she instructed, handing the bread over. "And this for later." She pressed the sausage into his hand. Finally she pushed her way to the opposite wall, weaving through the press of kitchen servants with the ease of long practice. There she opened a wooden hatch, revealing a series of shelves exposed to the chill winds that always blew in the highlands surrounding the castle. From this special larder she grabbed a sizable clay jug and, shutting the hatch once more, made her way back. She handed it over as well. "Enough to share. But mind you bring me back the jug."

"I will," Pocket told her through a mouthful of moist bread.

He looked beyond her and saw the other kitchen staff casting quick, disapproving looks in their direction. Some of them landed on Moragh's back, but most were meant for him directly.

"Moragh," he said quietly, causing her to lean down to his eye level. "They are all angry at us again. Maybe you should take these back." He held up the jug and sausage.

"You will not be telling me what to do in my own kitchens."

She smiled, her good eye winking. "And neither will they. Off with you, now."

Pocket left the kitchens, chewing happily on the fresh bread, the jug of milk clutched beneath his elbow, cool and sloshing. He made his way back down the way he had come, but instead of ascending the stairs to the Under Hall, he passed them up, entering the long dark hallways that connected the lower reaches of the castle.

The Roost was old, over seven hundred years if the tapestry in the Great Hall was to be believed, but Pocket knew every turn.

He often wished he would come across some forgotten vault or hidden passage, expanding his world, but after close on nine years, none such had been discovered.

He made his way assuredly, taking the time to produce a candle from his pocket, lighting it with what he knew to be the last burning torch in the passage. It was not long before he came to a sizable, round chamber, where a great construction of wooden stairs and platforms hugged the inner walls, spiraling upwards.

When Pocket first discovered this place, some time ago, he was not entirely sure where he was, but quick exploration confirmed that he was inside one of the Roost's many drum towers. The find had saved his life. Moragh had looked out for him as best she could, but the years passed and the older Pocket grew the more dangerous the servants' quarters became, full of spiteful looks and vicious intent.

Pocket went around behind the first flight of stairs and crawled between the wooden support beams, working his way towards the stone of the tower wall. Now he was just beneath the first landing and could stand upright. Going over to the little curtain he had hung from the woodwork above, he pushed it aside, entering the nook he called home. He set the milk jug on one of the wooden beams he used for a shelf and plopped down on his little bed; a feed sack stuffed with feathers on the floor. With the help of his candle and clumps of old wool he kept in a box, he kindled some coal inside the bronze brazier, quickly warming the confined space. He sat for a moment, plucking his tiny wooden horse from the mattress and galloped it across his lap, clicking his tongue to the rhythm of its hooves.

The Roost was no orphanage, but Pocket had known no other place. Sir Corc had brought him here from Airlann, an island somewhere to the west. He was just a babe at the time, the memory impossible to capture, but Pocket had come across a crude map of the isle while cleaning near the Campaign Hall. It lay crumpled, torn, smudged and forgotten beneath a discarded bookshelf.

Rescuing it, Pocket hung it across from his bed. He stared at it now, a flat, mysterious scribbling of a place he had once been, ragged proof that he came from somewhere.

A yawn came unbidden and Pocket lay back on his bed, cradling the sausage Moragh had given him. He was fearful to close his eyes, worried that he would sleep through the funeral. But close they did and Pocket dozed in half-sleep, warm and protected, rolling to his side, curling into himself. He became aware of a softly stuttering breath near his ear and smiled, waiting. Seconds later, a clipped yowl demanded his attention. Pocket rolled over to see Napper's orange, whiskered face, staring at him expectantly.

"Hello, handsome cat," Pocket said in a gleeful whisper, reaching over to scratch the soft fur between Napper's ears. The cat continued to stare at him, eyes narrowing slightly at the sensation of Pocket's fingers. Changing his approach, Pocket hooked his fingers under Napper's jaw, the cat lifting his face cooperatively, allowing his favorite spot to be tended. The scratching ceased as did the contented purring and Pocket hooked his arm in front of him on the bed. Napper walked into the space made for him and circled it twice before lying down, snuggling into Pocket.

"I nearly forgot!" Pocket admonished himself. "I have something for us." He sat up, receiving an annoyed look from Napper. "Oh, you will forgive me when you see what it is."

He fetched the clay jug from its perch and pulled the cork free of the wide mouth. Pocket took a healthy swallow from the jug, the milk pleasant, thick and still cool. Napper had risen, suddenly alert and reached up to place a paw on Pocket's chin. Pocket giggled, echoing softly into the jug. Removing it from his lips, he tipped the jug so that the milk was just about to pour free, then held his hands steady as Napper nosed in, licking at the liquid.

When the cat was finished there was still a good deal left, which Pocket drained between mouthfuls of the sausage, occasionally pinching off bits of the meat for Napper.

"We should go," Pocket told his friend, who looked up seeking more sausage.

Taking only his candle, Pocket left his sanctuary, Napper following close behind. They climbed the stairs of the tower to the fifth landing, opening the heavy wooden door onto a dark hallway.

Cradling the candle flame, Pocket shouldered the door closed behind them and set off down the passage, the patter of four clawed feet sounding steadily behind him. The windows in the hall were little more than arrow slits, but they afforded enough view to assure Pocket he was not too late. Night, seemingly the longest in his life, still held dominion outside.

Luckily, the servants were all busy in the lower levels among the living areas of the castle and he met no one. It was not precisely forbidden to wander, but Pocket did not want to answer any questions about why he was awake and not working. The rare times anyone spoke to him it was always to accuse him of some mischief, real or imagined.

He was just beneath the north wall in a section of the Roost constructed solely for defense. Of course, the castle had not known a single siege in its long history and there had not been a standing garrison for over a century. Now, it was a headquarters for the Grand Master and the Knights Sergeant, a training ground for the squires and a rally point for the Knights Errant, who returned only once every two years, unless there was a matter of great importance—like the death of a former Grand Master. The knights had gathered four times in Pocket's life, only the last two of which he actually remembered, but the event was sacred to him. Sir Corc would return with all the others with news of the world, tales of their deeds, fresh scars on armor and flesh. Pocket was saddened by the passing of Coalspur, but his excitement about seeing the knights so soon after their last reunion was undiminished.

Pocket had scouted his route days before and made for a window in an old turret that opened onto the roofs near the eastern gate. He scooped Napper from the ground, draping the cat over his shoulder and climbed out. The wind was too strong for his candle, snuffing it mercilessly the second he was outside, so he made his way in the dark, the silhouettes of the castle architecture black against the star filled sky.

The Roost was built atop a high, rocky crag. A slip in either direction would likely be fatal. The mere thought of the dizzying height past the outer wall was too much for Pocket, so he stayed to the side of the roof which sloped towards the interior of the castle.

Thankfully, Napper did not grow restless or try to dislodge himself, trusting to be carried along.

The castle was a confusing marriage of original stonework fortification and more recent structures of wood and plaster, creating a chaotically layered jumble of battlements, casements, spires and shingles. Pocket planned his route so that he ended up above the fortified bulk of the east gate, easily able to clamber down and gain the flat roof. He ducked low and crossed to the outer facing edge, peering cautiously around one of the merlons.

A wide, rocky bluff lay below, jutting from the cliffs at the base of the wall, facing east. Below and beyond, lay the highlands of Albain, lost for now in the final darkest hours of night. There was no approach to the castle from the east, no road, only sheer cliff face. The east gate, above which Pocket sat, served only to access the bluff from the inner courtyard of the castle. At the edge of the bluff sat a pedestal of stone, simply stacked, devoid of ornament or carving, but surrounded by large bundles of wood packed with straw. The squires were already in attendance, waiting along the processional way leading from the gate to the pedestal, bearing their iron tipped quarterstaffs, their combs covered by leather caps, fifty in all. The two nearest the pedestal held torches, the light from the flames sparsely illuminating the bluff.

Pocket caught sight of Áedán mac Gabráin, chief of the Dal Riata, standing off to the side with some of his clansmen, each holding a bladder pipe. The knights must have broken with tradition, allowing the humans to attend in honor of the allegiances Coalspur made with their clans during his tenure as Grand Master.

"We made it," Pocket whispered to Napper, clutched firmly against his chest. "Shouldn't be long now."

True to his word, mere minutes passed before the unseen tunnel of the gate below echoed with a sharp clacking, metal on stone, the noise created by many small sources, amplified in unison.

Pocket felt his heart jump and could not keep himself from leaning over, craning to see the tunnel entrance. In they marched, the banner of the Order leading, held aloft by Sir Kortigern Hatch, the rest following two by two. Each pair bore a torch between them, uniting them. They wore no helms, their combs proudly exposed atop heads held high. Their armor captured the torch light, plates of polished steel from shoulder to waist, their legs covered in shining skirts of mail, slit in the back, allowing the plumage of their tail feathers to remain colorfully displayed. The long hind-spur on each foot was capped in a finely wrought steel sleeve, denoting their knighthood. Tall, powerful, the ringing of their march never faltering, they marched out onto the bluff, splitting to left and right by pairs.

The Knights of the Valiant Spur.

Pocket tried desperately to see each one as they emerged from the tunnel, his excitement growing. He pointed. "There's Bronze Wattle!" he told Napper, barely able to whisper. "And the one with him . . . with the double-headed axe, that's Poorly Well!

And see there, the Dread Cockerel! I heard he may challenge Lackcomb for the place of Grand Master." He could not help but bounce slightly up and down on his toes as he named each in turn, trying not to miss a single one, but fearful he would overlook his favorites, sharing them with Napper as they came into view. "The black one there, that's Pitch Feather. Ha! Look! They have matched him with Sir Barn Lochlan, whom they call the White Noble on account of *his* feathers! Sir Corc! Two behind with the longsword . . . he's the knight that brought me here! Oh! And there's Blood Yolk and the fat one behind him . . . the Mad Capon! It is said he gelded himself so that he would never take a mate, one of the Order's strictest vows!"

Soon they were present and arrayed, thirty-six in all, the surviving Knights Errant of the Order. Two knights were missing, Sir Hauncicleer and Sir Tillory the Calm, both present at the last gathering barely half a year ago. Sir Tillory was thought to have been slain in the rocky wastes of Kymbru, and of Sir Hauncicleer there was no word. After several days with no sign of the absent knights, Lackcomb could wait no more and had ordered the funeral to commence. The failure of two such formidable fighters to return was disturbing. Fewer of the Knights Errant made their way back to the Roost each two-year.

A keen whistle rose into a sharp wail as Áedán's clansmen worked their bladder pipes, giving birth to a haunting dirge. The six grizzled veterans of the Knights Sergeant came slowly forward, pulled by the music. These were the instructors and weapons masters responsible for the training of the squires, their questing days long since over and permanent residents of the castle. Pocket knew them well, introducing them to Napper with hushed reverence.

"Stoward Thom. Banyon Deaf Crower. Yewly the Salted. Mallander Smokebeak. Worm Chewer. And the Old Goose."

Many times he watched them deliver the harsh lessons of combat to their squire pupils in the training yards, pupils who now grew even more rigid as the Knights Sergeant passed. Whether it was in fear of the veterans or in respect for the burden they carried, Pocket could not say.

Coalspur's body lay upon a litter, born aloft on the shoulders of the old knights. He was dressed in full armor, his greatsword resting on his chest beneath lifeless hands. Even from a distance and in the poor torch light, Pocket could see the ravages left behind by the fever. The body looked drained, wasted and thin.

The breastplate was ill-fitting, gaping at the neck and under the arms. The castle gossip was that Coalspur's feathers had all but fallen away in his final hours, leaving a flushed, bald, pitiful thing behind to die. If this was so, measures had been taken to ensure his dignity, for the body, despite its withered appearance was still thick with white feathers. Still, some things had been overlooked. Pocket noticed that Coalspur's beak was slightly open, as if he was snoring softly, but his chest did not rise nor fall. The sight was pitiable, making the once fearsome warrior look vulnerable and weak.

Pocket felt a rush of anger.

"Someone should have closed it," he said aloud, almost wishing to be heard.

The pallbearers carried the litter to the far edge of the bluff and lowered it slowly to rest upon the stone pedestal, then joined their brother knights. The whine of the bladder pipes faded, and, as one, the squires struck the butts of their staffs sharply on the stone, then knelt low, heads bowed.

Grand Master Lackcomb strode through the gate, the crimson surcoat and cloak of his office hanging heavily over his burnished armor. His legendary pole axe, the Coming Dawn, rode his fist as he came forward onto the bluff.

Pocket shivered, suddenly grateful for the furry warmth and comfort of his companion cradled closely to him. Lackcomb ignored the crowds' presence, looking neither left nor right. From his vantage, Pocket could not see Lackcomb's eyes and he was grateful, knowing the left was milked over and dead, the flesh surrounding it horribly scarred. He did have a clear view of the ugly, puckered bald strip on top of the Grand Master's head. It was said he cut the comb from his head with his own hands so that he would be less vulnerable to his enemies. Pocket did not dare even a whisper to Napper while Lackcomb was near. His mind conjured up the story of the Grand Master's ascension and it squatted there in his imagination.

Never a squire, Lackcomb simply strutted into the Roost one morning, strange looking with his bald head, and offered challenge to the reigning Grand Master, the legendary Coalspur.

Tradition demanded that the Grand Master accept any challenge to his rule and defend it in single combat. So it was in the Great Hall of the Roost, among the squires and Knights Sergeant of the Order that a self-mutilated youth of no renown threw down the greatest warrior of the coburn, winning himself the right and title of Grand Master of the Knights of the Valiant Spur. He was seventeen years old.

Of all the legends and stories Pocket knew regarding the knights, this was far from his favorite, but he loved hearing the part where Coalspur, in humbled awe, became Lackcomb's shield bearer and boon companion, remaining a loyal retainer until his death.

A death that claimed him eight days ago.

Lackcomb had retained his position of Grand Master against all challengers for over fifty years and commanded the respect of all within the Order. Despite the rumors and the Grand Master's advanced age, Pocket doubted even the Dread Cockerel could defeat him. He made his way steadily up to the pedestal where his predecessor now lay, and turned, acknowledging the others for the first time.

"Words were not Coalspur's weapons!" Lackcomb's voice, gravelly and shrill, pitched across the bluff. The sky behind him had turned an inky purple with faint traces of pink and orange outlining the horizon. "And neither are they mine. It is enough to say that our brotherhood must bid farewell to one of the finest knights ever to wear the Spurs. I became his superior. I was never his equal. There is no dishonor in how he died as there was none in how he lived." Lackcomb gave his knights a baleful stare, as if daring any of them to refute his words.

None did.

"Now, he is free from his sworn service. A service he was not ready to relinquish. His final wish was that his sword not journey with him, so that a part of him might still serve the championed causes of this Order. To that end and in honor of his last instructions there shall be a tourney, open to all, squire and knight alike. The champion will receive as prize . . ." Lackcomb tenderly lifted the greatsword from Coalspur's chest, turning back to hold the weapon aloft, ". . . his blade, which shall from this day forward bear his name."

Pocket found his mouth was open. A tourney! Excitement bundled up inside his chest, worked its way into a tight coil, preparing to spring forth and escape past his lips in a cheer of delight, but it slammed silently into the roof of his mouth to be swallowed safely back down into his gut.

"And now let us send our brother on his way," Lackcomb said solemnly. "May the glory of his deeds outshine the sorrow of his passing." The Grand Master stepped to the side, allowing the knights to move forward, each pair lowering their torch at the base of the pyre, bowing low before stepping back to their places. The straw and wood caught quickly, surrounding the body in smoke and flame. All eyes were fixed on the burning pedestal, the sky continuing to brighten in the east.

"Knights of the Valiant Spur!" Lackcomb cried. "Lift your voices to the fallen! Let him leave this world to the sound of our salute!" He raised the Coming Dawn high over his head. "For Coalspur!"

As one, the knights threw back their heads, opening their beaks wide and threw the war cry from their chests, the throttling screech rising to its triumphant peak, piercing the sky.

"For Coalspur!"

Again they challenged the fleeing darkness.

"For Coalspur!"

Thrice they cried and thrice the hairs on Pocket's neck stood up in a tingle of pride. Upon the final and loudest salute, he could not help but punch his fist into the air.

Dawn had come, but it seemed the sun had not risen. In its place, the pyre stood blazing at the center of the horizon, the sky beyond awash in smears of morning color. The fire burned and the memory of Coalspur lit the new day. Pocket let the tears fall and said goodbye to one of his heroes.

FIVE

Rosheen wrinkled her nose. "Hog's Wallow."

"Hog's Wallow," Padric agreed with a frown. "Abandoned."

Who would stay? Rosheen fluttered next to Padric as they made their way toward the center of the small hamlet, the ground a clog of thick, black mud. She could hear Padric's boots struggling free with a sucking sound after every step. The simple dwellings on either side of the quagmire were empty, without fire or hearth smoke, their cold doorways pleading and threatening.

After weeks of hard, tedious travel, they had crested a small rise to find the village below at last and Padric breathed a curse.

They knew immediately. No herds, no children, no dogs, not even a chicken. No movement at all, save the slow, dumb turning of the mill's water wheel, forced by the Trough's current to labor on. The other structures huddled pitiably together, shrinking away from the surrounding landscape. After a moment of weary silence, they went down the rise and into the village.

"No corpses," Padric said darkly, after leaning into one of the little huts.

Rosheen knew there would be none, even from the rise.

There were no crows. Fled, then. "What now?" she called across.

"We stay here," Padric said. "No other choice. A day or two to see if anyone returns . . . then gather what we can and move on." *Sounds familiar.* He said the same at the woodsman's hut, but they left as soon as the sun rose, after burying the man and what was left of his poor child. They took nothing.

Padric came back to the middle of the sodden thoroughfare, looking back the way they had come. He shook his head for the tenth time since they came within sight of the village. "No walls. Not of wood, earth or stone. Not even a ditch."

"Didn't need one," Rosheen said, nodding toward a low bump of earth with a door in the center. *A gnome hole.* "This place was Fae-friendly. They must have had a guardian of some sort, if they kept to the old ways. A fomori most likely, or maybe a Waywarder passed by regular. Someone kept them safe."

"Or made them believe they were," Padric muttered.

Or made them believe they were. Rosheen looked at the door to the gnome hole sadly . . . and then shook the feeling away. *Damn Padric and his mood!* Both were beginning to get to her.

"Let's find that alehouse," she said, a little too loudly for their surroundings. "Even that wretched stuff will taste sweet after all this bitter company." She flew off without waiting to see if he followed.

The River Trough bordered the village to her right.

Rosheen followed it up past the mill. It was a large, three tier construction of solid wood, its heavy wheel groaning steadily around. The alehouse was just beyond, a long, squat building of thick wooden beams. Attached to one side was a stable made of stacked stone with a turf roof.

The door to the alehouse was unbarred and slung inward with a slight push, revealing a spacious common room filled with long benches and tables, all of them upright, disturbingly well-ordered for a place with no people. Rosheen landed lightly on the dirt floor and stepped a few paces inside. It was colder in the shadowy alehouse than it was without, where the afternoon sun was hidden by a thick smudge of grubby clouds. The fireplaces were stacked with fresh turf, ready to be lit and clay flagons hung neatly on pegs over the serving table.

"Just like all the others," Padric said from the doorway.

"Undisturbed. Just empty." He dumped his pack and went over to one of the fireplaces, pulling his flint from his belt. Rosheen regarded him as he worked, kneeling before the fireplace, grimy and soiled from traveling.

Padric had not taken a blade to his face since they departed his home and a thin layer of black whiskers now shadowed his chin, lip and jaw. Coupled with the hair falling to his shoulders, black as ink, and the ever-present brooding of his eyes, the growth on his face made him look wild and more than a little dangerous. The slaying of a gruagach made it less an illusion and more a hard truth.

Rosheen's heart fell as she said goodbye to the innocent boy she knew, and not for the first time. *Will I be able to love the man as much?*

Or at all? She shook the thought away and found another barely more appealing.

He stood up, the fire now rising steadily, and turned to her.

Rosheen nodded. "Drink?"

"Right. Grand." Padric went around behind the serving table to where the large kegs rested heavily in their cradles. "These are all untapped. Need a mallet." He cast around for a moment before reaching toward the floor, pulling the cellar door open.

Rosheen could feel the cold underground air leak up from the opening. She tensed. *Why is there light?*

"Padric," she whispered.

"I know," he hissed and drew his long knife. He held his free hand out toward her, indicating she should stay up top and ducked his head, cautiously descending the steep stairs. The narrow passage was clearly illuminated by the flickering of firelight and Rosheen could see where the stairs ended facing an earthen wall.

Padric crept down quietly and stayed on the last step as he peered around the corner into the cellar. Knife ready, he stepped down to the right and out of sight. There was a moment's pause and then his head poked out from behind the wall, looking up at her.

"You better come down here."

As she flew down the cold closeness of the tunnel, she caught the pungent aromas of fresh ale and musty earth. Reaching the bottom, she looked. It was a roomy cellar, tightly packed with stacked barrels. Padric stood in the center, his back turned, the knife returned to its sheath. One of the wooden support beams held a bronze lamp, the burning animal fat spewing greasy smoke into the air, staining the ceiling. At her approach, Padric stepped aside and Rosheen looked down.

Should have guessed.

The clurichaun lay over the top of an empty side-turned barrel, his back bending with the curve of the wood. His swollen belly bulged toward the ceiling, expanding hugely with each deep snore. His feet were dangling towards them, one missing a shoe, his head lost from sight over the other side of the barrel. A clay jug dangled loosely from the tip of a relaxed finger. Another barrel stood open next to the clurichaun's makeshift bed, still upright. It was not simply tapped, but the entire top was pried off, showing the contents of dark ale near half gone.

"Relative?" Padric asked, a wry grin cracking his face. It was the first time he had smiled since killing the skin-changer.

Rosheen snorted and grabbed the clurichaun by the ankles, tugging sharply. The barrel rolled forward, dumping the wretch onto his rump on the ground. His head fell back against the barrel, but he kept snoring. Coarse stubble covered his face, his curly hair oily and matted. Rosheen grabbed the front of his stained shirt in her fists and gave him a good shake. His head thumped soundly on the barrel with a woody echo, but he did not wake. She released him and slapped him across the face, giving a second strike with the back of her hand on the return. The clurichaun rewarded her efforts with a reeking belch, but slumbered on. She brought her fist back and took aim at his nose.

"Rosh!" Padric admonished her.

"Oh keep quiet," she replied, but dropped her fist. "He is well beyond feeling anything. Now help me."

"Help you what? I'll not beat on him!"

"Don't be daft. Pick him up."

Padric frowned at her and leaned over, grabbing the back of the clurichaun's vest, hoisting him from the ground one-handed.

The little sot dangled at the end of Padric's outstretched arm, oblivious. "Now what?"

Rosheen tilted her head toward the open barrel and raised an eyebrow.

"Waste of good ale," Padric said.

"From the smell of him, he's already been swimming in it," Rosheen countered. "Now dunk him."

Padric sighed and held the clurichaun over the barrel.

"Head first," Rosheen corrected.

Padric reached down with his other hand and gripped the clurichaun's ankles, slowly spinning him around until his arms were swinging freely towards the ground. Wrinkling his nose distastefully Padric lowered his burden into the barrel. The curly head went under, the open mouth sending up a deluge of fat, gurgling bubbles.

Padric held him under for some time, looking more sheepish with each passing second, but the clurichaun did not wake. No ale erupted in a fit of froth and waves, the stubby legs did not kick or jerk in Padric's grasp. Padric gave Rosheen a withering glare and pulled the clurichaun dripping from the barrel.

"Mayhaps he can breathe it, too . . . like a fish," Padric said.

"Very well," Rosheen said tightly. "Get the lamp, while I take his trousers down."

Padric did not reply to that, just stared at her blank and horrified.

"We'll just singe his bollocks. Should be enough to . . ."

"Inna wake!" the clurichaun declared suddenly, still upside down.

". . . bring him right 'round," Rosheen finished victoriously.

Padric looked disturbed.

"I don'wan n'more soup!" the clurichaun said, his eyes blinking hard.

"Wake up and pay attention!" Rosheen stepped up.

"You leaf tha' broom a'there, Jileen!" the clurichaun complained thickly. "I had'no but tha'three pints and thas'all!" His face was swelling up, turning a strange shade of red and pale purple.

"Let him down," Rosheen told Padric, who looked greatly relieved as he eased the little fellow to the dirt floor. The clurichaun lay on his back, breathing heavily and muttering incoherently to the ceiling.

"Not like to get much out of him," Padric said.

Rosheen shook her head. "If the ale here is as good as that dwarf of yours claimed, this sodden wretch is the reason. I've no doubt he made a deal with the brewer—his enchantments for a place to sleep and a share of the stock. He's been living here a while now and knows what happened. Clurichaun are not always drunk, but they are enough of the time as makes little difference. He knows."

Padric nodded once and bent down, propping the clurichaun up against the barrels.

Rosheen approached and stood over him. "Can you tell us where everyone went?"

The bloodshot eyes rolled lazily around, missed her and pulled focus on Padric. The clurichaun squinted up hard and slack-jawed. "Lurvely voice for one s' large . . . an' bearded."

"*I* want to know what happened here, you crusty toadstool!"

Rosheen leaned in and said loudly in his ear.

A grin split the clurichaun's lips, revealing perfect white teeth. *Fae-folk. Even our drunks are comely.* "Pretty pishkie, give us'a kiss." He puckered wetly at her.

"I'll plant something on those lips if you do not begin talking sense." She pulled her fist back again.

"Fishhh fffoood wuzza dead man, heelz kissin' the sky!" the clurichaun sang tunelessly. "Fly, fly, mortals run, fear'n ev'ry eye! The 'ollow man has gon'away, left his masser drowned! The metal man has come'ta play, red death for'all around!" The clurichaun broke off his slurred song and slumped into a gurgling chuckle.

"He's mad," Padric said.

Rosheen was not so sure. She knelt down, slow and careful, reached out and placed a cool hand on the clurichaun's brow. His head rolled towards her unsteadily and he looked her in the eyes.

Sad. His eyes are sad. "Please," she whispered gently. "Tell me."

He stared at her and smiled. "Knew you'd take my trousssers down."

Padric was on him before she could blink. He grabbed the little fool up roughly, slamming him against the support beam, causing the lamp to shake, the light in the cellar fluttering wildly.

"Tell me what you know!"

The clurichaun gawked at him for a moment, wide-eyed and fearful, then burst out laughing full in Padric's face.

"Scared!" he chuckled. "So scared! They all were! No'me. I no'scared a'you, mortal boy. What'er you? Nowt is'what! No'when I dinna run from liffing iron!"

Rosheen felt her spine go taut. *Living iron?*

"I'll tell Jileen," the clurichaun kept on. "I'll tell'er and no drinks for you."

"Where is she? This Jileen." Padric's teeth were clenched, Rosheen could hear it, but her mind was elsewhere. . . . *metal man has come'ta play . . .*

"With the men," came a strange, lilting voice behind them.

"At the burial."

Burial. . . . red death for'all around . . .

"Fafnir," Padric said, looking around and lowering the clurichaun to the floor.

Rosheen turned. *The dwarf.*

Stocky and broad shouldered, Fafnir filled the width of the doorway. He wore traveling clothes of sturdy wool, a grey cloak about his solid frame, the hood pulled up over his head. His clever eyes sat above a bulbous nose and a shaven lip, but his jaw and chin were covered in a short, spade-shaped beard, rust colored and pointed at the end. Padric moved forward and the two clasped wrists. Fafnir's head barely reached Padric's chest but his hand was a ham hock, Padric's arm a twig.

"It is pleasant to see you again, friend," Fafnir said. His Middangearder accent created strange swells in his speech, instantly annoying Rosheen.

"I hoped to find you here," Padric said.

Rosheen glowered. *And found him you did. Him and no one else.*

"It is only ill-luck that you did," Fafnir replied. "I have been delayed. Many days now. Dark days for the people here."

Rosheen saw Padric's face fall at the words 'ill-luck', the foolish beliefs of his people falling on him like a sudden rain. *He will blame himself. Well done, dwarf.*

"What people here?" she demanded. "We have seen no one. Save *that.*" She jerked a thumb at the clurichaun who was staggering back to his barrel-bed. Clumsily, he attempted to mount it, belly down, but as he reached the top, his weight caused the barrel to roll. The clurichaun farted and fell out of sight.

Padric and Fafnir both looked over to her, the dwarf with a smile and the man with a distant stare, which dispersed in an instant.

"Fafnir," Padric said. "You remember Ro—"

"Rosheen," Fafnir finished for him and bowed his head toward her. "My honor to be at your service."

"Grand," Rosheen replied flatly. "Now, please. What happened here? You mentioned a burial." . . . *red death for all around . . .*

Fafnir considered her for a moment. "Come. We will talk upstairs."

Fafnir produced a clay pipe from his belt and filled the bowl with leaf before lighting it with a brand he took from the fireplace. Padric settled down on a bench and marveled inwardly at how good it felt to sit up off the ground after so long. Rosheen sat on the serving table behind him.

"I arrived a fortnight past," Fafnir began, the pipe clenched firmly in his teeth. "I had a sword to deliver to a fomori here. One Faabar. He commissioned it when I passed this way a year or more ago." Padric could feel Rosheen cast a look his way, but kept his attention directed entirely on the dwarf. "I am told that the fomori is injured, so I wait. But I do not wait long, before . . ." Fafnir took a long drag off his pipe and shook his head gravely. "One of the women found the village elder dead in the eel pond, the same day I arrived. A man named Brogan."

"The eel pond?" Rosheen asked.

Fafnir nodded. "The lord who resides near here bids the villagers breed them. Developed a taste for them while warring in Sasana, I am told."

Rosheen gagged slightly. "I hope the man was dead before he fell in." Padric tried not to smile.

"The herbalist claims he was drowned," Fafnir said.

"The villagers . . . they fled after the body was found?" Padric asked.

"They did," Fafnir replied. "The women, children and the old among them.

To the holdfast of the same eel-eating lord, Kederic the Winetongue. The herdsmen stayed behind, taking their flocks out into the hills most nights for safety."

"Why leave over one dead man? Did they fear a pox?"

"It is possible. The herbalist spoke heatedly with the men after he saw the body and it was on his instructions that the villagers fled. They have all since returned, hale and healthy. More than that I cannot say, the herbalist is a gnome and has little love for me. He tells me nothing and will not let me deliver the blade, for the fomori, he claims, is grievously injured."

Fafnir blew pipe smoke out of his nostrils. "But, the herdsmen gather here most every night. I hear gossip from them when they drink. They say Faabar is not like to recover, although never within the gnome's hearing. They also say that the elder was murdered. Slain by his husk servant. This they say for all to hear."

"This Brogan must have been a rich man," Padric huffed.

Fafnir shrugged. "I know little of him, save that he sent the husk to me with a request to replace the iron plough blade that caused hurt to the fomori with one of steel. Hours later, the man was dead and the husk could not be found."

Padric had only seen husks once in his life. Four of them helped construct the fort near his village when he was just a boy, adding stone fortifications to the existing wooden stockade. For years after, when he passed one of the scarecrows in the fields he would stop and wait for a while, watching to see if it might come alive. Rosheen explained to him that the Magic used to give the husks life was old and nearly forgotten and would not quicken on common scarecrows. Padric was disappointed but not surprised.

The farmers hung rush bundles on poles, poorly formed and bloated looking, all but shapeless, giving only the vaguest impression of arms and legs. Sometimes they would paint an ugly face on a feed sack to serve as a head, but most did not bother.

By contrast, the husks laboring at the fort were tall and gangly, deft, nimble and precise in every movement. Their stuffed bodies were not overly strong, but his father told him they were exceedingly clever and understood how to raise the fort up solid and level. Padric remembered they took no refreshment when the men of the village rested, but sat talking and even laughing among themselves. He wanted to approach and talk with them, but was too afraid they would shun him or cast cruel japes in his face as the villagers often did. Even if they were kind, which he suspected from the jovial expressions on their pumpkin faces, Padric feared he would only invite more suspicion from the men by speaking with them. Husks were not Fae, but were created with their Magic and could be trusted only so far. When the fort was completed, the man who owned the husks was paid with goats and pigs and wool.

The husks were given nothing and left with the man, carrying the wool and herding the stock. Padric had not thought of them in years.

"The gnome would not allow Brogan to be buried until today," Fafnir continued. "So the people have gone to the barrows. I was not asked to attend. There is a decent forge here, so I have worked steel, passing the days trading and teaching when the men are around, hoping the fomori will mend or that I will be permitted to see him."

"Why not leave the damn sword in someone's keeping and move on?" Rosheen asked.

Fafnir loosed a smoky chuckle. "This is what the gnome would have me do, but I see my goods delivered to their owners and none else."

"Probably hasn't been paid yet," Rosheen muttered to Padric's chagrin, but if Fafnir heard he gave no sign.

"I hoped to enter into your service," Padric said, trying to keep any nervousness from his voice.

"My wares would be the safer for it," Fafnir replied. "The roads are ever perilous and it seems not even the settlements are safe. And you might have better luck than I with the gnome. In dealing with these Fae-folk, you are skilled."

Padric smiled at that. It was a lie of course, but a lie that allowed Padric to gain Fafnir's attention in the first place. Fafnir had come to his village to peddle steel to the warriors of the fort and was met with little warmth. A few dirks sold, an axe head or two and little else, but while there, he happened to hear of a Piskie-kissed youth who was friend to the Fae.

Fafnir sought him out.

In the closeness of his father's hut, Padric and his parents listened to the dwarf's proposal. He told them it was often difficult to trade with humans and nearly impossible when dealing with Fae-folk. He saw a lad like Padric solving both problems. What Padric saw was an out. And so did his father. Little matter that the only Fae Padric knew was Rosheen and that he was not likely to sow welcoming feelings among his own kind.

Now it seemed he would be tested at last and he welcomed the chance. He would see the sword delivered so Fafnir could be on his way to the next town, the next fort, the next distant country, taking Padric with him.

The sound of approaching voices ended their conversation.

They all went outside, Fafnir leading, to find the villagers returning from the hilly country to the north. Padric counted barely a dozen families and what appeared to be a husky child with thick white hair, which could be none other than the gnome herbalist. The group made straight for the alehouse, but Padric noticed the gnome pull up short at the sight of them and strike off alone down a narrow track leading away from the village. Padric thought he heard him muttering as he went. The rest of the group came steadily on.

"Still here, master peddler?" one woman said when the group stopped in front of them.

"I am," Fafnir answered simply. "Along with my new apprentice and his companion."

"They're welcome, of course," the woman said. "Come, let us make our introductions within. We all have a thirst and a good man to remember this night." She gestured towards the alehouse door with a small, but genuine smile and the men made their way inside, each giving Padric a friendly nod as they passed, and some even bowed slightly to Rosheen.

Soon the common room of the alehouse was humming with low voices and the soft, warm glow of the hearth. Padric and Rosheen were introduced to the woman Jileen, who then acquainted them with the herdsmen. Most were older than Padric; simple, honest looking men. They gripped his wrist firmly and looked him square in the eyes when they spoke, asking about his home and his family. They were equally courteous with Rosheen, but their speech became formal and a little nervous when speaking with her. Rosheen, amused and charming, set them to ease quickly and had them all laughing before the first tankard was drained.

The light faded outside as the ale flowed and two of the men, Laoire and Dolan, left to relieve their fellows out in the hills watching over the flocks. Jileen filled Padric's cup for the third or possibly fourth time.

"So you come from Stone Fort?" she asked. Jileen was a fine looking woman, with a flashing smile and a thick mane of deep auburn. Her nose and forehead were a little broad to call her a great beauty, but Padric liked her capable manner and the way she navigated her curves between the men in the bar while serving the ale.

"Yes," he answered, his head swimming pleasantly. "But it was not called such when I was a boy. The fort was little more than a low wooden wall surrounded by a ditch."

"Stone Fort is a freehold, is it not?" Ardal threw in. He was a big man with retreating hair and a thick brown beard to make up for the lack on his head. He seemed to be in charge now that Brogan was dead.

"It is," Padric told him. "The warriors of the fort are fed by the farmers, who rule by council. The warriors give protection, we give food. Some of the farmers in my village were once warriors themselves, laid down the sword for the plough."

"Would that it were so in Hog's Wallow." Ardal lifted his mug to his lips.

"Kederic Winetongue offers you no protection?" Padric asked.

"He did," Ardal said, draining his ale. "And for years we had no need of it. Then Faabar suffered injury and Kederic sent his men to see us safe. Gone now, of course." Ardal stared into his mug, Jileen watching him intently. There was an uneasy silence and Padric felt it best to say nothing, turning his attention to the common room. One of the herdsmen played a decent wood flute and Rosheen danced with another, standing upon one of the tabletops to give her some height. The other men drank and clapped around them. After a moment, Ardal took a deep breath.

"We are all free men, the land gifted to us by the gnomes who once dwelt here. They went back to their underground city when my grandfather was a boy, and we have worked these lands, tilling, building, raising our flocks and children. Kederic arrived some . . . what? Ten years now, Jileen?"

"Near enough," Jileen said as she refilled Ardal's mug.

"He had warriors, a fair size herd of cattle and all manner of treasure from fighting across the water. Made himself known to Brogan and offered his protection. Protection we did not need, what with Faabar here. Brogan said as much, but he welcomed Kederic to these lands as was his way. We fostered his cattle while he built his fortress not twenty miles from here. Gifted us with a good smithy within a year."

"This place, too. And the stables," Jileen added.

Ardal nodded. "He was generous and we repaid his kindness with our own. Wool, candles, grain. Welcomed he and his men to our festivals, shared what we had, traded with the warriors. Some of our daughters are now their wives. But relations between the Winetongue and Brogan cooled after the first year or so. Both men have . . . had honor in them, but pride as well. Soon it was all land rights and whether we were Kederic's tenants or he ours. Kederic calls us bondsmen and Brogan took a sour view of that quick enough. But having his warriors here made Kederic bold, pressing Brogan into acknowledging him as lord of these lands. Wants to be a right and proper Thegn, like they have in Sasana and Middangeard, rule by his own hand. Brogan refused and the warriors were called back."

"And Brogan is dead soon after?" Padric asked.

"Same day," Ardal said gravely. "But don't let your mind run with suspicions. Weren't Kederic that did for Brogan. Those two known each other ten years and quarreled for all but one of them. Kederic is a warrior and killed plenty of men in battle, but murder is not in the man. No. The husk is at the end of that foul doing."

"Slouch Hat." Jileen all but whispered the name, her eyes on the serving table.

"Aye," Ardal snarled. "Saw his chance for freedom and took it. I'd stake my daughters on it. Faabar laid up and the warriors gone, none to stop him. Kederic will find him though. Set riders and that huntsman of his on the trail. They'll run that husk down and then we'll get justice for a good man." Ardal pushed himself to his feet and clapped Padric on the back companionably.

"Welcome to Hog's Wallow, lad. Wish it were in happier times. Here's to Brogan!" He threw back his cup, draining it down and with that he turned, before lumbering over to join the revels. Jileen stayed behind the serving table, clutching the flagon and staring sadly at nothing.

"I am sorry for his passing," Padric said after a moment.

"He taught me my letters, when I was a girl," she said softly, almost to herself.

"That is a rare skill and a wondrous gift," Padric said, hoping to sound comforting. "He sounded an honorable man and a fine leader."

"It *was* a gift. One he gave to all the children of this village who wanted to learn." Jileen looked over at him and gave a resigned smile, "But it was not Brogan who taught us. It was Slouch Hat."

". . . town's just resettled and what do we get? Visitors! No sense in it. None at all. A body can't even get a drink in his own home after burying a friend without stepping on a stranger. Dwarrow and piskies! Soon it'll be banshees and selkies! What's to follow? Giants and trolls? Or worse? Hobgoblins?!"

Deglan spat.

Bulge-Eye slept.

The pair sat outside Faabar's hut and would have been sharing the whiskey skin back and forth, but the great toad was not much of a drinker. Inside, the fomori slept deeply, compliments of the elixir Deglan mixed up when he returned from the barrows.

The wound had stayed closed, thankfully, but the fevers still came and went, much to Deglan's frustration. But he was patient.

"We must stare down injury and illness and never blink," he said aloud, quoting the old herbwife that taught him so long ago.

He took a pull off the skin and looked over at Bulge-Eye. "You'd make a fine healer."

The whiskey burned a little going down, but settled warmly in his chest. The night was fresh and crisp, chill, but dry. Excellent weather for a good sit and a few pulls off a skin.

"Mind if I join you?" asked a playful voice.

Deglan looked up. It was the piskie from the village, perched in a tree near the eaves of Faabar's turf roof.

"Yes," Deglan answered sourly.

She flew down heedlessly, landing on the toad's head.

Bulge-Eye awoke with a grumpy croak and rolled his eyes upwards, trying to see what was bothering him. The piskie leaned down and rubbed him enthusiastically between the eyes.

"He's adorable," she cooed. "Been a long time since I've seen a riding toad."

"Funny. He told me the same thing about piskies. Has a weakness for them. Likes the way the wings crunch."

She paid the comment no mind and continued to stroke the toad's lumpy head. A strange expression of calm contentment seemed to come over Bulge-Eye's face. If it was possible, the beast seemed even more at ease than usual.

Piskies kept to ancient traditions, continuing to live rough in the wilds long after the elves and gnomes and the other Fae had built magnificent cities. This piskie was as feral and youthfully beautiful as any he had ever seen. Her skin was pleasantly darkened by the sun, unclothed save for the intricate blue markings painted in sparing patterns across one shoulder and thigh. Her hair was a tangled pile of deep chestnut, festooned with braids, beads, bones and feathers. Her entire body screamed blissful abandon and Deglan found his loins stirring, unbidden and unwanted.

Thankfully he knew a tea that would solve the problem and made a point to remember to brew some when he returned home.

"What's in the skin?" she asked without taking her attention from the toad.

"Root whiskey," Deglan said and held the skin towards her.

Even half full the skin outweighed the piskie, so she tilted her head back and opened her mouth while Deglan poured a thin stream from the spout. She made a face as the whiskey went down and shook her head with a hard sniff.

"Potent."

"Brewed it myself." Deglan took a long pull. "Jileen's ale not enough for you?"

"It was fine," she replied. "Clurichaun knows his craft."

"Who, Two Keg?" Deglan could not help but laugh. "Old bugger's been drunk for a decade or more. Thought he would keel over and die the day that alehouse was built. Now *he* was sick of root whiskey. Comes up sober once in a harvest moon to lay fresh charms on the ale and then dives right back down again. But, yes . . . the results are impressive."

"Doesn't seem to have addled his wits any," she said and Deglan saw the bait.

"Name's Deglan Loamtoes," he dodged. "Master herbalist."

"Rosheen," the piskie winked at him. "Unwanted stranger."

"Do you always eavesdrop on folks at night, Rosheen?"

"Only on gnomes who talk to themselves. Likely to hear something interesting that way."

"Well, not from this gnome." Deglan stood up and stretched, walked a few stiff paces away from the piskie. She was entirely too close.

"So, you stayed behind?" he heard her ask behind him.

He turned back. "Pardon?"

"When the gnomes left, you stayed?"

Deglan gave a self-mocking bow. "I did. My kin up and packed off for Toad Holm and I remained. Me and the fomori."

And Two Keg, Deglan thought, but he was wary to bring the clurichaun back into the conversation. "And what of you? Why are you here, Child of Summer? To converse with a dwarf and that ill-favored looking mortal youth?" He wanted to turn the talk away from himself and quickly.

"Child of Summer? You honor me. Would that I were so young." She smiled coyly at him. Deglan tried to keep the surprise from his face. She saw Spring, then. An Age before his own birth.

"The dwarf is nothing to me," Rosheen continued lightly. "But the ill-favored mortal youth is my friend and where he goes . . ." she motioned to herself and the surrounding air.

Deglan grunted at that and turned back to the night, took another drink.

"Why did you stay?"

Deglan wanted to scream. The endless questions! He spun on his heel. "What?"

"I was just wondering why you stayed," she pressed on innocently. "The fomori, I imagine, stayed to protect the village even though there were no more Fae-folk. Honor-bound to some oath . . . fomori are funny that way. But why you? Was it the humans? They do get sick quite often. And hurt. Did you stay to help them? Deliver their children? Soothe their fevers? Close their wounds? Protect them from Unwound?"

62

And there it was. Thrown out carelessly and casually into the night, like the rind from a fruit. He found himself standing, looking at her, saying nothing and she stared back. Not accusing, not victorious. Simply knowing.

"You saw one?" she asked gently.

Deglan looked to the ground and shook his head. "I thought I did."

"I have been around these people most of the night. They think you had their families flee because of a murdering husk."

"They came up with that on their own!" Deglan was growing angry, the tension of the past weeks piling in on him. "I had a mind to tell them it was the flux or plague, but when the husk turned up missing it was on everyone's lips. But I couldn't worry about that, I had to get them out of here! For all I know the husk did kill Brogan. There is no reason to suspect otherwise! But telling them one of those . . . those things was on its way here to slaughter them all would have been madness. They don't know what an Unwound is . . ."

"They've heard . . ." Rosheen cut in.

"Stories!" Deglan rode right over her. "Legends! So far away from their ken as to be nothing but crouching fable. They've fought barghests and ballybogs, wielded iron against them and emerged alive and victorious. They fear them, but they fight. And they would have tried to fight this! And for what? To die? To watch everything die? What good is an iron sword or sickle against an Unwound? Against living iron? The only man who would have listened to me was floating dead among the eels. So I let them believe what they wanted and had them flee, for all the good it did. They are all back now, every last child. All in danger."

"Have you seen it since?"

Deglan shook his head wearily. "No. And feel grateful for it."

"An Unwound would have been here by now," Rosheen said. "They do not rest."

"I know what I saw." Deglan glared at her. "It walked from Bwenyth Tor. Heading for the village. What else could it be?"

"The Forge Born did not fight at Bwenyth Tor," Rosheen claimed.

Deglan strode fiercely towards her. "You think to tell me? I was there, piskie! At the siege and well before. Trapped on that blasted hill for months, Red Caps all around, starving us out! It would be folly to charge, too many of them. We were Wart Shanks, born in the saddle, every last gnome, riders to the blood. We vowed we would die before we ate our mounts and we choked on that vow as we choked down toad meat! Faabar was there, too. He'll tell you. But I didn't see you there! No Forge Born at Bwyneth Tor? True. But they were coming. We had word. A runner got through, little fella, drunk a lot, you might have met him. He told us they were on the march. Liked to have pissed ourselves. Better to have died in a charge then suffer those metal monstrosities!"

"But they never came," Rosheen said. It was not a question.

Deglan lost some of his wind. "No. They never came. Thank Earth and Stone. I don't have to tell you, you seem to know your history. Might be you lived some of it yourself. The spell against the Forge Born was completed and they quit the battlefield. The Gaunt Prince recalled the Red Caps from the Tor to fight at his side and . . . we were saved. That sorcerer's bastard got himself good and killed. Gnome King did that, thank you very much, and the Rebellion ended. Irial Elf-King was put back on the throne and we were heroes one and all." He looked at the whiskey skin scornfully and threw it into the bushes. "Heroes who rode to the Tor . . . and *walked* away from it."

"Dark days," Rosheen whispered.

"Dark days," Deglan agreed.

"And nine hundred years in the past," Rosheen said.

Deglan laughed bitterly at that. "That's the thing about living iron. When a Forge Born goes Unwound, it goes more than blood crazy. It seeks to do what it was meant to do before the burden of a heart . . . of a conscience. Carries out its last order, killing everything as it goes, never stopping. Far as I'm concerned, those things were on their way the day Two Keg told us they were coming. It's just taken them nine hundred years to get here."

"What will you do?" Rosheen asked.

Deglan tried to answer, but the words would not come. He did not know.

"We hunt it down," the harsh growl came from above them.

Deglan looked up. Faabar stood looming in the doorway, large and powerful, a blanket around his shoulders, a burning behind his bestial eyes.

SIX

The tourney fields were set up a good mile from the Roost.

The rocky highlands of Albain were rarely cooperative when it came to expanses of flat ground and the Grand Master had asked leave of the Chief of the Dal Riata for the use of one of his larger grazing fields. The shaggy cattle were herded off, allowing the servants of the Order to set about the simple work of making the field ready for the contest. Colored pennants were hung from poles driven into the mud to denote the boundaries of the combat grounds, and a raised platform was constructed for the Grand Master and the Knights Sergeant so they might view the combats unobstructed. A separate, larger area was cordoned off with the same pennant poles for the squires' melee. All in all, it was a drab affair; a damp field dotted with sad looking flags under an overcast sky, the Roost squatting gloomily atop its craggy perch in the distance.

Pocket was disappointed.

He had expected a grand festival of music and banners, amusing performers and sweets for sale. But the tourney it seemed was to be a dour event, unadorned and without fanfare. He walked around in the cold, moist air of the early morning and tried not to let the dreary surroundings dampen his excitement.

What matter if there were no songs and banners? The knights would fight and that would be grand enough. As for sweets, Moragh had made him up a batch of apple cakes, fresh baked and well spiced. He carried them in a sack, desperately wanting to eat them, but holding off so that he would have them for the tourney. He had asked Moragh to come with him, but she balked at the prospect of a mile trip in the cold, only to have to walk the distance again on the return and uphill besides. So Pocket came down alone and paced about, bored.

The squires' melee was still hours off and only a few servants were to be seen, making the final preparations to the fields by removing stones, shoveling cow droppings, spreading rushes and wood chips over the muddier patches in the grass and roping off the area designated for spectators. Pocket did not want to have his view blocked by the throng of mac Gabráin's clan folk that were likely to attend the contest. Everyone would be taller, so Pocket stayed close by the tourney field, ready to claim a spot at the front, watching for when the crowds began to gather. He found a rock to sit on, up off the wet ground and settled in to wait, hoping it would not rain.

Pocket found it odd that the feast following Coalspur's funeral was a boisterous spectacle compared to the tourney that was to come. The Great Hall had been packed with long tables and benches, each filled to bursting with noisy feasters. All of the knights and squires had been there, shoulder to shoulder with mac Gabráin's clansmen and even the more important of the Roost's servants, the Mumbler among them. Lackcomb and the Knights Sergeant had a table to themselves. Áedán mac Gabráin sat with them, gravy in his fiery beard. Pocket wished he had been selected to refill their cups, but the Mumbler had him serving the squires at the far end of the Hall. Cocky and boisterous, they all had a great thirst and Pocket was kept busy, his arms aching with the weight of the flagon, but he cast an eye at the Grand Master's table whenever he was spared the slightest moment.

Sir Corc sat with the other Knights Errant, not drinking too much nor eating too little. Sir Corc the Constant, his brothers called him. Pocket had not yet had a chance to speak with the knight since his return for the funeral, but he dared not approach him during the feast lest the Mumbler see his dallying. Sir Corc only looked his way once, along with the rest of the Hall, when Pocket tripped on the outstretched leg of a squire and fell hard to the floor, smashing the empty flagon. He felt shamed as he picked himself and the broken pieces off the floor, all eyes on him, the Mumbler staring hardest of all. Seconds later, the feast resumed and the eyes turned back to their drink and company, but Pocket saw Sir Corc's face, turned over one shoulder, linger a little longer before turning back to his food.

When the feast was ended Pocket was sore and weary to the bones, wanting nothing so much as his little bed and Napper's furry company, but before he made it out of the Great Hall, the Mumbler called him over, babbling in his low incomprehensible voice. Pocket did not need to understand the words to know he was being chastised. The Mumbler hated waste and a broken flagon was a waste. Pocket had been a waste of time ever since he was put into the Mumbler's service, and the one thing the man hated wasting most was time. As punishment for breaking the flagon he was to help clear the Great Hall. And on it went, Pocket not hearing a word of it. The Mumbler was not cruel by nature and never struck him, but his disapproval was a living thing. Nothing would satisfy the man, leastways nothing Pocket ever did.

He kept himself well away from the Mumbler's notice over the following two days, so that he had a good chance of going to the tourney without some useless chore getting in the way. In truth, Pocket knew he would not have missed the tourney for anything and would simply have neglected any assigned task. Whatever punishment the Mumbler cooked up would be worth suffering to see the knights compete for Coalspur's sword. During his years at the castle, Pocket had watched the squires train for endless hours, drilling in quarterstaff, sword, spear and mace. But a true combat between knights, sworn and spurred, was something he never dreamed would happen. Unlike the funeral, the tourney was open to all whose duties did not prevent them from attending. Pocket was out of the castle and down the mile or more to the field not long after the sun came up on the appointed day.

And now he waited.

He might have dozed on his rock, but it was too cold for sleep, so he sat and tried not to look at his bag of cakes. An eternity passed before the squires came marching down from the castle, all fifty of them, not a one passing up the chance to win glory for himself. Pocket stood when he caught sight of them on the road from the Roost. He took up a place right behind the rope and it was not long before a sizable crowd of humans from the neighboring villages packed in behind him and all around. He was jostled and pressed, but held firm to his spot, clutching the rope with both hands, the scratchy fibers rubbing against his chin.

The squires split into two equal groups and gathered on opposite sides of the field. Most bore mace and shield, but a fair number carried only their iron tipped quarterstaffs. The heads of the maces were smooth and round, covered in leather with neither flanges nor spikes, but they looked heavy and stout enough to drop an ox if swung with enough force. The squires wore their traditional skullcaps and quilted jerkins over hauberks of studded leather. Over this light protection each group wore colored surcoats, one side wore black, the other green. The two groups milled around, some joking at one another, others stood silent and focused. Pocket wondered if any of them were afraid. *He* would be.

But knights, even would-be knights, were not small, like he was.

They were bold, courageous and trained at arms, eager to win their spurs and Coalspur's sword. Pocket could never win that sword, but he was here and would see who did. He smiled and looked about to see if anyone shared his enthusiasm, but no one met his eye.

Soon, Grand Master Lackcomb and four of the Knights Sergeant took their places on the platform. They were dressed simply in wool tunics, lacking the armor and finery displayed at the funeral, but they were armed as ever. Yewly the Salted and Mallander Smokebeak wore swords, Worm Chewer bore a monstrous maul on his shoulder and the Old Goose leaned on his spear. The Grand Master carried his heavy pole axe, but of Coalspur's sword there was no sign. There were no stools or benches, not even a chair for the Grand Master, so Lackcomb and his officers stood just like the crowd on the ground. Lackcomb spent a moment surveying the field and the two teams of squires, his dead eye sweeping over them and then he nodded to the Old Goose. The aged coburn stepped forward, his head and neck devoid of feathers, his comb shrunken and blackened; the effects of a horrible burn suffered during a siege, Pocket knew. In commanding tones he addressed the squires, announcing the conditions of the melee.

Twenty-five per side and only the last four standing would go on to the knight's tourney. Lack of consciousness or a declaration of yield removes a combatant from the contest. Killing blows, thrown weapons, dishonorable attacks to the back and the use of spurs to injure were all prohibited. The squires listened intently and with respect, but Pocket had little doubt they had been told all this before, likely more than once. The Old Goose wished them all skill in battle and the courage to fight with honor.

The squires formed up and Pocket felt a tightening in his gut. The squires in green aligned in a block, five ranks of five, while their opponents, the black surcoats, formed a tight wedge. At the head of the wedge was a large squire, brandishing a mace in each hand. Pocket did not know many of the squires by name, but he knew Gulver. Thick of neck and shoulder with feathers of a brown so deep they were almost black; he was big even by coburn standards, towering above the others behind him. He smashed his maces together and waited for the signal.

There were only thirty yards of ground between the groups and the damp air between seemed to grow heavy, stiffening as the squires prepared to charge. The sudden horn blast made Pocket jump and a terrifying screech split his ears as the two sides rushed at one another. For a moment it seemed neither group was gaining ground, their legs pumping in place, their talons scrabbling ineffectually in the mud and then they collided. Gulver, at the tip of the black wedge, smashed into the front rank of the green squires and went flying over when his opponent ducked, slamming a shield into his chest and heaving him into the air. The force of his own charge carried Gulver over and he landed hard in the mud behind the last rank of green surcoats, but he was up in an instant bellowing a challenge. Two of the green squires peeled off the back rank and engaged him, their quarter-staffs whirling. The black wedge had failed to penetrate the block of the greens and broke upon it like a wave. The black surcoats fanned out, attempting to surround their enemies and then all was chaos.

Pocket lost the individuals and saw only the mob, weapons rising and falling, the harsh sounds of wood and metal striking together. The mud was thrown in angry gouts between the fighters, covering them in thick grime, making it difficult to tell green cloth from black. Pocket heard cries of pain and triumph, calls of "Yield!" sprang from the din and the battle played out in vicious scenes that jumped from the teeming mass of pressure and violence. Pocket saw one squire take a mace blow to the face, his beak spraying blood and then he went down, lost from view and the attention of his attacker. Two squires fought back to back against a dozen or more, pivoting endlessly around to fend off the crushing numbers and then they were gone, lost in the press.

Another pair, muddied and bloodied, rolled on the ground, not four yards from where Pocket stood. They beat at each other with fist and elbow, shoulder and head, as they struggled in the muck. One wrestled atop the other and his fist closed around the haft of a discarded mace, its head broken off. As the heavy wooden handle was raised to strike, the squire on the bottom cried, "Yield!" his hands flung up in pleading defense. Heedless, the other struck downward. There was a sickening crack and the defeated squire lay still. The victor stood and was casting about for another foe when Worm Chewer knocked him to the ground. The Knight Sergeant stood over the squire, cursing him for a dishonorable coward. He raised the huge wooden maul high over his head and the squire begged for mercy. Pocket prepared to look away, his eyes half closed, waiting for the heavy weapon to drop. Worm Chewer froze and slowly lowered the maul.

"You have mercy, bantam!" Pocket heard him snap, using the demeaning name for squires. "I give it to you, as a true knight should! As you should have done! Now get your brother to the leech and see he does not die! Go!" The old knight kicked at the squire until he gathered up the foe he had bludgeoned and fled the field. Worm Chewer ducked under the rope and stalked back to the platform, reaching into the pouch at his belt to fill his beak with a fresh wad of the pink crawlers that gave him his name.

Pocket turned back to the rest of the field and found the melee had shrunk to only a few fighters. Nearby, he watched a squire with a quarterstaff hook the end of his weapon behind the lip of his opponent's shield, flinging it away before spinning to deliver a solid strike to the gut with the other end, laughing all the while. His winded opponent went down, holding up a hand in defeat, unable to speak. The staff wielder helped him to his feet and clapped him on the back as he hobbled from the field.

At the center of the field, the huge squire Gulver was still standing, only he had lost one of his maces. His latest opponent was pinned under his talon, unconscious. Three others were harassing a single warrior at the far end, his shield taking a good deal of the punishment, but the blows rained down and he yielded quickly. The trio turned and stalked back to the center of the field.

Gulver nodded to them and they formed up behind him. Those four and the laughing squire where all that remained. The four wore black. Small patches of green showed through the mud on the garb of the loner. The crowd was silent, watching. Pocket held his breath.

"Best to yield now, Flyn!" one from the trio called out. "We got you four to one and Gulver counts for three all to himself!"

The laugher, the one called Flyn, did not respond. He wiped some mud off his staff and peeled his skullcap from his head, shaking his comb free. Without warning he bolted forward like an arrow, straight toward the four. Gulver braced himself, his mace held low and ready. Flyn did not break stride, closing the distance swiftly, vaulting sideways as the hulking squire swung the mace in a vicious arc toward the ground. Flyn was in the air, the mace passing harmlessly under, and landed next to Gulver, delivering a hard strike to the brute just above the hip. The staff never stopped moving, the iron tip coming around to land solidly on Gulver's wrist, disarming him and then sweeping like a broom at his feet, spilling him over facedown. Flyn landed a final blow to the back of Gulver's skull before he hit the ground, where he landed hard and did not rise. The trio never moved.

"And I count for ten." Flyn laughed and turned his back, walking from the field.

"Four remain!" the Old Goose declared from the platform.

"Four for the knights' tourney!"

Pocket let his breath rush out and cheered with the rest of the crowd, remaining at the rope long after the others dispersed.

He watched the squires muster on the other side of the field, those that could still stand talking among themselves and congratulating the four victors. Flyn's display was impressive, but none of the squires stood a chance in the knights' tourney. They were good fighters and well-trained, but not yet admitted into the proud ranks of the Order. The Knights of the Valiant Spur were fearsome, every one tried and tested in the harsh wilds of the world. Many of them had fought giants in Middangeard and emerged victorious.

The Dread Cockerel often quested in Outborders, Blood Yolk slew a half dozen baobhan sith single-handedly. In his day, Yewly the Salted killed a kraken and the Grand Master himself used to hunt Unwound in Airlann. It was noble of Coalspur to grant the squires a chance for glory with his final request, but what could these young struts do against such seasoned warriors?

The squires made their way back to the castle, some limping, others carried. The captains of the Order had long since departed.

The knights' tourney would not commence until noon, so Pocket was again left to wait. There were more people about now and some of the villagers had come with pushcarts and wagons, forming a small market to tempt the tourney goers with food and trinkets, clothing, tools and charms. He wandered through with the rest of the crowd, wishing he had coin or goods to trade. He would get a knife or a thick, warm shirt or maybe something for Moragh if he could do ought but dream. The sellers kept casting dark looks his way and guarded their goods closely when he passed by, so Pocket decided to leave the little market before too long.

Remembering his apple cakes, Pocket found a quiet place by a low stack stone wall that bordered the field well away from the suspicious eyes of the villagers. He untied the string around the bag, pressing his face into the opening to smell the sweet, bready aroma, before reaching in and selecting a cake. The dough was cold now, but still soft and sweet, the apples sharp and delicious. He munched happily, feeling instantly warmer and wondered what the rest of the day would bring.

Bronze Wattle would win the tourney, of that he was certain. He was the bravest of the Knights Errant, his deeds already lauded in song and tale. The Dread Cockerel was the deadliest sword, but some whispered he was a merciless killer, lacking in honor. Surely the blade of one as valorous as Coalspur would not be won by such a knight. Both Stoward Thom and Banyon Deaf Crower of the Knights Sergeant were said to be competing as well, which would explain their absence on the platform during the squires' melee. Those old war birds were still formidable and would likely give the younger knights a beating, but Pocket doubted they would walk away with their former Master's sword. Of course, if Lackcomb himself fought none stood a chance. Not since Mulrooster had a Grand Master been so deadly and so feared, but Pocket did not think he would fight today. Any knight who challenged the Grand Master to single combat and bested him was granted leadership of the Order. A tourney fight might not hold with the tradition, but if Lackcomb were beaten, his days would henceforth be plagued with challengers.

Pocket's musings were interrupted when he saw a group of human boys coming towards him. He tensed and waited. Why now? He was just eating, not bothering anyone. He had spent most of his life alone, wishing for company, for friends, but he learned long ago he was not meant to have such things. If these five boys were coming to ask him to join a game or share a jest, then the hope of lonely years would come joyfully true. But that was not what they were coming over to do, and Pocket knew it.

"Look it here," said the tallest boy when they got close.

"What you doin' now?" The question was directed at Pocket, but it was the boy's companions who responded with sneers and side glances at one another.

"I am waiting for the knights' tourney," Pocket told them with a smile, hoping it would shield him. "Are you going to watch, too?"

They ignored his question. "He's that changeling's get," said the sickly boy with cruel eyes. "The gurg what lives up in the bird's castle."

"That true?" asked the tall boy. "You a skinchanger?"

"My mother was human," Pocket said, struggling to keep his forced smile. "I do live in the castle. I have a cat."

"He's a mutt," said the pale, grinning one. "All that hair on him, look. He's half dog."

They all laughed. "Must be," the tall leader leaned in. "That why you're so hairy, gurg boy? Was the gruagach a dog when he rut with your mum?"

Pocket did not answer. They would not have heard him if he did, with their laughing. His responses were meaningless. These boys had chosen this course and nothing he said now would make any difference. It was only a matter of how far they might take it and that uncertainty did not ease his mind, but he sat and waited, keeping his eyes wide, his face open, acting as if he did not understand, hoping they would tire and go away. A foolish hope.

"So you come to watch the cocks fight?" said the handsome boy with the sandy hair. "See the sport?"

"It is not sport," Pocket said. "It is an honorable trial to find who is worthy of the sword of Coalspur, so that the legacy of his valor may live on and bring justice to the world."

They did not laugh, just stared at him stupidly, their eyes narrowing.

"What you got in the sack?" asked the shortest one with the thick eyebrows.

"Oh," Pocket said pleasantly, looking into the sack and trusting to kindness. "Apple cakes. I only have three left, but maybe if we split them in half, there will be enough." He reached in and pulled a cake out and tried his best to split it in two equal parts, holding them out to the tall boy. He waited with his hands outstretched and the smile on his face, but the boy just stared down at him with loathing.

"I'm not going to eat anything you touched with your filthy gurg fingers." He kicked his foot across Pocket's hands. The cake halves fell on the ground and the pale boy stamped them into the mud, grinning all the while. Pocket watched and tried to hold back his tears. Moragh made those and they were his favorite, better than anything these boys had tasted.

"Why did you do that?" Pocket asked and stood up, his mouth full of spit, thick from the effort of not crying.

"You stole them cakes!" said the grinning one.

Pocket bristled and tried to respond, but choked on anger and bottled tears. He tried to step forward, to defend himself, call them all liars, but he was rooted in place, paralyzed by fear and persecution.

The sickly one scooped a wad of mud into his hand and slapped Pocket hard across the face. He reeled and almost fell over, but the grinning one shoved him the other way, while the handsome one cheered them on. The tall boy grabbed for the sack and tried to pull it from Pocket's hands, but he held tight. His hair was grabbed from behind and jerked hard, bending him backward, something pressing into his back, unyielding. It felt as if his spine would break. Pocket cried out in pain but would not let go of the sack. The jeers continued from the hand-some boy, calling insults at Pocket and encouraging his friends. Pocket's face was covered in mud, forced upward by the unseen hand pulling his hair, a fist or knee grinding into his backbone. He had offered them the cakes, he was kind to them! Why could they not have left him alone? What had he done to them? He hated them! Hated them for their cruelty, for ruining one of Moragh's cakes and he would not let them take the others! They could snap him in two, but he was going to keep the sack!

The handsome boy's jeering ceased and Pocket felt the pain in his back lessen, then he was released. Everything was quiet and still. He wiped the mud from his face and looked up. The boys were still there, the short one with the thick eyebrows behind him.

He must have been the one who grabbed him. But they were paying him no mind, just standing nervously, tight-lipped and staring. Pocket followed their gaze.

"Boys that look for trouble often find it," Sir Corc said, his voice low. "And sometimes that trouble is more than they can handle." He stood glaring at the boys, his eyes piercing. The knight's broad shoulders and thick arms were covered in brown feathers, one hand resting on the pommel of the longsword at his side. "Get you gone."

They ran.

Pocket felt even more ashamed than when he tripped in the Great Hall. He wiped at the mud on his face and looked away. He was surprised to find the sack still in his hand.

"It was just a game," Pocket said, eyes downward.

Sir Corc was silent for a moment. "To them it was."

It was true and the weight of that truth pushed the tears free. "Why do they hate me?"

"They are too young to hate," the knight answered. "They borrow the feelings of their elders."

"Like the Mumbler," Pocket said and kicked at the dirt.

"Master Bannoch," Sir Corc corrected.

"Master Bannoch," Pocket repeated. "But he does hate me. You didn't say he doesn't."

"I do not speak for Bannoch," Sir Corc said and Pocket felt a rising panic.

"I'm allowed to be here!" he said quickly. "I do not have chores today and the tourney is open to all!"

"It is," Sir Corc nodded. "Moragh told me I would find you here."

Pocket breathed a little easier and finally had the courage to look up. Sir Corc was unarmored, dressed in a long, grey woolen tunic, belted at the waist.

"Would you like an apple cake?" Pocket asked him.

Sir Corc approached and leaned against the low wall, shaking his head. "I would not take that which you fought so hard to keep."

"I don't mind sharing with you," Pocket said. "And I offered to those boys, but they . . ." He broke off. He did not know what to say about them.

"They are cowards," Sir Corc said flatly.

"They were not afraid of me," Pocket said sadly. "They ran because you were here. I was scared of them even before they tried to take the cakes."

"You were generous and courteous. And stood your ground, five to one. That is bravery worthy of a knight."

Pocket could not keep the smile from his face. "Who will you fight in the tourney today? One of the squires who won the melee is very skilled, but you could best him. Do you think you will fight Bronze Wattle or the Dread Cockerel? Do you need help with your armor? I know how it all goes on. I studied the suits in the old armory. When is your first fight?"

Sir Corc looked off towards the tourney field, his comb moving slightly in the cold wind. "I will not be entering," he said at last.

Pocket gaped at him. That could not be right. Why would he not want to fight? Surely he was not afraid! Even if there were no songs sung about him or tales told of his deeds, he was courageous and skilled and true.

"You must," Pocket managed feebly. "I will cheer for you. It is the sword of Coalspur, surely . . ."

Sir Corc shook his head. "I do not need a tourney to tell me I am not worthy of that blade. Come, I shall escort you back to the combat grounds."

As they set off, Pocket worried over what Sir Corc had said, but try as he might, he could not bring himself to understand. Sir Corc was one of the greatest knights in the Order. Or was he? It suddenly occurred to Pocket that he knew very little about him, beyond the fact that he was the knight that brought him to the Roost as a babe. He quested often in Airlann, the Source Isle of Magic, across the narrow sea to the west, but what he did there Pocket did not know. He never heard tell of Sir Corc performing feats of arms, slaying beasts or rescuing villagers. Some of the other knights in the Order were living legends, but Sir Corc was not famed for any particular victory or defeated foe. He was simply Sir Corc the Constant. Could he be craven? Pocket could not believe that. Sir Corc looked cross and Pocket worried he had offended him. "I must return to the castle," Sir Corc declared abruptly. "You will not want to miss the tourney." With that, the knight walked away.

Pocket stood for a while quite puzzled. Noon drew closer and it was true, he did *not* want to miss the tourney.

The human clansmen turned out in far greater numbers for the knights than they had for the squires and Pocket found it difficult to find an open spot to watch. There were two separate combat grounds for the knights and they would both hold bouts simultaneously. The final victors from the two fields would become the champions that would fight for the prize, but there was no way of knowing who would fight where, so Pocket found the best view he could and trusted to luck that his chosen field would host the knights he most wanted to see.

Again, he was disappointed.

The first match he saw was between Sir Pyle Strummer and one of the squires from the melee. Pocket grimaced. It would have been better if the squire was the flamboyant staff wielder Flyn, whom Pocket wanted to see again, but it was not. This squire looked small and awkward in full armor, the breastplate engulfing him. He held the blunted tourney sword with a shaking hand, his face all but hidden behind his shield. Sir Pyle was not a great favorite of Pocket's, but next to his opponent he might as well have been the Grand Master himself. The whole sorry display lasted all of half a minute, before the squire was on his back, talons kicking in the air. Sir Pyle was to continue on, the squire was eliminated from the contest.

Pocket heard cheering from the other tourney ground and hopped up and down, desperately trying to see what heroic match he was missing, but the gathered mass of spectators foiled his efforts. Crestfallen, he turned back to his chosen field.

The wrong field.

The field that was now hosting Sir Kortigern Hatch and Sir Pikard the Lucky. Sir Hatch was a large knight and young, but he acted as the Order's standard bearer, eschewing the questing life for the humble, yet honorable duty. By contrast, Sir

Pikard was getting long in years and might have served as one of the Knights Sergeant had he not stubbornly refused to leave the Errantry life behind.

The fight lasted longer than the first, but Sir Pikard's title did not prove true and he was forced to yield when his tourney sword snapped in two.

Pocket looked again in the direction of the other fights and scowled when he saw the pale boy who had attacked him sitting atop a man's shoulders. The boy's eyes were full of wonder and awe, a broad smile on his face as he watched some glorious duel from his high vantage; a duel hidden from Pocket's view by distance and a teeming mass of legs and backsides.

Rumors began circulating through the crowd that Bronze Wattle had just defeated Banyon Deaf Crower in the opposite field and the White Noble was made to yield by one of the squires!

Pocket listened with growing apprehension. He was missing it! All the best fights were happening without him! He lived with the knights, he knew of them and their deeds. These unwashed humans were just here for the sport with no notion of what they were witnessing. It was unfair! Pocket thought about pushing his way out of this crowd and finding a way to get close to the other field where the true feats of the day were being performed. But what if he could not get through? What if the people barred his way or accused him of picking pockets as they had done before? He would lose his only spot and not see anything at all and the day would be ruined.

A hearty cheer mixed with laughter went up from the people around him and Pocket turned back to his chosen tourney ground. A smile broke his face. Maybe this was not such a bad place to be after all.

The Mad Capon was the fattest thing Pocket had seen, coburn or otherwise. He waddled out onto the field, his bulbous body encased in armor designed to encompass his prodigious girth.

Like many of the knights, he wore no helm to show off his comb, but his pudgy face and fat neck made his eyes and beak seem ridiculously small. Even the tail feathers sprouting from the slit in the back of his straining mail skirt appeared tiny next to his broad haunches. Despite his globular physique, the Mad Capon was said to be a deadly fighter and was feared by many of the other knights.

After all, any coburn that would castrate himself to ensure his vow of celibacy was daunted by neither pain nor fear. The fat knight bore a flail and shield, the blunt head of the weapon already swinging lazily around on the end of its chain.

Pocket's heart leapt when he saw Stoward Thom enter the field. One of the Knights Sergeant against one of the most colorful and famous of the Knights Errant! This was going to be grand!

Stoward Thom was short and compact, but still quite strong. He bore shield and tourney sword, his armor well-used and well cared for. He wore a mail coif over his head, covering his comb and he saluted his opponent with a smile.

"This could get brutal, Capon," Stoward Thom said lightly.

The Mad Capon chuckled, his belly bouncing under his armor. "It was always so under your tutelage, sir." He charged the older knight.

Pocket was taken aback by how fast the Mad Capon moved.

He fought wildly, the flail swinging in all directions with reckless abandon. Stoward Thom was quick as well, dodging where he could, interposing his shield where he could not. The head of the flail hammered down and around and down again. Pocket could feel the impacts in his teeth and the crowd instinctively stepped back from the ropes. Stoward Thom could do nothing but defend himself as the fat knight's onslaught pressed him backward. One clever swing snaked the chain around the older knight's shield, the head of the flail slamming into his shoulder. Stoward Thom grunted, but his spaulder took the brunt of the blow as metal rang on metal and still the Mad Capon came on. Stoward Thom had not yet made a single attack and Pocket winced as another blow from the flail whipped into his breastplate. Surely he would yield soon! If this kept up there would be naught but jelly inside the Knight Sergeant's armor. Maybe the Mad Capon would feast on that jelly after the fight was done. But, as Pocket watched, it seemed that the Mad Capon was tiring. His blows came less sudden, striking true less often and he was certainly slowing, his ponderous body moving more to its nature.

And then it was over, as quick as it had begun.

The flail came across and the sword met it in the air, the chain wrapping around the blade. The Mad Capon jerked hard and the sword was wrenched from Stoward Thom's grip. The move left the fat knight open and Stoward Thom did not hesitate. He bull rushed, his shield a battering ram and the Mad Capon fell in an avalanche of flesh and armor, landing in a heavy heap. Stoward Thom pinned the Capon's weapon arm to the ground with a talon, bashing him in his small face with the edge of his shield, again and again. It took eight squires to carry the fat knight from the field.

Things got much better after that.

Knights fell and victors were named and Pocket felt his luck change, witnessing skill at arms he once only envisioned in his imagination. In a furious battle, Poorly Well disarmed Blood Yolk only to have his own axe snatched from his grasp and used to defeat him. Pitch Feather and Sir Adelard the Pure agreed to fight without weapons in a strange, yet fascinating match where Pitch Feather emerged the victor, but Sir Adelard was so soiled from the mud he looked as black as his opponent. Pocket never saw Bronze Wattle, who battled in the opposite field, but news traveled quickly between the crowds and word was the famous knight was winning every match with honor. The lineup of knights in Pocket's field was not without renown.

A hush fell over the people when the Dread Cockerel strode into view. Pocket saw him at the funeral, but only from a distance and in dim torchlight. In the light of day, the knight looked out of place, unwelcomed and unwanted. He was tall and rangy, with a sinister, smoke-like grace to his movements. Coburn resemble nothing so much as monstrous roosters, but there was something of the hawk in this one. His armor was the color of soot, unadorned, scarred and ugly; the mail around his legs was made of blackened rings. His feathers were a dirty grey, flecked with white and black, the long, usually vibrant tail feathers completely lacking in color. On his head was a leather coif, similar to the skull-caps worn by the squires, only this one was studded with metal and long in the back, falling around the knight's shoulders. The Dread Cockerel's deadly skill with a longsword was almost legendary, but for the tourney he wielded a cruel looking cudgel with an oaken handle and a head of iron. He did not carry a shield.

Pocket watched with horrible fascination as he laid his opponents low, one by one. Sir Kortigern Hatch and Sir Pyle Strummer acquitted themselves valiantly, but in the end they fell before the inexhaustible prowess of the grim knight. Neither of them left the field under their own power. Pitch Feather was no match for him, nor was Blood Yolk's fury enough to win through.

Not even Stoward Thom emerged victorious and he staggered from the field coughing up blood. The Dread Cockerel was indomitable and he alone stood when the matches were completed.

And so it would end as Pocket knew it must. The only way this day could end and the outcome was certain. Pocket listened. The other field was silent. Bronze Wattle must have won his last match as well and now he would face the Dread Cockerel.

The final duel was to take place on the same large field as the squire's melee and Pocket made his way over with the rest of the crowd where they mingled with the spectators from the other combat ground. Pocket shoved his way through, heedless of the curses and got right up to the front. Grand Master Lackcomb and the Knights Sergeant had once again taken up their position on the platform. Pocket saw Banyon Deaf Crower among them, looking none the worse after his bout with Bronze Wattle. Stoward Thom was not on the platform, hopefully recovering from the injuries suffered at the hands of his unstoppable foe. That would now be remedied, for the Dread Cockerel's next opponent was not old, nor a squire, nor fat. He was the greatest knight of the Order.

The crowd settled and the Old Goose stepped forward. "It has been a day worthy of the knight it honors! Both our remaining champions have refused a period of respite and so the tourney will proceed directly!" A roar went up from the crowd and the Old Goose stepped back. The cheers died as the Dread Cockerel took the field, but Pocket could feel the anticipation growing as the people waited for the next champion to emerge. He felt he would burst as the nervous energy and the whispers grew around him.

And then he was there, walking proudly and the voices exploded.

Pocket threw his small voice into the tumult.

"Bronze Wattle!" he cried, but his cheer was drowned out, lost in the maelstrom of deeper, larger exclamations.

"Flyn!" the crowd cried. "Flyn! Squire Flyn!"

Pocket lurched. The coburn coming onto the field was slight, his walk a swagger. He wore neither plate nor mail and carried only a quarterstaff. It was the laughing squire from the melee! Pocket looked around at the humans to his right and left, his mouth agape.

"That little cock's good and buggered," he heard one man say. "The grey one's a right monster."

"Nah," another man replied. "That Flyn is something. We seen him all day. Quick as lightning!"

"He'll have to be," said the first man, "if he plans on staying alive."

"Well, he knocked that one with the shiny helmet on his back sure enough."

Pocket whirled on the man. "Bronze Wattle!? He beat Bronze Wattle!?"

The man looked at him dubiously and put a hand on his coin purse. "Aye, he did and many others besides."

Pocket turned back around and watched as the Old Goose walked onto the field carrying a tourney sword, breastplate and shield. He went directly to Flyn, holding the armaments out. Pocket could not hear their words but it was obvious the Old Goose wanted the squire to use them and Flyn was refusing. The Dread Cockerel was a terror and this cocky scoundrel was going to fight him with nothing but a stick and some leather armor.

"Madness," he heard a man say.

All around him, the crowd started arguing. The people cheering Flyn's name were sure he would walk away with the prize.

Those like Pocket who had seen the Dread Cockerel fight were horrified, knowing that the match would only result in a dead squire. Why was he out there in the first place? Pocket was sure it should be Bronze Wattle, not some mirthful upstart. How could he have been beaten? And by a squire? The Old Goose continued to try and convince the stubborn squire to better arm himself while the Dread Cockerel stood unmoving, staring implacably. Coalspur's sword was as good as his.

At last, Flyn's protests won through and the Old Goose turned back to the platform. Flyn spun his quarterstaff and said something to the Dread Cockerel that Pocket could not hear. The knight made no reply but took a step towards the squire, the cudgel riding his fist. Pocket did not want to watch.

"HOLD!"

The crowd gasped and spun at the voice behind them.

After a moment of shocked silence they parted, allowing a figure to pass and approach the field. It was a coburn, dressed in mail and blue surcoat, both travel-stained and speckled with mud. A sword hung from his belt and a spear was propped on one shoulder. He was a good height and well-built, yet stooped and weary, his face stricken with exhaustion. He came within a few feet of Pocket as he ducked under the rope and walked to the platform where he knelt before the officers.

"Forgive my intrusion, Grand Master," the newcomer said with respect, but loud enough so that the crowd could hear.

Lackcomb's face was unreadable. "Rise, Sir Tillory, and be welcomed. We feared you lost." Pocket leaned forward. Sir Tillory the Calm, thought to be dead.

"Not lost, Grand Master," Sir Tillory replied as he stood.

"Only delayed in Kymbru. But I have come and wish to enter the tourney."

Murmurs began spreading through the crowd, but Lackcomb focused only on the knight standing before him. "The champions of this tourney have already been decided, sir. I fear you are too late."

Sir Tillory looked the Grand Master in the eyes. "I have heard that the tourney was open to all who might wish to enter, including the squires." His voice was even and steady with no hint of irritation. "All I ask is a chance to win the prize as is my right as a sworn brother of this Order."

"The tourney is near an end. The Knights Errant must return to their questing ere long. We cannot delay this decision further."

"Nor do I wish to," Sir Tillory said placidly.

"Very well," Lackcomb replied. "But you shall have to defeat both champions to win the prize and you look hard used."

"I will fight as I am."

"Very well. Whom will you challenge?"

Sir Tillory turned and faced the would-be champions. After a moment he turned back. "I do not know the youth. I shall fight the Dread Cockerel."

The crowd buzzed and Lackcomb nodded. Sir Tillory stuck his spear into the earth and removed his sword belt, doffing the stained surcoat as well. "Might I have use of those, my old teacher?" he asked the Old Goose, motioning to the arms the Knight Sergeant still carried. The Old Goose smiled and helped Sir Tillory into the breastplate. The knight took the tourney sword, but refused the shield and saluted the Grand Master before walking out to where the champions stood.

Flyn hesitated a moment, reluctant to leave the field, but after a moment he gave ground. It was the first time Pocket had seen him without a smile. The Dread Cockerel stood stark still, his face giving no hint as to his feelings regarding this new adversary.

Sir Tillory circled to the left, his legs spread, sword at the ready. The Dread Cockerel only turned in place, keeping his opponent in view. Sir Tillory was the broader of the two, but the Cockerel towered over him. Sir Tillory would need every inch of the tourney sword's length to get past the reach of that ghastly cudgel. Pocket set his jaw and resolved not to blink.

Sir Tillory lunged, but his thrust was a feint and quickly turned into a backhand cut. The cudgel knocked the blade aside lazily and then swung up in an arc only to descend in a crushing strike. Sir Tillory pivoted out of the way, but the Dread Cockerel checked his downward swing and spun, delivering a glancing blow.

Sir Tillory stumbled and almost lost his feet. The Dread Cockerel pressed the attack, the heavy cudgel swinging at the end of his long arm as if it weighed no more than a switch. Sir Tillory fell back, desperately trying to keep away from the flying iron. He did not attempt to parry, lest his sword be knocked clear from his hands.

The Dread Cockerel threw a ferocious forehand swing that came inches from Sir Tillory's beak. The force of the attack caused the Dread Cockerel to overextend himself and Sir Tillory's sword hammered twice into the side of his breastplate. The Dread Cockerel brought the cudgel around for a backswing, which the shorter knight ducked and then made a low slash of his own. The mail skirt around the Cockerel's legs took some of the impact, but the blade struck true and the grim knight drew back, hobbling slightly. Pocket felt his breath catch in his chest. It was the first time all day anyone had landed a blow on the fiendish knight.

Perhaps he could be hurt after all.

But Pocket's hope withered quickly. The Dread Cockerel advanced like a cat stalking some vermin prey. He did not attack, but simply waded in on Sir Tillory, allowing him to attack, turning the sword blows aside with ease. The shorter knight tried to stand his ground, but he dared not let the cudgel come within reach. The sword struck out, again and again with little effect. It was a strange dance; the Cockerel advanced and defended while poor Sir Tillory retreated, trying to attack. It was only a matter of time before he stumbled and then it would be over. He had come late, tired from traveling and whatever perils he must have suffered along the way.

He could not keep this up for long. In contrast, Pocket had watched the Dread Cockerel fight for the better part of a day and his strength showed no signs of flagging. He was no longer limping from the blow he received mere moments before.

And then it happened.

From his vantage Pocket could not say whether it was a stone that tripped Sir Tillory or a mudhole or simply a misstep, but he went down hard. He managed to get up on one knee before the cudgel came screaming down, and he raised his sword to block.

The heavy iron head crashed into the blade, bending it horribly before slamming into Sir Tillory's head. The knight's limbs went oddly limp as he fell, flopping in a manner that made Pocket queasy.

The Dread Cockerel stood over him, staring downward and remained there as the Knights Sergeant came running, dropping to their knees in the mud around the fallen knight. The Grand Master stood on the platform, waiting. Pocket watched as the Old Goose rose from the mud to face the platform and slowly shook his head.

Pocket stood, silent as the rest of the crowd. Sir Tillory the Calm, thought dead only this morning. *If only he'd stayed away*, Pocket thought.

SEVEN

It was windy on the Tor. The trees hissed in complaint, their branches bending, throwing their leaves into the air, flights of red and gold. Padric tied his hair back to keep it out of his face, but the wind plucked ceaselessly, and soon errant, wispy tendrils broke free to tickle at his eyes and lips. He shivered. The ascent had been tougher than he expected and when they reached the top he was sweating freely. Now the chill breeze cooled the moisture that clung to his skin and Padric found himself wishing for a dry tunic.

He considered sitting on one of the pieces of broken wall, somewhere out of the wind, to ease his quivering legs but dismissed the thought quickly. Faabar stood in the overgrown center of the ruined castle, his back turned. Padric would not rest so long as the fomori was on his feet. The steep grades to the top of Bwyneth Tor were taxing even with two good leg. Padric did not know how Faabar managed the climb.

He could do nothing but gawk for a moment when he first laid eyes on the huge warrior. Fafnir had instructed Padric to deliver the sword to Faabar's hut the morning after he and Rosheen arrived in Hog's Wallow. When the fomori came to the door, Padric almost dropped the blade. At least seven feet tall, he dwarfed even the biggest men Padric had known, his father among them. Faabar's shoulders were broad and sloping, his neck corded with heavy muscle. His skin bristled with coarse hair, like a cow or goat's hide, while a thick black mane fell across his entire back.

From this mane sprouted two sweeping horns, like a ram's, and below was a bulging brow. Faabar's nose was flat and broad, while two curved fangs poked out from his thick lower lip. His eyes were gold flecked with jet, an animal's eyes. A predator.

And now the predator hunted across the top of the Tor, his head uplifted, his body still, sniffing the fierce wind. Faabar wore loose fitting woolen breeches and soft leather boots, but he was bare from the waist up save the leather harness that held the greatsword strapped firmly to his back. Fafnir's work was impressive, it could not be denied. From pommel to tip the weapon was as tall as Padric, the blade almost as wide as both his hands and solid steel. Padric's steel knife was a weapon of utilitarian beauty, but next to the colossal sword, it looked fit for nothing but spreading butter. In addition to his new sword, Faabar also carried a long hafted maul of heavy wood with a head banded in bronze.

"A keen edge and sharp point are little use against a foe without flesh," the fomori had said when Deglan kept complaining about the excessive arms. The herbalist was worried about the extra weight and the strain on Faabar's injured leg. Had the gnome his way, Faabar would have stayed in bed entirely, but the fomori had been firm in his determination. Deglan only relented on the condition that he go along as well to tend the wound. They were freed from his fretting when they reached the Tor and the gnome refused to go up. He was waiting now at the bottom astride his huge toad. As they started up the steep trail, Padric thought he heard the cantankerous little man muttering something about the last time he had ridden to the top and a vow never to do so again.

The climb had taken the better part of the morning and the going was difficult. Faabar carried the maul in his right hand, using the haft as a makeshift crutch as they hauled themselves over boulders and root-choked inclines. Padric wondered if that was the true reason he refused to leave the weapon behind. Rosheen had an easier time of it, her wings carrying her almost effortlessly up to the summit where the ruins lay waiting.

And the wind.

Rosheen was grounded by the force of the gusts as soon as they reached the top and now huddled at the base of a gnarled tree growing within the broken leavings of what was once a standing tower. She sat well away, not looking in his direction, still wroth with him for coming along. That was fine by Padric. He was cross with her for trying to leave him out of the hunt.

They had been several days in the village, and Jileen offered them a place by the fire in the common hall of the alehouse. Ardal insisted that Fafnir reside in Brogan's house for his comfort until he took his leave. So Padric's days were spent helping Fafnir at the forge and his nights in the companionable warmth of the alehouse.

He saw little of Rosheen who remained strangely absent. She claimed to be helping the gnome with Faabar's healing, but Padric had known her long enough to detect things unsaid. On the fourth morning, Padric entered the oppressive heat of the smithy to find the dwarf already hard at work on a plough blade. The same blade commissioned by Brogan just before he died.

"Too much of the wilds?" The dwarf barely looked up from his labors.

Padric feared there might be a jibe in the comment and was tense in his reply. "Not at all. I am ready to leave whenever you are. I will not be going back to Stone Fort. You have my word."

"Oaths," Fafnir said between hammer strikes. "No need for those tricky things. Ingot and I are glad of your company. No one need bind themselves to me. Our travels will take us back to your home one day and it would be a pity if you could not see your kin because of an oath sworn in haste." The dwarf worked the tongs deftly as he spoke, turning the hot steel and hammering it into shape. It would be a fine plough, well-tempered and strong. Padric laughed at the thought; the habitual musings of a farmer's son.

"And it was not the wilds ahead of us that I was meaning, but the wilds surrounding us today. The wilds your piskie means to wander with Faabar and that sour gnome."

"Was that today?" Padric went to the coal scuttle and began shoveling so Fafnir would not see the confusion on his face. "I had forgotten." In truth, he had not known at all. Where would Rosheen be going with those two? And for what purpose? He had suspected she was hiding something, but willful as she could be, it bothered him that she would keep her journey a secret.

"Not how I would spend my day, for certain and sure. Out hunting a husk," the dwarf grunted as he bent the glowing metal.

"A fool's errand and wise of you to see it, boy. He is well away from here by now. Husks do not eat and need little rest, unlike men. You must be weary of such travel. Kederic Winetongue has men out looking and dogs too, Ardal tells me. Why would a wounded warrior, an herbalist and a piskie newcomer go out in search of a quarry long gone and well sought for?"

Padric continued to shovel as the question gnawed at him.

Now Fafnir was the one leaving things unsaid. Why all the dissembling? Padric heard the sharp, angry hiss as Fafnir quenched the blade in the water barrel. The answer came to him. He turned.

"Because they are not looking for Slouch Hat."

Fafnir looked up through the steam. "Then why say so? And why should you not believe it when the herdsmen so clearly do?"

"You do not believe it either," Padric said.

"No, but I am well-traveled and weary with the world. I see brigands and deceit everywhere. I am a dwarf, a mercenary people it is said, who seek only to sell their loyalty. Who am I to be trusting? Or trusted?" He fixed Padric with a friendly, knowing look. "Not much to do today, anyway. I can finish this alone. Take the day if you like, rest up . . . or whatever you like."

Padric made for the ale house and begged some food from Jileen before grabbing his pack, axe and knife. He caught up with the trio an hour later. Faabar's hut was vacant, but the fomori's heavy steps and the splayed prints of Deglan's giant toad were easy enough to follow. He found them on a meandering goat trail, headed up into the high country northwest of the village. Faabar was the first to turn and see him coming, but it was Rosheen who flew back to meet him.

"Go back," she said firmly, but Padric hiked right past her without a glance. "Padric, this is no game. Go back."

"Bugger off." It was harsh, but Padric was angry, sick of being disregarded. He made his way up the trail, eyes ahead, where Deglan and Faabar stood watching and waiting.

Rosheen was fluttering at his side. "Padric! Look at me! We will be back tonight, just wait for us in the Wallow! There is no reason you should go! Padric! Would you stop a moment? Look at me! Dammit! Padric!"

He ignored it all and only stopped when he reached the daunting pair. The gnome looked annoyed, but the fomori's face was still.

"Where she goes, I go," Padric told them. It was the only explanation he could give.

Deglan sucked at his teeth. "Then neither of you go."

Padric wished the gnome luck with that declaration.

Rosheen was as unstoppable as the tide when her mind was set. "I go where I wish, Master Loamtoes," she said and turned her fuming face back to Padric. "I am sorry, but this is no place for you. For a mortal. You must trust me, it is too dangerous."

"What is, Rosh?" he kept his voice even. "What is too dangerous? Hunting a man made of straw? You will need to do better than that if you want to frighten me off. I am not a boy anymore."

"This is not like fighting a gruagach, Padric!" Rosheen's voice was growing thin with impatience. "This is . . ."

"Is what?" he would not let her finish. "The truth of it now! I may be mortal and too foolish . . . too . . . unskilled for this company, but if you are all so wise, so powerful, why would I be in any danger from a lone husk? Even one that has killed? Answer me that, Rosh! Or else get used to me being here, for I am going with you."

"I cannot let you, Padric."

"Why?"

"I promised . . ."

"What is so damned dreadful that you would keep me from . . ."

"An Unwound!"

Padric laughed. He was so embarrassed for her that he could not even meet Rosheen's eyes. He kept laughing and looked at his feet, shaking his head. She truly still thought him a mewling child, frightened by stories. His laughter turned bitter in his throat and he did finally look her in the face. "An Unwound? Why stop there? Why not Festus Lambkiller or the Gaunt Prince himself? You really do think me a fool."

"She says it true, lad." It was Deglan who spoke, regarding Padric with a withering look, part pity, part disdain. "And you *are* a fool. I do not know any in the race of man who is not, but you are a prize among buffoons, not trusting the word of one you have known your whole, miserably short life. A life that will end even sooner if we find this thing, so do as you're told and go back. We have no use for you here." The gnome turned his toad and started up the trail. Padric turned to Rosheen, but now it was she who could not meet his gaze. Padric spared her the effort and started back toward the village.

"Wait," Faabar's voice rolled deep and wet in his throat.

Padric turned and the fomori limped down towards him. He came up and regarded Padric with his golden eyes. "Is it true? Did you battle a skinchanger and live?"

Padric struggled to hold the fomori's gaze. "I did."

"And the gruagach? Did it survive?"

Padric clenched his teeth. He had not been proud of killing the gruagach and the face of the little girl came to him in his sleep, forcing him to split it with his axe again and again in a nightly struggle of bad dreams. He was not proud, but the act had given him a sense of prowess, of courage. A sense that shrank away while he stood in the shadow of the huge fomori. Faabar's arms were slabs of muscle, thicker than Padric's waist, his weapons larger than most men. What was Padric's deed compared to this fearsome brute? But he answered all the same.

"No."

Faabar looked down at him for a moment longer then turned and began struggling up the trail. "He comes."

And so he joined the hunt, finding himself atop the Tor, in the wind, waiting on the fomori. During the trek, Deglan remained bad-tempered, Rosheen stayed in her huff and Faabar was intent on his tracking, so Padric marched in silence. He gathered from the few exchanges between the others that Deglan had seen the Unwound coming from the Tor, so the search would begin there.

They had been on the summit for the better part of an hour and the ruins did not seem to be yielding any trace so far as Padric could tell, but he was no tracker. Rosheen's patience broke long before his. She stayed on the ground, marching over to Faabar, who stood still as a statue.

"Anything?" she asked. Padric smirked. The fomori towered over *him*, next to Rosheen, he was a mountain. The piskie did not seem to notice.

"There are traces," Faabar said. "Even in these strong winds, the scents are here. Iron. Rust. Oil."

"Sounds right," Rosheen stated.

"No. There is something missing." Faabar looked down at her. "Blood. Unwound always smell of it, from many different sources. It would be the strongest scent. There is none in this air."

"There are none up here to kill."

"Perhaps." Faabar looked doubtful. Padric stayed where he was. He had nothing to offer but another pair of eyes and some stories about the Unwound.

They were soldiers of living iron brought to life by the human sorcerers that ruled the goblins in bygone days. They were said to be monstrous large and unstoppable. There were hundreds of them and they marched forth to slaughter the Fae that were fighting to put the Elf King back on the throne. The Fae rebels defeated them with Magic; working a spell to give them a heart. It is said they threw down their weapons in shame for their bloody deeds and abandoned the Goblin Kings. It was not one of Padric's favorite tales, but a good one nonetheless. He kept his mouth shut as the others spoke. He did not want to look the fool twice.

"Still," the fomori went on, "we will follow the scents that *are* here. They lead down from the old gatehouse." Faabar motioned to the ragged remnants of three stone walls, irregular in height and crumbling. Padric tried to detect even the shadow of a gatehouse in the ruins and failed. ". . . down the opposite side of the Tor. The boy and I will follow." Faabar turned to Padric and bid him approach with a jerk of his hand, then turned back to Rosheen.

"If you will go down the way we came and tell Master Loamtoes to meet us at the foot of the hill near Bairn's Babble. It is a spring. He knows the place. Circle around the northern edge of the base and do not split up."

Padric thought Rosheen would argue, but she surprised him and merely nodded before heading off back down the path they had ascended, leaving Padric alone with the fomori. He grew a little uncomfortable as he stood there in silence. It was not fear, but a gnawing apprehension. Over the past weeks, Padric had learned much about himself. The journey to Hog's Wallow had hardened him, both in body and resolve. He felt more competent and sure in his actions. He had never been overly strong, but he found that he possessed a well of stamina and a deep capacity to struggle through hardship, pain and toil. In Faabar's presence, all of that seemed to melt away. The fomori made him feel even more a witless child than his father ever did. Padric worried he would say or do something foolish, proving the gnome's harsh declaration that he was of no use. Faabar had spoken up for him, allowed him to come along and Padric feared he would disappoint.

"Come," Faabar said. "Our way will be more difficult."

Padric followed as they picked their way through the shattered gatehouse and on into the encroaching tangle of bracken and thorns.

"There was once a donkey track that led up to this point," Faabar told him as they made their way through the overgrowth.

"Narrow and winding, it was only used to bring supplies up to the fortress. But the gnomes wove their spells when we heard the goblins were coming, asking the Earth to swallow the path so that our enemies could not use it. Nature, it seems, has continued the work of Magic in the centuries since."

Whether it was the work of spells or natural growth, Padric could not say, but their way was certainly impeded. The downhill was choked with fallen limbs, dense hedges, tripping tangles of thick weeds and everything was covered in the ever-present flood of fallen leaves. Each step was a challenge and a threat, forcing Padric to think about every motion. He was so intent on placing his feet that he almost lost an eye to the jutting branch of a dead tree.

It caught him just below the eyebrow, forcing his head backward and his feet out from under him. He slid onto his backside with a curse, but recovered quickly. Thankfully, the fomori did not turn, but continued down, going sideways, his injured leg leading, keeping the knee straight as possible. The hillside was unforgiving and soon Padric could hear the fomori breathing heavy, giving the occasional grunt of pain.

They pushed on and before Padric knew it, he had pulled well ahead. He stopped to wait, grateful for a chance to catch his breath. When Faabar caught up he stopped for a moment as well.

"Better I should lead," he rumbled.

"In case we run into the Unwound?" Padric asked.

"No," Faabar gave a tired smile. "So I can slow you down, instead of chasing you down this damn mountain."

Padric laughed at that. He took two hard-boiled eggs from his pack and offered one to Faabar. The fomori nodded gratefully and popped it into his mouth, shell and all. Padric looked down at his own egg doubtfully, then bolstered himself and bit into it, unpeeled. The shells were sharp, but tasteless and the egg went down fine, if a little gritty. They shared a waterskin between them before resuming their descent.

"Padric, was it?" Faabar asked from the lead.

"That's right."

"Were you a hunter before joining with the dwarf, Padric?"

"No," Padric admitted. "My father was a farmer. We grew our crops and raised our meat. We traded with hunters for game sometimes." Padric had been shown how to use a sling as a child.

It was a skill meant to drive off animals that might harm the livestock. Padric had never even picked up a bow.

"I am not a hunter myself," Faabar continued. "Too much patience is needed. But I learned some woodcraft from those I have known. In war, there are few skills that are not useful, so I listen and I learn where I can. So, you and I are hunters today. Would you learn?"

"Gladly."

In truth, Padric had never been one for learning. He had grown up too mistrusting of others to accept their wisdom. Not that there were many in his village eager to take him under their wing, unless it was to teach mockery, scorn and accusation. He learned some from his father, but only grudgingly after he failed to surpass him in anything. His mother taught him many things through her kindness and her gentle, unyielding manner, and some tangible skills he was forced to hide lest he be seen as only capable of woman's work. Rosheen was more playmate than mentor. Now that he had joined with Fafnir, events were taking him on a wild hunt through the forest with an immortal warrior hunting a creature that was not supposed to exist. Padric smiled ruefully at his chance to be an apprentice.

"Know your quarry," Faabar began. "It sounds simple and should we be stalking a deer, it would be. But savage as it might be, our prey is no animal. What do you know of the Unwound?"

Padric took a moment before he answered. He had a sudden, foolish obsession with answering correctly and did not want to misspeak. "Before today I would have said they were myth and what knowledge I do possess comes from stories, nothing more."

"Tell me."

So he did, starting slowly. He told the story he knew from childhood, feeling quite the mooncalf when he was finished. "I am sure it is mere fable," he said sheepishly.

"It is not," Faabar said. "But there are errors in your telling. You relate the tale of the Forge Born. It was of the Unwound I was asking."

Padric frowned. "Are they not the same?"

"As the faithful hound is the same to the rabid dog. As you say, the Forge Born were soldiers. Disciplined, controllable, little more than puppets, but the spell which instilled them with a heart also freed them from their thrall, giving them a will of their own. Some did cast their weapons aside in grief, others turned those weapons on their former masters in vengeance and some took their own lives out of guilt, unable to bear the blood on their hands. When the war was done, the Forge Born remained and many in the newly restored Seelie Court called for their complete destruction. But Irial Elf King decreed it would be a wicked act to bestow them with goodness only to punish them for their unwilling servitude. The Forge Born were spared and allowed to find a place in the world."

"I have never seen one," Padric said earnestly. Fearing Faabar would take that as disbelief he added, "But I have not seen much."

"Nor would you have. It has been almost a thousand years since the Restoration and in that time the Forge Born withered, slowly succumbing to the wasting influences of long years. They were as much machine as Magic and there were none left with the craft to maintain them. There lies the other error in your account. The Goblin Kings did not create the Forge Born, but the goblins themselves."

"But there are goblins still in the world." Padric was certain of it. He had seen one when he was a boy, at least he had seen its head rotting on a pole.

Faabar grunted. "Oh they're numbers remain undiminished. All folk thrive during times of peace and goblins thrive at the worst of times. Might be there are more now than there were during the Rebellion. They cluster in the ruins of the elf cities to the north, like Black Pool. Some have even returned to the fold of their ancient kin, the gnomes, but save yourself a tongue lashing and do not mention such to Master Loamtoes."

Padric would remember. The gnome had shown him nothing but scorn since he first delivered Faabar's sword. Padric felt no need to further that ire.

Faabar picked his way carefully with the haft of his maul and continued. "For all their masses, goblins are a hopeless rabble, squabbling and leaderless. And what is true today was true a thousand years ago. That is how they came to be led by the warlocks. Ambitious men and powerful, they learned their Magic under the tutelage of trusting Fae-folk, all the while lusting for control of the isle. They were cunning and knew potent crafts, but they were still mortal men and could not hope to overthrow the Seelie Court without help. The goblins were many and easily swayed, so the warlocks marshaled them to their cause and went to war, wresting the crown from the elves and abolishing the Seelie Court. They became the Goblin Kings, usurpers and oathbreakers all, oppressing the Fae for long centuries, ending the Age of Summer and ushering in this . . . Age of Autumn.

"At last, when the suffering grew too great, we fought back and began slowly retaking what had been stolen. We were dubbed rebels," Faabar practically spat the word. "In truth we were liberators, sworn to overthrow the treasonous tyrants that put us under their heel. The goblin armies were numerous, but their masters were mortals and despite their spells, could not cling to life forever. A succession of weak Kings left the goblins divided, while we *rebels* grew in strength. Victory was in our grasp, or so we believed. And then came Jerrod the Second and his son, the Gaunt Prince. Our hopes turned to ashes."

Padric had heard much of this tale before, but never told like this. Faabar's slow, rumbling voice seemed to settle in Padric's chest and camped pleasantly in his ears. He was not hearing the tale, he was feeling it. It was not legend or history or fireside fancy, it was living and real and suddenly not so long ago. Faabar was there and saw it all. As had Deglan. And Rosheen. Padric was sure of it now. Never had she spoken of it so openly as the fomori did now, but it was a part of her all the same. They all shared it, gnome, fomori and piskie alike. Even the drunken clurichaun Two-Keg held it close. It was just behind the eyes. A haunting sadness wrought by the terrible events of days past and a deeper sadness beyond, of the better days before. Days that would never return.

Faabar stopped on the hillside and gestured around them.

"Gnomes guard the Earth. Sylphs are in the Air. Undine deep in the Water. But thousands of years before the warlocks rose, the goblins went deep underground and took the power of Fire from its former stewards. That is a long tale and not for today. It is enough to know that they retained their mastery over the purging element in the days of the Rebellion and were instructed by King Jerrod to harness it to create for him an army. The goblins obeyed the madness of their human over-lord and shaped the Forge Born in their blistering foundries deep below the Earth. Victory was torn from our hands on the day they first marched and we knew many more years of suffering."

"But the Fae King refused to destroy them," Padric repeated thoughtfully. "Even after the war was won." He absorbed the tale, nodding darkly to himself. *Mankind should not be blamed for the actions of Oathbreakers.* Those were Rosheen's words. *The Court understood that.* It seemed they forgave the Forge Born as well.

"Some helped us to rebuild," Faabar answered. "Others left the isle for lands not scourged by their hands. The goblins who made them were powerful Flame Binders and the Keepers of Fire. They were killed during the war or hunted down and executed for their creation. Without them the Forge Born declined, their slumped, lifeless remains standing like statues across the land."

Faabar's face grew grim and his voice low. He scowled at nothing.

"But for every ten that simply rusted to stillness there was one that went Unwound. Not even the wisest can say why, but all can agree that a Forge Born gone berserk is a ruinous storm upon everything unlucky enough to fall in its path."

Something occurred to Padric then. "You picked up a scent on the Tor . . . we have been following it. If an Unwound is so destructive why is there no evidence of its passing? This hillside is overgrown, thick with bramble and hedge. Nothing has come this way."

Faabar stared down at him for a moment, then nodded with approval and set off again. He did not continue downwards but set off across the hillside. Puzzled, Padric followed. It was not long before the fomori stopped again and Padric was forced to do the same. He halted abruptly and stared. There was a scar running down the hillside, a swath of churned leaves, trampled hedge, felled trees and broken limbs. Padric swallowed hard when he saw that there was not a tree branch remaining at least a foot above Faabar's head. Whatever had come this way was taller than the fomori. They had been hiking next to this destruction for hours, not fifty yards removed.

"When hunting dangerous prey," Faabar instructed. "It is best to track it. Not follow it."

Bairn's Babble was choked down to little more than a pitiful gurgle. The water trickled down the rocks and was then lost in a morass of mud covered leaves. Deglan cleared away some of the debris and used a few of the leaves to make a channel for the scant water, diverting it to fall over a jutting rock. He was able to get his waterskin under the flow, but it was some time before the slight trickle filled the skin even half way. Deglan waited, his arm cramping, his brow furrowing. When the skin was full at last, he moved so Bulge-Eye could take a drink, his tongue a pink, fleshy wad pressed between his wide toad lips. The piskie fluttered and paced and fluttered again, casting eyes up the wooded slope of the Tor. She was never still.

"Would you sit," Deglan barked. "They'll be here."

Rosheen shook her head disapprovingly at the Tor. "He should not have come."

Deglan eased himself down on a dry rock. "My thinking is none of us should have."

She stopped pacing long enough to give him a dose of the glare she was giving the Tor, then went back to her midair dance of worry. She cared for the boy. Deglan found some spit in his mouth and shared it with a leaf on the ground.

Mortals brought strange feelings to Fae-folk. Always had.

The elves used to view them almost as amusing pets. To the gruagach they were a sickness. Goblins would have worshiped the most powerful and kept the rest enslaved. Faabar protected them like lost lambs, even though it was his own people that tried to fight them off when they first reached Airlann's shores several millennia ago. The cliff dwelling fomori clans still clashed with human raiders from Middangeard, but Faabar had left the rocky shores long ago. Deglan had never seen him wroth with an Airlann-born human. Deglan's own people felt a need to teach and trade with mortals, placating them like younger siblings. The humans' knowledge of healing *was* appalling and Deglan never turned a patient away, but he bore no great love for mortals.

Not like the piskie. Especially *this* piskie.

"They're here!" There was relief in her voice. Deglan craned around to look, not bothering to rise. He scowled at the sight of Faabar sliding stiff legged down the slope. "Should never have allowed it," he muttered at Bulge-Eye. The boy was trudging dutifully behind, trying to look for all the world like he wasn't having fun. He never made a move to help Faabar, but Deglan did not miss the look of concern on the boy's face. He's been watching him, Deglan realized and wondered what the lad intended to do should the fomori have truly ailed. He could not have supported even a quarter of Faabar's weight. Still, there was something to be said for good intentions.

The pair came out of the tree line and onto the flat ground surrounding the Tor. Rosheen went to meet them while Deglan sat and waited.

"Best let me change that dressing," he said when they drew close.

"In a moment," Faabar said, breathing like a bellows. "I must needs sit for a time."

Deglan stood. "You sit while I work." He made a dropping motion with his finger. "Breeches."

Faabar hesitated.

"No need to be bashful," Deglan mocked, "The sun has not yet risen on the day that made a piskie blush." The boy snorted and received a flick in the ear from Rosheen.

Faabar frowned down at him, then dropped his weapons and his clothing. Padric had to help him remove the boot on the injured leg. Faabar reclined as best he could against the rocks.

Deglan was glad to see there was no blood blossoming through the bandages, but changed them just the same and moistened the poultice beneath. While he worked, Faabar related his findings.

"So there is one around?" Rosheen asked after the fomori told them of the destruction in the forest.

"Possibly," Faabar replied. "Whatever made that trail was taller than I."

"So, why the doubt?" Rosheen pressed. She was sitting on the boy's shoulder, the grudge from earlier in the day forgotten.

Faabar looked up at her. "Because Hog's Wallow still stands."

"And the trails we found do not head towards the village."

It was the first thing the boy had said.

Deglan clenched his teeth. "I saw it going there myself. I may be shorter than you son but I am not blind. If you think . . ."

"Wait," Rosheen cut him off. "Trails? More than one?"

The boy nodded. Faabar turned to Deglan.

"No one thinks you did not see it true," he said. "But Padric is right. We found evidence of its passing on several separate trails going up and down the Tor. Whatever it is, it has been ranging all over, but going nowhere near the Wallow."

"Do all of you have tadpoles for brains?" Deglan was fed up. "Hog's Wallow did not exist during the Rebellion! The Wart Shanks settled it after the siege." He threw an exasperated look at Faabar. "Remember!? It was a cavalry outpost long before the humans came with their . . . *sheep!* The Forge Born did not know about it, because it wasn't there! Their orders were to take the fortress and that is what an Unwound would do—fulfill that order! It's stalking around up there looking for the defenders of Bwenyth Tor, the gnomish cavalry and the warriors of the Brindleback clan!"

He thumped Faabar in the chest with his knuckles then himself.

"Us! We are all that remains!"

Their eyes held for a long moment and Deglan saw that Faabar knew he was right. The fomori stood and dressed, slinging the greatsword over his shoulder and taking the maul in his huge hands. "Then we shall attend to our duty with the same vigor as our once and future foe."

Deglan rose himself and glared at the warrior. "You pull those stitches and I'll skin you alive. I don't care how much vigor you have!"

"There is still daylight remaining," Faabar judged the sky. "I have a mind to follow the most recent trail." He looked at the boy.

"What say you?"

The youth nodded, his face full of determination. *Such valor*, Deglan scoffed inwardly, and then cursed himself for a bitter old cuss.

"Do you not have duties with the dwarf?" Rosheen said critically from the boy's shoulder.

The boy smiled wolfishly. "Who do you think told me about all this?"

"Meddling dwarf," Deglan said, just as Rosheen said the same. He grinned at her and she winked at him. But then her face froze, her gaze behind him. The boy drew his long knife.

Deglan turned quickly and found two lean, shaggy hounds not ten yards off, standing at the edge of the forest opposite the Tor. They were long of limb and snout, the muscles visible beneath their wet, grey fur. There they stood, so very close and had never made a sound. Deglan knew them.

"Sweat and Panic," he whispered.

If they were here then *he* could not be far behind. And then he saw him; a sinewy, compact man, crouching just inside the tree line. Matted, straw-colored locks grew past his shoulders. Thick whiskers covered his cheeks, but his lip and chin were shaved. He wore hunting leathers and a short mantle of animal pelts. In his hand was a stout spear, its head a broad point of thick, black iron.

Madigan the Sure Finder.

"Sheath your blade, Padric," he heard Faabar say. "You will not need it."

"Oh . . . he might," Deglan said softly.

Neither Madigan nor his hounds made any move towards them. They remained three sets of eyes, all of them watchful, patient and calmly feral. Sweat and Panic panted slightly, never blinking. Madigan could have been carved from the bark of the trees around him.

"Who is that?" Padric asked, his voice taut.

"Kederic Winetongue's huntsman," Faabar answered. "We had best be off. Riders will not be far behind."

"Too late." The heavy sounds of horses moving through the trees reached Deglan's ears. They rode past the huntsman and reined up at the spring. There were eight of them, all told, each wearing a tall helm, the faces beneath grim and bearded. They wore woolen cloaks and brigandine armor over their riding breeches and boots. Each held a boar spear in their fists, their saddles adorned with various other axes and swords, cold iron every one. Deglan tensed as one of the riders approached. He nodded curtly, recognizing the man.

"Acwellen."

A crooked toothed smile split the man's brown beard. "Ho, lads! It's the Faery Doctor! Out to gather pansies in the woods today, little man?"

"Actually," Deglan replied cheerfully, "I am looking for more codsoothe root. Just in case you decide to get amorous with *another* of the shepherd's stock."

Acwellen's face darkened as only the face of an oaf can when insulted.

"You should be careful, gnome," the smallest man with grey in his beard said through yellow teeth. "These lands belong to Thegn Kederic. You might get lost . . . and never be seen again."

"I doubt it, Drefan," Deglan replied. "I've been riding these lands for more years than you can count. Which is to what, ten? Before you have to take off your boots and use your toes?"

"We are on the hunt," Faabar put in loudly, drowning out Deglan's last remark. "Same as you."

Acwellen made a show of seeing the fomori for the first time. "And the guardian beast! My, my, this is quite the gathering. I last saw you bleeding in a shit smeared field, lowing like a calf at market."

The pale tub of suet named Fat Donall laughed at this, his tiny pig eyes squinting with mirth. Deglan recalled this cruel man laughing when a pack of wolves ripped a lamb from its mother mid-birth. Next to him, the gawky, chinless wretch known as Poncey Swan grinned arrogantly.

"And last we saw you," Deglan told the lot of them, "You were riding out of town before dawn, your horses' tails tucked firmly between their legs. Least they showed some shame in leaving. Unlike you lot of cowards."

Acwellen's face turned red as he stood in the saddle, brandishing the boar spear. The other seven riders formed up behind him, anger on every face.

"Peace!" Faabar shouted, stepping between Deglan and the horses. "Acwellen, do you seek the husk?"

The man nodded, still glaring at Deglan. "By the Thegn's order."

"And have you any sign of him?"

Acwellen shot a glance at Madigan's hounds, somewhat nervously to Deglan's mind. "It's only a matter of time."

"Slouch Hat's been gone well over a fortnight now," Deglan jabbed. "Might want to try looking back in Sasana."

"I don't need advice from a herbwife!" Acwellen snapped. "It's your kind should be leaving these lands! Your damn unnatural slaves, murdering decent folk! The Thegn will see a stop to it, hear my word!"

Deglan was growing tired of this lout. "Slouch Hat was no slave of mine. But

I am glad to hear the Winetongue is so grieved at Brogan's passing as to send his men out in search of his killer. Interestingly, the same men he ordered away from Hog's Wallow the day we found Brogan dead."

Acwellen's voiced dropped to a contemptible snarl. "That tongue's going to get you killed one day, little man."

Faabar stepped close to the man. "I have oft told him so," the fomori's voice was distant thunder. "But it will not be today."

Acwellen was ahorse, Faabar standing. The two were eye to eye.

Acwellen blanched and then turned his horse, giving his men the signal to ride on. He paused long enough to call back, "Go back to that sheep shit village of yours and leave the husk to us!"

Deglan shook his head as he watched the back end of the horse trot away. "If he ever falls under my care again, remind me to render him impotent. I know a plant that would do it."

Remembering the huntsman, Deglan turned back to the trees. Sweat and Panic were gone, as was their master. Deglan's thoughts went to Slouch Hat.

"May Earth help you if you are guiltless," he muttered to himself.

They lost the trail just as the last hazy light of a purple dusk dwindled in the sky. They had come across a small branch of the River Trough, narrow and easily forded, but beyond they found no sign of the Unwound's passing. The trees were undamaged, the leaves on the forest floor undisturbed. Faabar squatted in the shallow water, searching for a sign. Padric heard him growl in frustration.

They were all tired. The day had been long and the effects were showing in their little band. Deglan had not groused for several hours. Even his toad seemed ragged and sleepy. Rosheen had fought her weariness stubbornly and valiantly, but eventually collapsed on top of Padric's pack. He could feel her behind him, leaning against the back of his head. Padric ached all over, his feet stone bruised and sore.

They were countless miles from the village with night falling quickly and Faabar appeared to have no intention of turning back.

"It is following the stream bed." The fomori said this almost to himself, but Padric heard.

"Upstream or down?" he asked.

"Up," Faabar answered. "The silt is deeply furrowed, the stones turned."

"It doesn't want to be followed," Deglan said, stifling a yawn.

"But it leaves so clear a path," Padric said. "Once it leaves the water, its destruction will continue."

"But in the dark," Faabar said grimly, "we could miss it and pass right by without ever knowing."

"Or it could be waiting to ambush us," Padric said. The thought had come to him suddenly and he voiced it without thinking, immediately wishing he had not.

"Either is possible. And both are cunning." Faabar stood, his scowl burning in the last rays of dying sunlight. "Unwound are not cunning. This has been thought through, purposefully planned to throw us off and plant doubt in our minds. A bloodthirsty machine does not do this. They seek, they slaughter, they seek again. That is their way. This . . . is something else."

"What then?" Deglan asked, some of the bite returning to his voice.

"We won't know until the trail ends." And the fomori was off. Padric heard Deglan groan then spur his toad onward, up the stream bed.

"Are we really going to do this?" Padric asked his unseen passenger.

"You had your chance to turn back, farm boy," came her reply.

Padric smiled and followed after the toad.

The moon rose, bathing the stream in soft, cold light.

Padric could see where the blackness of the treetops gave way to the star encrusted sky and the fire of moonlight dancing in the water ahead, but naught else. The rest of the world was ink and mystery.

Faabar's huge silhouette led them, the great blade on his back gleaming sharply when he turned to check for signs of their quarry's egress. Padric wished he could ask Rosheen for her Faery-fire, but knew it would only draw attention should something be waiting for them in the dark, so he followed blindly, his once sore feet numb from the knee deep water. He trusted Faabar had a reason for traveling in the stream and avoiding the banks.

They traveled in silence, stopping occasionally to let Faabar scout the woods to either side. With each foray the fomori was gone longer and longer, while Padric and the rest waited in the water. They waited now, growing more impatient with each long minute. Padric felt his body flagging while his mind grew more anxious. This trek through the dark was beginning to spark of madness and Padric could not help but recall the last night he spent with Rosheen on his back traveling through a darkened forest.

Faabar returned at last, moving low and careful. He rejoined them in the stream bed and motioned them to gather. His voice was a wet whisper in the dark.

"Follow me and move silently. Padric remove your pack. Deglan you will have to leave Bulge-Eye here."

Something in the warrior's voice killed any complaint the gnome might have given. He kicked his mount over to the bank and dismounted. Padric followed close behind and dropped his pack near the toad. Rosheen took to the air once again.

"He will stay," Deglan whispered, patting Bulge-Eye's lumpy head.

"Follow," Faabar repeated. "Low and silent. Our lives depend upon it."

Padric did as he was told, hunching low as he entered the woods, stepping softly as possible. Faabar led them through the trees, winding his way silently between the trunks. He seemed to go in random directions, never staying long on a straight path. Padric was surprised how silently the large warrior moved despite his size and his injured leg. The gnome crept just as quietly and Rosheen was smoke on the wind. Padric felt he was crashing through the forest, making a tumult of snapped twigs and fallen leaves. *Our lives depend on it.* Padric expected to die at any second with the noise his feet were making.

They came to a rise in the land, the trees marching dutifully up the slope. Faabar led them down a gully at the base of the rise for some time before stopping. He turned to face them and put his finger to his lips then pointed up the rise. Finally, he spread his fingers and pushed his splayed hand slowly towards the ground.

Silence. Up the hill. Keep low. Padric nodded in the dark and swallowed his fluttering breath. They followed the fomori up the hill, three scared, blind goslings. Padric could see the lip of the rise ahead.

The trees stood at the crest, black columns edged in the flickering burn of firelight. Padric's mouth turned sour. More fires. More forest. More death.

Faabar bellied down to the ground and crawled to the lip.

Padric followed his example. Deglan beat him to the top and lay to Padric's left. When he settled in Padric looked over to catch the gnome's eye and recoiled, clamping his teeth shut against a cry of alarm. It was not the herbalist lying next to him.

The body was of a size with Deglan, but where the gnome was solid and husky, this creature was wiry of limb and ill-formed.

It wore a leather jerkin, studded with metal and on its feet were armored boots of heavy iron plate. A vicious looking billhook lay clutched in its knobby fingers. But the worst was the face, pinched and narrow, ears and nose sharply pointed, a wide gap-toothed mouth lying open and slack. The body was belly down on the ground, but the pale eyes stared up at the night sky, the flat head turned completely around on a broken neck. Padric had seen a face like it once before, rotting on a pole. That goblin, like this one, had been dead. The dozens in the small valley below were very much alive.

They thronged around a large bonfire, the blaze illuminating them in a harsh, hot radiance, their twisted shadows stretched and capering. The leaves of the trees, normally soft gold and honest orange, were molten hands shimmering above the furious clamor of the goblins. All were armed and armored similar to the corpse next to Padric, their heavy boots stomping, spears, scythes, bills, halberds, all thrusting into the ember filled air. The goblins cavorted and cheered. The fire burned and everything was awash in red anger; the boulders, the dirt, the trees, the skin of the goblins and the rough, shapeless bonnets atop every head. Padric locked his teeth together.

Red Caps.

Padric learned today that not all fables are false; that history and legend are sometimes one, but he needed no tale to tell him these were dangerous creatures. These fanatical killers had plagued the mortals of Airlann for generations and were spoken of with as much fear and disdain as the gruagach. But where a changeling worked its evil with trickery, deceit and quiet murder, the Red Caps brought theirs with the torch and the sword, razing whole villages, using the blood of their victims to dye their hats that horrible color.

Even the warriors in Stone Fort grew grim at the mention of Red Caps. Padric heard they slaughtered other Fae-folk with equal impunity.

He looked over at his companions. Piskie, gnome and fomori. Each face a carved mask of disdain, the firelight etching their features in burning shadows. Rosheen felt his gaze and looked over. Her expression was pained, almost shameful, her eyes wishing him a thousand miles away. Beyond her, he saw Deglan lurch forward, his eyes wide, the muscles of his jaw working beneath the skin. Padric turned back to the valley and saw the goblins settling as one of their number stepped next to the bonfire.

He seemed larger than the others, but that might have been due to the suit of heavy bronze armor that covered him toe to throat. On his head, he wore the same dreaded hat as the others, but a brazen helm, fashioned in the likeness of a snarling boar was tucked under his arm. He turned slowly in place, taking in the goblins around him, waiting for the din to die before speaking, his voice even, calm and dripping with malice.

"Promises, my cullies. Promises. Who keeps them?" He paused, his pale eyes gleaming, searching his band. "The Lord of the Pile?"

There were hisses, angry jeers, cursing and spitting.

"The fat lord of our mud brothers, King Hob?"

More screams of dissent and several of the warriors pulled their members out and pissed in the dirt. The speaker nodded slowly, a thin satisfied smirk on his face.

"Promises . . . who keeps them?" He thumped his chest, his bronze gauntlet ringing on his breastplate. "Torcan?"

The Red Caps erupted, their weapons pumping with each shrieking cheer. A few began shouting over the others, "The Swine's Wife!" and soon the cry was taken up by all, each goblin adding his voice to the call. "Swine's Wife! Swine's Wife! Swine's Wife!"

The one called Torcan held out his armored hand and a goblin stepped from the throng cradling an ugly battleaxe of pitted iron. Torcan took the weapon and held it aloft, the goblins surrounding him yelling madly, stomping their heavy boots.

"Swine's Wife! Swine's Wife!" Torcan's lips were moving, but Padric could not hear his words over the triumphal wails. The Red Caps quieted in order to listen.

"Torcan is your captain," Torcan said, "Torcan leads you. Torcan . . . and his wife." He hefted the axe onto his shoulder, leering at the blade. "She is a wanton slut, my cullies and so unfaithful . . . she kisses all of Torcan's enemies."

The goblins cackled in agreement, making rude gestures with their own weapons.

"She kisses them, but she does not love them. She lets Torcan caress her, but she does not love him. She has but one love, my ghobs. One for whom she pledges all her wet, red kisses. Her rightful lord, aye . . . and yours." Torcan paused, then took a deep breath and raised his voice for the first time, his axe hitting the sky as he screamed, "His Grace, the Gaunt Prince!"

Padric winced at the goblins' response and feared his ears would begin to bleed.

"Torcan promised to serve him! Torcan promised to fight for him! Torcan promised to see him king'd! But the mud brothers stole him away! Their dirt king and that elf slattern murdered him and on that day Torcan made a new promise! A promise to find our prince's heirs and see them sat back on the throne! To recruit all true goblins to his cause and swell his armies once more! To free our Prince's most trusted follower from his long imprisonment!"

Here he paused and faced the great bonfire, staring into the flames with eyes that reflected the heat. He took a slow step backward, his gaze never leaving the fire. His voice dropped with reverence and when he spoke again, his words were no longer directed at the assembled goblins.

"Promises. Who keeps them?"

The bonfire jumped and blazed brighter, causing Padric's eyes to pulse in pain. The goblins squealed with rapture, but Padric could not hear them over the growing roar of the fire. It licked higher into the night sky, red flames towering over a core of white heat. Padric squinted, but would not turn away, for a terrible truth lay within the flames. It was not wood that fueled it, no logs, nor limbs, nor kindling. The life of the fire was unnatural and impossible, for at its core sat a figure. It moved, uncurled itself and stood, stepping from the infernal cradle. It was a goblin, naked and hunched, his sagging flesh unmarred by soot or burn. Filthy tangled locks of hair dripped from his scalp, hanging almost to the ground, covering him like a foul cloak. He spoke, his voice a mushy croak.

"Smoke," he said slowly, the smile on his face growing from a sour grin to a wet, toothy display of pleasure. "And Fire."

"SMOKE!" the goblins screamed, "AND FIRE!"

EIGHT

The feather inched across the stone floor but the hunter remained still, green eyes held wide, watching. Only the tail moved; swishes of anticipation behind furry haunches bunched up and ready to pounce. Napper darted, but Pocket was ready and jerked on the string at the last moment, sending the feather flying across the floor. Seeing his prey escape, Napper redoubled his efforts and made a mad dash, but the feather reached the tower wall first and Pocket reeled it up. Napper was forced to check his speed before colliding with the stonework and performed the awkward yet agile sideways bounce that is known only to cats. Pocket sat on the first landing of the tower stairs and looked down at the expectant face of his best friend, full of whiskers and wide-eyed wonder. He lowered the string back down and laughed aloud as Napper tried to stand on his hind feet to swat at the feather with his front paws.

It felt good to laugh.

The castle and all within it had been infected with a depressing solemnity since the tourney. The Roost was not the most cheerful place in the brightest of summers, but the past few days had caused it to feel less a fortress and more a tomb. The servants had never been pleasant to him, but he would often catch them smiling and jesting with one another when they did not know he was around, but of late every face was grim. They passed each other without a word or a nod, going about their chores in silence, ignoring the presence of their fellow servants as they had once ignored him.

The tourney had ended a scant five days before and already Pocket had been forced to flee to his under-stair sanctuary, abandoning his chores in order to avoid the abuse from the tongues of the servants and the hands of their children. As always, the young were the first to harass him; shoving him aside, should he be unlucky enough to pass them in the halls, kicking over his water pail while he scoured the ovens, one pair of boys had even spit on him from a covered bridge as he dallied about in the castle yard. The first gob landed wetly on his foot, alerting him to the danger and he was able to avoid the second disgusting attack. He danced out of range and looked up to see their gloating faces staring down. With the children, this sort of thing was expected.

Their parents were not so bold, but no less cruel. Where once their eyes passed over him as if he were invisible, now they fell upon him with disdain, some even seeming to search him out as they would a spider that needs to be stepped on. He had learned years before that he could not trust the cooks and only ate meals he could scrounge himself or those Moragh prepared for him. He was careful never to be alone with any of the men for too long, lest some accident befall him.

Accidents were becoming common place in the castle. A fire broke out in the kitchens the morning of Sir Tillory's funeral and the next day two of the hunting hounds escaped from the kennels, bringing down several of some poor shepherd's stock before they were rounded up again. The blacksmith's daughter fell down the well in the outer bailey and near drowned. She was still sick with fever, lying in the leech's quarters in a bed next to the Mumbler. Both were raving, throwing exclamations in fits and spurts at the ceiling, neither aware of the other yet seeming to try and out-do one another with their fretful ramblings. The Mumbler had gone to the leech complaining of pain in his ear and within hours was reduced to a sweat-covered pile of gibbering nonsense and twitching limbs.

Pocket was blamed for all of it.

Suddenly, he was no longer just the changeling's get, an unwanted reminder of the foul couplings of mortal and Fae. He was the skulking doom of the entire castle, death in the shadows, misfortune made flesh. All of the castle servants knew he answered to the Mumbler, and when the old man was laid low by his mysterious ailment, their accusations turned towards Pocket. As the other incidents stacked up, their suspicion increased. The blacksmith sent him fleeing the leech's quarters, his tear-streaked face swollen with red fury, his weathered hands leaving his daughter's limp fingers and curling into tight promises of pain. The big man knocked over half the leech's stock of unguents in his attempt to reach Pocket, his violence fueling the mad ranting of the two unfortunates lying in their cots. Fortunately, the blacksmith was blind with despair, clumsy with grief and Pocket escaped amidst the breaking of pottery, the splintering of wood and the cries of the stricken. He had only tried to bring the girl some flowers.

He fled to the safety of his tower hideaway and remained there, but he was quickly facing the need to return. His meager food stock was gone and the empty rolling in his guts was usurping the fears in his head. Were he a proper changeling, he could become one of the castle children and roam free, never hiding, never starving, never fearing, but the ability to hold a human's form was as elusive as their trust. So he stayed and hid and slept. He looked at his map, played with his wooden horse and with Napper when the cat was around. He envied the little ratter's freedom, wishing he could fill his belly on a whim, but as yet, the notion of dining on rodents was unappealing. But in a day or two more, who could say?

"You will have to teach me how to hunt soon, little sir."

But Napper was not listening. He was staring, intently and unmoving, ears pushed forward, hunched and watching, watching the dark tunnel that led into the abandoned tower.

Someone was approaching!

Pocket pushed forward off the landing, spinning about to catch hold of the lower cross-brace where he dangled for half a heartbeat before dropping noiselessly to the ground. He dashed forward, scooping Napper up into a bundle then turned on his heel and fled underneath the stairs. Keeping Napper close, he squatted in the shadows of the scaffolding, facing the tunnel mouth.

The light came first, a creeping glow infecting the secure blackness. Pocket had borne countless torches and candles down that very passage, the flames a welcome companion, but in the hands of the unknown, that same light was a dreadful threat. No one ever came down here! Not in years! Pocket drew further back into the stairs, struggling to keep Napper still.

The light drew closer, trapped behind the iron shutters of a lantern, held aloft by something large and shuffling, a terrible silhouette that came steadily on no matter how much Pocket willed it to stop. The figure stopped just outside the tower proper, looming in the passageway, only the lantern came forth, stretched out by a cloaked arm. Light invaded the tower, forcing Pocket to retreat as far back into the foundation as he could go, his back pressed against the stones. He would be discovered! And then there would be no place to hide! His fear mounted, a fear matched only by the trepidation in the invader's voice.

"Child?" It was a reluctant whisper, tremulous and uncertain. "Child?"

Pocket's whole body relaxed and Napper hopped free, striding out into the light without a care to rub against Moragh's leg.

She stepped into the cavernous chamber and set the lantern on the ground, rubbing between the cat's ears in the same stoop. She was breathing heavily, her body and head wrapped in a heavy woolen shawl to guard against the chill in the stones. Pocket crawled out from under the wooden beams, his relief doing nothing to dispel his confusion. Why had she come? He never told anyone about his haven. Not even her. How had she known? But his questions fled when he saw the small clay pot in her hand, the aroma of stewed kale tickling the air between them. Pocket hurried forward and she handed the pot over without a word. There was a wooden spoon inside and Pocket tucked into the stew with a vengeance. It was barely warm now, but he did not care, it was painfully delicious. He looked up at her and smiled, trying to get words of thanks past his lips, but he was too busy with his first real meal in days, barely chewing before swallowing and shoving another spoonful into his mouth. Moragh watched him eat, her expression fixed, almost blank. The pot emptied quickly and Pocket raked the spoon around the edges for every last clump.

"Thank you," he said at last. "I will help you back to the kitchens and scrub this out." He went to grab her hand, but Moragh avoided him and took a half step back, blocking the tunnel.

She tried to force a smile but it turned into a sad twitch across the palsied half of her face. His shoulders slumped, the brief respite from his isolation and despair fleeing him.

"It is still not safe." He forced himself to say it aloud.

Moragh remained silent while Pocket stared at the broken floor. It was nigh on a week now. It should have passed. It always passed.

"When?" he asked. "When can I return?"

There was a pause and then her voice came in a broken whisper. "Never."

His head shot up. "Never?"

She nodded in the dim light of the lantern, looking old and worn, her face a melted candle.

"Wh—but, why? I did not . . . I'll stay out of sight. No one will . . . no one will know I'm there. They won't stay angry forever. It passes. It always passes! I won't come . . . I won't, not to the kitchens and I'll do all . . . all my chores. Master Bannoch will never have to wonder where I am . . ."

"He's dead, child."

Pocket's mouth snapped shut. Dead? The Mumbler? He stopped himself from saying it aloud. Moragh had not liked him to use that egregious title when the man was alive and Pocket knew she would not suffer it now that he was gone.

Gone.

Coalspur. Sir Tillory. And now the Mumbler. All dead. All gone. Maybe the castle *was* cursed.

But not by him!

"It's not my fault." He meant to scream it at her and then scream it again at the walls of the tower, raising his head, spinning in place, washing the dark stones with his protestations. But all that came out was a weak mumble and his only move- ment was to drop the pot, the clay breaking sadly on the stones. "It's not. What am I to do, Moragh?"

She came forward then, her expression strange, relieved.

"Do you know the old sally port? Behind the northwest tower?"

Pocket nodded. No one knew the castle better than he did.

"Go out there," Moragh continued, each word more hurried than the one before. "And down the rock until you come to the trees at the base. There will be someone to meet you, but you must hurry. All has been arranged."

"Arranged?" Pocket asked. "Who is meeting me? Moragh, what? I don't . . . you want me to leave?"

"It is the only way now."

"No . . . I don't want to! Surely there is another . . . why do you want me to go? I don't understand! What did I do? Are you angry? What did I do?"

She knelt down and took his hand in hers, shaking them with every word. "Listen to me, now! You must go! There is no choice left. Master Bannoch is dead and the smith's lass is like to follow before nightfall. When that happens . . ." Her voice clipped in her throat and she looked away for a moment, then swal- lowed and looked back. "I cannot protect you anymore. I am too old and without Master Bannoch there is no one else here to help me. For your life child, you must go!"

Her fingers squeezed his hands past the point of comfort, but the pain in Pocket's fingers was nothing compared to that in her eyes. His whole life he had known her face, careworn and tired always, but also strong, full of determination and a stubborn challenge at anything that might attempt to lay her spirits low. But he had never seen her despair, never watched her bend to the sorrow that forever lay scraping under the surface. He would not be the cause of her pain. He owed her that. That and so much more.

So he nodded. "I will go." He watched her pain worsen and loved her for it.

He felt a brushing at his leg and looked down into Napper's open face, the natural curiosity reflecting Pocket's own questions.

He scooped the cat up into his arms and hugged him close, breathing deep of the familiar fur. His eyes were growing hot and he had to fight back against the quivers in his chin. He needed to do this quickly or he would never do it at all.

"Would you hold him?" he asked Moragh. "He will follow me if you do not."

She held out her arms and Pocket passed the cat over.

Napper gave out a cry of complaint, but Moragh held him firm.

Pocket took a step back and looked into both of their beloved faces, committing them to memory. Moragh knelt in the lantern light, her own face battling against unwelcome emotions. Napper stared wide-eyed and agitated, protesting with his little voice. *Why?* He seemed to say. *Why?*

Pocket lurched forward and Moragh caught him up with her free arm, pulling him tightly against her. Pocket's forehead pressed into her broad cheek, his eyes closed tight and felt her tears fall. He buried his nose in Napper's head and he kissed him again and again, hating and cherishing the moment. Moragh held the three of them together and Pocket said good-bye to his family. He tore away and fled down the tunnel, heedless of the dark. Napper continued to call after him. *Why?*

Pocket pushed open the heavy door to find a morning grey and damp, the wind thick with spitting rain. He hesitated in the archway, his heel wedged between the oak door and the stone jamb.

Biting his lower lip, he stepped forward and winced as he heard the latch fall with a heartless click. He did not want to look back at the castle for fear of what he might see; a home lost forever or a bastion of wet unwelcoming stones? So he trudged down the narrow path of weeds and broken rocks that wound down the slope and away from the castle without a backward glance. Pocket knew the path led to the base of the mountain where a small copse of scrubby trees dwelt.

His feet slowed.

What if no one were there to meet him? Or worse, what if the blacksmith was waiting in ambush with the other men so they could murder him? Moragh said the castle was no longer safe, but it had never been safe, so why send him away? Why must he leave, unless they truly meant to kill him, and what better place than in the trees far away from the castle? They would cave in his skull with a rock or drown him in a milk bucket or hold his mouth shut while they stabbed him with knives, ridding themselves of the filthy gurg-child for good. His mind reeling with horrible fates, Pocket looked to both sides of the path for a means of escape, but the way was too steep and rocky, uphill or down. The Roost was built atop the mount for a reason, and where no army could tread, Pocket alone had little hope. He could run back up the path and pound on the door, trusting someone would hear and let him back inside! But who? Who would let him back in? Moragh was the only friendly face in the castle and she had sent him away. Napper would come, he would hear! He would hear and be helpless, standing on the other side of the thick oak listening to the pounding of Pocket's fists, mewling sadly, unable to open the door.

Pocket found himself running, but it was not up the path, back to the castle. No, it was down he ran, heedless and headlong, hot tears of hopeless anger mixing with the cold rain on his face. If he was to die then let it come! He was tired of being afraid, unwanted and distrusted! Let them kill him! All their hate and loathing and disgust, let them open his throat with it and see if his tainted blood could cleanse it all away! He bit back his tears as he saw the trees and almost lost his feet on the final yards of the steep path. His stumble turned into a leap and he screamed as he landed in the shadowy confines of the copse. Let them come and find not the scared little boy! Let them see the horror they all thought him to be!

Sir Corc stood next to a laden mule. He looked down at Pocket for a moment, a frown threatening to crack his feathered brow. "Good morning," the knight said.

Pocket froze. He found himself in a crouch, his breath pushing out from the bellows his chest had become.

"It is not necessary for you to be armed," the knight said flatly, before turning to the mule and tightening the load ropes.

Puzzled, Pocket opened his mouth to explain he possessed no weapon.

And then he noticed his hand.

His left had hit the ground when he landed, bracing him, but his right was pulled back behind and raised high. Seeing it now, Pocket straightened quickly, sheepishly trying to hide the transformed appendage behind his back. He could feel his fingers tingling beneath a slight burning sensation and there was an unpleasant pulling at his fingertips. Sir Corc appeared busy with the bundles on the beast's back, so Pocket risked a look. He brought his hands around, the left cradling the right, just in time to see the claws receding. They were black, thick and cruelly hooked, the tendons on the back of his hand thick and swollen beneath the skin.

His stomach churned sickly and Pocket looked away, rubbing at the flesh until the burning ceased. He was ashamed and more than a little disturbed. He had never formed anything like that before and certainly not without trying. What must Sir Corc think? That he was moon-brained! Addled in the wits! A wild and pathetic thing, displaying ugly and futile ferocity just like the rats before Napper killed them. He glanced back down. His hand had returned to normal, but he hid it anyway when Sir Corc turned around again.

He always seemed to embarrass himself in front of this knight. The knight who saved him as a babe and seemed to be saving him once again.

"Can you tend a mule?" the knight asked.

Pocket had been a scullion his entire life, not a stable boy.

He nodded anyway.

"Good," Sir Corc said. "You will lead him and feed him. Brush him down at night. Mind his hooves for stones. His comfort will come before your own. On a journey such as this, it must be so. Understand?"

Pocket nodded again. "Does he have a name?" He knew it was a foolish question. Sir Corc would never name an animal.

Pocket was already thinking of what he would call him.

"Backbone," Sir Corc said. "I call him Backbone." Pocket was pleasantly surprised and managed not to show it. "This too shall be yours," the knight said, handing him a bundle.

This time, Pocket failed to keep the shock and joy from his face. It was a long jerkin, sized to fit him and made of finely woven wool, lightweight yet sturdy and warm, but it was not the quality that made him marvel, it was the colors. It was deep crimson and pale grey, quartered in front and halved across the back; the colors of the Valiant Spur!

Pocket held it up reverently in front of him, unwilling to take his eyes off it, lest it vanish from between his fingers like smoke. All his life, his clothes had been threadbare and tatty, the rough garments of an orphan. His shirts were little more than sacks, his breeches castoffs that Moragh had washed and repaired. He had never owned shoes. Not until Sir Corc handed over a solid pair made from hide and leather, along with a wide belt complete with pouch. Pocket donned them all, the jerkin sliding over his servant's garb, hiding it from view. Knights were given to a little vanity and for the first time, Pocket knew why. He could not stop looking down at himself and wished he could run back to the castle so that he might admire his new raiment in a looking glass, and if the other castle servants should happen to see him, then so much the better.

Suddenly, the prospect of leaving no longer frightened him.

He felt prepared for the road and the world it traversed. He was so unconcerned with the perils of the journey the jerkin might as well have been mail. He strode over to Backbone's bridle and took the thick guide rope in his hands. He looked Sir Corc full in the eye.

"Lead on, Sir. I am ready."

The knight nodded, but remained where he was. "Soon," he said looking back towards the castle. "We await one other."

Pocket's mouth twitched. One other? The Knights Errant always traveled alone! But then again, *he* was here, why not one more? But he could not help but feel disappointed. Sir Corc could be taciturn, but the idea of sharing the journey, just the two of them, was an exciting one and this mysterious third felt like an intruder. He was about to ask Sir Corc who would be joining them when something caught his eye among Backbone's saddlebags. A well-worn scabbard was thrust through the ropes and Pocket's eyes fell upon the wide cross-guard, long grip and round pommel of a very familiar sword. But why did Sir Corc have it? He did not even fight in the tourney! That sword belonged to the Dread Cockerel.

Only it didn't. He did not win the tourney, at least not with honor. And Pocket himself had spied the deadly knight leaving the Roost in the pre-dawn hours two days after the tourney. He had been hunting bird's eggs in the nests clinging to the castle's eaves, risking the venture only in the bitter watches of the night. He froze at some movement in the Inner Bailey below and then shivered when he saw the tall, terrible form of the Dread Cockerel, striding out the gate like a threatening storm cloud. And he had not borne the sword, Pocket was certain. By rights it belonged to . . .

"Squire Flyn," Sir Corc said flatly.

Pocket turned and saw the young coburn amble confidently into the trees. He bore his quarterstaff in hand, a rucksack slung over one shoulder. Pocket felt his hair tingle at the memory of the squire's skill in the melee. Four against one and he emerged the victor! Pocket found he was feeling more agreeable to the prospect of a third traveling companion after all.

Flyn approached with easy strides then stopped before Sir Corc, an amused expression on his face. Sir Corc was broader across the shoulders, but Flyn was of a height with the knight and looked him boldly in the eye.

"The Grand Master explained this arrangement to you?"

Sir Corc asked.

"He did," Flyn said with a laugh.

"And you agree with it?"

The same laugh, "I don't."

"All squires must go on errantry before they are spurred, young Flyn. It is tradition."

"Alone," Flyn countered, his tone friendly. "It is tradition they go alone."

"And in their sixth year," Sir Corc said, his voice rising slightly. "You have squired only two years. You travel with me."

With that Sir Corc turned and started out of the copse.

"I won the sword," Flyn said to the knight's back.

Sir Corc stopped and it was a long moment before he turned. "You did. You won it. Because a good knight died at the hands of one not worthy to wear the mantle of this Order. But seeing as the death of Sir Tillory was not enough to strip one knight of his spurs, I see no reason why it should cause another to win his. Your valor and skill at arms has been noted and rewarded. You are going on your errantry and should you return, you will be knighted. Be content with that."

"I would have beaten him," Flyn said lightly.

Sir Corc's eyes narrowed. "What?"

"The Dread Cockerel," Flyn shrugged. "I would have beaten him."

Sir Corc shook his head slowly. "Valor and skill at arms. The Grand Master said nothing about brains."

Flyn laughed at that with genuine amusement. "Well put! You have me! Indeed it is you who has been given the least courtesy by our Grand Master, saddling you with my thankless company. My apologies, sir." Flyn extended his hand. Sir Corc regarded it for a second or two and then took it wordlessly.

"But," Flyn added as they clasped arms, "Coalspur is mine."

Pocket watched as Sir Corc's expression curdled. He released the squire's hand, stepped over to the mule and pulled the big sword free from the harness. He tossed it to Flyn with a jerk of his arm. "Then you can carry it." With that the knight turned and began walking away.

Flyn stood cradling the weapon and looked at Pocket for the first time. "I guess we had best follow." Then he winked.

Pocket could not help but smile. He pulled on the guide rope and Backbone responded, plodding dutifully along. Flyn walked next to him, using his quarterstaff as a walking stick, the great blade propped up on his shoulder.

"I fear I owe you an apology," he said after a dozen paces.

Pocket furled his brow. "Me?"

Flyn smiled. "Well, the mule has nothing but to thank me. I lightened his load, after all. So yes, my apology is for you."

"For what?"

"You served the squires at Coalspur's funeral. I'm afraid I was responsible for that nasty fall of yours . . . or rather my leg was. Very sorry about that."

Pocket remembered feeling such shame at the time. It all seemed so petty now. "It's fine."

"I thank you for your pardon," Flyn said. "If it is any consolation, I fell many times myself that night and unlike you, I have no one but myself to blame."

Pocket smiled again. It was hard not to in Flyn's presence.

"What shall I call you, my generous little friend?"

"Pocket."

"Very well, Pocket. And you may call me Flyn . . . or Bantam Flyn if you prefer. In fact, I think that's what *I* prefer. Yes. And why not? All the greatest knights have titles and it appears I am the greatest of all squires! Best to embrace it, eh? After all, I am to be the wayward babe in this trio of travelers. And we certainly have our wet nurse." Pocket followed Flyn's gaze up to where Sir Corc marched well ahead. Flyn laughed and gently bumped Pocket with his staff. "I hope that does not make you the whipping boy!"

"I am the page," Pocket said.

Flyn looked down at him, his face a mask of exuberant curiosity. "Indeed?"

Pocket gave a deep, assured nod of his chin. "Yes." He pointed at Sir Corc, then at Flyn and finally at himself. "Knight. Squire. Page. As it should be."

Flyn repeated Pocket's indications with his staff, but he said, "Wet-nurse. Stripling. Whipping boy." And they both laughed. "No, I jest! You have the right of it. Much more suitable, Master Page. Well then, do you know any songs?"

"A few," Pocked replied.

"Excellent! You will teach me your few and then I shall teach you my many dozens!"

They walked the day away, passing over the rough highlands and windswept hills that surrounded the Roost. The castle must have disappeared from view at some point, but Pocket never noticed. He led Backbone along the rocky trails and talked and sang with Bantam Flyn. Sir Corc stayed well in the lead, rarely even wasting a glance back. They hiked through the herd lands of the Dal Riata, the shepherds and their children watching them as they passed, some of the men raising a hand to Sir Corc in greeting.

The knight always returned the hail, but never stopped. He set a brisk pace, familiarity with the land giving speed to his steps.

They reached the coast just before dusk, the boulders grudgingly giving way to flat ground just before the surf. The sun had deserted them not long after midday and now they faced the ocean under a sky choked with grey clouds, spitting rain. A small fishing village squatted miserably on the shore, the stones of the little huts turned black in the rain. As they approached, Pocket saw several men standing out in the weather next to a small wharf. They wore thick woolen cloaks against the rain. Their beards were long, ragged and dripping and in their hands were thick spears with heads of pitted iron. A currach was tied to the wharf and Pocket saw two figures huddled in the vessel, clutching each other against the sea spray. Sir Corc had reached the village ahead of them, but stopped some distance from the wharf. When Pocket and Flyn reached him, the knight was staring at the small boat.

"Come with me," he said. "But say nothing." He snapped a look at the squire. "Do nothing." And with that he headed for the wharf. Pocket followed, apprehension growing with every step. He glanced up at Flyn who gave a simple shrug. As they approached, the four men stood where they were, staring like wet beasts. Sir Corc walked purposefully forward and Pocket noticed he wore only a dirk at his hip. Sword, shield and mace were still strapped securely to Backbone.

"Which of you are conducting these two across?" Sir Corc demanded.

None of the men answered, but one held up an arm. The knight approached him and began speaking in low tones, the wind and roar of surf swallowing their words. Pocket and Flyn stood among the remaining three, who stared with the blank boldness Pocket had grown to recognize in the pitiless bullies of the castle.

Three pairs of sunken, dim-witted eyes looked down on him, the thoughts behind them shallow and violent. None of them were even glancing at Bantam Flyn and took no notice when he drew the greatsword.

"Coalspur kept very good care of this blade."

Every head turned to find the squire casually inspecting the steel.

"Sharp," Flyn continued, thumbing the edge. "Sword this big . . . doesn't need to be sharp in truth. But it is. That is admirable dedication to one's weapon." Flyn seemed to come out of his revelry, noticing the men for the first time. He smiled at them in a self-effacing manner. "And look at me mistreating it! Baring this fine, sharp steel in the rain? In the salt? I must be a fool!" He fixed the men with a hard stare and his voice dropped. "Why else would I do it?"

The men found they had better things to stare at than Pocket. He looked at Flyn and nodded his thanks.

The squire winked. "You get to oil it," he said as he returned Coalspur to its sheath.

A long, low moaning drifted over the crashing water and drew Pocket's attention to the boat and its occupants. He could see them clearly now. A woman clutched a young girl, faces and hands fish-white in the wet cold. The woman shivered, her face drawn, lined with anger and grief, but she did not weep. Her energy was placed into the embrace, holding the girl to her, struggling to keep her still. The moaning came from the girl, a toneless, almost bestial sound pushing past her thick tongue. The poor child's face was witless, the skull underneath misshapen and over-large. She moved in a constant, clumsy jerk, fighting incomprehensibly at the world around her. The woman grappled tirelessly, at once calming and restraining.

"Pocket!"

Sir Corc's voice made him jump.

"Bring a blanket from the mule!"

He jumped to the task, fetching it quickly and jogging over to where the knight stood staring balefully at the man. Sir Corc took the blanket from Pocket and shoved it roughly into the man's arms.

"Now," the knight all but spat the word. "Have you been properly paid?"

The man looked down at the blanket, his thumb running over the thick weave. He looked up at Sir Corc, a grin splitting his sopping beard, teeth gapped and rotten.

"There are two of them."

Sir Corc seethed, but the man just stood there grinning his ugly grin. Pocket looked at the knight, water plastering his feathers, his comb quivering with barely contained rage. Sir Corc ripped the dirk from his belt and Pocket flinched away. When he chanced a look, the man was still grinning, holding the weapon greedily.

"See they make a safe crossing," Sir Corc warned him and walked away. Pocket followed and they went back to where Flyn waited with the mule.

"We will stay the night here," Sir Corc said. "Tomorrow, we hire a boat to take us to Grianaig."

"And whither are *they* bound?" Flyn indicated the two in the currach with his head.

Sir Corc looked at the boat for a long time. The man to whom Sir Corc had given the blanket and dirk was walking down the wharf, laughing and chatting with the other three. He climbed into the boat and unfurled the single sail while the others untied the craft from its moorings. The woman clutched the girl and looked at nothing as the craft left the wharf. Her face was placid, but her arms continued to stave off the girl's awkward struggles. That face haunted Pocket long after it was lost from view. The boat was barely visible when Sir Corc finally answered.

"They are banished. Sent to live as exiles, along with all the others on some accursed island in the Knucklebones."

"Others?" Flyn asked. "Other what?"

"Women," Sir Corc answered. "The cast offs. Poisoners. Those whose insanity make them too dangerous to live among others. Those given to sorcery or who couple with . . ." He broke off and glanced down at Pocket.

"The gruagach," Pocket finished the statement.

Sir Corc nodded. "The place they are taken, taken . . . and left, is called the Isle of Mad Women."

Pocket looked out over the flinty waters. The boat was gone from sight.

"That girl was simple!" Flyn declared. "Simple and misshapen! But she was not mad!"

"I know," Sir Corc replied, his voice full of disgust. "It is not the girl who is deemed touched. It is her mother. Who else but a mad woman would refuse to abandon so flawed a child?"

"You paid them!" Flyn took a step toward the knight. "You paid that cur to dump them on some island?!"

Corc's voice remained steady. "By human tradition, the women must pay for their passage. If they do not, it is likely the boatman will throw them over the side before they reach the isle. The woman had nothing to give."

"How do you know that wretch won't take your trifles and then dump them over just the same?!"

"Humans are a superstitious lot," Sir Corc replied. "A blood price has been paid. He will not break such a bargain."

Flyn was incensed. "We could have saved them! You! You could have saved them! Cut down those four dogs, not buy them off! This should not stand, sir! The Order should do something!"

"What?" Sir Corc asked flatly. "Do what? This stands, my young squire, because it has stood for hundreds of years. It is human tradition at its most cruel, but it is *their* tradition. There are places like this all across the Tin Islands. Not just here in Albain, but all over. Sasana, Kymbru, Airlann. They all have wharfs like this one and boats full of sorrow and they are all bound for that one isle. What can our Order do against that? Go to war with every human clan that casts off its undesirables? With fifty knights?"

"We could go to the isle," Flyn said defiantly. "Rescue them! Take them away from there! Where is your courage?!"

Sir Corc approached the squire, leaning forward until they were almost touching beak to beak.

"It has been tried," Sir Corc told him, "and failed."

Bantam Flyn did not flinch from the closeness of that stare.

"Isle of Mad Women!" he scoffed in the knight's face. "Where do they send their mad men?"

Sir Corc was quick to answer.

"They sit on the councils that judge the women." With that, he turned and walked away.

NINE

Deglan thanked Earth and Stone for the great toad's excellent vision. They crashed through the dark forest, the unseen leaves above jealously guarding all starlight, banishing the face of the moon. Deglan saw quite well in the dark, but at this speed he surely would have dashed his skull into a tree by now. Not so for Bulge-Eye, who charged between the rushing trunks with the full might of his back legs. Deglan leaned forward in the saddle, his face near touching the back of the toad's lumpy head. He did not need a low-hanging branch knocking him from the saddle, nor a broken neck. He would breathe easier when they reached the plains of An Curragh, where no obstacle would stand between them and the fort.

He parted from the piskie not an hour ago, trusting she could find her own way back to the Wallow and raise the alarm. In truth, he had no doubt she would succeed, but whether the stubborn herdsmen would heed her was another matter. They had suffered the need to flee already. Twice in less than a moon's turn was enough to turn their pride against them, force them to dig in and stand their ground. Without Kederic's warriors they stood no chance and even with them, there was little hope. Hope turned to an elusive cinder caught on the wind when a Flame Binder was on the loose.

"Buggery and spit!"

The thought of one of those mad bastards running free was the most infuriating kind of jest. A jest Deglan had seen coming for centuries. And there were times when he hated himself for being right.

The Red Caps were on the move. They cheered and cackled, waving their weapons, their torches dragging harsh light through the forest. They were not difficult to follow.

Padric kept close to Faabar and out of sight as they shadowed the boisterous horde, using no light of their own, staying on higher ground, keeping the trees between them and the goblins as much as possible. They were regularly forced to halt and keep low when small groups of Red Caps broke off from the main body in twos and threes.

"Scouting parties," Faabar whispered as they hunkered down in the underbrush, hoping they would not be stumbled upon and discovered.

Padric did not need to be told their destination. The Red Caps had been making their way steadily towards Hog's Wallow ever since the bonfire birthed its terrible predicant. The hunched goblin was given a robe, then helped onto a crude wooden litter and carried out of the gully, his followers saluting him in a frenzy.

They were on the warpath, marching boldly with no care taken for silence or subterfuge. Padric and the others waited on the ridge until the raiders were out of sight then rushed back to where his pack and Deglan's toad lay waiting. Decisions were made quickly; arguments flared and were snuffed in a few words and before Padric could make sense of it, Rosheen and the gnome were gone and he was chasing after the goblins, Faabar's hulking shadow leading him through the darkness.

Padric had lost all sense of time, but it seemed they had been tracking the Red Caps for hours. His back was sore and cramping from running while bent low, his wet clothes steadily working a chill into his bones. Surely they were near the village by now. Surely they would find it abandoned; the people forewarned by Rosheen and fled for the safety of the Thegn's fort. Fear had long ago given way to fatigue and now Padric just wanted an end to it. An end to fires and wizards and blind pursuits through the night.

The Red Caps seemed to be taking the most direct route, eschewing the winding game trails and sheep runs. They cut straight through the forest, over streams and gullies, ridge and rise, riotously bushwhacking towards their bloody purpose.

And still Faabar followed.

Padric was stone bruised and thorn scratched from a thousand unseen assailants by the time the goblins finally halted.

They were on the edge of the forest; the stone-walled meadows that marked the beginning of the herd lands lay unprotected before them. Bwenyth Tor loomed off to the right, a mute and useless sentry. Hog's Wallow was still some distance away, lost to sight over the rolling fields.

Damn fools! "Damn fools! You cannot stay here! They will be coming!"

"And we will be waiting," Ardal said without turning.

Rosheen's wings were tired from her long flight through the wilds and now she was forced to chase this mule-headed man all over his precious hamlet. The people of Hog's Wallow were emerging from their houses, confusion and fear dispelling the bleariness of waking. Ardal had wasted no time when she rousted him from his bed and set about the manful business of dooming his neighbors. He strode purposefully from door to door, pounding until he was answered before moving on, spreading the call to fight, a woodcutter's axe riding one shoulder.

"Every moment you delay brings them closer!"

But it was useless. The lout kept walking, summoning the townsfolk to meet before the alehouse, instructing the men to arm themselves.

The gnome was right. They will fight. And they will die.

"Ardal!" she flew around, forcing him to look at her. "Do not do this. You have families to think about. They must make for the fort."

He stopped. "I will not send them out into the plains at night unguarded. They will be safer here with us."

This foolishness has no end. "There is no safety here!"

Ardal's face remained resolute. "If Master Loamtoes went to warn the fort, as you say, then there is nothing to fear. Kederic will send his warriors."

"You are quick to put trust in a man who so readily abandoned you."

Ardal continued walking. "He will come."

Rosheen followed him to the alehouse. The wives and children were gathered, their faces flickering with uncertainty in the light from the building's fat lamps. The men were rushing over in singles and pairs, pitiful weapons in hand.

"Faabar bid me advise you to flee," Rosheen pressed on, hoping her words would reach someone of sense. "He is out there now. Padric, too. Shadowing the goblin advance. Giving you every chance! Would you throw that away?"

"We must defend what is ours!" Ardal countered, making sure the crowd heard him. "We have flocks and homes here. Would we give those up so willingly? See it all destroyed and ourselves with nothing but the Thegn's charity? Then we really are his tenants for good and all! Brogan did not want that. I do not want that."

"Ardal is right," one of the men declared. *Laoire. His name is Laoire.* "We will drive them back. With iron!"

Someone laughed.

It started small, and then grew to an obtrusive cackle. Every head turned towards the sound. Two-Keg stood unsteadily in the door of the alehouse, his face flushed with mirth and drink. He teetered out into the middle of the crowd, barely the height of the smallest child. He swept the people with heavy-lidded eyes, chuckling sourly, stopping when he found Rosheen.

"Best let'em stay, lass. They can do it! They's shepherds, affer'all. More than a match for what's coming. Only Red Caps. Pfssh!" He waved his hand dismissively in the air. "They've only been fight'n wars, murder'n folk, burning life to the ground for . . . A . . . THOUSAND . . . YEARS!"

He screamed at the assembly, his face a twisted mass of disdain. "You fuck'n fools! What will ya do here? Stand? With your pitchforks and peat cutters? With your . . . IRON? They won' care! They'll run right over you and rip those tools from your hands . . . use them to butcher your children! And they'll laugh. Think it merry sport. 'Cause that's all you will be. They'll set your precious sheep on fire while they're still livin' and delight as they run around, bleating as they burn. They'll kill you men, but not before you been good and scalped . . . given the same red hat they all wear. They'll rape your wives and your daughters . . . savage them mercilessly with hands covered in the ash of your homes!"

The crowd stood silent. The faces of the men were a mix of fear and fury. Tears fell silently down the mothers' faces, the sobs of their little ones giving voice to their weeping. Two-Keg gave them all one last pitiful look, then seemed to shrink.

"You can all stay for that . . . if you want," he mumbled.

"Not me. I seen it all before." The clurichaun shuffled off, away from the crowd and into the dark.

The villagers stood unmoving, heads bowed, eyes lost and wide.

Scolded children.

Ardal's face was the worst, all resoluteness vanished, replaced with doubt and defeat, the axe hanging limply at his side.

It was the alewife, Jileen, who spoke. "Ardal. We should go. All of us."

And then one of the men cursed, his voice feeble and afraid.

His arm was outstretched, pointing out into the night-covered fields. A fire burned out in the dark, just passed the last house.

Another gasp, another fire, this one just over the river. And yet another on the hill to the south where Rosheen and Padric had first spied the village. Then they were everywhere, surrounding them. A dozen red, angry eyes opening in the death mask of night.

Watchfires. Too familiar even after a thousand years of peace.

Rosheen had hoped never to see them again.

"It's too late," she said. "Ardal, listen to me! You cannot flee now." She pointed out to the fires. "The goblin magus can see you through those flames. He is watching and will know where you go! The Red Caps will not stop here, but follow you into the fields where you have no hope of defense. They will run you down before you reach the fort. You wanted to stand and fight . . . and now you have no choice."

Ardal stared at the nearest fire. "There is a choice," he muttered gravely and then turned to his people. "Women and children to the fort! You men, to me! We will stay and give what time we can." He looked to Jileen. "Be swift as you can. You need not cover the whole distance. The warriors from the fort will be coming on swift horses and will reach you 'ere long."

The woman looked as if she might protest, then nodded and began marshaling her charges.

"They will never make it," Rosheen told the man. "Even if you can stall the main force, the scouts that lit the watchfires are out there waiting. Who will protect your people from them?"

Ardal did not answer. He was not even looking at her. His gaze was fixed behind her.

Rosheen turned.

The dwarf had donned steel mail under his traveling cloak, a heavy bladed sword hung from his belt, along with a quiver full of grey goose shafts. His hands were covered in thick gauntlets of leather and metal plating, one of them clutching a stout bow.

"I will," Fafnir said.

Padric rushed across the fields, the stars and moon revealing less than his instincts. His breath burned in the canals of his ears, accompanied by Faabar's ragged gasps, drifting farther and farther behind. He had dropped the pack his mother gave him, his father's rope within it, left them behind somewhere in the dark. He ran with only his axe and his knife gripped tightly in his fists. The black mass of a field wall squatted before him and Padric vaulted it without breaking stride, leaving the limping fomori farther behind.

"We may not make it," Faabar's words haunted him. "We may not make it, but we must try."

They had waited and watched, every moment more horrible than the one before. Padric saw the armored goblin barking orders, his voice echoing mercilessly inside the swine-shaped helm. He saw the goblins form up in bands and despaired as he tried to count them, each one a tally to hopelessness. Three score torches hungry for life, three score weapons thirsty for blood. And above it all, sitting atop his litter, the twisted goblin craned forward, leering at the dark horizon. Without warning, his eyes erupted into tongues of sputtering flames, smoke billowing from the sockets. It made Padric jump, hairs prickling. The armored goblin, the one called Torcan, approached and knelt before the litter.

"What would you have of us, my lord?" he asked.

The goblin on the chair grinned, his eyes still ablaze, watching something only he could see through vile sorcery. "The mortals remain," he said. "They send the sows and sucklings away, but the men stay behind. Two dozen, no more . . . your lads may have them."

Faabar cursed and drew Padric off with a touch. When they could no longer see the goblins, the fomori squatted and leaned into Padric's ear.

"We must make for the village while his attention is diverted," he hissed. "They will be slowed by that damnable chair and that gives us a chance. Go with all speed. Do not wait for me. We may not make it, but we must try."

And so they snuck away. Snuck away and ran, determined to reach the village ahead of the Red Caps. Padric could not hear the fomori behind him anymore, but he did not slow. They had ventured out hunting a threat to the village and found another entirely. He did not understand much of what he had seen, but he knew the Wallow was in great danger along with everyone who called it home, so he ran on. There was only the breath in his lungs, the fall of his feet and the weapons in his hands. He had time for nothing else.

They were clear of the trees and flying across the flatness of the plains when Deglan spied the torches. They were moving fast, held too high off the ground to be goblins.

"Riders," he told Bulge-Eye. "Cut them off you tub of guts."

The toad surged ahead, covering the distance in moments.

The lead horse spooked and reared when Bulge-Eye leapt into its path. The rider struggled to get the animal under control, cursing as he pulled at the reins. Deglan did not waste breath on pardons.

"Hog's Wallow is threatened! Goblins are on the raid!"

The riders clustered around, torches fluttering. Deglan knew them and he knew the man who spoke for them.

"Then it is a day of bad omens," Acwellen said. "And piss-poor luck."

The man was smiling and Deglan's patience evaporated.

"Did you not hear me? Red Caps threaten the herdsfolk! They bring Fire and Magic and death! Even now, Hog's Wallow could be burning!"

Acwellen swept his men with a theatrical look, his smile contagious.

"Goblins," he said and they all laughed, Fat Donall loudest of all. "Magic." More derisive chuckles. Acwellen looked back at Deglan lazily, mouth twisted with amusement. "And gnomes . . . lost in the fields at night. What are we to do?"

"Ride for the Wallow, you daft prick!" Deglan had no patience for this fool. "Should I beg? Pay for your service and your loyalty like the Winetongue? Well and good, name your price! But waste no more time!"

Deglan watched his pleas fall on deaf ears. Acwellen continued to grin down at him, unaffected even by insults. This man's pride was as thin as his intelligence, usually rankling at the smallest slight, but now he remained calm, even relaxed. And then Deglan realized his mistake. He had been distracted by that damn smile, concerned with the safety of the village and the desperation of his message. He had not noticed Acwellen's eyes.

He saw them now.

"You knew," Deglan's teeth ground into each other.

"Damn you, Acwellen! You knew!"

Poncey Swan's spearhead caught Bulge-Eye just behind his right leg. The toad let out a high-pitched shriek of agony, lurching away from the villain who drove the weapon deep. Horses whinnied and reared, men shouted and Acwellen cursed as Bulge-Eye spun and lunged. The toad's bulk slammed into the chest of one of the horses, knocking it to the ground in a kicking mass of legs and panic. Deglan clung desperately to his mount as the toad barreled out of the encircled warriors, leaping away from the spears, the torches and the trap.

He heard Acwellen shouting orders and the horrible thundering of pursuing hooves. Another thrown spear shattered off a boulder to the left, but Deglan did not look back. The An Curragh was leagues of open plain, but still treacherous, especially to galloping riders with nothing but torchlight to guide them.

Bulge-Eye's surefooted and powerful leaps should have quickly outdistanced the horses, but Deglan could feel the injured toad flagging. They could not run forever. The sky was already beginning to turn the deep blue that heralds the sun and soon there would be nowhere to hide. If they could make it back to the forest, then there was a chance.

The shouting grew closer as the toad grew slower and the sounds of hoof beats drummed into the back of Deglan's head.

One of the rider's overtook them and came up on the left side, the horse frothing as it kept pace. The rider had abandoned his torch in favor of a sword and Deglan ducked the first vicious swipe. Bulge-Eye did not give the man a second chance. He leapt sideways, his weight crashing into the horses pumping legs, knocking it into the air. Something cracked hard into Deglan's head as man and animal lurched overtop, landing in a horrible chorus of snapping bones and helpless screaming.

Deglan's skull was throbbing, but he thought he could see the dark line of trees ahead and felt Bulge-Eye surge ahead with newly-found vigor. He leapt erratically in haphazard diagonals, scrambling as he landed, almost spilling Deglan from the saddle.

There was no controlling the toad's headlong rush and they crashed into the trees. Deglan was pitched forward and thrown off the toad's back, his face punching into the unforgiving turf. His mouth filled with blood and the gritty fragments of shattered teeth. He rolled to his feet and tried to rise, but the ground seemed to tilt and he pitched back over. He lay in the leaves, willing his head to stop spinning, but waves of nausea overtook him if he so much as moved his eyeballs. Bulge-Eye lay on his back not far off, the stark white of his belly strangely grotesque. Deglan crawled over, dragging himself along by his fingertips. One of Bulge-Eye's legs was outstretched, quivering uncontrollably. Deglan pushed himself to his knees beside the toad, his skull and stomach trying to switch places in his body.

"Got . . . to roll over," he placed his hands under the toad and lifted vainly. "Need to see . . . the wound. Come on, you old sack . . . get up." He strained, ignoring the lancing pain in his head, but he could not budge the toad's weight. Bulge-Eye's mouth was closed tight, his front feet moving slowly, pawing feebly at the air.

His breathing was loud and labored. "Don't you give up, you lazy lump of lard! Don't you do it! I can fix this. I can . . . but you have to get up. Bulge-Eye, I can't see the wound unless you get up!"

The sounds of men and horses drifted into the forest.

Deglan looked out across the plain. They were coming swiftly.

"No! No . . . more lying about! We have to go! Now get up . . . please old friend, you must get up." He heaved again, the effort sending an avalanche of dizziness through his head. He fell over in front of the toad's large face. Bulge-Eye stared back at him, but his eyes were empty and his breathing had ceased. Deglan pushed himself up, made a silent promise and ran unsteadily into the forest.

The men were clustered near the alehouse when Padric sprinted into the hamlet. Ardal had chosen their position well, backs to the stone wall of the stable, pitchforks and makeshift spears leveled at the ready. Half a dozen men with bows crouched on the roof, arrows nocked. The river flowed protectively behind the building, guarding against any attack from the rear.

"They are coming!" was all Padric said in way of greeting.

"How many?" Ardal demanded.

"Sixty or more."

The faces blanched before him, every man seeming more a boy.

"And there is something else with them," Padric was getting his breath back. "One of them can command Fire."

Ardal nodded. "Your piskie told us."

Padric looked around. "Rosh . . . where?"

"She leads our families to the fort. She and the dwarf. Where is—?"

He was cut short by a wordless whimper from Laoire.

Padric looked and felt a sickening in his bowels. The lights of three score torches danced over the fields, a swarm of huge drunken fireflies. They could hear the goblins' laughter.

They came screaming between the buildings, tossing torches atop the sod roofs and into doorways. The small houses went up in seconds and the entire town was revealed with the light of their destruction. Padric had spent the entire night in silent vigil, watching these crazed creatures with a detached fear. That fear turned to barely controlled panic as they charged towards him, mouths full of teeth. The bows above him thrummed, six arrows swallowed by the teeming mass of sharp metal and gleeful howling that barreled towards them. Padric bent his knees, flexed his fingers around the hafts of his weapons and prepared to sell his life for the families of strangers.

"SONS OF GHOB!"

The Red Caps ground to a halt, turning towards the bellowed challenge. Padric looked to the south and there, standing on the hill, was a towering shadow, broad shoulders draped in steam, horns gleaming with moonlight, sword and maul raised in defiance.

Faabar's voice boomed. "I am a servant of the Seelie Court, guardian of the Source Isle of Airlann! This trespass will not be suffered! Be gone! Your enslaved Fire shall not burn here, thralls of Penda!"

The faces of the goblins curdled, their confusion turning to outrage. Suddenly, they turned and charged up the hill towards the fomori, leaving Padric and the other men forgotten. Faabar did not wait for them. He bull rushed down upon them, the maul swinging in vicious arcs, scattering the goblins to left and right. Many fell broken to the ground and did not rise again. He towered over the mass, quickly surrounded on all sides. They stabbed with spear and pike, slashed with pole-axe and billhook, but the force of his charge was unstoppable and he won free, tearing a swath through the horde. Smashing through their rear ranks, Faabar continued his rush until he reached the stable. The big warrior's body was covered in a hundred small wounds and Padric saw blood running freely through his bandaged leg. Faabar did not appear to notice.

"You men!" he yelled at the bowmen on the roof. "Thin these vermin out!"

The archers reacted quickly, sending arrows into the goblins before they could regroup from the fomori's assault. Padric watched the shafts fall. There were so many goblins, the arrows could not miss, nor make a difference.

"Stay behind me," Faabar ordered. "Guard my flanks. Do not let them surround us or we are lost." Without waiting for a response, he turned back to face the Red Caps.

They came more cautiously this time, spreading out in a wide front. Padric looked into their gray faces as they drew near.

There was no fear, only a cold cunning, a calculation of the killing stroke. Each was half the height of a man, but they carried long hafted weapons that could disembowel a larger opponent with ease.

Boiled leather, studded and plated in bronze, hung filthy and worn upon their bodies, more protection than could be boasted by any of the shepherds. They made horrible bestial sounds as they advanced, barking and hooting, catching the attentions of the men and demoralizing them with promises of painful death.

And then they charged.

Padric saw Faabar's weapons swing in mighty strokes, but almost instantly the goblins were past him. The men of the village gave a wordless bellow and surged forward to meet them and Padric went with them.

A Red Cap cackled at him, thrusting a rusty halberd towards his face. Padric knocked the blade aside with his axe and slashed back with his seax, but the stroke did not have the reach, whistling harmlessly past. Pain cracked through his ankles as the halberd haft swept low. Padric fell hard and waited for the heavy blade to cleave his skull, but the blow did not come. He stumbled to his feet and found the Red Cap lying on his back, an arrow in his chest. There was no time to thank the men on the roof. Padric saw Ardal fending off two goblins, his heavy chopping axe barely able to parry the swift thrusts of his assailants. Padric ran to his aid, bringing his own hatchet down into the back of one goblin's head.

There was a woody clunk, followed by a revolting squeal as Padric pulled the blade free of the skull. The remaining goblin cursed, turning to face this new attacker when Ardal's axe took him in the shoulder. The force of the blow knocked the goblin to the ground, his arm twisted and broken. Ardal raised the axe high and dispatched him with a brutal downswing.

Padric took a quick look around. Faabar was continuing to hold the bulk of the Red Caps at bay, his greatsword sundering their polearms before they could reach him, the maul in his other fist sweeping into their ranks, breaking bodies. The goblins danced around, looking for an opening, stabbing at the fomori's face to distract him while others slashed low, trying to bring him off his feet. Their numbers were many and for every two that Faabar killed, three slipped past.

Their arrows spent, the men on the stable roof could only yell out warnings when a goblin broke through. Already the men were hard-pressed to deal with the interlopers. Laoire lay squealing against the wall of the stable, his left leg gone at the knee. Several others lay motionless on the ground, brained or gutted or with no visible injury at all. Somehow, those were the worst. Padric's innards felt full of putrid liquid and it was all he could do to keep the shit from running down his legs in stinking relief.

Defying his weakness, Padric leapt into the fray, charging four goblins that threatened Faabar's flank. He threw his axe on the run, the weapon whirling end over end to catch a goblin in the hip.

Padric closed the distance and kicked the wretch in the face, bowling him over. Before the other three could react, Padric was upon them, punching the long blade of his knife into an exposed neck. Hot blood squirted over his hand as he ripped the blade free.

A man he did not know ran up beside him and engaged one of the remaining goblins. The last got his billhook up in time and Padric was forced to check his charge. The hideous face beneath the blood colored cap smiled at him, crooked teeth full of rot and mockery.

The billhook made a swipe for his collarbone, but Padric stepped into the attack and dropped to a knee. The wooden haft of the weapon struck him, dull pain welling, but Padric ignored it, grabbing the shaft with his free hand. He yanked hard and pulled the goblin towards him, already stabbing forward with his knife.

The blade caught the plating of the goblin's jerkin and the grip fumbled out of Padric's blood slick hand. Shrieking, the goblin threw himself forward, slamming his broad head into Padric's cheekbone and they toppled backwards. The goblin was on top of him and they wrestled with the shaft of the bill hook, free hands punching and clutching. Padric buffeted the goblin across the mouth with his elbow. It laughed, blood thick with drool dripping onto Padric's face. The goblin released his hold on the billhook, snapping his hands into Padric's hair, yanking his head forward, then slammed it back down into the ground. Light burst into his vision, a swimming dizziness. He barely felt his head raised and slammed again. Pain-blind, Padric rolled, scrabbling and thrashing at the wiry mass trying to kill him.

When his vision cleared he found himself on top of the goblin, its eyes bulging, face swelling. Padric's forearm was across its throat, his full body weight crushing into the windpipe. The goblin hissed and spit, his hands gouging feebly at Padric's face, legs kicking in the dirt, snot tossed out of its bulbous nose. To his right the fallen seax lay within reach and Padric snatched it up, keeping the goblin pinned. The struggling bastard managed to catch his wrist, but there was no strength left in his arms. Slowly, inevitably the blade pushed downwards and the goblin watched helplessly, feebly trying to move his head out of its path. The steel was halfway through the eye socket when the goblin went limp, dropping Padric's entire weight into the knife, pinning the twitching head to the ground.

He yanked the blade free and staggered to his feet. Smoke from the burning houses was thick in the air, flecked with glowing embers. Nine of the villagers still stood, Ardal among them. A hole in the side of his head wept blood where his ear had once been.

The others were dead, dying or too wounded to keep their feet.

Laoire was no longer screaming. He lay silent against the stable, eyes staring sightlessly. Faabar still stood, dead goblins lying sprawled at his feet. The remaining Red Caps, some three dozen Padric guessed, had withdrawn from the fomori's reach. They stood back, malice and murder in every face, the knobby knuckles of their long-fingered hands caressing the hafts of their weapons.

"What have we, my cullies?" Torcan stepped through the ranks of goblins, striding boldly towards the fomori. His hideous helm rode the crook of his arm, the large war axe propped across his shoulders. "The mortals keep a guard dog?" He swept the bodies of his fallen soldiers with a face full of mock surprise. "And it bites!"

The Red Caps laughed, unconcerned that half their number lay slain.

"You would stand against us, fomori?"

"Aye, Swinehelm," Faabar's voice rumbled hoarsely. "Until you and all those who follow you lay in this pile of stinking meat."

He kicked one of the goblin corpses contemptuously and it rolled limply over to rest at Torcan's feet.

The Red Cap leader regarded the grisly carcass for a moment, and then swung his axe lazily down as if he were reaping wheat, severing an arm cleanly from the body. He kicked the appendage back at the fomori. "Have a last meal, elf's pet!"

Torcan grinned wickedly and stepped backwards, watching Faabar all the while. The Red Caps were parting, making way for something coming through the smoke, which appeared to gather unnaturally. It rolled thickly, defying the wind, coalescing around a nimbus of flame that made its way through the curtain of burnt air, which grew oppressively dry. Padric felt his throat and lungs begin to burn with each breath. The black cloud swelled then sucked into itself towards the fiery center. Four burly goblins stepped out of the smoke bearing that horrible chair on their shoulders, and seated upon it was the lank-haired goblin, his eyes the approaching flame.

Faabar turned sharply towards the men behind him, but it was Padric's face he looked into. "Run!"

A hissing roar erupted from the litter and a gout of flame spewed from the goblins burning gaze, blasting into the roof of the stable. The squeal from the men perched there was cut short as the top of the building was blown apart. Padric dove to the ground as chunks of blackened stone, burnt timbers and charred bodies fell around him.

"We must make for the river!" Ardal's voice yelled into his ear and he felt strong hands lifting him to his feet. They ran clutching each other, keeping their heads low, heading for the safety of the water. A concussive wave of heat threw them into the air as the alehouse erupted. Padric felt the sharp slap of water and choked as liquid filled his throat. He rose coughing among a sea of wriggling death. He was in the eel pond and it was steaming. The eels thrashed about all around him, hopelessly struggling against the boiling of the water. Padric vaulted out of the pond, throwing his arms up to shield himself as the wheelhouse burst into flames.

Ardal lay next to the eel pond, his brains dashed against the stones.

The men were fleeing, several of them burning as they ran, their tortured screams mixed with the perverse laughter of the Red Caps.

Padric heard Faabar bellow with rage and looked up to see the warrior hurl his maul at the litter. The weapon whirled through the air, a deadly windmill of heavy bronze. The wizard only smiled as it spun savagely towards him and Padric stared dumbly as the wooden haft turned to ash in mid-flight, the metal head falling to the ground in a molten puddle. Howling in fury, Faabar charged, his greatsword held high. A bolt of fire punched into his shoulder and he staggered, but managed to keep his footing. A second caught his injured leg and he fell to a knee. The goblin magus stood, his arms held low and outstretched, fingers curled. The air between the fomori and the litter began to shimmer and distort as waves of heat danced mercilessly in Faabar's path. Rising slowly, the warrior snarled and pressed on.

Padric watched as Faabar's tough hide began to blister and peel, sweat falling in torrents down his face. The hair across his shoulders smoldered yet still he planted one foot forward and then the other, dragging himself inch by inch. The Red Caps stood around, stamping their feet and the butts of the weapons, jeering as Faabar labored onward. A grunt of frustration and pain issued dryly from Faabar's nostrils and the sword fell from his hand, the metal glowing red as from the forge. He was two steps from the litter when he fell face first into the earth. Torcan and his Red Caps threw dirt, spit and insults as Faabar attempted to rise again. He managed to push himself to his knees, but his injured leg buckled when he tried to stand. Faabar's proud, horned head did not bow, but looked the goblin wizard in the eye.

"Irial Ulvyeh is King . . . of this isle. His . . . undying justice will fall upon you."

Screaming flames burst from the goblin's hands and Faabar was catapulted backward, thrown through the air to slam into the wall of the stable. The stones collapsed and the fomori was swallowed by the burning building.

Padric ran for the river and threw himself into the drink, the frigid waters an excruciating relief. He let the current take him, treading water to keep his head from going under. The village dwindled as the river swept him away and became nothing but a burning glow in the distance.

Two dawns crept over the horizon. In the east, the glow of the true sun lightened the sky. To the south, a baleful orange mocked the new day. Rosheen looked south.

Padric.

"All the curses of the Earth upon goblin-kind." She had not heard the dwarf approach, but she did not take her eyes off the false dawn.

"Must you give them curses because you could not give them steel?"

"Aye," Fafnir replied. "And truly they deserve both."

The dwarf had scouted ahead several times during their long flight from the hamlet. Always there were watchfires and always he returned with no arrows spent, no blood on his blade.

They suffered no ambush along the way and the abandoned fires were the only sign of goblins.

Oddly fortunate.

The refugees had stopped to rest and to watch and to weep when the glimmer of their village's fate appeared behind them. The Red Caps would be coming, Rosheen was certain, but the men had done their job, giving them time to escape. The wives and old men said the Thegn's fort was near. They would reach it and they would be safe, free to live new lives as widows and orphans under the care of a foreign warlord.

"We need to keep moving," was all Fafnir said before turning his back to the south.

Rosheen watched for a moment more.

He is safer with the fomori. She did not often lie to herself and the comforting delusion did not hold long in her mind. *The time for keeping him safe slipped by long ago.*

Morning had fully blossomed when the fort appeared across the plains. Chill mist clung to the man-made hill that the great wooden walls perched upon. The structure dominated the landscape, hunkered protectively above the partitioned fields where cattle and sheep pulled at the dew-damp grass. The villagers produced pitiful expressions of relief and quickened their pace, making for the hill and the uninviting fort with more speed than when they fled their homes. Fafnir took the guide rope of his mule from the boy who had led the animal during the flight. Rosheen turned her back in disgust.

Must have his goods. Plenty of trade to be had in a fort.

The people were halfway across the fields and riders were already coming out the gate to meet them. Riders that were looked for throughout the length of their harrowing journey. She had a moment's worry for the gnome, but there was little room in her heart left, so long as Padric's fate remained a mystery.

Rosheen made to follow the villagers when she was grabbed from behind and pulled backwards. Thick, powerful fingers clutched her from shoulders to thighs, pinning her arms and her wings. The dwarf's strange, lilting voice whispered closely to her. "Oh, I do not think you will be going up there."

TEN

Padric could not remember what it was to be warm. The suffocating horror of the burning village was a misremembered nightmare. The real world was uncontrollable shivering, spasms of numb pain and building panic that could only be calmed if he surrendered to death.

And Padric did not want to die.

He stayed in the river as long as he could, hours or minutes, he did not know. The sun had risen, barely discernible behind a film of cloud, ashamed to look upon the doings of the night. He struggle to the nearest bank and hauled himself out of the current.

The icy waters were a warm bath compared to the shock of the morning air. The slightest breeze sliced into his bones and his shivering turned into violent convulsions, his teeth drumming against each other in clacking mockery at his helpless condition. He lay curled tightly into himself on the bank, eyes and fists clenched painfully tight, willing the cold to leave him alone. It was no use. If he lay there, he would die.

Fighting for control of his limbs, Padric rose and stripped to his skin, fingers useless shards of blunt meat. A pained whimper came unbidden from his lips and holding his clothes in a sodden bundle, he ran. The air against his wet skin was excruciating, but that was only the surface. His survival lay deeper, in his muscles and his blood and the heart that fueled them. He ran, forcing the warmth to pump through him. His breath wheezed in his chest, his nostrils ran with stinging fluid, but he kept running, ignoring the awful slap of his numb feet against the grass.

He forced himself to stop when he saw the strays, four ewes and two lambs, huddled together near an outcropping of boulders. He crept up carefully, the cold instantly returning. If he spooked them, he was lost. It was difficult to keep his voice calm, his wordless sounds seeming harsh in his ragged throat, but he managed to get within arm's reach of the biggest ewe. He soothed her with his voice and with gentle strokes, edging closer. At last he was able to kneel down and place his arms around her body, pressing himself into her wool. The sour, earthy smell was intoxicating and he drank it in as warmth and feeling began to slowly return to his body.

The other sheep remained close, more at ease in his presence. They were fellow survivors of the Wallow, truly lost without the company of dog or man. Padric wondered if they were of Laoire's flock, or Dolan's or Ardal's or some other man whose name he never knew. They were all dead now. The smoke from the village was visible in the distance. He did not know where the Red Caps would go next, but he had to find safety and shelter.

Ardal had said the fort was a twelve-mile journey and Padric thought he had a rough estimation of where it could be found.

Warm enough to function, he wrung his clothes out as best he could and spread them on the boulders. The sheep stayed close, nipping at the grass. He had no provisions, no weapon and no idea if the Red Caps were close to heel. He would have to leave the strays behind if he was to make any speed. The thought pained him suddenly and he sat against the boulder, tears coming. He wept and then laughed at his own absurdity, the chuckles coming between sobs. In time, he donned his damp clothes and turned his back on his saviors. They followed him, at first, but Padric refused to look back and quickened his steps.

He traveled throughout the day, following the Trough, hoping that the fort would lie close to its banks. He wished often for his pack and the food that it contained, the warm cloak, his father's rope. All of those were now gone, along with the seax, left amidst the ashes and the bodies. He had eaten nothing since the Tor and could not remember the last time he was allowed to sleep.

Night came and he had neither the tools nor the stomach for a fire. He huddled through the cold, windy night, small and exposed in the middle of the fields. He plodded dumbly throughout the following day, each step feeling more pointless than the last. He was hollow, empty of nourishment, hope and reason.

The river, the endless plains, the steely sky, they remained constant and tireless while he slowed and shrank. A wet cough took up residence in his chest and soon he was sweating, shaking with fever.

His joints ached deeply, robbing him of strength and the molten sloshing in his ears imprisoned his senses. Sound and sight bled together into a queasy morass of sensation. His head was heavy and hot, boiled raw through throat and nostril. His ribs quaked with chill, weak hands clutching to hold them still.

Stumbling, bent double with racking coughs, he trudged miserably on, dimly aware that he had lost a direct course miles ago.

He careened, drunk with sickness until the crushing wool in his skull and the swamp in his lungs, sent him to his knees. Yet still he rose, stubbornly forcing the feeble steps, only to fall again.

And rise . . . and fall.

He awoke coughing, terrible visions of flames and burning corpses fleeing his mind, replaced by the smoldering coals of a hearth pit. Blankets covered him and Padric could feel the forgotten softness of a straw mattress cradling his back.

"Try not to move," a man's voice told him as a strong hand pressed gently into his chest. "The compress will loosen."

Padric became aware of a cool tingling in his torso and the tightness of linen bandages. The cloud of feverish sleep was lifting, allowing the pounding of his head and the soreness of his throat to make themselves known.

The man stared down at him, features lost to the deep shadows of the room. "Can you drink?"

Padric nodded and tried to answer, but a painful croak was all he managed. He was lifted easily from behind his head and a steaming cup was held to his lips. The brew was scalding, going down in a cloying torrent of bitter herbs and strong spirits. He swallowed and tried to lie back, but was held upright, the cup still under his chin.

"Breathe," the voice instructed. "The vapors will help."

Padric did as he was told and soon he found his head clearing, his lungs opening. There was still pain, but it no longer threatened to engulf him. After a while, he was guided back down and lay back against the mattress.

"You are fortunate." The voice moved about the room. "Now rest."

Padric must have slept. Through his closed lids, he perceived the room brightening and when he opened them fully, a gray sky floated in the window. The room was small but well-constructed; walls, floor and beams all strong wood. Padric's mattress lay atop a thick pallet of animal hides. A simple stool sat next to a small table with a copper basin and various clay jars resting atop. The man had pulled the hide curtain away from the window and was standing with his back to Padric, staring out into the wet day. Seeming to sense Padric's eyes on him, the man turned calmly. He was tall, long waves of flaxen hair half tied behind his head. The simple belted robe he wore revealed broad shoulders and a slim waist, a physique defying the weathered lines of a face well into middle years. A short and neatly trimmed beard covered a strong jaw beneath proud cheekbones and hunter's eyes, sharp and deeply lined at the corners. He fetched a cup from the table and filled it in the basin, bringing it over and kneeling beside the mattress.

"Water," he said, offering the cup.

Padric pushed himself up, finding the compress gone. He reached out and took the cup, drinking the contents down in long pulls.

"I thank you," he managed, his voice oddly pitched with disuse.

The man nodded and took the cup back, setting it on the floor. "Lean forward."

Padric did so and the man placed a broad hand across his back. "Breathe thrice deeply."

As Padric took the breaths, the man kept his face down and away, eyes closed in concentration. After the final breath he removed his hand and looked at Padric.

"Good," he said with some pride. "Some hot food and all will be hale."

"How did I come to be here?" Padric asked.

"You were within sight of the walls when you collapsed."

"Walls?" Realization struck him. "The fort! This is the fort of Kederic Winetongue?"

"It is."

"I must speak with him. Hog's Wallow has been razed!"

"Yes," the man replied. "Four days ago."

"Days? But the Red Caps . . ."

"The goblins have moved on. They did not risk the defenses here."

"The families . . . did they arrive? Are they safe?"

"They are."

"There was a piskie with them . . . Rosheen. Is she here?"

"No."

"But Ardal said she led the villagers here."

"And the villagers say the same, but when they arrived there was no sign of any piskie."

Worry quickly replaced relief. Had she gone back? Thrown herself into peril for fear of his own fate? Were she and Fafnir caught by the Red Caps to be tortured and set ablaze, like the poor shepherds?

"The other men?" Padric asked suddenly. "Did any of them survive?"

The man's broad shoulders dropped slightly and a resigned expression filled his face. "I thought to ask you the same question."

Padric had known the answer, of course, but this man must have held out some hope. A hope Padric had just dashed with his own pointless question.

"Faabar . . . he might have . . ."

The man waved him off. "Warriors were dispatched to the village. They returned and reported nothing of the fomori. Only the burnt bodies of good men."

Anger flared up in Padric. This fool did not need to tell him, he had been there.

"Good men that stood alone while the Thegn's warriors hid here and did nothing!"

The outburst did not change the man's expression. "How were they to know?"

"The herbalist . . . he rode here to raise the alarm."

The man shook his head. "He did not come."

Padric's face fell, his anger dissolving. "But, he . . ."

The man stood and went to the window, looking out as he spoke.

"We awoke to smoke on the horizon and the warriors marshaled . . . but the women and children of Hog's Wallow were outside the walls before they could ride. They said a piskie had come and warned them of a Red Cap attack and then led them to safety with the help of some steel-mongering dwarf. The fate of the town was written on the morning sky, but of a helpful Fae-girl there was no sign. Goblins have raided and vanished. And now you say the gnome was sent here as well? The Fae have ever been practiced at elusiveness."

Padric had heard enough from this leech. He flung the blankets away and spotting fresh clothes folded on the table, he rose. He managed one step and then his quivering legs betrayed him. The man caught him as he fell and guided him back to the pallet. Padric felt a helpless babe, naked and weak in the man's stable grip.

"Food would be wise before attempting that again. I shall have some brought up to you." The man rose and went to the door.

"But after," Padric said before he could leave. "I would still speak with the Thegn."

The man inclined his head without mockery. "And so you have," he said. "I am Kederic, called by some the Winetongue and you are welcome in my holdfast."

The food came, but the Thegn did not. Padric had hoped to see a familiar face, maybe Jileen, but the girl who came with the bread and broth was not from the village. Perhaps the daughter or young wife of one of the warriors. She smiled shyly and left quietly.

Padric was ravenous and ate with vigor, but his stomach was quickly filled by the broth, so he left the bread untouched. He dressed, finding the boots and breeches to be his own, but the shirt and long, sleeveless jerkin were new. They had the cut and durability of soldier's garments and Padric felt awkward in them.

He was uncertain if he was to wait for the Thegn's return or if someone would send for him, but after a few minutes Padric abandoned any thought of patience or decorum and went out the door. A narrow and short hallway led to a large vaulted hall, empty but for a few dogs drowsing among the floor rushes. Long benches stood around a circular stone fire-pit, lit and smoking up towards a hole in the thatching.

Padric crossed the length of the hall and pushed open the heavy double doors at the far end. Outside he found a windy morning, devoid of rain and sun. The hall was built atop stout beams, overlooking the interior yards and affording Padric an expansive view of the fort. It was easily twice the size of Stone Fort, but still constructed entirely of wood and Padric noticed no sign of work being done to reinforce with masonry. The smaller buildings were built against the interior of the defensive wall, their turf roofs nestled comfortably under the walkways. Men with spears, cloaked against the wind, walked steady patrols and there were archers in the half dozen sturdy watchtowers. Women, children and livestock could be seen going to and fro across the yards. A generous stable and its surrounding paddocks dominated the western side, and Padric could see the most activity lay there. He descended the stairs of the hall, his legs still quivering slightly, and headed for the stables.

Kederic Winetongue was indeed within, looking intently into one of the stalls. Several other men were gathered around, talking casually of foaling with the same voice Padric had heard his father use so many times. They had never owned horses, but the forced confidence in the voices of the Thegn's grooms was identical to the farmers of Padric's childhood during lambing.

Padric approached and saw a mare, swollen and still, her time clearly near. The Thegn did not look his way when he spoke.

"Do you know of horses, Padric?"

"No," he replied, less than surprised at the knowledge of his name. He wondered what else the refugees had told this man.

"Swine and sheep. And crops. These I know. Horses are for a man who means to travel far."

A smile turned up on the Thegn's profile. "And you have not travelled far?"

The events of the last moon's turn fell heavily into Padric's thoughts.

"Farther than I ever expected," he answered after a moment. "A horse . . . would have helped."

Kederic breathed a quick laugh and turned to his grooms.

"Keep me informed," he instructed before looking at Padric for the first time. He gave a quick appraisal before nodding with satisfaction. "Much improved. Please, walk with me."

The Thegn left the stables with long, easy strides and Padric followed. When they were out in the yard, Kederic slowed his pace and Padric came up alongside.

"My thanks for your attentions," Padric said. "I did not expect to be tended by my host."

"The best man for the right job," Kederic said. "It is important to know a man's skill . . . his worth, be he Thegn or stable boy. Titles of leadership do not matter when another's life is in balance. I have been through many wars and several plagues. None here know herbcraft better than I, and it would be unjust to put a sick man in less capable hands.

"Had you been a horse about to give birth," the Thegn waved over his shoulder at the stables and smiled. "I would gladly have stepped aside."

They ascended a set of steep steps to the top of the wall.

Padric saw a staked ditch just below, thick with muddy puddles and an earthen mound beyond. The fort stood atop a high hill and Padric had an uninterrupted view of the An Curragh plains, cold and green and boulder-strewn. To the south Padric could see no smoke, no sign of Hog's Wallow. The Thegn's gaze rested on the same horizon.

"A cruel fate," Kederic said softly, his voice barely audible in the wind. "You are much blessed to have survived it."

Padric's hair blew into his face. "Cursed, you mean. The widows will hate me for breathing while their husbands' blackened bones lay scattered in muddy ash. A coal-headed stranger who brought nothing but ill-omens and death. I ran while others fell."

"Every man runs from the battles he survives, Padric."

Kederic told him. "How did you come to be there?"

Padric snorted at that. He was not sure himself. But he told the tale as best he could. About his home and family, the mistrust of his neighbors and Rosheen's friendship. He told of Fafnir, the journey to Hog's Wallow and the changeling child in the woods. He told of the hunt for the Unwound and meeting the Thegn's own men at Bairn's Babble. Finally, he told of the terrible night in the forest and the emergence of the goblin wizard from the flames and Faabar's unrelenting protection of the village. As he spoke, he grew disturbed, the words forced through gritted teeth. This man had saved his life and deserved answers to his questions, but Padric deserved answers as well. He finished his tale and then looked the Thegn boldly in the eye.

"Why did you not help us?"

Kederic returned his stare, but did not bristle at its harshness or the angry tone in Padric's voice. "Some of what you have said was known to me. Much and more was not. For some time, I have pleaded with the people of Hog's Wallow to live under my protection, but they refused. Brogan was the largest voice of protest, but I believe they all felt as he did, believing themselves safe from the abominable horrors that stalk these lands. They put their faith in immortal champions and the mystical arts of Fae-folk, all the while ignoring that the greatest threat to their lives was that very allegiance.

"The Fae are wondrous beings, Padric. Immortal and fair, they have crafts and knowledge beyond the ken of man, and for years too impossible to count we have been caught in the middle of their wars and jealousies. They claim this isle to be under the stewardship of their Elf King, but he has not been seen since before my grandfather's time and Airlann falls deeper into turmoil with each passing year. I have sailed across the waters to the east and seen the other Tin Isles and there are strange creatures that reside in those lands as well. Aye, even beyond in snow-covered Middangeard, giants and trolls roam the mountains. And it is said there are worse things in the deep forests of Outborders, where even I have never set foot.

"But nowhere, Padric . . . nowhere does the Magic of the Fae hold such sway as here, trapping the land in this perpetual season, ever-dying. They claim rule over this island, these immortals, but we are abandoned, left to defend ourselves as best we may among enmities forged thousands of years before our most distant ancestors were born. Once long ago, a handful of mortals dared to rise against this mysterious Seelie Court. It was men who marshaled the goblins and overthrew the elves. They were wicked men for certain, dabbling in dark sorcery never intended for mortal hands and eventually they were laid low, but their betrayal . . . their boldness is remembered and cursed by the Fae-folk to this day. Do you think they do not hate us for that? Do you think we are not attacked at night, murdered by changelings in vengeance for the actions of those long dead warlocks who defied them?

"These Red Caps would see the heirs of those men restored to power, but the rest of us are fit for nothing but slavery and slaughter. Fae-folk are powerful. They can change their skins, wield the elements as weapons and they feel no disease or infirmity. They are stronger, faster, wiser and keener than even the best warrior born to a mortal mother. But there is a weakness . . . a single gift that we might harness to protect ourselves. Iron is poison to them and it is only that discovery that has saved mortal-kind. The dwarves have smelted a stronger metal and they peddle it across the Tin Isles, trading to mortal and Fae alike, but you will find no weapons of steel in the hands of my men. It is with iron that we place our trust, for there is more need of it now than ever.

"I told Brogan as much many times, but he would not hear me. He would not see that living among the Fae was folly at its most deadly, for even those immortals that claim friendship are hated and hunted by those of their kind who would rid the world of humanity. I could not threaten the safety of those already under my care by tending to those blinded by Faery magic, so I withdrew my men from the Wallow."

Padric listened as the Thegn spoke with passion and watched as the shame of his decision settled over him. Kederic stood on his wall and looked to the horizon, eyes narrowed against the wind, jaw set in contemplation.

"And then Brogan was slain," he continued with ire in his voice. "That walking scarecrow servant of his murdered him and I sent my own men out to hunt him down. They are still out there, Acwellen and his huscarls, along with the Sure Finder and those damn dogs of his . . . might as well be Fae themselves for all their queer cunning. I have chewed at these events Padric, worried at them and I do not like what begins to unravel. You say the gnome claimed to have seen an Unwound and took the fomori in search of it, all the while my riders search for the husk . . . and the village is left undefended, giving the Red Caps every chance to burn it to the ground. This is not passing chance. Something is set against us."

"The goblin in the fire," Padric said.

Kederic nodded. "With the help of the husk and the gnome."

Padric started. "Deglan? Why would he . . ."

"Who else saw this Unwound? Who took the fomori in search of it? You said it yourself, he was headed here with a warning . . . a warning that never came."

"Rosheen and Fafnir did not come either," Padric said.

"That does not put them in league with the Red Caps."

"Careful," Kederic said. "Do not put so much trust in Fae-folk and dwarves. That was Brogan's mistake, as well."

"I cannot vouch for the gnome," Padric countered. "But I have known Rosheen my whole life and she arrived as I did, a stranger with no knowledge of any of this."

"No knowledge?" Kederic scoffed. "She is Fae. I do not place blame upon her for the dealings here, but it troubles me you never thought to ask her about yourself."

"Ask her . . . ?"

"Raven-touched." Kederic gestured at Padric's head. "Your neighbors thought you cursed and you have grown up believing it. Padric, I have travelled enough of the world and seen that the beliefs of men are as varied as the flowers in spring. But here on this Island where there is no spring, we grow superstitious and place foolish predictions on the hair color of babes and read auguries in the entrails of animals. Among the tribes of Middangeard, where the raven is revered, a man born with black hair is thought to be a great chieftain and destined to bring woe to his enemies. That might have been you, but by chance you were born here; not among warriors in Middangeard, but among farmers in Airlann, a land where the seasons never change and peasants are forced to find explanations for Magic, a land where the Fae are at once respected and feared. Your own neighbors curse you for a Fae-friend, while the shepherds of the Wallow think you much favored.

"If your people think you cursed, Padric, there is a reason. A reason for which the Fae are to blame, mark me. You should discover why you have been so ill-named. And who better to ask than an immortal? One who was around the day you were born and thousands of years before. This Rosheen knows, Padric, but she has left you to suffer in ignorance. Such are the games played by the Fae."

ELEVEN

Deglan chewed willow bark to ease the pain and swelling in his mouth. His tongue kept wandering his aching gums, probing at the salty gaps where four of his teeth used to sit. Three were completely gone and he had been forced to yank the jagged remnants of the last out by hand. Thankfully, he still had his satchel and the prepared willow, but the slow working herb had not yet reached his head. A dull pain, fed by a sizable knot, still pulsed through his skull. It would fade given time.

There was no balm for the pain he felt when he finally reached the Wallow. Even from a distance, the destruction was absolute; a greasy black stain on the landscape. Deglan walked the ruins, struggling to see some semblance of the place that had been his home for over eight centuries, but everything was utterly laid low by Fire. Only a skeleton of the windmill remained standing, two tumbled stone walls barely managing to lean against the other.

Deglan plodded numbly into the shell and poked around the morass of wet ash, fearful in the certainty of what he would uncover. Most of the bones were reduced to little more than charred fragments, but the skulls were unmistakable. He had known these men, treated their hurts as boys and delivered them as babes. Now their empty sockets stared back at him from a charnel pile of soot. Some of the skulls were clearly goblin, but Deglan could find no joy in the sight. There was no more honorable pyre for a Red Cap than the flames of destruction they lived to create.

In the mud outside were the prints of many horses. He had lost Acwellen and his band of brigands in the forest, but he was on foot and they must have reached the village well ahead of him.

Come to see the spoils of their treacherous act and gone away, leaving Deglan to stand in the vestiges of Hog's Wallow and try to make sense of it all.

He had never trusted Kederic Winetongue, not from the first day he arrived with promises of protection and friendship, but he never thought the man capable of this much evil. Consorting with Red Caps and sorcerers! Deglan let out a choked grunt and kicked savagely at one of the goblin skulls, sending it bouncing through the muddy ash. It rolled to a stop still facing him, grinning at his despair.

He found the tunnel to his house choked with rubble, but was able to struggle through and gain entry. The Red Caps' hatred of gnomes was apparent in the destruction. Smoke still hung lazily in the underground dwelling, mingling with the stink of excrement.

Deglan's bed was burnt, his stores of herbs as well. The shelves of potions, unguents, salves and liniments had been ripped from the walls, broken into splinters. He had known comfort here. Safety and warmth. He lived and worked in this home, using his craft to heal, ease and sometimes prolong the fleeting life of mortal-kind.

There should have been memories in the very walls, phantom feelings of past days echoing in the familiar space, wailing in pain at its degradation. But Deglan was passed all feelings of loss. The memories that returned to him now were not of happier days, but of days before. Days of war and fear and hunger. His body and mind slipped back into the old rhythms with tragic proficiency.

There was no more time to mourn. Survival was the only concern.

He salvaged what little he could and tucked the rescued medicines into his satchel. He scavenged in the ruins for warm clothes, taking anything he could find, heedless of the burns in the wool or the reek of goblin piss. The heavy, bronze-bladed cleaver he used for amputations lay in a corner and he snatched it up, a tool of grim purpose now a much-needed weapon. As he turned to leave, his eyes fell upon the large nook where Bulge-Eye used to sleep. Strangely, it was untouched, free of offal and scorching.

Empty.

Deglan passed it without a pang of sorrow.

When he emerged from the tunnel . . . it was waiting on him.

Deglan froze, the instinct to fight or flee as motionless as his feet.

If he ran, it would catch him. Maybe not instantly, as they were not exceptionally swift, but it would pursue at its own tireless pace and catch up when Deglan was broken by exhaustion. To fight was ludicrous. It was huge and made of solid iron. Living Iron.

It faced him, the narrow black holes that served as its eyes staring at him and above him and beyond him all at once. The slim limbs of heavy, dark metal hung motionless at its sides, large hands tipped in long fingers. A shabby mantle of raw wool was draped formlessly over its torso, but underneath, the thick plating of its body gave it a powerful frame at shoulder and chest. The legs stuck out from beneath the makeshift cloak and appeared sparer, suggesting agility for all its weight.

Deglan had spent four miserable months in the fortifications atop Bwenyth Tor, tending to comrades, stitching wounds, staunching blood, removing limbs and burying friends as the goblins launched attack after attack at the defenses. They had fought, they had starved, but they had held and given as good as they got. When Two-Keg brought the word that the Forge Born were coming, Deglan waited for them to arrive with all the rest.

Waited to die. It seemed that death had finally reached him.

"To it then, you blighted metal bastard! You rusted, mindless goblin puppet!" He scooped up a clod of mud and reared his arm back to throw in a feeble, final act of defiance.

"I was asked to bring you."

The face had no visible mouth and Deglan was startled when it spoke. The voice that issued from the thing was slow and deeper than distant thunder. Each word hesitated into the next, grinding out unaccompanied by movement or mannerism, the sound threatening to fade to a halt at any moment. Deglan's arm hung in the air behind him, the clump of mud still in his fist. He was perplexed, afraid, tired and very angry.

"Kill me now, you walking anvil! I'll not be a prisoner to goblins!" He threw the clod as an afterthought. It did not have the distance and came apart in the air, dirty chunks scattering into the air between them. There was a long silence. Deglan's agitated breath expelled in vapor, while the Forge Born stared through him in mute judgment. Finally it spoke.

"The goblins march south . . . for now." The last two words lowered greatly in pitch as they slowed to a ponderous crawl. "We go north." Then it turned and began walking in the declared direction without ensuring that Deglan followed. In stillness, the thing was unsettling, but a shiver ran unbidden up Deglan's spine when he saw it in motion. Its metal legs carried it with steady, determined strides towards the river, its pace and direction set and sure.

"The world is mad," Deglan said as he watched the Forge Born walk away. "And I am its king." He set off after his guide.

One thing was for certain, it was not Unwound. At least not yet. All of their kind was built for destruction, but this one still had control of its faculties. After the Rebellion, the Forge Born were a common sight, but Deglan had done his best to stay well away from them. It had not been difficult. Despite the King's decree that they be granted mercy, there were few willing to endure their presence. The more vicious of the fomori tribes ignored the Court's laws and began hunting them, but it was a dangerous endeavor and many of the would-be predators fell prey to their quarry. For even with a heart, the Forge Born were dangerous.

Deglan had to jog in order to catch up with the long, mile-eating strides of the Forge Born. He scowled at its back, pondering the wisdom of his choice to follow it, angry at himself for finding no better option. Deglan noticed the throat of a metal scabbard peeking over the ragged cloak just beneath the Forge Born's right shoulder. Curiously, the scabbard was empty and Deglan could find no evidence of other weapons.

"It was you," Deglan accused suddenly. "I saw you coming from the Tor. You were up there!"

The war machine did not respond and kept its pace.

"We tracked you," Deglan said, his voice growing louder.

"And we found *them*. Were you following the goblins?"

"No." It was more akin to a bell toll than a word.

"Then how do you know they went south?"

"I watched."

"You watched? Watched what . . . watched the village burn, watched the men die?! You could have stopped it!"

The Forge Born halted so suddenly Deglan almost collided with its legs.

"No," it said without turning. "I could not." It resumed walking.

Deglan seethed and allowed the thing to go on without him.

"This is folly."

His confusion had caused him to follow blindly, but now he looked at the surrounding landscape and found it to be very familiar. They had left the fields behind and entered the rougher upcountry. The way was hilly and boulder-strewn with nary a path or sheep run to be found. A difficult stretch of land and one that Deglan had walked many times. They were heading for the barrows.

Deglan chuckled sourly. "A dead man wants to see me. Wonder which one has a complaint." He continued up the rocky incline.

The barrowlands were laid long before humans settled the area. Low mounds, completely reclaimed by dirt and grass marked the edge of the earliest burial sites. Many of the defenders of Bwyneth Tor moldered in these grounds, the final days of the war making it impossible to transport their bodies back to Toad Holm so that they may be laid to rest in the Ever Dark as was gnomish tradition.

Further in, the larger and more recent cairns of mankind bloated the countryside. Some were simple mounds of stacked stone covered in earth, with naught but a small opening to admit the dead, while others were vast, many chambered constructions with heavy stone lintels set above the entrances. Deglan grimaced.

Human lives were candle smoke on the wind, here and gone, yet they spent most of that life in backbreaking preparation for death.

He hated coming here. And he hated it more with his present company.

The Forge Born strode purposefully between the great mounds, never pausing nor wasting a sidelong glance at the cairns.

The pale grass was long, thin and weedy, flowing in spurts against the wind. The stones were the color of long years and between them the passages into the mounds gaped, at once hungry and gagging. How many such bleak places had this machine walked, uncaring? How many had its metal hands lain low with violence so that they must be placed within such houses of bones and dust?

Questions Deglan could not answer. Questions not worth posing to the thing walking in front of him.

It finally stopped next to one of the largest barrows and seemed to be looking down at something. A smaller mound blocked Deglan's view, but he made no effort to quicken his pace.

Slowly, he passed the smaller mound and the object of the Forge Born's attention came into view. Deglan rushed forward, cursing.

Faabar lay against the wall of the barrow, a filthy heap upon the grass. Even before Deglan reached him he knew the fomori was blind. His once magnificent horned head was tilted at an odd angle against the wind, straining to listen, to smell. Deglan had his satchel off his shoulder on the run and slammed to a halt next to his friend.

Faabar's face turned toward the movement. "I knew you would come."

"Quiet now," Deglan told him. He fumbled desperately around in his bag, never taking his eyes off the fomori, hoping that his hand would light upon something that could help. He had so little of use, and, for the first time in centuries, he hesitated. He did not know where to begin.

Faabar's face was a ruin of stiff, blackened flesh, red raw and seeping from where it peeled away from his skull. A sticky film covered his cheeks, the last remnants of eyes boiled from their sockets. The leg previously injured by the plough had been brutalized into something unnatural to look upon. The rest of his body was covered in horrible burns, skin slick as glass in places, bubbled with blisters in others. But even Fire could not cauterize the wounds suffered from iron blades. They crisscrossed his chest in a dozen angry rends, blood leaking weakly. Only Red Caps were crazed enough to wield weapons as deadly to themselves as they were their enemies.

Deglan's hand slowed to a halt within his bag, finally pulling something free. Faabar gave no reaction when the wet rag touched his brow. Deglan dabbed gently, uselessly.

"The goblins went south," Faabar rasped. "Kederic can overtake them if he rides now . . ."

"Kederic betrayed us," Deglan said flatly.

Faabar's face searched blindly for answers.

"I never made the fort. Acwellen ambushed me in the plains . . . I was lucky. He knew about the Red Caps, of that I am certain."

"Then the women . . . the children?"

"I do not know."

Faabar lurched, spasms wracking his body. Deglan could only watch. The sight of his friend's pain and his own helplessness were too much, so he cast a baleful glance up at the Forge Born. It seemed to be watching Faabar, unaffected by his agony. He settled at last, but the shivers of shock remained, seeming to shrink the proud warrior with every tremor.

"We . . . we must get word . . . to the Waywarders," Faabar managed. He looked up in the direction of the Forge Born. "Help me rise."

The machine leaned down and reached for the fomori.

"Do not touch him!" Deglan shot to his feet.

The thing stopped and returned to standing over them, as if it had never moved.

Faabar groped feebly for Deglan. "He is not . . . Unwound."

"I damn well know that. But *it* is still iron."

Deglan had no doubt the thing had carried Faabar up here, aggravating his already grievous injuries. The strength required to move the weight of a fomori was frightening to think about, but it was a task this Forge Born had done with ease. It did not have Faabar's bulk, but it was at least half a head taller and not subject to fatigue. Why it had done it was a mystery and one that Deglan had no time to unravel.

"You cannot travel," Deglan told the fomori, trying to keep the finality out of his voice.

Faabar shrank further into the barrowside, letting out a pained breath. "Then you must. Go to Court. Tell them . . . what has happened. Stop this . . . before it is too late."

Deglan watched the grass ripple in the breeze, trying to ignore the cairn stones and the sense of hopelessness in his heart.

"Sixty years or more since a Waywarder came through these lands. Over two-hundred since the last proclamation from the King . . . and near another hundred on top of that since anyone last laid eyes on him. He may be dead."

"He is not." Faabar's voice was weak, but not the conviction behind it. "The island clings to life. Winter has not yet fallen. Irial lives, Deglan . . . he lives."

It was still a gamble and Deglan had made up his mind. "I will go where I know there is help. For all the foolishness, there is still strength in Toad Holm. Hob will do something . . . he must."

Faabar's breathing was shallow and labored. "Keep your temper, Master Loamtoes. You must make them hear you. Remember . . . they are your kin."

Deglan kept his mouth shut. The gnomes were his kin, the rest were squatters.

"I wish . . . I . . . could go with you."

Deglan knelt and took one of the fomori's large hands in his own. "I wish that, too."

Faabar looked to the sky. "Do you remember . . . little Colm? He used to ride on my shoulders. He would laugh . . . such a joyful sound. He . . . is buried here."

Deglan did remember. The boy had been born sickly and lame. Deglan's best efforts had not seen him out of childhood.

They had placed him in one of these barrows on a day much like this one. Four hundred years ago.

Faabar spoke and Deglan held his hand, listening. "I am happy . . . to be here with him . . . and all the others. We . . . knew . . . them all. My sword, Deglan. Please . . . my sword."

Deglan looked around for it and was startled to find the Forge Born coming forward with the weapon in hand. It bent slowly and placed the hilt gently in Faabar's hand, then rose and drew back. Faabar smiled and pulled the blade close to his quaking chest. His hand squeezed Deglan's, strong to the end.

"It has been . . . my . . . honor, to call you . . . friend. Continue to serve. It is . . . a worthy life . . ."

Faabar inhaled sharply and shuddered to stillness.

Deglan's face tightened in grief, body rocking with sobs. He bowed his head and wept.

"May the rain fall and wash you with Water. May the wind blow and take you to the Air. May the grass grow and embrace you to the Earth. May you know no more flames and be free of Fire."

It was a long time before he finally turned his head. The Forge Born still waited.

"You did this," Deglan accused, unwilling to release his friend's hand and wipe the ugly sorrow that clung wetly under his nose. "You burned him with your damn hands."

"No worse than he already suffered," the thing answered.

It was true. And Deglan knew it. He turned back to Faabar and found his blurry gaze resting on the steel blade of the sword.

His mind suddenly turned to the empty scabbard on the Forge Born's back and rage flushed his face, boiling the already hot tears.

"You cannot have it!" he screamed, not turning, placing both his small hands protectively over the great blade. "I'll not let you take it from him!"

There was a long silence. When at last the Forge Born replied it was standing in front of him, cradling a large rock in its metal fingers.

"I have no use for swords," it said and bent to lower the stone next to Faabar. It turned without further comment, retrieving another stone from the grass and placing it next to the first. Deglan watched with numb perplexity as the thing worked.

"What are you?" he asked, knowing he sounded the fool.

There was the slightest pause. "I am Coltrane." And then it went back to building Faabar's cairn. Deglan would have laughed if his heart was not encased in suffocating pain.

"You did not know him," he stated.

"No."

"Then why?" Deglan growled. "Why bring him here? Why bury him?"

The thing with a name stopped then and regarded Deglan with its horribly blank face. "Because it is all I can do."

Deglan rose, weary to the bone, but more weary of his own questions.

"Well, you'll not do it alone."

He looked about for a moment until he found a rock he could lift. He winced as he bent forward, swallowing the groan that tried to escape as he heaved the rock upward. Hobbling under its weight, he placed the stone neatly next to those the Forge Born had already placed. The pile grew steadily and soon Deglan's back threatened to snap in protest as he set stone after stone. It would have been easier to let the tireless machine do all the work, but Deglan owed his friend so much. The least he could give was a few blisters.

At last, the cairn was complete; the fomori's body covered by a simple yet solid pile of stones stacked against the barrowside.

Faabar would have approved. Deglan stared at the stones, not wanting to turn his back on them and begin the long journey that awaited him. He felt movement to his right and looked to see the Forge Born marching steadily away. Deglan scowled at its back, glad to be free of it, glad to be free of the temptation to ask it for help. Let it go! Let it fade into the distance until it was nothing more than the tall, moving shape he had first seen that miserable day while eating a turnip with Bulge-Eye. And then Deglan noticed its direction. South.

"Damn it!" he yelled, running half a dozen paces after it.

"You said you were not following the Red Caps!"

The Forge Born continued on, heedless of his challenge.

Deglan pursued, but his exhausted body could not sustain the chase.

His legs gave out and he slumped forward in the tall grass, his breath coming in fierce, angry bursts.

"What do you know of all this!?" he called at the quickly receding machine and then with desperation, "Coltrane!"

The Forge Born did not stop.

TWELVE

Pocket was lost. Every street looked the same and his sense of north had become fuddled several wrong turns back. Maybe if he found the river again he would have some hope. But there were two rivers that ran through Black Pool. He had confused the two on his errand the previous day and did not have much hope he learned enough from that experience not to repeat the mistake. Sir Corc would be cross if he dallied. Only he was not dallying, not on purpose.

He was lost.

The city was vast and had filled him with a mix of reluctance and excitement when it first came into view from the deck of the ship. The voyage across the choppy water from Albain had been Pocket's first experience with the sea. At least the first he could remember. Certainly he had made the trip once before, as a babe when Sir Corc brought him from Airlann to live at the castle.

He had not known what to expect upon seeing the land of his birth, hither fore only dreamed of while staring at his old map under the tower stairs. But the sight of the city with its cluttered harbor and sprawling buildings eclipsed his initial vision of the island. So far, Airlann was Black Pool; a chaotic hive of ancient buildings, countless smells and many, many winding streets.

Pocket turned in place, looking all around the alley in which he found himself. He fought down a rising sense of panic as he realized he was no longer certain from which end he had entered.

He looked to the sky for an answer, hoping he might spy the sun, but the tired structures around him leaned so alarmingly that their eaves almost touched, leaving only the smallest strip of open air between them. Pride gnawed at him more than fear. He had memorized every twist and cranny of the Roost, able to get from one point in the castle to any other blindfolded. He had been in Black Pool eleven days now and still he was having trouble finding his way.

He was looking for the billier's shop in a section of the city known as Cauldron Town. Sir Corc had made him memorize it; a small shop under the sign of a black axe across from the bell-founder's. Cauldron Town, Pocket knew, was the metal working district of the city and could be found by following the smoke and clamor . . . or so the locals said. Pocket had been walking most of the morning, following these assured guidelines, but from what he could tell the entire city was filled with black air and loud noise.

The alleyway ended in a steep, irregular stair which dumped into the riverwalk. Pocket took a moment to look at the waterway.

It seemed to be smaller and slower moving, so he guessed it was the Poddle. The wider Hot Foot was filled with boats and bridges.

The deep, brackish pond that formed where the two rivers met gave the city its name. No matter where you stood in the city, the Tower of Vellaunus could be seen standing vigilant over all. It rose from the center of the pool atop an island of cut stones, crooked and leaning from long centuries and the weight of the atrocities committed within its looming walls. It was said to have been erected in a single night by the foul crafts of the Goblin King Vellaunus the Cackler, for which the tower was named. Long abandoned and reachable only by skiff, the Tower was avoided by the inhabitants of Black Pool as a cursed placed that tempted the mad, calling for them to jump from its uppermost chamber and break their bodies on the fortified island far below.

Pocket had learned that and a great deal more about the city since their arrival. Some from Sir Corc and more from Old Lochlann, the bent-backed old man who served as steward to the house kept in the city by the Order. The wrinkled villein, like many of Black Pool's human residents, was of Middangearder stock, descended from the original raiders that took over the harbor after the Rebellion left the city vulnerable. Before that, Black Pool was the seat of the Goblin Kings and had seen many dark periods of oppression, neglect, siege and civil war. At one point, the city was contested by two powerful human sorcerers both laying claim to the Goblin throne. Black Pool was divided not only by loyalty but by construction when the two contenders built a massive wall across the city, scheming on their respective sides against the other.

King Sweyn the Third and his upstart rival Hogulent the First and Only spent years enacting bloody violence and murderous plots trying to unseat the other and were eventually both brought low by the woman known to history as the Goblin Queen. The wall no longer existed but the division remained, with half the city known as Sweynside and the other, poorer half dubbed simply Hogulent after its former despot.

Cauldron Town was Sweynside and if the river in front of Pocket was indeed the Poddle, then at least he was on the right side of town . . . unless it was the Hot Foot, in which case he could be in Hogulent and therefore very off course. He shambled over to the water's edge and considered plopping down on the wet cobblestones in defeat, but he was wearing his livery and did not want to return from his errand both unsuccessful and with the colors of the Order soiled. Before his first errand, Sir Corc had told him that if he found himself to be lost, the best course of action was to ask a passerby for directions, but unless Moragh was somehow miraculously living in Black Pool, Pocket did not know who to trust. Any aid, asked or unasked, was not something he was used to receiving and eleven days was not enough to kill those instincts.

In truth, no one had cast so much as a sidelong glance at him since the day he got off the boat. Gurgs, it seemed, were not so queer a sight in Black Pool. Old Lochlann said there was an entire orphanage dedicated to them somewhere in Hogulent. The city stewed with all manner of folk, each more unique than the last.

Within minutes of the boat reaching port, Pocket encountered stern faced dwarf merchants offloading steel from massive barges, and, just beyond, a large cage next to a slaver's vessel housed a pair of trolls. The male raged against the bars, his long arms corded with muscle, his sloping forehead twisted in fury as he bellowed wordlessly against his captivity, heedless of the soothing sounds made by the diminutive female, who was as fair as her mate was brutish. Insular and elusive creatures, they were a rare sight even in the hoary wastes of Middangeard that was their home. Fascinating as they were, Pocket's attention was again diverted mere steps from the cage.

Tall, sinewy beings with pale blue skin and flowing hair the color of seaweed, moved gracefully through the crowds and Pocket had gawked when he saw them. They could be only undine, elementals trusted with the guardianship of Water as the gnomes were with Earth and the sylphs with Air. Before Pocket could marvel further, the bustling traffic of the harbor yielded more wondrous sights. Husk servants bore heavy loads upon straw-stuffed bodies, following closely behind their richly dressed masters who shuffled hurriedly past a rag-tag group of coburn leaning against the wall of a dockside tavern, their weapons near as filthy as their feathers.

"Sell-swords," Bantam Flyn said with distaste. Pocket pictured the Dread Cockerel feeling right at home among such a rabble.

Even the humans seemed strange to Pocket who was used to the ruddy, thick-limbed clansmen of Albain. The men from Middangeard were fair of hair and black of countenance, their mail shirts and long axes well-used. The merchants and sea-captains from Kymbru were lean of body and cunning of eye, haggling in their strange lilting language. The Sasanan warriors all strode with arrogant confidence, their long hair and short beards a sandy brown.

"Mortal men are varied as wildflowers," Sir Corc had told him. "And their lives are as short. But do not mistake, they are neither fragile nor weak." Pocket had never considered humans to be weak, but he said nothing and took in the sights as they made their way through the harbor and into the city proper.

The streets lacked the colorful bustle of the docks, but were nonetheless filled with more comings and goings than the busiest feast days at the castle. Beggars and urchins haunted grimy doorways, staying out of the byways where oxcarts loaded with the harvest plodded forward, urged on by rustics with switches. Shops and stalls of all kinds faced the choked streets, their vendors hawking all manner of food and sundries with as much fierceness as they used to keep the gangs of thieving orphans at a safe distance. And everywhere were the goblins.

Black Pool was home to the largest population of goblins in all of Airlann. Not even in Toad Holm, where many of them had returned to live in the more civilized culture of their gnomish cousins, could so many be found. Pocket had never laid eyes on one outside the embroidered hordes on the tapestries in the Great Hall, but that first day he saw hundreds of their grey-skinned, bulbous nosed faces. Some pushed carts loaded with tinker wares while others patrolled the streets in the uniform of the city guard.

They drank in the taverns and poled skiffs in the rivers, as common a presence as the humans that made up the second largest community in the city.

So it should not have been surprising that it was a goblin that broke him out of his morose reflection.

"I wouldn't." The voice came from behind.

Pocket jumped slightly and turned. This particular goblin was quite fat, a prodigious gut hanging over the front of his patchwork breeches from which a fishtail poked out of one pocket.

A frightfully large cudgel rested on his shoulder, festooned with ribbons of many very faded colors.

"Would not what?" Pocket managed.

"Jump in," the fat goblin replied. He faked a shiver, causing the gold ring in his ear to jiggle. "The Poddle is dreadful cold this time of year. And on this island it's always this time of year."

"Then this is the Poddle." Pocket was relieved.

The goblin looked confused. "What is?"

"The river."

"What about it?"

"It's the Poddle."

"Oh, I dunno." The goblin gave an enormous shrug. "I never thought to ask it its name afore."

"But you just said . . ."

"Don't jump in. And I wouldn't! Filthy blighter, the Poddle."

Pocket found his mouth hanging open.

"Now if I was to kill meself I would go with . . ." the goblin's fingers dragged at an imaginary beard, ". . . drowning!"

Pocket looked at the river and then back at the goblin.

"But . . ."

"Not by the river! By somewhat more exotic. Keg of ale, no . . . wine! Oh no wait, the blood of a thousand vanquished foes. No, too terrible. Fresh cream! Ooohhh!" Pocket watched as the goblin did a little jump and pointed at him in excitement. "Teats!"

"Teats?"

There was gold in his smile as well as in his ear. "Teats. Only way to drown, I say. In mounds of soft, warm, round, unblemished flesh." There was an awkward moment where Pocket watched the goblin close his eyes and revel in a pantomime of his preferred demise. The hand gestures were very specific. At last the goblin stopped the charade, but kept his eyes closed and his face uplifted to the sky as if bathing in the warmth of the sun.

"Sir?" Pocket asked after a moment.

The goblin opened his eyes and looked at him. "Sire!"

"Sire?"

"Are you not a king?"

"No."

"And I am no knight! No more *sirs*, sire."

Pocket was having trouble keeping up. "But I do not know your name."

The goblin leaned down slightly. It was not a long trip, he was hardly taller than Pocket, but his bulk made it a bit alarming. "I will tell you it today, since we just met, but henceforth you must guess it."

"All right," Pocket agreed reluctantly. "What is it?"

"You must guess."

"But you said you would tell me."

"Tell you what?"

"Your name."

"What is my name?"

"I don't know!"

"Well guessed! Clever lad, my name today *is* Muckle. How ever did you know? And what should I call you?"

"Pocket."

"Oh this?" The goblin reached in his pants. "It's just a fish."

"No." Pocket could not help but laugh. "It's my name."

The goblin straightened abruptly and wrinkled his considerable nose. "Your name is Fish?"

"No. Pocket!"

"Oh!" Muckle breathed a sigh of relief. "Thank Girth and Moan for that."

Pocket did not know what that meant but was afraid to ask any more questions.

"That's why I would not want to drown in the river," Muckle told him. "You'd be ate by fish." He regarded the dead one in his hand with intense scrutiny. "Fish are cheeky. They never blink. Nothing cheekier than a bloke who won't stop staring."

Pocket could not help himself. "Why do keep one in your breeches?"

"I like cheeky." Muckle winked and tucked the fish away.

"So, what do you reckon? A high fall? Poison? Tell a coburn it's nothing but an overgrown chicken?"

"What?"

"For how you want to kill yourself."

Pocket shook his head. "I'm not doing that! I'm just lost."

"Well," Muckle placed a broad, thick-fingered hand on his shoulder and made a grand sweeping gesture with his big club, "this is the grand city of Black Pool. It rests on the northeastern shores of Airlann, also known as the Source Isle. Cold winds and chilly rains are typical here especially during the current Age. It all began some four thousand years ago when—"

Pocket brushed his hand away. "No. I am looking for the billier's shop in Cauldron Town and I got confused. I have a message to deliver there and—"

He stopped himself. He was on an errand for Sir Corc and thusly, the Order of the Valiant Spur and should not be sharing that with anyone, much less a corpulent goblin who was obviously moon-brained. He tried to think of some way to excuse himself, but found he was standing alone. Muckle had already moved off down the riverwalk, his long, ludicrously pointed shoes flapping on the stones.

"Well I'm off," he called over his shoulder. "Have to see the bell-founder in Cauldron Town! Having myself cast in an enormous brass bell, you see! Thing of beauty! The crown will be fashioned after my own head and the clapper will be my . . . Anyway, pleasant meeting!"

This goblin may have been some kind of fool, but Pocket did not consider himself one. He saw his chance. "Wait!"

He caught up to Muckle and fell in beside him. The goblin said nothing, but began to whistle jauntily, leading them away from the riverwalk and towards a flight of steep stone stairs. He was quite nimble despite his weight, but Pocket had to fight back the giggles as the goblin let out a short, sharp fart with every step upwards. Muckle stopped at the top of the stairs to catch his breath, causing Pocket to bump into him.

"Pardons."

"Why?" Muckle replied and then leaned down to whisper.

"Did you fart?"

Pocket allowed himself to laugh then and continued to do so for most of their trek through the city. Muckle knew every street and turn and made a point of greeting everyone they passed by name, which drew a great many confused expressions and more than one angry glare. There was a tense moment that Pocket thought might come to blows after Muckle hailed a passing Middangeard raider as Lord Sweetmeat, but following a brief exchange and several bawdy jests the man parted smiling, clapping the goblin heartily on the back. Pocket learned several shameful poems and more than a few ribald songs during their walk and ate a good many treats from street vendors that Muckle managed to acquire. Pocket never actually saw him at any thievery, nor did he ever see him pay, it was simply that the normally suspicious shopkeepers were filled with a good-natured generosity when the fat goblin spoke with them and soon pies, tarts, fruits and other morsels were offered up as earnest gifts.

Muckle was downing the last swallows from a yard of ale when they entered Cauldron Town and pronounced their arrival with a grand sweep of the club that Pocket had learned the goblin referred to as his "pompous knob." His words were lost, however, in the deafening sound of countless hammers falling upon stubborn metal. The lively din of the streets was nothing compared to the furious scream of industry. The pallor cast by thousands of turf fires within the rest of the city was a thin veil next to the ocean of forge smoke that churned within this one district. Men, goblins and dwarves trudged between the foundries, red-eyed and soot-stained, most clad in heavy leather aprons. Muckle leaned down in Pocket's ear.

"Come. You've an axe to grind and I've a beautiful bell of brazen brass to be boldly bestowed with the bulbously brave body bequeathed by birth to this both beloved and blessedly boastful braggart."

They dodged through the workers, shying away from showers of sparks and unpleasant spews of suffocating heat. The bell foundry was a massive structure of plastered stone with large openings at regular intervals along the walls. Within, Pocket spied great scaffolds and huge cauldrons of molten metal around which an army of workers labored. And just across the way was a little storefront, above which hung a wooden sign fashioned in the likeness of an axe, painted black. Pocket turned to thank Muckle only to find him in a heated argument with his fish.

"I know a bell is round! That is no reason why I cannot be riding a rearing horse and playing a harp!" He seemed to feel Pocket's eyes on him and broke off his debate momentarily. "Can you find your way back?"

"Yes," the lie came easily. He liked Muckle, but the thought of what Sir Corc would say if he returned in such company was too much to risk. "Thank you for your help."

"Pfshh!" Muckle waved him off. "I didn't do much. Except save you from jumping in the river and that's . . . well, yes, pretty damn impressive, but small on the long list of greatness I perform daily. Luck to you." And with a wave he turned away, passing the bell founder's completely. Pocket could hear him even above the clangor. "I *can so* play the harp, but now you've gone and spoiled it. No! I don't want to be a bell anymore. Don't you try and apologize to me you wall-eyed bastard! I'll have you know . . ."

Pocket delivered his message to the dwarf that ran the billier's shop and waited among the racks of various axes while a reply was drafted. He tucked the missive into his jerkin and promptly asked the billier for directions.

He found Bantam Flyn at practice when he returned. The squire had taken to drilling with his quarterstaff in the little walled courtyard at the front of their quarters, his frustration taken out on stuffed sacking nailed to several posts. The results of this day's exercises were spread over the yard in pitiful heaps of split hemp and scattered straw. The dull smacking of wood continued as Flyn worked the now unprotected poles, his staff a whirlwind of stroke and counterstroke.

"Hello, carrier pigeon," Flyn said as Pocket entered the yard, not taking his eyes off his target nor halting his strikes. "Come back with another love letter?"

It was said lightly, jestingly, but Pocket noticed that the squire's staff struck harder with each word, the iron tips sending splinters flying.

"A message, yes," Pocket told him, trying not to be awed by the speed of the quarterstaff. "I best get it to Sir."

"Best wait," Flyn grunted between swings. "*Sir* is occupied with guests . . . again."

Pocket nodded. Sir Corc had hosted a steady stream of guests since their arrival, often spending hours at a time shut away in the small receiving room at the back of their quarters. Pocket's curiosity could not overpower his sense of place and he never asked what was happening in those meetings. Bantam Flyn had no such qualms. On their second morning in the city after a pair of undines had departed, the squire flat out asked what Sir Corc was doing behind closed doors.

"Listening," was all the knight had said.

Pocket sat on the ground, his back to the courtyard wall and felt his feet begin to bark sorely from the day's long ordeal on the cobblestones. Flyn continued to hammer away, his body in motion, his face restless. Pocket looked over and saw Coalspur leaning a few feet down the wall. The sword was still encased in its old scabbard, but now a belt and harness of new leather was affixed, so that the blade might be worn across the back. It was simple work, but likely the best the squire could afford.

"Had to send Lochlann out for it," Flyn stopped his practice and strode over.

"It's quite handsome," Pocket told him.

"Might as well be hanging on the wall in the Marshal's Hall for all the use it's getting." Flyn leaned his quarterstaff against the wall and sat down next to Pocket.

He had a point. When they left Albain, Pocket had imagined grand adventures in snowy mountains and dark forests, duels on bridges and quests to lonely towers. Running messages through a maze of smelly buildings was certainly not in his musings and he was barely a page, with no hope of ever wearing the spurs.

He could not help but feel a little pity for the squire.

"How fares Black Pool?" Flyn asked.

"Big," Pocket responded. He did not want to say too much.

Sir Corc had not allowed Flyn to go out into the city without his presence and the knight had hardly left his rooms since their arrival.

Flyn plucked pebbles from the ground and tossed them halfheartedly at nothing. After a while, Old Lochlann shuffled out the doorway, knobby knees poking through his thin hose. He squinted at the pair of them sitting against the wall.

"There's fish stew above the fire if you've a mind," he told Pocket. Bantam Flyn gave his arm a subtle squeeze in warning.

"Thank you," Pocket said with a smile. "I am all right for now."

The old man gave a quaking nod, his lank, white locks swinging and went back inside.

"He is trying to murder us," Flyn said with feigned concern.

"Wants the place back to himself."

Pocket smiled but did not laugh. He had taken quickly to the steward. When they arrived he had not so much as blinked when he saw Pocket, but simply tucked his cap with mumbled courtesies and shown him to the garret where he was to sleep. He was nothing like Moragh, but nor was he anything like the other humans Pocket had known.

"He cannot smell or taste so good anymore," Pocket said.

"I think that is why his cooking is so bad. I'll make us something when he is not around."

"Be careful where you dump that stew," Flyn said. "If any of the locals' animals die, they'll seek recompense."

"Sir Corc doesn't seem to mind the food."

Flyn scoffed. "That one could live on dirt and rainwater. Tough old bird . . . and a damn fraud."

"Fraud?"

Flyn did not answer for a long moment, but when he finally spoke his voice was bitter. "You hear a lot about the knights, as a squire. The Knights Sergeant are forever in your face, training you, but it's the Knights Errant that everyone talks about at meals and after the curfew bell. The long dead legends like Mulrooster, sure . . . but the living ones, the knights out in the world, those are the ones we aspire to be. You hear such deeds . . . how Pitch Feather hunted a pack of barghests to their lair and slew the den mother. About the time Blood Yolk single-handedly boarded a slaver's ship, cut every man down and liberated the holds. The Mad Capon drank a giant under the table . . ."

"Bronze Wattle once rescued Áedán mac Gabráin's daughter from the grua-gach," Pocket threw in. "And Poorly Well prevented a grove sacred to the wood-wose from burning."

"Yes!" Flyn agreed. "The White Noble outwitted the Slip Noose Gang, Pyle Strummer saved the flocks of the Dal Riata from a vargulf and—"

Pocket waited for him to continue, breath held. He had heard about all of these deeds, but never from one so close to them.

Surely Flyn knew more and Pocket could not wait to hear the details of these exploits. But the squire had stopped completely, an angry and sullen expression creeping across his face.

"And?" Pocket urged.

"And," Flyn locked his attention. "Of all those stories, not one of them relates to our laconic ambassador. No tales are told of Sir Corc the Constant. No songs or poems. But despite that, there was one known fact about our knight that could not be denied and we squires spoke of it with as much reverence as any of the others. Of all the heroes of the Order, Sir Corc stays on errantry longer than any other, often gone for years at a time. I once heard the Old Goose say that he used to not return even on the two-year, sending only written notes as evidence that he still lived."

Pocket frowned. If that was true, then it must have been ages ago. The Knights Errant had returned to the Roost twice in Pocket's memory and Sir Corc was there both times.

"That was dedication to the quest that could be boasted by no other. That was a true sense of duty. But . . . now we know where he goes," Flyn gestured dismissively at the house. "This is where he goes . . . what he does. Meetings. Sitting. Nothing. A fraud."

As if conjured, the door opened and Old Lochlann escorted two men and a goblin through the yard and out the little gate. The trio did not spare a look for Flyn or Pocket. Sir Corc came out directly, looking very tired. Pocket stood when he saw him. Flyn stayed where he was, throwing pebbles. Sir Corc held out his hand and Pocket approached, placing the note the billier had given him into the knight's broad palm.

"Will Sir be wanting any supper?" Lochlann asked as he returned from the gate.

"No," Sir Corc said as his eyes scanned the note. Then he looked up. "On your feet, Bantam Flyn. Pocket, please fetch my sword."

Pocket hesitated for a moment, but Lochlann cast him a "get to it" look and he rushed into the house, quickly gathering Sir Corc's sword belt from the wall peg. When he returned to the yard, Flyn was standing, the hilt of the greatsword towering over his right shoulder. Sir Corc took his own weapon from Pocket and buckled it on.

"We will be back before dark, Lochlann," Sir Corc told the steward. "Do not admit anyone until my return. You two, with me."

The knight walked purposefully out the gate without waiting to see if they followed.

This time Pocket did not wait for an urging look, but went right on out. Flyn drew even with him, his face unable to contain his excitement. The easy smile was back, the swagger returned to his steps. Pocket smiled when the squire thumped him companionably on the back.

Sir Corc led them competently through the streets, avoiding the larger market squares, but also keeping out of the narrow alleys.

His pace was steady, never halting to check a street or his direction.

Soon they came to a bridge which Pocket, thanks to Muckle, knew to be the Goat's Tongue and Sir Corc led them over, crossing the Poddle and into Hogulent. Pocket had yet to set foot on this side of the city, but he quickly saw why it had a reputation for being the worst end of Black Pool. The buildings were little more than lean-tos next to the river and housed a thriving community of the city's most destitute, but Sir Corc passed the forest of begging hands and pressed further into the slums. The choking reek of the tanneries that operated in the district threatened to gag Pocket and though Flyn put on a brave face it was obvious he was suffering as well. Sir Corc did not appear to notice.

They wound their way through the cattle pens bordering the tanneries, the poor doomed beasts staring at them from their muck-ridden confines. Beyond, Pocket could hear the dull thud of the maul and the desperate lowing of the soon to be slaughtered.

Sir Corc approached a low wooden shed among the myriad of outbuildings and leaned near the filthy curtain that served as a door.

He whispered something that Pocket did not catch, but the reply was loud enough.

"Come ahead," said a strangely accented voice.

Sir Corc pushed back the curtain and held it open as Flyn ducked inside. Pocket followed closely behind. He was not surprised to find a dwarf inside. He had seen many since coming to the city. Finding him brushing down a mule inside the shed was a bit odd, but nothing was as shocking as the small, naked girl with wings trapped in a bronze cage hanging from the wall. She looked up when Sir Corc entered and despite her size, Pocket had to take a step back when she yelled.

"Stop staring, you sword-wearing game cock and get me out of here!"

THIRTEEN

"Pains in that tender hide, boy?"

Padric ignored the jibe and the mocking chuckles of the other men that followed, silently cursing Drefan's sharp eyes. The sour, old warrior must have spied the wince that played across his face when he shifted in the saddle. Almost a fortnight of daily rides and still Padric's body protested at spending hours astride a horse.

His legs had grown stronger and the tight, painful pulling of the previously unknown muscles down the insides of his thighs had lessened mercifully, but the soreness in his back and hips seemed to worsen with each day. The rain only made matters worse. His clothes were soaked through and clung to him, the wet wool rubbing his skin raw where it touched the hard leather of saddle and harness. Still, he never complained outwardly and found he had a natural skill while ahorse, a feeling validated when Kederic granted him permission to accompany the patrols.

He could feel Drefan's stare, the bastard waiting for a reaction, but Padric would not be baited and focused on the entrance of the crofter's dwelling. After a moment, Aglaeca emerged from within, sword still in hand and shook his head.

Acwellen ran a hand down his face, pulling the rainwater from his beard, then spat onto the flooded ground. With a jerk of his head, he signaled Aglaeca to mount.

"Fled or dead?" Drefan asked whimsically and even without looking Padric could see his slimy grin.

"Both." It was Banan who answered; his first word of the day and likely his last.

Padric thought he had the right of it. If the crofter and his family had been killed here then there would be some sign. Padric's mind went unbidden to the memory of the pig keeper they found not a week before. The goblins had nailed him to the door of his cottage and set him on fire. The blackened remnants of his arms still hung from the wood, a pile of greasy ash and bone below. That unfortunate man had lived barely two days ride from the fort. The croft where they now stood was several days further distant and Padric could not help but think that it was unlikely its former inhabitants made it to safety. More than likely they were hunted down in the forests or harried into the bogs. Padric hoped they did not have any children.

He thought of his own family, and, not for the first time, was thankful they lived in the shadow of Stone Fort, many miles away. If the Red Caps would not attack Kederic's wooden holdfast, they would not dare attack the fortifications that guarded his home.

He had grown up despising the warriors that mocked him, hoping that some bloody conflict would lead them far away and claim their lives. Now he was grateful that so many spears stood between his parents and the brutal acts he had witnessed since leaving them.

Besides, he had new men to despise.

"Come lads." Acwellen jerked the reins of his horse. "Let's turn these nags to home. Nout to find here."

The big man led them away from the croft, each rider falling into his designated place. Padric's horse was square in the center of the line, four warriors before him, four behind. After their initial meeting at Bairn's Babble, Padric had not been keen on accompanying Acwellen and his men, but the Thegn had insisted.

Padric could not well refuse after asserting his need to help so strongly. Kederic had saved his life, clothed him and fed him and offered him lodging. In no small way was he beholden to the man and Padric would not dishonor himself by balking at the duties given him.

Acwellen's riders were a grizzled bunch, each a veteran of numerous wars across the breadth of the Tin Isles. Once there were forty men under Acwellen's command, but only seven had lived to see the Winetongue come into prosperity and retire in Airlann. A decade of peace and good living had done nothing to soften them. Padric had slain a gruagach and survived a Red Cap raid, but next to these killers he might as well still be on the teat.

They rode hard through the day, making for the holdfast direct. Acwellen did not seem interested in retracing the circuitous route of their patrol, although Padric privately thought a second look at the places where people were known to live was worth taking. But he said nothing. He learned quickly that his opinion was neither valued nor welcomed in this company.

They made a rough camp that night among a pitiful copse of trees. The men went about their preparations with the belligerent ease of old campaigners. As always, Padric was ignored and left to tend his horse with no offer of aid or advice. He brushed the beast down after removing the saddle as Kederic had taught him and watered and fed her. He did not rush for he was in no hurry to join the others around the fire, but nor did he tarry overlong lest his extended absence be mistaken for incompetence.

Dallying as long as he could, Padric left the horses and trudged the short distance to the camp.

"Fine night," Seon said as Padric passed him in the dark.

"Fine," Padric agreed without pausing. Seon was the most pleasant of the bunch, but Padric knew he mocked along with the rest when they suspected he was out of ear-shot. Padric would be spared his fake smile this evening as the man had drawn horse watch. It was a small mercy.

The stew pot was already steaming by the time he walked into the firelight. Acwellen sat talking in hushed tones with Aglaeca while Drefan and Big Cunny pretended to laugh at something Poncey Swan said. Fat Donall stirred the pot and just outside the ring of light, Banan stood with his back turned, staring out into the night. Padric never thought he would yearn for the nights when he and Rosheen had camped out in the dark during their journey to Hog's Wallow, but looking at these men he wished for nothing more than to be with his best friend and away from them.

He sat himself down as far from Poncey Swan's mewling voice as he could manage and pretended to look busy oiling his sword. It was a borrowed blade, given to him by the Thegn the morning Padric left the fort. Wearing three feet of solid iron was strange and uncomfortable. Acwellen's men had gotten a good laugh on the first day when Padric dismounted and the scabbard became entangled in his stirrup strap. He had never wielded the weapon, so sharpening it was pointless, but he made sure he kept it well cleaned, making a nightly ritual of the task, drawing ridicule from his companions, but he paid no heed. He would not return a rusty sword.

As he worked the oil into the metal with a rag, his mind turned once again to Rosheen. He constantly wondered what had become of her, and during his first days at the fort he resolved that he would find out. Initially, his plan consisted of thanking the Thegn for his hospitality, begging some provisions and striking out on his own in search of the wayward piskie, but deeper reflection on his lack of knowledge concerning the surrounding landscape and the very real danger that was loose in those lands forced him to refine his purpose. He would brave anything to find her, but setting off blindly would benefit nothing. He fancied he could hear Rosheen's voice chiding him to just that effect.

Kederic's words still troubled him, but he would never discover if Rosheen had any answers concerning his life if he never saw her again. The thought soured his heart. They had rarely been apart and it was all he could think on. He was tempted every morning to walk back to Stone Fort, embrace his mother and help his father with some familiar labor. But he could not do that. Not without Rosheen. So he endured the sneers, the spiteful stares, the mocking comments, and he rode, hoping that the long, wet patrols would offer some sign as to where she had gone, and eventually lead him back to her careless smile.

There was a sudden change in the sound of the camp. It was too quiet. Padric looked up just as Big Cunny threw the dagger.

Reflex caused him to jerk his limbs ineffectually and the blade buried deep into the sodden ground, not a hand span from where he sat. Laughter once again filled the camp, Big Cunny's loudest of all, his witless face looking around at his compatriots for approval.

Slowly, Padric pulled the dagger from the mud with the intent to simply toss it back without a care. These men were dogs. Fear only made them more likely to bite. But when he saw the blades in Drefan and Fat Donall's hands he paused, his grip tightening on the recently flung dagger. Big Cunny must have won the toss to see who would throw first, which was fortunate. Fat Donall would have sent the blade into Padric's gut for the sake of a bigger laugh.

But it was not the deadly game at his expense that most angered Padric, it was the weapon he saw in Drefan's hand. Over a foot of sharp, smoke colored steel.

"That," Padric said, flicking his eyes at Drefan's hand, "is mine."

The old man's yellow teeth grinned back wetly, and Padric saw he had just made the game much more amusing. "Well then," Drefan said. "Pup's after me property."

"Stupid move, mate," Poncey Swan said smugly while Fat Donall chuckled, his pale chins wiggling. Padric knew he was pushing this situation beyond good sense, but the sight of the seax in Drefan's boney hand was more than he could stomach. Padric looked into the old man's face and tried to keep his voice even.

"You found that in the Wallow."

"No," Drefan's tongue slid across his chapped lower lip. "I found it in some burnt out pile of sheep shit that was once the Wallow."

"Burnt out pile," Big Cunny repeated as Fat Donall guffawed.

"Still mine," Padric said.

Drefan's teeth grit together, but the grin remained. "And I've a mind to give it back to you." The murder in the man's eyes was naked.

Padric jumped to his feet, brandishing Big Cunny's dagger and Drefan followed him up. Fat Donall seemed to think this was the most amusing turn yet and continued to laugh, jowls flushed.

Big Cunny smiled gormlessly, but his eyes were confused, darting around the camp. Poncey Swan watched with his arrogant face, his weak chin. Banan had turned around to watch, but made no further move. All of this Padric saw in a glance, trying to gauge if anyone would come to Drefan's side. Acwellen and Aglaeca were beyond Padric's periphery and he fought down a rising panic, suspecting a blade through the back with every breath. But it never came. The men seemed content to watch, offering only crude shouts of encouragement. Drefan and Padric watched each other over the campfire as the others made sport.

"Ooooh! I think he's angry with you, Drefan."

"Cut his bollocks off!"

"Pull his breeches down and shag him like a girl!"

Padric ignored them.

"It belongs to me," he told Drefan firmly. "On the pommel is a dwarven rune . . . the mark of the maker and the one who gave it to me."

"Aye?" Drefan sneered. "Then why do I have it, eh? It was in the mud. Could it be because you left it behind when you ran a craven from the battle?"

That drew jeers from the others and Padric fought the urge to rush the man.

"Yes," Padric said. "I ran from the battle. But I also ran to it. I do not recall you being there at all, old man!"

Drefan's face darkened. "You're about to die bloody, boy."

Padric thought that was true. "I'll carve you even uglier before I do."

Drefan snarled, leaping over the fire, kicking the stew pot over to hiss in the flames. Padric darted backwards, away from the long reach of the slashing seax, but the stroke never fell.

"Enough!" Acwellen's voice barreled over the cheers of his men as Aglaeca stepped in, grabbing Drefan's arm and near throwing him to the ground. The camp went quiet, every man looking to Acwellen except for Banan who simply turned his back once again. Acwellen pushed himself to his feet, while Drefan breathed hard, splitting his glare between Aglaeca and Padric. The old man huffed when his leader approached and held out a hand for the seax, but handed it over without a word. Acwellen took a moment to admire the blade before squinting down at the rune etched into the pommel.

"It is as he says," Acwellen said. He looked at Padric and walked over, thumping the hilt of the weapon against his palm. "It was yours."

Padric smiled gratefully and held out his hand for the weapon.

"What do you have to give for its return?" Acwellen asked.

Padric looked up at him, mind searching, but Acwellen did not wait for an answer.

"It is not right that my men should suffer loss of spoils without recompense. You are a stranger here. And a pauper. What have you to offer this man in trade?" Acwellen leaned down, his large frame blocking the firelight. "Nothing. Your clothes, your boots. Horse. That sword. Your life! All gifted to you by the Winetongue. You own nothing but your own cursed head. And you will not look to take gifts from me and mine the same as you take from our Thegn."

Acwellen loomed over him for a moment longer, then turned and flipped the seax back into Drefan's hand before resuming his seat.

Padric spent that night in furious silence. None of the men spoke to him, not even Seon, but Drefan kept throwing amused leers his way, sharing nudges and whispers with Poncey Swan.

Padric could taste the need to kill them and put an end to their gloating for good and all. His days were spent in the saddle, lost in dark thought. At night, the saddle was traded for his blanket, but the thoughts remained the same. Faabar would have known how to deal with these churls, but he was gone and Padric had only himself for council. By the time they reached the fort, he was still uncertain of his course.

The warrior's camp had grown larger since last they were there. The steady influx of refugees from neighboring settlements seeking solace had forced Kederic to order his own men to sleep beyond the walls, keeping only a small contingent inside at night to man the watchtowers. It had been a difficult choice for the Thegn, but he deigned that no women or children should sleep without, and the fort soon grew overcrowded. Already many of the surviving husbands and fathers had taken to sleeping in the camp with the warriors. The Thegn's prodigious cattle herds were now swollen with the beasts brought by the dispossessed. Herds of sheep, goats and swine clustered thickly in the fields surrounding the fort and the camp doubled as a means of protecting the animals from predators both four and two legged.

It was near dusk when they rode through the gate and found Kederic waiting on them.

"Red Caps are still out there, Winetongue," Acwellen reported as he dismounted, handing his reigns over to a ready groom. "But we never saw 'em. Nor anyone alive. Any that would have made it are here already, reckon. T'other riders?"

"Orvin brought in a few," the Thegn replied. "And one of Warian's men found a lad surviving in the bogs. The rest found their own way. They all tell the same tale."

Padric could imagine. Watchfires in the dark. Torches and cruel laughter. Fire and slaughter. The Red Caps had turned the countryside into an abandoned expanse of burnt homesteads, scattered herds and the footprints of the fled. They were everywhere and yet still unseen by any of Kederic's men. They came, killed and vanished and everyday saw new survivors find their fearful way to the Thegn's protection.

"Sleep in the hall tonight. Rest." Kederic swept the men with a glance and gave Padric a brief nod before turning and heading back to the hall, Acwellen close at his side.

The others followed, cheered by the promise of warmth and ale, but Padric remained in the yard. He had wished a word with the Thegn, away from the others but was not entirely sure what he wanted to say. Informing him that his men were thieving bastards seemed a guarantee of ill favor. Padric was not certain he even cared to please the man any longer. Mayhaps it was better to take his leave.

Deep in thought, he followed the grooms to the stables, leading his own mount. He tended the animal himself, ignoring his hunger through the work. The prospect of the warm hall and hot food was tempting, but the thought of having to spend another second with Drefan and the rest was enough to keep him away. He did not know where he would sleep tonight and was avoiding the search for a place. Maybe he would simply bed down in the stables with the grooms and their charges. He was tired. Not just in his body, but straight through. He had thought to find a new life, but instead the world had gone mad. His one companion was gone and people were being butchered and burned all around him. He was just another refugee, adrift in a sea of survivors with no possessions and earning nothing but the enmity of the men around him. He had traded the mistrust of his neighbors for the hatred of strangers and found himself returning that hatred tenfold. Only briefly had he found acceptance and possible friendship, before both had been taken in the flames.

Padric had been avoiding the survivors of Hog's Wallow since his recovery. Shame and guilt and fear kept him away. The chance to ride with Acwellen was more than a means of finding Rosheen, it was an escape from the faces of the women whose menfolk had died around him. Ardal had almost made it out with him. Padric could still see him lying motionless, his skull caved in.

It seemed impossible now that he still had his own life.

A new life. And as trapped as he was in the old one.

He snorted derisively at himself and gave the horse a final pat on the flank before leaving the stables. Evening had settled silently over the fort and everywhere people surrounded tiny cook fires, preparing meager meals. The refugees huddled anywhere they could find space, some lucky enough to shelter in the smithy or one of the granary huts, but many and more were tucked under the stairs to the ramparts or among the support pylons of the hall.

Mostly, they squatted miserably under makeshift lean-tos at the base of the wall or even in the thoroughfares. Padric wound his way through the clusters of desperate faces, feeling they searched him for answers. He wore a sword, the quilted jerkin and leather hauberk of a warrior, looking like he belonged to this place, a source of strength and protection. If only they knew the truth.

The former residents of Hog's Wallow occupied the bakery and a quarter of one of the warrior's barracks. As the first refugees to reach the fort, they had quickly made themselves useful, slipping into the daily labors of the place with ease. As Ardal had told him, many of the herdsmen's daughters were now wed to the men in service to the Thegn, turning neighbors into family. These ties had quickly established the survivors of Hog's Wallow as liaison for the Thegn and the refugees from other parts. With many of the men dead, this duty was shouldered firmly by the women and Padric found a long line of folk waiting before the bakery. The women of Hog's Wallow worked feverishly in front of the ovens every night, making as much bread as they were able to help feed the unfortunates from other hamlets. Padric found Jileen milking a goat while Ardal's widow distributed clay jars of the milk to the children. The two women had decreed that every child have a full belly before any others were allowed to eat.

"Thought you to be in the hall with a trencher and a full horn," Jileen said when she saw him.

Padric curled his lip and shook his head.

The former alewife smirked at him. "Warrior's life not to your liking?"

"It never was," he replied.

"Any sign?" the widow Móirne asked without taking her focus from the children.

"No," he answered, unsure as to what she was referring. It did not matter. There were no signs. Not of goblins nor survivors and not of Rosheen.

"There's food," Móirne said. "If you wait until we get these wee ones sorted out."

"Thank you, no," Padric told her.

"Nonsense," she declared, taking her eyes off her work for the first time. "You will stand right there until we're through and then you will have your supper. If that does not suit you, then you can lend a hand and then . . . you will have your supper. Those are the choices, Padric. Make one."

He smiled. She was a great deal like her husband. He helped where he was able, taking over the milking from Jileen while she fetched more jars, the udder of the animal feeling more familiar in his hands than a sword ever would. The sky was full dark by the time they were through and could take their own repast of bread and cabbage. There was even some ale to share and they passed the horn, drinking to their beloved dead into the late watches.

He and Jileen remained awake after the others had stolen away to their pallets. The ale ration was long since gone, so they sat around the last embers of the cook fire listening to the odd silence of a place full of sleeping people. Padric was dozing when Jileen finally spoke.

"So many times," she said, "one of the Thegn's men would come down to the alehouse . . . offer himself as husband. And I turned every one of them away. Now . . . here I am. Living in this fort anyway." She curled into herself, then looked at him and smiled, rolling her eyes at her own words.

"I am sorry." He did not know what else to say.

"No fault of yours."

"It feels like it is," he said before he could stop himself.

"Móirne is so kind. And I watched her man die."

"You had no choice in that, Padric." Jileen shifted closer and ducked her face to his so that he had no choice but to look at her. "You are Fae-touched. It is more than fortune that watched out for you. Móirne and all the others are grateful you were there. Someone who can speak to the bravery of their husbands and sons. It is a gift to them."

"Fae-touched," he snorted. "They are all gone now. Faabar and Deglan. Even that drunken clurichaun. Rosh. We cannot even find the goblins. Kederic may be right. Mortals are better left to themselves."

"We are certainly alone now," Jileen replied.

Padric looked around the yard at the mass of sleeping bodies and gave her a pointed look.

She laughed. "You know my meaning."

"I do," he said with a smile and stood up. "I am for the stables, I think. My thanks for the hospitality."

She rose. "I will walk with you."

"I would just have to escort you right back," he told her.

"Too many unfamiliar faces about to have you walking alone."

"Well then," something happened to her eyes, "I will not come back."

She was bold and Padric was tempted. Her thick auburn hair promised warmth, her smile spoke of welcome abandon. He had tasted his fill of harsh company and underneath her woolen dress, Padric was sure she would be soft to his hands.

"Forgive a tired man," he said, inwardly cursing himself for a fool. "I think the horse got the best of my strength for the day."

Her face remained amused and playful. "Is that a refusal?"

He laughed. "It is a plea. Not to take offense to either of the poor choices I would undoubtedly make tonight."

He was relieved to see she was indeed unhurt. She smiled and shook her head. "You are a strange one, Padric Piskie-Kissed."

"I know," he said walking backwards, still smiling. "It is a burden."

He made his way back to the stables, immediately regretting his decision, but he did not turn around and make himself twice the fool. The grooms were all asleep in their bunks off the tack room, so Padric crept by and made for the stalls. Kederic would not risk the welfare of his steeds and had forbidden anyone from sleeping in the stables, but Padric did not care. Disobeying the rule gave him a petty satisfaction and maybe his defiance would lead to an audience with the Thegn away from his men. The possibility that he would be flogged passed through his mind, but he was too weary to worry overmuch. He made for the rear where a large stall was used for feed and fodder storage, unbuckling his sword belt and letting it fall. A long sigh of comfort escaped from his lungs when he settled into the soft mound, sleep quickly dimming his vision. Something pressed into his lower back and he dug halfheartedly into the hay to retrieve it.

The mound erupted and something leapt on top of him!

The hay fell in over his head, blocking his sight and he felt his left hand pinned fast. He swung blindly with his free arm and buffeted into the thing, but could not dislodge it. He tried to raise his face out of the pile when a hand gripped his throat, shoving him back down. He thrashed and punched in a panic, vision and breath cut off. Another hand clutched his free wrist and pinned it down, rendering him completely helpless. Choking and sputtering, his mouth filled with dry strands, gagging him. His right hand closed on something and his dimming brain recognized the feel of leather.

He grasped it and kicked his body upwards with his legs, desperate to throw off whatever was crushing the life from him. His knees struck it in the back and the pressure flew away from his throat, his wrists. He rolled out of the hay, drawing in dry breaths of dust, coughing back to life.

The sword belt was still in his hand and he fumbled to draw the blade as the figure recovered and dashed at him from the top of the pile, arms outstretched and grasping. Padric stumbled back and thrust with the naked iron. The figure did not check its headlong rush and the blade slid in easily through its chest up to the hilt. It fell forward and knocked Padric back into the wall. Shoving the figure away, Padric lost his grip on the sword. His attacker stumbled back on unsteady feet, the blade still imbedded deep in his body. He was so thin, Padric did not know how he managed to fight at all. Some old man? It was difficult to tell with the face concealed beneath the wide brim of that rumpled hat.

Padric held his bruised neck and sucked in air, waiting for the wretch to fall, only to have his newly found breath catch in his throat when the man kept his feet and slowly pulled the sword from his own body. No blood ran from the tear in his filthy shirt, no drops ran red from the blade as it issued from the wound, unblemished. It took the sword out and into hand before raising its head. There was no face! Only a sack stuffed and stitched with the semblance of human features, dead pits of blackness for eyes beneath the floppy brim of a . . .

"Slouch Hat," Padric croaked.

The husk hesitated at the sound of his name, but Padric did not. He launched off the wall, swatting the sword out of the scarecrow's hand before barreling him over. The stuffed body was heavier than it looked, but Padric still outweighed Slouch Hat by several stone and once they were down Padric pinned him fast.

"Murderous maggot," he rasped at the husk.

"Padric!" a sharp whisper came from behind him. He turned his head and found Jileen in the entrance to the stall, eyes wide, white knuckles clutching a shawl about her. Her gaze shifted to the form pinned beneath him and she rushed forward, dropping to her knees next to them.

"Stay back," he hissed.

"Padric, let him up."

"What? Jileen . . . it just tried to kill me. It *did* kill Brogan."

"Liar." The word came from below him in a voice thin and reedy. Padric shivered, reluctant to look down at the formless face.

Jileen placed a hand on his arm and was about to speak when they both caught the glow of a light coming towards them.

Jileen shoved Padric away and threw her shawl over Slouch Hat then grabbed Padric by the tunic, dragging him down on top of her.

Her mouth found his, lips parting, her body pressed upwards seamlessly into him. They rolled and she was now astride him, hay caught in her tousled hair, dressed bunched up around her thighs.

She breathed in little laughing gasps and did not stop when one of the grooms poked his head into the stall, lantern in hand.

"Oi now! What's this, then?"

"The lord's come a'callin'," Jileen giggled, her voice slurred.

She poked Padric clumsily in the chest. "Yer t'be flogged."

Padric watched the groom's grin begin to overpower his scowl. "Beg an hour?"

The groom gave him a knowing nod and went his way.

Jileen waited for the lantern light to completely fade before ceasing her mummery.

"Boy," the reedy voice issued from under the shawl next to Padric's ear. "Would you get off me?"

Jileen stood up, allowing Padric to roll away. He retrieved the sword out of the pile, but did not sheathe it as Jileen uncovered the husk and helped him to his feet.

Slouch Hat was shaped like a man, albeit a gangly one. He was barely taller than Padric, but there was something queer about the way he moved, an unnatural smoothness that sent hackles up the spine. His tunic and breeches must have once been finely made, but were now soiled and torn. Padric watched as he methodically picked every last piece of debris out of Jileen's shawl before handing it back to her.

"How did you get here?" she asked as she wrapped herself back up.

"I snuck in," the husk replied, the folds of his sack face moving disturbingly as he spoke.

"But the Sure Finder?" Jileen's hushed voice was worried, almost desperate. "Slouch, what if . . . how were you able—the—"

"Not with ease," the husk cut her off gently. "Madigan has had his beasts on my heels since I left. I barely managed to stay ahead of them. They harried me through the forests and back again and then . . . several days ago, they just stopped."

"He has not returned to the fort," Jileen said.

"Then the Winetongue has him hunting other prey."

"Goblins," Padric put in.

Slouch Hat's laugh tore almost noiselessly at the air. "He knows well where they are."

"Speak plainly!" The night's events had killed any patience Padric possessed.

The husk fixed him with the holes in his face. "Kederic commands the Red Caps."

It was Padric's turn to laugh. "Madness! The man distrusts the Fae. Why would he ever conspire with goblins?"

"To rule them," Slouch Hat said. "To become a Goblin King."

Padric struggled to keep his voice down. "I'll not listen to slanderous words from a thing that murdered its own master."

"He didn't," Jileen said. "Padric, Slouch Hat did not kill Brogan."

"How do you know?"

"He was on an errand for me when the body was found."

She suddenly seemed to remember something and looked to the husk. "Did you find them?"

"No," Slouch Hat replied. "It was as we feared. They were gone."

"Gone?" Padric was confused. Angry and confused. "What was gone? What errand? Jileen!"

"There is no time to explain this to some warrior whelp," the husk snapped. "Jileen, we must end this now, before it is too late."

Jileen hesitated before speaking. "What do you propose?"

"I will kill Kederic."

Padric brought his sword up so rapidly Jileen jumped.

Slouch Hat remained perfectly still. "I will not allow that."

"Do you really think *that* will work on me, boy?" the husk stepped towards him. "My home has been burned, my friends have been slain, I have been branded their slayer and the man responsible is sleeping peacefully within a bowshot of where we stand. If you think you can keep me from him, I will show you how mistaken you are."

Jileen stepped between them. "Enough! Padric, put that down. Slouch, listen to me. Padric was there. He fought with the others. He tried to save us. Faabar trusted him . . . *we* can trust him."

"I will not be a part of your murderous plot," Padric told her. "Murder?" the husk returned. "This is beyond that, beyond vengeance. Kederic must die if you do not want what has happened to these lands to occur across the whole of Airlann. If you do not trust my word, trust what is in front of you. The countryside burns, yet this fort remains untouched and the people who survive have no choice but to come here. He is master of more today than yesterday and much more than a moon's turn before. Kederic's own riders hunt the goblins but never find them. You say he distrusts the Fae, this we have known for years, but now he uses their greatest enemy against them. If the goblins put a throne under him, he need not love them. He owns them and he will use them to rid this isle of Fae-kind forever. Already, Faabar is dead and . . ."

"What?" Jileen pressed.

"I found Bulge-Eye," Slouch Hat said slowly. "While I was on the run. And I can tell you it was no goblin spear that I pulled from his corpse. I have lived around the Thegn's men long enough to know their arms."

"And Deglan?" Padric found himself asking.

Slouch Hat shook his head. "I found no sign."

Padric went cold. Kederic told him the gnome never made it to the fort and now he knew why. The villagers said Rosheen led them to safety, yet . . . The man had lied to him! They called him the Winetongue and Padric had become drunk on his words, senseless to the truth. He thought of Rosheen, hunted by the Thegn's men, ridden down like an animal and pierced with cold iron. Was she lying out there now? Moldering in some lightless track of woods?

Slouch Hat was wrong. This was not about the fate of the island.

Airlann could rot! Padric thirsted only for vengeance.

"We move now," he told the husk. "Acwellen's dogs are the only ones in the hall and stupefied with drink by now. He will never be more vulnerable."

The husk nodded grimly and snuck quietly out of the stall.

Padric made to follow when Jileen caught his arm. She said nothing but the meaning in her look was clear.

When they reached the yard, Padric took Slouch Hat by the wrist and looped an arm over his shoulders. The husk's limb felt fragile, devoid of muscle or bone, but there was strength when he tried to pull away. Padric held tight.

"Just act drunk."

Slouch Hat must have understood, for he went limp, stumbling along as they made their way to the hall. Some of the refugees under the support beams were awake and watched them from the dark, but Padric paid them no mind. They just needed to reach the Thegn's bedchamber. After that, Padric saw only red.

They dropped the act after opening the heavy doors and slipping into the hall. It was black as pitch inside, the central fire cooled to embers. Padric crept close to the wall, leading Slouch Hat, hoping they would not tread on someone sleeping in the dark. He felt his away along until they came to the side passage which led to the Thegn's quarters. Padric paused to listen for any sign that their passing had made a disturbance. Silence met his ears and he breathed easy. Nothing stirred, no footfalls, no mumbles of wakened sleepers, no snores. It was completely quiet.

Curse his stupidity!

He turned to flee when the torches flared. Banan stepped out of Kederic's chamber, an axe riding one fist, a sword the other.

Poncey Swan had an arrow trained on him from across the hall, his smile willing Padric to run. Seon and Big Cunny stepped forward with leveled spears, and behind, Fat Donall lounged on a bench with his torch held lazily. Drefan almost danced as he approached and held his torch close to Slouch Hat, who backed as far into the wall as he was able to avoid the flames. Aglaeca relieved Padric of his sword then hauled him roughly to the center of the hall and threw him to the floor.

"These actions grieve me, Padric," Kederic Winetongue said. "I did not want to believe you capable of this."

Padric struggled to his knees and looked up to see the Thegn standing over him, Acwellen close to heel.

"I believed too much of you," Padric spat on the Thegn's foot. Aglaeca cuffed him heavily across the face and Padric met the floor again. This time he spat blood.

Kederic knelt down in front of him. "I thought you stronger than this. Past being taken in by the lies of these creatures."

"I know the truth when I hear it," Padric told him through sore teeth.

"What have they promised you, Kederic?" Slouch Hat demanded from the wall. "You speak of lies! What falsehoods were you fed to birth so much evil?"

Kederic rose. "Bring that thing here."

Drefan herded the husk over with his torch and forced him to kneel before the Thegn. "I suffered your presence for Brogan's sake," Kederic said. "But now that he is gone, I see no more use for you. I will light a fire in his honor with your unnatural carcass."

"Honor the man you murdered?" the husk replied.

"I murdered no one," Kederic said through clenched teeth.

Padric tried to rise again, but Aglaeca put a boot to his chest, so he tossed his words at the Thegn from the floor. "Then which of these whoresons did it for you? I know the men you keep, curs all! Fat Donall would drown a man for an onion!"

The man named chortled heartily from his bench.

"Poncey Swan's too much a coward," Padric pressed on.

"And Big Cunny too daft. Drefan more than likely did your skullduggery. All for a pat on the head! Be proud of them, Thegn. Men such as these will be fit for your court. Only they would serve a Goblin King!"

Kederic snatched Padric by his tunic and hauled him upright. He shook him, their noses almost touching as he yelled in his face. "You would say this to me? You! Fae's pet that you are! I saved your life, boy! How dare you! How dare you!"

Padric did not struggle, he did not pull away. He just looked into that red face. "I would dare anything for Rosheen."

Kederic's face fell, his eyes filled with sorrow. "She has you bewitched." He released his hold and motioned to Aglaeca. "Get these cutthroats out of my sight."

Acwellen strode forward. "That will be difficult, my lord."

Kederic turned. "Why?"

Acwellen's fist slammed into the Thegn's jaw, showering Padric's face with bloody spittle. Kederic stumbled but did not fall until Aglaeca kicked his legs out from under him. Padric stood stunned but that did not stop Drefan from planting a knee into his gut and sending him to the floor beside the Thegn.

"Because," Acwellen leaned over them smiling. "You will be seeing them right up until the end."

"Acwellen!" Kederic's voice was full of fury and blood.

"You cannot expect to get away with this."

"You'll not be talking your way outta this one, My Lord Winetongue," Acwellen chided. "I got all me boys here. Where're yours?" He straightened as he laughed, full of himself. "Seon, run along and let our guests in! They've been awaitin' too long."

Big Cunny went to work binding all their hands while Acwellen seated himself and pulled deeply from a bottle.

"The other carls will not stand for this," Kederic said as his bonds were pulled tight. "They will never accept such treachery."

Acwellen ignored him and shared rude jokes with his men.

Padric lay on the floor, numb and uncaring. He had failed. Had he succeeded, his world would have still been darker. Maybe he would have gone home and seen his family. Found some days of solace before the wickedness that plagued these lands reached their doorstep. But even that fleeting chance could not eclipse his desire to see every man in this room dead by his hand. He should have fought back. Death was certain, but maybe he could have run Drefan through before they brought him down. That would have been something.

The doors to the hall opened and Seon returned, his face nervous. Padric craned his head to look upon the figure that followed and his guts churned. The heavy bronze boots thudded across the hall as he approached, the battleaxe propped casually over a shoulder and that damned unmistakable helm, forged in the likeness of a boar, was cradled in the hook of his arm. Kederic saw the goblin and began screaming, cursing Acwellen's name, kicking at the floor, trying to rise, but was held fast by the spear tips of his traitorous warriors.

The goblin paused when he reached the center of the hall, half the height of the men who all shrunk slightly away from him.

Even Banan took a step back.

The goblin pointed to Kederic. "This him?"

Acwellen nodded, trying to hide his apprehension. Kederic did not cower. Heedless of the spears he pushed himself to his knees and looked at the goblin in the eye.

"Be gone from here, filth! Or my loyal men will see your head mounted on a spike come daybreak."

"Oh, I think we will be away long before then, as we have just one question for you." Torcan Swinehelm placed the blade of his axe under the Thegn's chin and leaned in close. "Tell me, Kederic Winetongue. Where is your wife?"

The Thegn craned his head away from the bite of the blade, face full of loathing and did not answer.

"Where?" Torcan coaxed, pressing the axe upward until a thick pool of crimson welled upon the blade.

Kederic grit his teeth through the pain. "Dead."

Torcan laughed. "No, no. That she is very much alive, I know for certain. Where you have hidden her, this I will have from you." The goblin ground the blade deeper and Kederic's eyes ran with fury and pain, but he said no more. "Very well," Torcan looked at Acwellen. "The Thegn is to come with me, so we may . . . talk more. You have your fort, mortal. But remember, this ends not our bargain."

Acwellen nodded and Padric saw sweat running freely beneath his beard. "What of these two?"

Torcan did not bother to glance at Padric and Slouch Hat.

"Kill them."

Padric heard Fat Donall laugh, followed by a wet noise of glee in Drefan's throat, but it was Poncey Swan that he watched.

The weak-chinned bastard's face was full of lust as he approached, laying the bow aside and drawing his skinning knife. Padric waited, ready to kick Poncey Swan off his feet as soon as he was near. This one, he would take with him.

"My Lord Swinehelm!" Slouch Hat's voice cut through the hall. "You need not Winetongue's wife, when you have her son!"

The Red Cap looked up and squinted hard, then rushed forward, knocking Drefan and his torch away from the husk.

"What did you say?"

"I tell you," Slouch Hat said firmly, "you let them kill that boy . . . and you kill the Gaunt Prince's heir."

Padric watched, full of confusion and fear, as Torcan Swinehelm turned and looked at him for the first time.

FOURTEEN

"Them's loaded, they are," Canker complained.

"Shit-liar, you," Nape spat back. "Now roll."

Canker snatched up the dice irritably and cast them in the ash pit.

"Ruttin' hell," he cursed the result.

"Smoke and Fire!" Nape cheered. "There's a right measure. Nape wins!"

"Nape's a smug fuck," Canker muttered.

"Smug or no, I gets the honors when the cat comes back."

"If'er she comes back."

"She will. You watch."

Canker glanced around the clearing for the twentieth time.

"Still thinkin' we ought have a look-see."

"Bugger that! And you. Through marchin' in the woods, me. Got the finer's all right here. Wait in comfort and see a proper result, mark me."

Nape stretched and lay back, resting his head on the corpse of the collier's wife. Canker remained restless, shifting on the seat he had made of the dead dog.

Nape looked up at the sky, scratching between his bandy legs. "Think I fancy a little throttling."

"Whatta you on now?"

"The cat," Nape replied. "Gonna takes me time. Get a good long strangle outta her. Watch her eyes pop! This'n dropped too fast when you poleaxed her." Nape reached back and punched into the woman he used as a pillow. "And that bastard had to be stuck quick. Fast fucker."

Canker looked towards the forest's edge where the body of the collier still lay, spear sticking straight out his back to mark where he fell. "'Twas a right good toss," he admitted.

"If I may say," Nape giggled.

"You're the shit-liar now, Nape! 'Twas Midden's throw that did for him. I saw. Yours lost in the trees somewhat."

Nape's head craned off the woman to glare at Canker.

"Mine struck home, I says, and Midden missed."

"Not the way of it!"

"Was! And Midden's not here to say otherwise."

"No," Canker said pointedly. "He ain't. But we are. Got left behind to clean up. If that don't speak to the truth of your aim, nout does. And we should be runnin' down that rascal cat and getting back before Swinehelm has us branded for deserters."

Nape settled back down with a careless sigh. "Swinehelm's on his own errand. Don't give a fig for us out here. Been more moon's turns than I can count, runnin', scoutin', trackin' and hard camps at the end o'every day . . . and more often we march through the night as well! No, says I. No more. Not until I can enjoy me a little leave time."

Nape closed his eyes and Canker just watched him.

"Drowning," Nape said after a moment. "That would do for our cat. I'll make like some filthy gruagach . . . hold her head down in the rain barrel."

"Shouldn't talk such," Canker mumbled.

"Why and not?"

"About *them*. 'Tisn't right."

Nape sat up on his elbows, grinning. "I could be one. Some skinchanger out here in the wilds! Real Nape is lying over in that stream yonder. Poor Canker . . . you'd never know it. Not till I was behind ya and turnin' yer head backwards!"

"S'not funny!" Canker jumped off the dog.

Nape laughed at him. "If'n you're too craven to wait with me, go ahead into them woods while we still have some day left. Might be you'll stumble on that cat. Just remember, I won them bones so I gets to do her proper."

Canker snatched his poleaxe off the ground and made for the trees.

"Watch for changelings!" Nape advised before he got there.

Canker stopped and stood for an uncomfortably long moment. He pulled the grimy, blood-colored hat off his broad head and fidgeted, glancing at the trees and then back to where Nape lounged in the dying sun. Finally, Canker went back and sat on the dog without a word. The goblins waited.

And Deglan waited with them.

He could see them. He could hear them, forced to listen to their foul tongues wag for hours. The collier laid not a dozen steps away. He had not died straight away. The spear Nape had claimed to throw had pierced a lung and Deglan had watched as the helpless man twitched, trying to pull himself away by his fingertips, slowly, almost noiselessly, drowning in his own blood. He was still at last, but his paling eyes stared at Deglan, pitiful and accusing.

Deglan tried to ignore the dead gaze. Even in the man's final moments it would have been impossible for the collier to see him.

The Earth embraced him. Hid him. Allowed him to watch from safety as this innocent man died within reach while he did nothing.

He had been traveling through the wilds for near a fortnight and everywhere was signs of Red Caps. Homes and villages were razed, livestock herded over cliffs and the half-burnt bodies of travelers hung from trees. Deglan had not dared use the old elf roads, but even in the backcountry the goblin presence harrowed his steps. He should have reached Toad Holm by now, but too often had he been forced to hide from a patrol or go long miles out of his way to skirt a goblin encampment.

Deglan now realized the band that had burned Hog's Wallow was just the tip of the sword. There was no way to know how many goblins Torcan Swinehelm had wearing the Cap. The presence of a Flame Binder would have brought fanatics out of hiding from across the isle, all ready to marshal under such power. The exact count made little difference. When it came to goblins, you were always outnumbered.

But two to one were the best odds Deglan was likely to get.

He had heard the attack through the trees and cursed himself for being unaware the enemy was so close. Had it not been for the charcoal burner's hut, Deglan might have stumbled on the raiding party unawares. Lynched and burnt was a merciful end compared to what Red Caps were known to do to gnomes. He asked the Earth to accept him and hid, waiting for the sounds of slaughter to cease and soon the patrol marched past, blood on their weapons, laughter on their lips. He hated them almost as much as his own helplessness. There was little hope of survivors, but the habits of a healer do not cower and Deglan snuck close to have a look. He found these two murderous lice taking their ease among the remains of their victims. He could have snuck off and been back on his path, but this was a rare chance and Deglan meant to take advantage of it.

The Red Caps had not yet burnt the collier's hut, nor the pair of outbuildings. Likely these two meant to spend the night in the hut before putting it to the torch, but for the present they sat outside, making it difficult for Deglan to make any move. His skin had darkened to the color of rich soil and his body was entwined with a thicket of brambles and saplings. Dead leaves crowded around him as he lay close to the ground, shielding him from Canker's nervously roaming eyes. It was blood Magic, ancient and pure, but only effective if he remained quite still, so he waited and watched.

Soon, Nape was snoring and Canker paced about, bored and agitated. He kicked at stones, poked at the dog's remains with the butt end of his poleaxe and nosed through the outsheds. When he finally shuffled into the hut, Deglan wasted no time. Careful, cleverly timed plans had their place, but also too many details that could go wrong. Sometimes, it was better to simply move.

He darted out from the tree line, bent low and felt the Earth release its ward. Keeping his eyes fixed on the sleeping goblin, Deglan plucked the spear from the collier's back on the run.

Nape's eyes popped open the instant before the spear head pierced his throat, bursting out the back of his neck to imbed in the woman's corpse behind. Nape's cry of surprise died in the ruin of his jugular, his hands jerked up to the spear shaft, but the spasms of his dying fingers would not allow him a proper grip. His frothy tongue pushed forward, flecking blood into the air as he gagged on a foot of metal. The wound hissed and burned around the broad iron head, the pumping blood steaming as it flowed down Nape's chest. Deglan gave the haft a sharp twist and wrenched the spear free. Nape vomited a torrent of thick crimson and went limp. A quick glance to the door of the hut showed no signs of Canker.

Deglan caught Nape's ankle and dragged him into the trees, dumping the spear in the brush alongside the corpse. Snatching the shapeless cap from Nape's head, Deglan donned it with repressed revulsion. Wordlessly, he asked the collier's wife for forgiveness and lay down.

It was some moments before he heard the door to the hut creak open and Canker's heel-dragging steps. Deglan kept his eyes closed, feigning sleep and tried not to think about the heavy poleaxe that was doubtless in the goblin's hand.

"Found some turnips in'ere," Canker said as he approached. "And some beans. What say to a little pottage, eh? I fancy we . . . bugger me!" The footsteps stopped abruptly and there came the dull thuds of dropped turnips. Deglan willed his heart to calm and stretched slowly, opening his eyes lazily.

"Sounds grand."

Canker's mouth went from gaping to tight-lipped and back again. The poleaxe was nowhere in sight. The goblin's hands hovered empty near his waist, clutching turnips that were no longer there.

"Well," Deglan said. "Fetch some water."

Canker blinked and the air pushed around in his throat with half formed words.

"N-nn-nuh-Nape?" he finally managed.

"What?" Deglan aimed his voice for mild irritation and hit ignorant anger. "Fetch the water, I said."

"Fire claim me," Canker stammered. "Please don' drowned me!"

"Why would I?" Deglan made a show of looking at his hands, then put them to his face, feeling his features. "Oh! Well, that is what I get for sleeping. Gone and formed a gnome. So similar to you goblins! Both despicable, stunted. It is a disgrace to wear your skins, a humiliation!"

Canker tried to glimpse the trees without moving his head and Deglan saw his weight shift.

"Do not try and run. I would be upon you before you could make a pair of steps. We gruagach are very fast, Canker."

Canker did not run. His legs gave out and he hit his knobby knees, his hands raised in appeal. "No! Don' drowned me! Don' I beg, don' . . . don' drowned me!"

"I'll not," Deglan said and hope flitted across the goblin's face. "If you answer my questions."

"Yes! I will. Ask anything, I'll speak it true by my bones. I'll speak it true and if I says a'right you'll not drowned me?"

"No, Canker. I will not drown you. Now into the house so we may talk."

Canker went within all too eagerly. Deglan asked his questions and Canker answered them. He had to keep his face a mask as the goblin spoke, but his guts turned to sickening liquid with every response. Deglan got his answers and kept his promise.

He did not drown Canker. He slit his throat to the bone with his cleaver.

Night was coming, but Deglan remained in the hut, his thoughts spreading as darkly as Canker's blood. Lingering was likely to prove fatal if the main group came back in search of these two, but he could not bring himself to stand. It felt as if he had been on the run forever, as if the intervening years of peace between the last war and now had never transpired. It had felt good killing Nape; a tiny measure of revenge against all the sorrow goblinkind had heaped upon him. But by the time he opened Canker's throat, vengeance offered no more succor. All the blood in the world would not be enough to weigh against what had been and what would be if Canker's final confessions could be believed.

And Deglan believed.

He shook his head roughly. "Enough of this wallowing! Miles to go and sitting here will not remedy that."

Deglan pushed himself to his feet and went out the door.

A little girl stood next to the corpse of the collier's wife, looking with lost eyes around the ruin of her life in the last ugly orange light of dusk. Deglan froze, afraid she might bolt, but she did not seem to see him. She walked in a nightmare, a frozen painting of the familiar posed in awful mockery of itself. Physically, she was unhurt, but Deglan's eye took in deep injuries of the mind.

So, this was the cat. Deglan should have taken more time with Nape and Canker. They died too easy, damn them.

He approached at a careful pace, not so fast as to frighten her or so slow as to appear the hunter. She did not resist when he scooped her up, her face vacant. She could not be more than three, which was fortunate. Mortal children grew so quickly. Any older and Deglan would have been hard-pressed to carry her, but carry her he did, out into the woods and away from the gory remains of her world.

He walked for a few hours through the night with no direction in mind. Putting some distance between the child and her home was his only concern, so that she could not find her way back.

Eventually his arms began to quiver from the limp burden and he stopped walking, settling down into the cradling roots of an ancient alder filled with fallen leaves. Breathing a sigh of relief as the tension left his muscles, Deglan risked a glance at the girl. She did not sleep, as he hoped, but continued to stare into the trees. He held her close with one arm and used the other to pull the leaves about them for cover. Deglan settled back and closed his eyes, stroking the child's smooth cheek with his thumb and asked the Earth to guard her against the perils of a long, chilly night.

He awoke to mist laden rays of sun rippling through the branches. A warm weight lay comfortably atop him and he looked down to find the girl sleeping soundly. She still had the chubby cheeks of youth, rosy from the cold air, and her hair was the golden red thought to be lucky by many human tribes. She certainly was lucky to have survived, although she may well wish she had not.

Deglan was tempted to let her sleep, but they had to be on their way. Placing a finger gently between her eyes, Deglan lightly rubbed down her nose.

"I am sorry, seedling. It is time we were awake and away."

The girl's eyes fluttered open, cloudy and unfocused. They were the color of burnt chestnuts and Deglan smiled down into them. His smile faded when the blankness returned to the child's face. He rose and carried the girl up with him, but immediately placed her on her feet. She stood silently, barely taking in her surroundings. Her dress was simple, but sturdily made of wool and her shoes were still sound. Deglan pulled a piece of cheese from his satchel and held it out to her. She looked at it and then up at him, but made no further move.

"My name is Deglan," he ventured. "Deglan Loamtoes. What is your name?"

She blinked.

He nodded. "Blink it is then. Well met. So Blink, I need some help. I have a long way to go today and no one to talk with, which can be very lonely. But if I had you to keep me company, then I believe the day would be much brighter." Deglan held out his hand. "Will you walk with me?"

Her little hand came up and clutched his gently. He nodded and started off at an easy pace and the girl stayed right by his side.

As the morning drew on, they stayed hand in hand and Deglan told her the names of every tree and plant they passed, trying to sound as light as he could while still staying alert for danger. While he spoke, he casually offered her the cheese again and this time she took it, munching quietly as she put one small foot in front of the other. She never looked around, her gaze fixed at a point just beyond her feet, but she trudged dutifully along, keeping the pace.

Deglan stopped regularly to make sure he did not overexert her and managed to get her to take some water from his skin. He had little in the way of provisions left, but the forest would provide long enough for them to reach their destination. Or so he hoped.

Deglan had not been this far away from Hog's Wallow in centuries. He did not know which of the human clans, if any, dwelled in these lands or what their customs were. And he would not have left Blink with them even if he did. No one was safe in any community. Their only hope was Toad Holm, if it was still there.

After the revelations of Canker, Deglan was more anxious and determined to reach the city than before. He had intended to deliver a warning, but now it was impossible to fathom that the whole isle was not aware of the Red Cap's presence and still none stood against them. Surely, there was enough strength left within his people to resist one Flame Binder. The thought set Deglan's teeth to grinding. They were fools for ever locking him away and allowing him to live. Should have taken his head off and had done!

Too many acts of mercy followed the Restoration of the Seelie Court. Irial's benevolence was well chronicled, but the forbearance he showed his enemies at war's end bordered on madness. Elves were a strange lot, for all their wisdom, and Deglan often counted himself lucky not to be born among their number, preferring the more practical ways of his own people. That is, until that practicality was replaced by the same blind acceptance that Irial preached. Madness, it seemed, was contagious.

Deglan glanced down at Blink and it occurred to him that he had a problem. She was the daughter of a charcoal burner, spending her heartbeat of a life in relative seclusion. Deglan did not know if she had ever met any other mortals besides her parents, much less Fae-folk. Certainly there was a settlement near to her father's hut where he went to trade, but how often had she been there with a mind to remember? She seemed to have accepted his own presence, but he was quite sure her mind had been damaged by the loss she had suffered and there was no way to tell if that damage would ever mend. He was trying to save her life, but where they were bound contained sights that might destroy what was left of her sanity forever. Goblins lived in Toad Holm. Or hobgoblins did, if you used the proper term, but the difference would be lost on her. And why should it not? It was lost on Deglan. Still, she deserved every chance. If there was a shred of rational thought left in her wee skull, she needed to be prepared.

"I have a story for you, Blink. Would you like to hear it?"

She did not divert her attention from the spot in front of her feet.

"Many, many years ago . . ." he began, feeling foolish, but why bother explaining the Age of Spring, tens of thousands of years ago, to a child not yet four? ". . . the elves ruled this island that we now call Airlann. They were good rulers and just and everywhere was sun and warmth and bounty. The elves were the stewards of Magic, which made the world, and the tools it used were the Elements. The Elements were powerful and precious and needed to be kept safe, so the elves entrusted them each to a separate race. My people, the gnomes, looked after Earth and lived deep underground. In the seas and lakes and rivers, the undine watched over Water, while high above in the sky the sylphs guarded the secrets of Air. And far, far below at the core of the world was the source of Fire and its keepers were the dragons!"

He gave the last word a wondrous quality and leaned in close to the girl, wiggling his fingers like some daft hedge magician.

Blink was unimpressed. Deglan's face withered. Faabar would have been better at this.

"The Elemental Guardians," he continued, more subdued, "were allowed to govern themselves and each had a king or queen of sorts to lead them. The gnome king at this time was named Ghob, and Ghob was a right greedy bastar—that is, Ghob was greedy. He went to the elves and asked permission to delve deeper underground so that he might expand the holdings of the gnomes and make them richer, but the elves refused him, fearing he would encroach . . . I mean, bother the lands of the dragons. Ghob bowed his head and left the Seelie Court, that is what the elves called their kingdom, and he vowed to obey, but when he returned to his own kingdom he announced to the gnomes his plan to go against the wishes of the elves and venture deeper underground. Many of the gnomes were angry with King Ghob and called for his removal, and Ghob soon found himself an outcast without a crown or a throne. But there were those loyal to him, and in disgrace, Ghob took his few subjects with him into exile, sneaking away where the elves forbade him to go.

"Many, many years passed and Ghob was forgotten and the land was peaceful. Until one day, a group of strange buggers came up from the deepest tunnels of the gnome city. They were grey and bent and misshapen and spoke queerly. They claimed to be Ghob's kin, but to everyone it sounded as if they said *goblin*. Somehow they had survived and even thrived as there were many and more than what had followed the fallen king so many years before. But more terrible than their numbers was that they wielded Fire. How the goblins could have taken it from the dragons is not known and the elves were deeply disturbed, but they allowed the goblins to live in Airlann, which was bloody stupid and they paid for their mistake.

"The goblins helped some evil humans take over the isle and called them their Kings. A terrible war was fought over many years, and eventually the Goblin Kings were all defeated. The last was called the Gaunt Prince, and he was slain by the gnome king of that time, a powerful warrior named Goban Blackmud. A damn fine king! After the war, Goban took his hammer and struck off for the center of the world, claiming he would not return until Fire was taken away from the goblins, and, if they still lived, placed back under the care of the dragons. He has not been seen again to this very day, but do not give up on him, Blink. Some of us never have.

"Now Goban had to leave his crown to someone before he left, so he put it in the hands of his brother, an empty-headed lack wit named Hob. Hob got to talking with the newly restored king of the elves and thought that it would be a right grand idea to offer an invite to any goblin who wanted it, to come back and live with the gnomes, so as to get reunited with their long-lost cousins. Nevermind that the goblins were responsible for hundreds of years of oppression and bloodshed and were nothing but an unwashed rabble of bandy-legged, sister-shagging, gap-toothed, flat-headed, Fire-loving murderers!"

Deglan stopped. In his tirade he had let go of Blink's hand while flailing his own angrily above his head. She had stopped walking and was now standing motionless several dozen paces behind. Deglan's heart sank. It was all a waste of breath and there was nothing he could do to change that. There was no herb that could cure this poor child. And what had he hoped to accomplish?

To explain that she would have to see goblins again? The same pug-nosed bastards that had slain her parents and found the act a lark? But that they were different from other goblins, because they had chosen to accept Hob's decree and come back to gnomish ways? That they were good goblins? She had no reason to trust that, and Deglan would be lying to her if he said she should, because he did not believe it himself.

"Forget the story," Deglan said and walked back to where Blink stood. He squatted down and placed one hand on her face and the other he cupped under her chin. Gently he raised her head until she looked him in the eye. "If you hear nothing else, sweet one, hear this. No matter what we see or who we meet . . . I will not let anything happen to you. I *will* keep you safe . . . or you can kick me in the shins."

They spent another night in the woods and this time Deglan risked a fire. They both needed some hot food, so he boiled up a broth with some leeks and tubers he found during the day. It was bitter stuff but Blink put it down without a sign of distaste or approval and slept through the night. The next day brought them to an area of the forest covered in steep rolling hills. The trees marched up the leaf choked embankments and down again, forming deep valleys in the forest floor where thin creeks gurgled with dark water. It took Deglan the better part of the day to find a gate.

Toad Holm's greatest defense was its difficulty in locating.

There was no great wall or castle or main gate, the city was entirely underground, and though its tunnels sprawled for miles and miles, there were few entrances. Deglan had not been back to the ancestral home of his people for several centuries. In fact, he had vowed never to return, but the most earnest of vows make fools of the forsworn and so here he was, poking around the hills, looking for a way inside. Finally, he discovered a large fallen oak that made his ears itch. The great tree had toppled and its massive tangle of roots now faced Deglan, resembling the tentacle laden maw of some beast. A large furrow was left in the ground where the tree once stood, filled with muddy rain water and forest debris. Deglan let go of Blink's hand and left her standing on the edge of the depression. He skidded his way carefully down the side and sunk up to his waist in the muck when he reached the bottom of the bowl. He spent a long time inspecting the roots until he was sure.

Reaching into his satchel he pulled out one of his bronze lancets and pierced the meat of his palm. Squeezing his hand into a tight fist, he let the blood fall into the water below.

"I am a rightful guardian of Earth. A chosen protector of the Molding Element. By rights gifted to my people by Magic, I bid you open. Mud for blood. Stone for bone. Soil for soul. Open."

The water churned as the red droplets struck and the roots of the fallen tree stretched down, burying deep in the sodden soil of the bowl. Quickly the water drained as the dead tree drank deeply and soon the depression was no longer flooded. A great stone lay near the base of the bowl, just below the roots of the tree.

Deglan reached up and helped Blink down as the stone slid open to reveal a damp tunnel, glowing with a soft blue light. Taking Blink by the hand, Deglan led them inside. The stone slid back into place and he breathed a sigh of relief. The forest was behind them and nothing could follow.

Deglan looked down to make sure Blink was not frightened by the tunnel. He expected to find her usual blank stare, but was surprised to see the little girl wore an expression of mild curiosity.

She was staring at one of the large grubs lazily crawling across the tunnel wall. Its entire body shone with a pale blue luminescence, and it, along with the dozen or so of its comrades were the source of light in the tunnel.

"They are called moonbacks, seedling. My people keep the soil around these tunnels filled with their favorite food, so that they will live here and help us to see. You may take one with you, but do not crush it."

Deglan gently scooped up one of the grubs and placed it in Blink's hand. It all but covered the little girl's palm, but she held it tenderly and continued to gaze at it with the first real emotion Deglan had seen.

"Come," he said, taking her free hand. "Let us see who else we can find."

They struck off together down the tunnel, Blink's moonback providing adequate light to guide them. The tunnel was raw earth and barely twice Deglan's height. Thin roots poked through from the ceiling and there were no stones paving the way.

It was only wide enough for two riding toads to travel side by side, telling Deglan that this was a remote passage. The absence of sentries was puzzling and he expected they would be challenged at any moment. He was not wrong.

At the first intersection, they found the tunnel barred with a bronze gate and four guards stood watch, each wearing the heavy leather armor of the Worm Guard.

"Halt there!" one of them yelled when Deglan and Blink drew within a spear's throw of the gate. "Who goes?"

"I am Deglan Loamtoes, master herbalist and former Staunch of the Bwenyth Tor Wart Shanks. Open up! I have information for the Wisemoot."

He heard the creak of a key being turned in the gate lock and the bars swung open. He led Blink through and had a moment of worry when he saw one of the four guards was a hobgoblin.

Thankfully, the girl was still fascinated by her moonback and took no notice.

"Which way?" Deglan demanded, looking down both forks of the passage. "I need to get to the Moot and speak with Durock Moundbuilder, if he still commands."

"He does," one of the guards said. "We will escort you."

"Not him!" Deglan pointed at the hobgoblin guard, whose face flashed with anger, then settled in an almost sad resignation.

The gate commander also shot him an impatient look, but Deglan held the stare and nodded down at Blink. "Red Caps."

"Understood," the gate commander said and looked to the hobgoblin. "Morel, you and Slevin have the gate. Master Loamtoes, if you would follow me."

Deglan could feel the hobgoblin's eyes on him as they left, but he did not return the look. The hobgoblin was quite young, no more than two hundred and was probably born in the city long after the Restoration, but Deglan had no time or inclination for sensitivity, and he meant to limit Blink's exposure to goblins, *any* goblins, for as long as possible.

The watch commander was still a bit put off by him. "May I ask," his voice was brusque. "What you have to tell the Wisemoot?"

"What is your name, commander?" Deglan asked as they came to a larger tunnel.

"Breasal, Master Loamtoes."

"Well, Breasal. I have to tell them that Torcan Swinehelm is ravaging the countryside with an army of Red Caps and he is aided by a Flame Binder allowed to escape from this city."

"Allowed is not the word I would use Master Loamtoes," Breasal said tautly. "And the Moot knows all of this."

"Well damn, then I have come all this way for nothing."

"You know more." It was not a question and Deglan did not bother to answer. "How?"

"I found a Red Cap," Deglan said. "And I asked him impolitely."

"What did he tell you?"

Deglan stopped and whirled on the commander. "That my people need to stop asking questions and start fighting back! Because if they do not, they and everyone else on this island will once again be crushed under the boot heel of oppression!"

He paused, reluctant to tell a gate commander before he had a chance to speak to the Moot. Then he damned his caution.

Let them know! Let them fear! It may be what forces them to act.

"Torcan thinks he has found the lost heir to the Goblin Kings. He means to bring the heir and the Flame Binder together and reawaken the Forge Born."

FIFTEEN

"There you go! Almost . . . No! Don't think about it, just . . . yes! Very good."

Rosheen laughed and clapped her hands together. Pocket's smile threatened to split his face in two as he turned his head from side to side, trying to see the mule's ears that now drooped down past his cheeks.

"I did it!"

"I told you."

Pocket giggled and Rosheen could not help but laugh again.

She glanced up and saw the younger coburn trying to suppress his own smile as he pretended not to watch the boy's progress. Pocket did not give him a chance to continue his feigned indifference. He jumped off the ground and ran over to where the squire trained with his quarterstaff. *Where else would he be?*

"Flyn!" Pocket was breathless. "Look!"

The coburn leaned on the training dummy and smiled down at the little gurg. "I have often been called an ass, but you my friend are the first to make me wonder if it was a compliment."

"I am sure it wasn't," Rosheen threw at him, smiling.

Flyn bowed grandly. "As my lady says."

Pocket was feeling the tips of his new ears, his face a mix of pride and amused confusion. "Now all you need is a proper tail," Flyn told him.

"A tail!" Pocket ran back over. "Can we? Rosheen! Show me how to do a tail."

"Show you?" she said with fake aghast. "I cannot do that. I do not have a tail!"

She heard Flyn whistle bawdily and fought to keep her eyes on Pocket's bright face.

"We can work on it," she promised. "You should run inside and show Sir Corc."

Pocket's face fell and she could feel Flyn shoot a look at her.

Curse me for a manipulative shrew.

"No! I have a better idea!" she rescued herself. "Run and find Lochlann. He will want to see. And then have him bring you to where Ingot and Backbone are stabled. If you can fool real mules, you can fool anyone!"

Pocket brightened and made for the door of the townhouse, then turned on his heel so fast, Rosheen thought he might fall.

"What about the tail?"

"Tonight," she assured him. "But let's see if you can hold the ears until then."

The wide smile returned and Pocket dashed inside.

"Backbone will never buy it," Flyn said, looking at the training post and rubbing his hand down the pitted wood. "He has almost less whimsy than his master. Almost."

Rosheen did not respond. If mules mocked their masters, then Ingot was likely to smile and promise the world. *And lie with every breath.* She had spent the better part of a fortnight bumping around in a cage hanging from that beast's back, but she did not begrudge the mule. Fafnir was another matter. He seemed to believe he had saved her from something, but neither asked for thanks nor offered apology for her confinement. She was out of the cage now, but felt just as trapped. Beyond the wall of the little courtyard, the sounds of the city quaked ceaselessly; empty-headed banging on cobbles, crying babes, hawking vendors, the splash of night soil thrown from upper windows. Rosheen loathed Black Pool. She never saw a reason to be here when it was an elf harbor, much less now that it was a sanctuary for the world's unwashed.

Bored with her own tedious thoughts, Rosheen flew over to where Flyn practiced, landing on the top of his training post.

"You beat most manfully at your pole," she said down at him. Flyn stopped swinging and looked up at her.

"Most perceptive of you," he said, impatience edging his courtesy. "And also distracting."

"Then I improve the exercise. You do not think it will be distracting when some frothing barbarian is swinging something heavy and sharp back at you?"

"That," Flyn smirked, "will just be amusing."

"Oooh. Such a cocky one."

"Please get down."

"I am quite comfortable."

"I might strike you."

"Well that would be most unseemly of a knight . . . in training."

"In waiting," Flyn countered. "Waiting for you to move."

"Waiting, yes," Rosheen sighed. "Seems to be a common pastime with you lot."

Flyn backed a few paces away from the post and leaned his staff against the wall of the house. He looked towards the door for a moment and then spoke without looking back to her. "It is at that."

Rosheen could almost see the frustration resonating off the young squire in waves. It was no wonder he worked constantly at the dummy; any less and he might burst. Rosheen followed Flyn's stare to the door.

"What *does* he do in there?"

"He listens," Flyn said, practically spitting the second word.

He stalls. "Has he always been this . . . sober?"

Flyn let out a noise that was half disgust and half dismissal, but said nothing.

He does not know. "And the boy?"

Flyn turned away from the door and the swagger returned to his shoulders. "Pocket was at the castle long before me. He and our goodly knight have a history of which the boy knows little and Sir Corc says nothing . . . not like him at all."

Damn peculiar. Rosheen's hopes had risen when she first saw the coburn and the colors they wore. The Knights of the Valiant Spur were a dwindling sight on the isle, but once they had commanded great respect and a reputation for righting wrongs. But this knight seemed content to languish in Black Pool holding councils, accompanied by a squire he kept in the dark and a gurg page with no talent in actually changing his skin. Sir Corc seemed to be respected by the myriad of visitors that occupied his time, but as for righting wrongs, he had done nothing that Rosheen could tell.

The door to the townhouse opened and Rosheen groaned audibly when the dwarf stepped out. She had spent enough unwanted hours with him and the pipe he was now filling. She hovered off the training post and then realized she had nowhere to go. *Damn all cities!*

Fafnir gave her a polite nod, which she ignored, then turned his eyes on Flyn who had given up trying to thwack away with his staff and now stood inspecting the blade of the massive sword that received the second half of his daily hours.

"Still a fine blade," Fafnir said as he approached. The strange lilting of his accent made Rosheen's fingernails grow.

"Still?" Flyn asked.

"Well cared for," Fafnir gestured appreciatively at the sword with his pipe. "Given how old it is."

"You will not find any notches in the blade on my account," Flyn said bitterly.

Fafnir seemed to find that very funny and let loose a smoke filled chuckle. "No, no. I very much doubt it."

Flyn's comb rose off his head and visibly darkened. He turned towards the dwarf, feathers almost quivering and looked ready to strike him. Rosheen was suddenly very glad she stayed.

Never seen a dwarf beheaded.

"Meaning?" Flyn asked.

"Meaning," Fafnir said nonchalantly, "*that* steel is as strong now as the day it was forged. Very difficult to put a nick in it. I had forgotten how sound it was."

"You have seen this sword before?"

"Not since the day I gave it to Coalspur," Fafnir tucked the pipe into his teeth and looked wistfully at the blade.

"You?"

"Oh yes. He bade me craft it when he became Grand Master. Near two years before I was done. May I?" The dwarf held out his hands.

"Oh," Flyn relaxed and handed the sword over. "Of course."

Rosheen's shoulders fell. *Looks like you are going to survive this day after all, you smelly dwarf.*

Fafnir inspected the blade with his hands and his eyes, his expression joyful and a little awed. *Meeting a long-lost friend.*

"It is truly a marvel, Master Fafnir," Flyn said, clearly trying to make amends for his hasty temper. The dwarf stared a moment longer then handed the blade back.

"I thank you," he said with a small bow. *His thanks is not for the praise, but for the chance to hold the weapon again.* Rosheen forgot her hatred for a moment.

"Well," Fafnir said with a deep sigh. "I must be on my way. Ingot and I have many miles to travel before we may go home again."

He is leaving?! "You are leaving?!"

"My goods are needed."

"But," Rosheen could not control her stammer, "but what about Padric?"

A glimmer of regret crossed the dwarf's eyes. "The boy is capable. If he is alive, then he will no doubt keep himself safe."

Oh no, I still hate you.

Rosheen cast daggers at his back long after he was out of sight. She could not seem to take her eyes off the gate, afraid to look away. She had never liked the dwarf, and those ill feelings had soured to outright disdain when he took her captive. But now that he was gone, she was frozen. Her world shrank to the court-yard and the wall and the gate leading out into the terrible clamor of Black Pool. Only there was no Black Pool, there was only the stone arch and the vines crawling across it and the swollen wood of the door beneath. There was only the space that Fafnir had just vacated, and he was her last connection. If she looked away, if she dared blink, then what thin tether remained might break, and her last link to Padric would be lost.

"I am sorry, my lady." Flyn's voice.

She turned sharply, looking away from the gate as quickly as she could, snapping the foolish hope she invented and breaking her heart. "You are sorry? Do you even know why you apologize . . . because I do not! For which of these grievous lack of deeds do you feel remorse? I asked! I asked for help! I never need help . . . and I need help! He is out there. He is out there because of me and I swore to take care of him and the last time I saw him . . . the last time . . . why will none of you help me?!" She flew right into Flyn's face, the tears she held back threatening to engulf her. "You train out here with your stick and your sword, when you should be practicing with a quill and parchment! You are not knights! You are councilors and speechmakers! You are useless and you sit idly by when earnestly asked for aid! There is a savage threat out there, running free, killing and burning without restraint or challenge. The dwarf told you I spoke true and still you do not stand. You are cowards!"

Flyn said nothing. His face was full of anger, but it was not directed at her. She followed his gaze over her shoulder and found Sir Corc staring at them.

"Bantam Flyn," he said evenly. "Where is Pocket?" And when he did not get an immediate answer, "Flyn!"

"At the stables," the squire replied, his expression unchanged. "With Old Lochlann."

"Get him," the knight said. "And then the two of you go to the chandler's under Ten Ferries Bridge. There will be a message for me. Bring it back here."

Rosheen felt the squire linger and look at her, as if waiting for absolution, but she had eyes only for the older coburn. When they were alone, she spoke.

"You heard?"

Sir Corc nodded.

"Good. Then you know what I think of you."

He regarded her for a long moment, his face impassive.

"Come with me," he said at last and was out the gate without looking to see if she followed.

She did.

It was late morning, and the streets heaved with all manner of dusty traffic. The poor and bedraggled mixed with the perfumed and powerful, every one of them a prisoner in the unnatural patterns they believed were necessary to survive in this hive of cramped filth. Rosheen had been in Black Pool barely a week and already she wanted nothing but to flee its walls, its roofs, its gutters, its canals, leave it all behind before she was smothered under a mountain of shingles, cobblestones and masonry. She would find a grove, an orchard, even just a field and she would breathe deeply.

Invite the clean air, the flowing water, the living world back into her body and hold it inside until she shuddered with exquisite relief.

But all of that would have to wait until she discovered where this coburn was taking her.

She wanted to laugh at her own desperation as she followed Sir Corc through damp, fish-reeking alleys and over pitted bridges spanning noxious waterways. The multitudes in the streets made way for the knight's broad shouldered advance, jostling one another to get out of his purposeful path. Soon, they came to a decrepit square surrounded by leaning buildings, the crumbling bricks seemingly held together by the vines that covered them. At the center of the square stood a small, chipped fountain covered in wet, dark mold. The water still flowed freely from a nearly headless statue carved in the likeness of a peeing clurichaun. Lying on the rim of the fountain, his mouth open to the statute's stream and gargling loudly, was the fattest goblin Rosheen had ever seen.

"Muckle," Sir Corc said as they approached. "Is it arranged?"

The gargling ceased and the goblin rolled his bulk out from under the flowing water. He reached up and patted the statue's protruding bare belly. "A fine vintage," he said with satisfaction and hopped down, retrieving a huge club of knotted wood that was propped against the fountain.

Rosheen looked him over and wondered if she were drunk.

He has a fish in his pants. He returned her stare, but incredulity did not fall upon his face as it must have on hers. His thick cheeks parted in an amiable smile.

"Nothing quite like the physical perfection of the piskie to make a body realize just how copious it has become." He sighed deeply, pouted his lower lip and hung his head, looking down at his enormous paunch.

"We should be off," Sir Corc told him without sympathy.

"I cannot now," the goblin whined. "I am not comely enough for such company."

"Enough of these games, Jester! Can we be off?"

"No!" a hand came up towards the knight, pudgy fingers splayed wide. "Do not try and compliment me further. Nothing you say about the strength of my character, my stolid resolve or the great feats of diplomacy, guile and charm I must have undergone to get you this meeting . . . none of these shall sway me. I am too wounded, too overcome, too—"

This is getting nowhere. "Handsome," Rosheen broke in.

The hand remained in the air, but the fingers turned and made a slight coaxing gesture.

"And stalwart," Rosheen continued, keeping her voice genuine while throwing her most bitter look up at the coburn.

"And quite clever. Full of natural grace . . ."

"More about my handsomeness."

Why me? "Such a fine, regal forehead. A firm . . . husky strength and an enchanting smile."

The goblin's head came up, wearing the only feature Rosheen had not invented.

"I would be most honored," Muckle said, "if you would accompany me this way." He motioned down a narrow lane leading away from the square and offered Rosheen his little finger. She smiled at him and hooked her arm around the offered digit. "You could learn from this one," Muckle said to Sir Corc as they left the square.

"What made him agree?" the knight asked from behind them.

"Other than my ceaseless badgering?" Muckle replied.

"Who?" Rosheen was tired of this mystery.

Muckle's voice took on the ringing shout of some pompous herald. "Only the most elusive and well-guarded figurehead in the history of Black Pool! Only the most influential individual in the city today! The singular body who might reasonably be said to govern the teeming masses that live betwixt these not so fair walls!

None other than . . ." Muckle put the end of his club to his lips and threw forth a terrible imitation of a trumpet, "the Lord of the Pile!"

Rosheen turned and looked back at Sir Corc, demanding answers with her face, but the knight's own face remained a wall.

She had agreed to follow in the hope that the knight would lead her to some means of aid, but instead he was serving up a dish of riddles and this preposterous goblin was the cook. Muckle led them through the city, keeping up a steady stream of stories and anecdotes about every structure they passed, but Rosheen had no ears for him.

She had heard of this Lord of the Pile. A goblin leader who had risen to prominence within the last hundred years, and guided the dealings of Black Pool with a long reaching, yet invisible hand.

Her mind went back to that harrowing night in the wilds near Hog's Wallow, and she remembered the leader of the Red Caps and his minions cursing the Lord of the Pile as vehemently as the gnome king. That level of enmity could not have been lightly earned and Rosheen could not help but wonder what manner of ruler they were walking so swiftly to meet.

They came to the outskirts of the city where large livestock yards sprawled in the shadow of the walls. Muckle made for a long building with low walls of stacked stone nestled under great wooden posts supporting a thatched roof. The building was open to the air between the stone wall and the eaves of the roof, and the wind coming through the structure carried the sounds and smells of swine. There was no door, only a wide gap in the wall beneath the apex of the roof, guarded by no less than ten warriors of Middangearder stock, their already large frames swollen by fur cloaks and coats of mail. They glowered darkly from behind their flaxen beards as Muckle approached. He leaned forward and growled low in his throat at each of them in turn.

"It's how they greet each other in their own land," he told Rosheen with a wink. The burly warriors did not appear amused.

"We are here to meet with the Lord," Sir Corc told them.

"Surrender your weapons," one of the men commanded, his sing-song inflection similar to Fafnir's.

"I bear no arms," Sir Corc replied and Rosheen fought the urge to look down at the foot long spurs sprouting from the back of the knight's feet. *A coburn is always armed.* Another of the men stepped forward and reached brusquely for Muckle's ribbon-festooned cudgel. The goblin snatched it away from his reach, launching his voice and pointing finger at the man.

"Seventy years bad luck to whosoever touches me club, A strange hand reaches out and pulls back merely a stub! Your teeth will loosen, your hair will grow sparse And blood will flow freely from nose, gums and arse! Be ye warned, whether man, girl or vicious mob, Such is the fate of all that touches my Pompous Knob!"

Muckle had grown louder and more incensed with every line and by the time he was finished, he was stretched up on his toes as close to the tall warrior's face as he could get, one finger poked firmly into the man's chest. The Middangearder stared back at him in shock and confusion, trying to lean as far away as he could without looking a craven to his fellows.

Muckle burst out laughing in the man's face. "I am only jesting! Here," he held the cudgel forth. "You can have it."

The man opted not to take the offered item and they were ushered inside. Four of the warriors escorted them down the central lane, while on either side countless pigs snuffled and squealed from behind the wooden fences of their pens. Muckle greeted several by name as they made their way to the end of the lane where a small group of figures looked into a wide enclosure that lay across the back of the building. Inside this pen, the largest hogs had been kept separated, and the shortest of the figures was pointing to individual animals.

"That one. Yes . . . and that one there. And there, no . . . the one with the black face, yes."

The speaker was a goblin, dressed in a simple black robe trimmed with grey fox fur. As he spoke, the human swineherds jumped to his bidding, wrangling the pigs he indicated and leading them out of the pen into a side enclosure where a dozen other monstrous hogs were already being kept. The goblin finished his selection and turned towards them. Other than a braided beard of white hair dangling from his chin, this was a most unremarkable goblin. Rosheen had passed at least a hundred just like him in the streets getting there.

"My Lord," Muckle said with a grand bow. "May I present Sir Corc, called the Constant. Knight Errant of the Order of the Vibrant Spurt."

"Intriguing," the Lord of the Pile said, looking directly at Sir Corc, his tone neither mocking nor apologetic. "I thought coburn to be prickly creatures. Easily slighted even if they lack a knight's vows. But this one," his voice pointed at Muckle. "He insults your order and yet I hear no reproach. I see no anger."

"I have known Muckle a long time," was all Corc offered for explanation.

"I feel as if I have, too," the Lord said wearily. "He has come to me with tedious regularity of late. Have I grown so esteemed that I warrant a visit from emissaries of both your Order and Toad Holm?"

"Your Lordship is much loved," Muckle said.

"Much scrutinized," the other goblin replied, his eyes still on Sir Corc. "Tell me Sir, what do you seek from me that you would send so persistent an envoy to plead an audience?"

"Many audiences have been requested of you," Sir Corc said evenly. "And refused. Only you can say why you granted this one."

The Lord of the Pile smiled thinly. "Perhaps I seek some recognition of legitimacy."

"That would not be for my Order to decide. The Seelie Court—"

The Lord held up a hand calmly. "The Seelie Court no longer has such power. If Irial Elven-King had anything to say regarding my governance he would have done so by now. I take his silence for acceptance, and any disapproval, if it exists, is lacking in sufficient strength to enforce it. Now, please. Tell me why you have come."

He is so calm.

"As you say," Sir Corc replied. "I represent the Knights of the Valiant Spur. Our Grandmaster and the oath we take ensure we keep a vested interest in the powers of this isle. I have standing instructions to speak with you and take your measure. You have refused us for years. There was no reason to suspect you would not again. Personally, I do not care if you choose to speak to me or not, but I do follow the orders that have been given to me."

More than six words. Impressive.

The Lord of the Pile must have thought so also, for his thin smile deepened. "And yet your actions betray your words. If you possessed such lingering apathy you would not have allied yourself with our fat go-between here."

Muckle's face jerked in overly acted shock and he looked from the Lord up to Rosheen and back again. "My Lord, manners! It is not polite to call her fat. I find her to be quite svelte . . . shapely certainly, but in all the right places and . . ."

"Please, enough," the Lord said as if someone were filling his goblet. He took a deep breath and looked up, fixing Muckle with a hard stare. "I ask you, do not bandy witless words at me. For all your foolery I know what you truly are Muckle Gutbuster. And I fear it not. Now," he turned back to Sir Corc. "You said that you were instructed to . . . take my measure, was it? And since I would not presume to imagine what that would entail from a group of chivalrous coburn, I wonder if you will tell me what these standing instructions require so we can bring this meeting to a desired end."

"The Grand Master wants to know if your designs extend beyond the walls of Black Pool," Sir Corc said bluntly. "If the agreements you have made with the Raider Kings of Middangeard are about more than trade. He also wants me to determine if—"

"I am a Red Cap?" the Lord offered.

Sir Corc did not blink. "Are you?"

The goblin folded his hands into the sleeves of his robe and looked at the ground. His eyes tracked slightly as if reading something written in the rushes. When he looked up again, he spoke in measured tones as if he expected his audience to memorize his words.

"I have ruled this city peaceably for over a century. The Raider Kings with whom I originally treated are long dead, their grandsons now stand on the decks of the ships which guard our port and protect the merchant vessels that transport all manner of goods to the markets for the good of the populace. Any designs of conquest would have to be refreshed with each passing generation of man and would spell the end of all I have struggled to accomplish here.

"Black Pool was an orphan. A cast off. Unwanted by the Seelie Court after the Restoration. Maybe they thought it had been stained by the Goblin Kings or maybe even then they were too weak to build it back to glory. I was born here, sir knight. I was born here when the city was divided between two lecherous humans; childish mortals playing with Magic too great for them to understand. I watched as over the decades my race licked the boots of these would-be sorcerers, and I came to a great understanding.

"We goblins have never had our own leader. We crawled up from the center of the world and followed anyone of strength. That is our pathetic legacy! The Red Caps would see us all cast back into thralldom and once again place a crown upon a mortal's head. Others," his eyes flicked over to Muckle, "would have us swear loyalty to the gnomes. Rejoin our cousins and our lost heritage and play into Hob's foul scheme to see the end of goblinkind by breeding us out of existence. I will not let that happen. Toad Holm is not a haven for us. Black Pool is! And I will spread that word to the corners of this isle and beyond. If you would report anything to your Order, sir, I hope it will be that. And you . . ." he said to Muckle, "can tell Hob the same. I will not follow a man. I will not follow a gnome. I am a goblin and my people can follow me."

Rosheen winced at the sound of Muckle slowly clapping his meaty hands together. *He is going to get us killed.*

"Will you fight for that belief?" Sir Corc asked.

The Lord of Pile regarded him for a moment, an expression passing across his face that Rosheen had not yet seen.

He doubts.

"The Red Caps," Sir Corc continued. "They are heading for the city in force. You have ten days, maybe less, before they are at your gates."

Rosheen felt bile rise in her throat. *Fafnir you fleeing coward.*

The Lord of the Pile searched the knight with his eyes. Sir Corc remained unreadable. "You know this? How?"

"Fat go-betweens have their uses," Muckle said, his smile not reaching his voice. The Lord's eyes flicked up to one of the Middangearder warriors and the man turned and left without a word. "I shall look into these claims. But be assured, even if you speak true this city is well defended."

"From without," Sir Corc said. "What about from within?"

The Lord found the question amusing. "You think I should fear insurrection?"

"Black Pool is home to many," was the knight's reply.

"And," Muckle put in, "a great many of them look a lot like you and I, my Lord." Muckle glanced down at his own ludicrously long shoes. "Well . . . more like you."

"Ah," it was the Lord's turn to feign surprise. He wagged a finger at them. "You think that a city full of goblins must also be rife with Red Caps."

Yes.

Sir Corc said nothing.

The Lord of the Pile smiled sadly. "Come with me, please."

They followed the Lord out of a small opening in the side of the building and came into a mud clogged field. The Lord of the Pile trudged away from the pens, the hem of his robe dragging through the filth. After a few dozen paces he paused and turned back towards the building, his gaze resting high and he motioned for them to do the same.

On the roof of the building seven goblins stood precariously near the edge. Two large men stood behind them, sharing a bottle back and forth. The goblins' hands were bound behind them and Rosheen shuddered when she saw that each wore a noose around their necks. The ropes fell down their chests, over the roof edge and looped back up under the eaves, tied to the rafters. A sack covered each of the goblins' faces, painted a garish red.

The Lord of the Pile extended a hand towards the roof. "Is this what I have to fear?"

"So they *are* in the city," Muckle said.

"Who?" the Lord of the Pile asked mildly. "Red Caps? It is possible. By your logic at least one of these seven must be." He waved a hand and one of the men on the roof lazily put a boot into the back of the left most goblin, kicking him off the edge. There was a squeal of terror from beneath the red hood, cut short when the poor wretch passed the eaves and the rope jerked taut.

"Stop this!" Rosheen said to Sir Corc.

"My Lord," the knight said. "You need not do this for our benefit."

"Yours?" the Lord waved again. The second goblin fell awkwardly, almost spilling from the roof. He dangled from the end of his rope, feet kicking hopelessly as he slowly strangled. "The benefit is entirely for my city."

"You cannot do this . . ." Muckle began.

"Without proof?" the Lord interjected. Rosheen winced as another spine snapped, but the goblin pressed on, unaffected.

"Why? You come to me with no proof. Only accusations. These seven are goblins. What more proof do I need?" He waved again and the fourth rope claimed a life.

"We came to you with a warning," Sir Corc said, anger spilling into his voice. "And you give us this vile show!"

The men on the roof were laughing now as they kicked the remaining three to their deaths. "The only warning, Sir, will be the bodies of these seven strung up on the gates and bridges of Black Pool. You tell me my people are sympathizers to an army of blind fanatics? After today, they will not dare."

Five bodies hung limply from under the thatching, the contents of their bowels running down their legs. The other two gurgled and twitched in the air, spinning hopelessly in agonizing death.

"Come away," Muckle shoved past the guards. "I am not one for gallows humor."

Sir Corc stared hard and the Lord of the Pile returned his gaze, the knight's face full of fury, the goblin's placid. The coburn turned and strode away. Rosheen followed him.

Even Muckle was silent as they made their way back to the city proper, but the time for tight lips was over. Rosheen wheeled on Sir Corc.

"Why did you bring me to see that?"

The knight stopped. "That madness was not expected."

"Then what? What did you expect?"

"You do not trust me," he replied. "You think I am idle in the face of danger. That I ignore it, but these threats are very real to me, piskie, and maybe now you can believe that. I am not going to help your friend. I ask your pardon, but if he did survive then he is in the Red Cap's wake and far safer than we are. You saw a village burn, I doubt that not, but this city is next and my duty is to the safety of . . . others."

Something crossed the knight's face that Rosheen could not place. He had almost said something else and then caught himself.

Frustration gnawed at his face and Rosheen waited.

"Also," the knight said at last, "I wanted your council. You are wise and I wager, a keen judge. So, I ask you. Is the Lord of the Pile a Red Cap?"

Rosheen did not hesitate. "No."

Sir Corc nodded, both relieved and troubled. "Will he fight?"

This time Rosheen did hesitate, but it was not for lack of certainty. *No.* She shook her head.

"As I feared," the knight said.

"What now?" Muckle asked.

Shame settled over the knight when he answered, but Rosheen did not judge him harshly. "We flee."

Pocket sat in the tiny garret room that served as his bed chamber, looking out the round window at the night-covered roofs of the city. He was supposed to be asleep, but he lay in his bed long after blowing out the candle. Bantam Flyn was silent at last, the sounds of his stumbling and drunken singing no longer coming up through the floor from the squire's room below. He had bought a flagon of wine from a street vendor on their errand for Sir Corc and happily told Pocket his plans to celebrate his brief freedom.

The squire's good cheer had soared upon their return when Sir Corc informed them that they were to be leaving the city within the week and he had spent the night passing the bottle with Old Lochlann.

But not everyone was filled with such gaiety. The piskie lady had barely spoken a word all day. Even now she sat out on the ledge under his window, staring mournfully at the stars. Pocket had not bothered her about teaching him to form a tail, although he had managed to hold the mule's ears the entire day. She seemed to want peace, so Pocket only smiled when she caught him staring and she always smiled back, but there was something missing. He could see the tips of her wings poking up from the bottom of the window and he watched them flutter slightly in the nighttime breeze for more than an hour before he made up his mind.

Pocket had spent a lifetime in long, quiet solitude; sitting in dark places, away from the world, hoping not to be disturbed by bad people . . . and all the while wishing someone kind would come and find him and talk to him and be his friend.

Rosheen looked up and smiled when he leaned out the window.

"Trouble sleeping?" she asked.

"Yes," he told her.

She nodded then turned back to the sky, her eyes careful never to look down at the jam of buildings. He watched her for a moment, nervous to speak.

"You miss him?" he finally ventured.

Rosheen looked over at him, puzzled but not angry. "Yes," she said. "I do."

"Me too," he said, then realized his mistake. "I mean, I miss my friends sometimes too."

He watched her watch the stars for a long time and worried that she was ignoring him, that he was bothering her. His heart fell, and he was about to duck back inside when she spoke.

"Everyone keeps telling me he may be dead," she looked over at him, her eyes bright and wet. "But I would feel it, were it true. I know I would feel it. He is alive." She nodded firmly, dislodging a single tear. "He is alive."

"Sometimes," Pocket said, "I talk about them. My friends that are not here. I tell Flyn about them or Lochlann. Sometimes even Backbone, because he listens best. He seems to like the stories about Napper."

"Napper?" Rosheen asked.

"He's a cat," Pocket said. "My best friend. He and Moragh. She was like you. She was very kind to me."

"I wish I knew them, then."

"They would like you," Pocket said. "But it helps. To talk about them with someone. It helps even if they do not listen. But I would listen." Pocket took another nervous breath. "Would you like to tell me about him?"

Rosheen smiled at him and this time, nothing was missing.

"Yes," she said. "I would."

SIXTEEN

It had been well over a thousand years since Deglan Loamtoes last set foot in the Burrow of the Wise. The vast, domed ceiling, roofed in intricate patterns of interlacing roots had been reshaped and restored to its former glory. The expertly carved lamps of thin amber were replaced, each hung from bronze fixtures and filled with a dozen mature moonbacks, casting a warm, steady light across the breadth of the cavern. All of the stone benches that were cracked or broken were now whole and covered with a cushion of fresh moss. In the center of the circular chamber, the Speaker's Mound was newly laid with rich, fragrant soil, giving and soft to ease long hours of standing.

Deglan's feet still hurt.

The chamber may have been lovingly crafted in the centuries since the Restoration, but the occupants had not been likewise improved. This place was still full of fools.

"Tell us again," Burden Dunloe droned from the third gallery. "Who this supposed goblin was that gave you this information?"

Deglan had to stop his eyes from rolling. "As I said . . . he was a Red Cap. Canker, was his name."

"And this Canker." Dunloe sounded as if he were about to fall fast asleep, "he was high in the Red Cap ranks?"

"What? No. He was a foot-stomper. Just another gibbering killer with a torch."

The assembled buffoons, crowded rump to rump on the benches, mumbled and murmured and harrumphed to one another.

Burden Dunloe sat back, resting his heavy lidded eyes along with whatever argument he thought he had made. For every ten gnomes in attendance, Deglan spied at least one hobgoblin wearing the robes of a Burden. Likely, they were none too fond of Deglan's last remark. Let them be offended. Deglan spoke only the truth.

Another of the King's advisors leaned forward. "And you say these Red Caps claimed to be under the command of Torcan the Swinehelm?"

Deglan did not recognize this particular windbag, but he grit his teeth and answered. "Yes. But that I did not need to be told. For the fourth time, I saw Torcan with my own eyes."

"On the same night you saw the Flame Binder?" Burden Windbag confirmed.

"Surely," Deglan said with a bitter smile. "I do not need to convince you I saw *him*. Unless I must offer proof of your own mistakes?"

Windbag's eyes widened as if he had been struck with a fistful of something smelly and the benches erupted with shocked cries of protest. Burden Dunloe woke from his nap long enough to calm the assembly and come to his offended colleague's rescue.

"And now you say that the Red Caps are marching on Black Pool! Tell me, Master Loamtoes, why would a powerful warlord like Torcan Swinehelm reveal such plans to some lowly follower?"

"I have a question of my own, good Burden," Deglan smiled bitterly. "Have you ever been to war?"

Dunloe seemed to find this question amusing and chuckled softly, looking around to see his fellows on the benches were equally entertained. "I was present during the Rebellion, Master Loamtoes."

"I remember," Deglan said. "And you sat around flapping your fat mouth then as you do now!" That sparked more grumbles, but Deglan rode over them. "There is such a thing as marching orders, Burden. I doubt if Canker was told anything by Torcan directly, but the Red Caps are spread out in raiding parties across the countryside. Their leaders would have been given a point of convergence. They are to gather four days march from the city. I tell you, Torcan means to take Black Pool."

"To what purpose?" Burden Calum asked. Deglan relaxed a little. Calum was old, but practical as ever. Maybe there was some sense left among the King's advisors.

"Recruitment," a gravelly voice answered. Deglan turned with the rest and looked to Durock Moundbuilder, standing by the entrance to the galleries. "If he can take Black Pool, then he can swell his ranks. Convince or threaten the goblins there to don the Cap."

Deglan nodded gratefully, taking comfort in the general's presence. Durock's broad forehead now sat below a bald pate, but the fierce, black hair that had retreated from his head now covered his cheeks in bushy whiskers.

"Which is why you must strike now," Deglan urged the assembly. "Before his forces gain further strength."

"We still have been given no proof to this report," Burden Dunloe said.

"Then send riders to confirm it!" Deglan thundered. "If my word is no longer good in this council!"

"No," a frail looking gnome said from the back gallery.

Deglan could not believe that after all this time Burden Feeney still shook when he spoke. "We must not send our forces out needlessly. Not with Red Cap patrols on the loose."

"So!" Deglan threw his arm angrily in Feeney's direction, causing the whelp to flinch. "The Red Caps are out there, after all. Just not where I say they are!"

"Sit down, Burden Feeney," Dunloe scolded and waited until his instructions were followed before turning back to the room. "If this army is marshaling where you claim, then it will reach the city long before our troops could muster. The Red Caps would hold Black Pool and we would be forced into a siege."

Dunloe hung his head sagely and then shook it before looking back at the assembly. "Too costly."

"You need not risk a siege if you ride now," Deglan could hear the plea in his own voice. "The Wart Shanks could cover the distance and with luck take the Red Caps by surprise. They would be caught between us and the walls of the city. You could end this with one crushing blow."

"We have no assurance that Black Pool will offer any resistance," Windbag threw down. "They may simply open their gates to the Red Caps."

"And," Dunloe added, "a foe as seasoned and dangerous as Torcan Swinehelm, if it is indeed he with whom we are matched, would never fall to such a trap."

"Perhaps," Deglan snarled, "we should let our own very capable General decide that. Durock," Deglan turned to the lined face of the old campaigner, "tell them—"

"General Moundbuilder," Dunloe snapped, "does not sit on the council that helps bear the King's Burden! He is here to answer questions regarding the strength of our troops and to march when and *if* the King so chooses. Nothing more."

Deglan looked into Durock's weathered face as the councilor spoke. The General did not look away, but in his eyes was a weary resignation, a shamed acceptance of the folly that surrounded them. Deglan had fled this inanity long ago. A wise choice if what he now looked upon was the result of dealing with such absurdity for centuries.

Deglan turned away and looked up to the King's Seat above the sixth gallery. Empty.

Empty as the heads of everyone in this room, including himself. He was the greatest fool for coming here. Airlann stood on the brink of repeating a nightmare. Already, the lives of mortal men had been pounced upon and what did his people do? They hid, content to keep their heads as buried as their city. King Hob was probably tending his mushroom garden, blissfully unaware that the world above was beginning to burn.

Burden Dunloe had continued to prattle on for the benefit of his captive audience and Deglan had ignored him until he heard the useless sack declare, "We dare not act upon the words of a Red Cap spoken while under torture!"

Deglan gawked. "Torture? I never said I—"

"Did he survive your interrogation?"

"No, but—"

"Do not try to dissemble with me, Master Loamtoes," Dunloe barreled over him. "Your reputation during the Rebellion is well known by this council as is your hatred for goblinkind. No doubt the grievous pains inflicted on your prisoner conjured up all manner of falsehoods just so you would put an end to his misery."

He swept the seats. "We cannot take faith in this report!"

"Then take faith in your own failure!" Deglan yelled back.

"You know a Flame Binder is free because he escaped from this city! Maybe you should be standing down here answering my questions about that!"

Burden Calum stood up, his hands raised in a calming gesture. "Master Loamtoes, please. You go too far."

"Forgive me, Burden," Deglan told the aged councilor, "but you do not go far enough. You must act! And swiftly. Torcan Swinehelm will soon have all he needs to subjugate this isle for a second time."

"Ah yes," Windbag seemed to have rallied himself for another assault. "An heir of the Goblin Kings. Tell me, how is that possible when the last of those despoilers was thrown to his death?"

"Jerrod the Second, you mean?" Deglan would put a stop to this worm's second bout of bravery. "Or did the history book not tell you his name, you suckling child! Yes, he was pushed from a tower and his son—"

"The Gaunt Prince," the stripling councilor cut in angrily.

"Very good!" Deglan praised him ruefully. "He was killed in the Battle of Nine Crowns. But . . . both King and Prince had children that were never found at war's end and fanatics like Torcan have never stopped searching for them."

Burden Dunloe scoffed. "Nine hundred and more years is a long span for mankind. Countless generations! It is most unlikely the line has survived." The gaggle of advisors surrounding him nodded most agreeably. Deglan wondered if Dunloe had their heads attached to a string running up the sleeve of his robe.

"If I may," Burden Calum cleared his throat. "The progeny of the Goblin Kings has ever proven more gifted than that of most humans. Their talents with Magic were beyond what most mortals could ever achieve and it did extend their lives most incredibly."

"At a cost," Burden Dunloe grumbled.

"True," Calum continued. "Madness, physical deformity, all of these maladies and more plagued the Goblin Kings, but even then they remained quite resilient. It is not impossible to believe that their descendants have managed to thrive. And let us not forget, the line of the first usurper, Penda Blood Coin, was not the only family to wield sorcerous powers. Twice there was a schism in the succession of the Goblin Kings. Once with Hogulent the First and Only and then again with the peerless rule of the Goblin Queen. Their seed, along with that of the Gaunt Prince and his father may very well endure."

"Well then," Dunloe's tone was placating. "Master Loamtoes, did your . . . *prisoner* tell you who this heir might be?"

Deglan swallowed hard. "No."

Burden Dunloe's grin widened as he allowed the effects of the admission to pass through the chattering chamber. "And why not? You seem to know everything else from his lips. Why not this most important of facts?"

"I asked," Deglan told him, "but he did not know."

"Because there is no such person," Dunloe told the chamber. "This heir is nothing but a myth told to the Red Caps to stir them into further frenzy. Well, I refuse to be taken in by such delusions! I will not believe it!"

"Nor I!" Burden Feeney squeaked.

"Hear, hear!" Windbag was on his feet along with the rest of Dunloe's sycophants. Support was spreading through the galleries, but there was doubt in the faces of many of the assembly.

Deglan needed to act quickly.

"Peace!" he yelled. "Peace! Listen to me! It makes no matter whether we believe. Do you not see? Torcan believes! And that is more dangerous than all the goblins under his command. Because a thousand Red Caps, a hundred Flame Binders, is nothing compared to the might of just ten Forge Born! And that is what Swinehelm intends to do . . . crush this isle under an army of living iron!"

"Do not embarrass yourself, Loamtoes," Dunloe chuckled.

"The Forge Born are no longer a threat to this isle. The Magic of the Seelie Court saw to that a thousand years ago."

"If you think they are not a threat, then you have clearly never seen the havoc a single Unwound is capable of."

"The Unwound," Dunloe spoke as if to a child, "were a rare abomination. The violent result of a few Forge Born in their death throes. There has been no report of an Unwound on these shores in close to a hundred years and no functional Forge Born has been sighted in twice that time. They are gone, rusted to pieces."

Deglan's mind went to the Forge Born that had dragged Faabar away from the devastation of Hog's Wallow. The one with the empty scabbard who had spoken to him and led him to the barrows and handed Faabar his sword, helped to bury him.

Coltrane. It had called itself Coltrane.

There was nothing rusted about it and if there was one there could be others. Deglan would make this council understand that if he had to stand on the Speaker's Mound forever.

He took a deep breath.

"Say nothing."

Deglan glanced up angrily at Burden Dunloe, but found he had once again taken his seat, conversing quietly with his lackeys.

"Do you have anything else to say to us, Master Loamtoes?" Windbag jeered.

"Yes," Deglan said. "There was—"

"They cannot be trusted."

Deglan whirled around to the seats behind him and found a hundred faces staring back at him expectantly.

"We are waiting, Master Loamtoes," Windbag urged.

Deglan turned back and opened his mouth.

"For Airlann's sake, say nothing of what you saw."

Deglan shook his head roughly, trying to dislodge the voice.

"If there is nothing more," Windbag said primly, "this council will conclude."

"Wait!" Deglan exclaimed.

"No!"

"I have other—"

"Silence! "

"There is—"

"I believe you. "

Deglan stopped. The Wisemoot stared down at him impatiently. Even Burden Calum seemed perturbed and Durock Moundbuilder would not meet his eyes.

"Look up," the voice urged. *"Fifth gallery. To your left. I am scratching my right cheek with two fingers. "*

Deglan scanned the fifth gallery and there, sitting among the rest, was a wizened hobgoblin scratching his face lightly with two fingers.

"This Wisemoot shall retire," Windbag declared. "And these matters brought before King Hob by the Chief Burdens."

Deglan remained on the Speaker's Mound as the councilors filed down from the galleries. He was confused and grew angry at each sidelong glance and backhand whisper cast in his direction. In retaliation, he shot a sharp look at Burden Feeney and was rewarded when the little squint tripped on the hem of his robe. It only made him feel slightly better. He caught sight of the hobgoblin again among the exiting crowd. He possessed the wide head, protruding nose and bat-like ears so prevalent in goblinkind, but unlike most of his race, whose skin was usually a mottled grey, this goblin's flesh was a dingy white, his pale hand poking out from the sleeve of his councilor's robe and gripping a gnarled root staff. He did not look at Deglan, but watched his feet as he carefully made his way down the steps.

"We must talk," the voice filled his head again. Now that Deglan could concentrate he found the tone gentle and refined.

"Meet me in two shadow's turn at Salt Well."

Deglan watched him descend the final steps and wondered what the old albino would do when he found himself alone in that briny cave.

"I am not an albino, Master Loamtoes," the polite voice corrected him . *"And you would be wise to meet me. Oh! Bring a fishing pole."*

Deglan scowled at the hobgoblin's back as he left the chamber.

Mind speech was a seer's trick and quite common among the elves during the height of the Seelie Court, but he had never known a gnome or a goblin to be capable of such craft. This hobgoblin deserved no more trust than the council he warned against, and Deglan had no intention of meeting him anywhere. He lingered a moment longer, taking one last look at the King's Seat. He remembered the days when a better gnome occupied the chair, wishing he still did, then turned his back and left the Burrow of the Wise. Durock Moundbuilder awaited him in the entrance tunnel wearing the heavy bladed falchion not permitted in the Moot.

Seeing the General armed and flanked by two soldiers clad in bronze plate and bearing menacing halberds made Deglan's heart jump to his throat, but he pushed it down.

"Am I to be taken into custody?" Deglan asked without breaking stride. He walked past Moundbuilder and his guards without waiting for a response.

The General caught up to him, his escort staying a respectful distance behind. "Still cranky as ever, Staunch."

Deglan kept his eyes forward. "I am not cranky. I got piss in my veins and shit in my craw. All I been fed for half the day."

Moundbuilder said nothing. After another dozen strides, Deglan stopped abruptly and spun to face him. "Since when is the Marshal General not also a Bearer of the King's Burden?"

Durock's jaw muscles bulged underneath his whiskers.

"Things have changed," he said slowly. "His Grace no longer feels the army should have a voice in such matters. We are the hammer . . . he is the hand. His words."

"Put a hammer in my hand and leave me alone with His Grace," Deglan muttered. "Knock some sense into him."

Moundbuilder glanced over at the soldiers standing fifty paces off, then back at Deglan. He took a step forward and Deglan was suddenly reminded why Durock had risen so high in the ranks.

He was bloody big for a gnome; thick arms covered in muscle and black hair. His flat face, framed in whiskers and dominated by dark eyes gave no doubt as to why his troops called him the Old Badger.

"Careful, Loamtoes," he rumbled quietly. "Not all ears are friendly. And I cannot protect you from your own treasonous tongue. For all his faults, I still serve the King and I will take you into custody if you insist on making more enemies."

Deglan nodded and Moundbuilder backed away. Then a grin split his craggy face, and he clapped a weighty hand over Deglan's shoulder. "It is good to see you again, Staunch. Did you not make a vow never to return Holm?"

Deglan could not return the smile. He shook his head and continued walking. "A vow I would have kept if you lot did not have rocks in your skulls. By the Stone! Durock, how ever did you allow a Flame Binder to escape?"

"Over eight hundred years entombed and then one day," the general punched his fist forward and splayed his fingers wide. "He was gone. Cell was empty and none of our own were dead."

"Why was he even here?" Deglan struggled to keep his voice down. "They should have all been put to death! Why did you not go after him?"

"I was forbidden," Durock said simply. "The Moot thought it best to wait for aid from the undine and the Waywarders, so that we might combine our strength."

"And have they come?"

Durock's brow buried itself between his eyes. "The undine, yes. Of the dusk elves we have seen naught."

"And while you tarry, Torcan is using the Flame Binder to turn the mortal world to ash."

"The Red Caps would not exist were it not for man," Durock said gruffly. "They are no strangers to war, fighting among themselves as they so often do. And they have their precious iron. Let them fend for themselves."

"They are not the only ones who suffer, Durock. Black Pool is home to mortal and Fae alike." He stopped and turned to the general. "That Flame Binder killed Faabar."

The Old Badger took the news like any commander.

"Shame. We could have used him in the times ahead."

"What times are those, General?" Deglan asked.

"Hunkering down here and holding councils? Faabar died fighting and he took a goodly number of goblins with him. To my mind, he struck the first blows of this war for our side. You say you could have used him? I say he could have used you. And where were you?"

"Serving my King," Durock glowered back. "Something you seem to have forgotten."

"Your king," Deglan countered, "is not his brother and last I knelt, it was to Blackmud. The King that fought. The King that had you on his council and not just as a tool to brandish. But this is not about rulers, Durock. Faabar remained loyal to Irial and the Seelie Court to his last breath, but I think he had a far deeper allegiance and one which no monarch can surmount. He was loyal to this isle, to Airlann herself and all her peoples. And he understood something that no one down here seems to comprehend." It was his turn to step forward and get in the general's face, thrusting a finger towards the roof of the tunnel.

"The mortals that are dying up there . . . Faabar gave his life to protect them. And why? Because he knew that not one of them was alive during the reign of the Goblin Kings. They are not responsible for the deeds of their ancestors. Ancestors that lived so long ago they appear as legend to mortal eyes. Mankind is guiltless, Durock. Can we, who have lived so long, say the same?"

Moundbuilder's jaws worked under his skin, as if chewing Deglan's words to mush. "What would you have of me, Staunch?" he asked. "Defy the will of Moot and King? Take the Wart Shanks into the field and make merry chase of Torcan and his army? Leave Toad Holm defenseless?"

Deglan smiled for the first time. "Sounds good."

The Old Badger snarled and turned away. "I cannot."

Deglan looked at his former General and did not recognize him. Durock stared at the ground, frowning at nothing but his own indecision.

"General Moundbuilder," Deglan began slowly, "I have removed no less than four arrows from your body. Not to mention the spear that took you through the shoulder. I brought you around when a goblin mace near showed your brains to the sun. I have stitched your wounds, reset your bones and relieved your fevers. And I was proud to be of service. But this wound from which you now suffer, no skill of mine can mend. I have no remedy for broken resolve. There is no cure for cowardice."

Moundbuilder's head shot up and his hands curled into meaty fists. "Burden Calum was right," he growled, eyes full of fury.

"You do go too far."

"I do not know which makes me angrier," Deglan said turning his back and heading down the tunnel. "That everyone keeps telling me how far I go . . . or that no one is willing to follow me there." He did not stop walking.

The tunnel contained no branches to left or right. There was only one route to the Wisemoot, and, at last, Deglan emerged into one of the many huge caverns that made up Toad Holm proper. The passage led onto a walkway along the rim of the cavern.

The ceiling was lost in deep shadows above, but the walkway was still high up the cavern wall and Deglan could look down upon the many layers of Toad Holm. Bridges of carved stone, stairs of coaxed roots and walls of molded Earth criss-crossed below, a harmonious jumble that gave shape to the city. Deglan traveled the walkway, heading down the wall in a gentle spiral.

Every street in Toad Holm was paved with flat, uncut stones of every size, each one painstakingly sought after so that it fit seamlessly among its brethren without the use of hammer or chisel. After three Ages and tens of thousands of years, there remained gaps in the pavement, brown earth showing through, marking where that one naturally fitting stone was yet unfound.

Deglan had almost forgotten how single minded his people could be and how lovely the results were.

When he turned his back on Toad Holm, the city was newly resettled after centuries of abandonment. The long neglect had caused widespread cave-ins, destroying entire districts and the already war-weary gnomes spent years driving off the unsavory creatures that had taken up residence in their absence. Burrowing ballybogs infested many a tunnel and covens of baobhan sith hid from the sun in the once resplendent halls. As Deglan made his way down, he found it difficult to imagine the once decrepit state of the place. He came down into the middle reaches, crossing over one of the many bridges and entering a typical living district. To his left the cozy market burrows bustled with gnomes trading for wool, vegetables and tools, the patrons taking their goods away down the well-lit side tunnels and eventually to the large caverns where their home burrows lay nestled comfortably next to those of their neighbors.

Deglan meandered around the market and considered making his way back to Ruhle Nettle's burrow. The fierce old herbwife who had been his unyielding mentor was long dead, but one of her many daughters now dwelt in her house and it was the best place Deglan could think of to leave Blink. She was in capable hands, Deglan was certain. Ruhle had made sure every one of her offspring knew the healing arts, but he still found himself worrying and felt a deep need to check on the child. Maybe he just needed a familiar face that did not fill him with disappointment.

"What may I interest you in, good gnome?"

Deglan turned and found a plump, smiling merchant at his elbow. He regarded the merchant for a long moment and just as the good-natured smile began to lose its sincerity he said, "A fishing pole."

An hour later, Deglan had trudged down into the lower reaches of the city. The tunnels remained wide and high, but there were fewer lamps, and large sections had yet to be completely cleared of rock spills and uncooperative roots. Feeling foolish with the pole in his hand and not entirely certain he wanted to go through with this clandestine meeting, he had taken a long detour.

Salt Well and that ghastly hobgoblin could wait. There was something else he wanted to see first.

The Gate of Lost Kings was housed in one of the largest caverns in Toad Holm, far below the civilized districts of the city.

The Earth of the cave was barely shaped and retained a wild, untamed appearance. Lit only by two large bronze braziers on either side of the Gate, this was the only place in Toad Holm illuminated by Fire and the great double bronze doors shone savagely in the light of the flames. Easily ten times the height of a fomori, the Gate remained a humbling sight.

No one knew exactly where King Ghob slipped away to delve deep into the core of world, but it was well known where his spawn reemerged. The great fissure now sealed by the Gate was the birthplace of goblins into the known world. Since that day, the Gate had been heavily guarded and was the permanent station of an entire contingent of seasoned gnome warriors known as the Kings' Butlers. Deglan walked past the long ranks of motionless troops, grateful that the right to visit the Gate was still allowed to all inhabitants of Toad Holm. These gnomes were the most well-disciplined veterans in the army, standing the long tedious hours of their watch in perfect silence. Encased in their hulking suits of armor, faces hidden behind the visors of their helms, they reminded Deglan of giant, brazen beetles. Their gauntleted fists gripped broad shields and ornate glaives. All of these armaments were powerful relics from the Age of Summer, emblazoned with protective wards.

As formidable as the Butlers were, they were far from the most imposing sight in the cave. The contingent was supported by two monstrous war toads. Flanking the Gate, each of these ancient brutes could swallow a human cottage whole and carried a fortified platform upon their backs where the Earth Shapers could wield their destructive Magic from safety. Even during the reign of the Goblin Kings and the long years of the Rebellion, when the rest of Toad Holm lay empty, the Gate remained secured by the Butlers and their wart-covered giants.

Originally dubbed the Gate of the Hated King, both doors had once depicted brazen images of King Ghob and his treacherous legacy. The arch of the doors showed him deceiving the Seelie Court, and further down, his banishment and flight deep underground. How Ghob stole Fire from the dragons was an enduring mystery but the sculptors had done their best, imagining the greedy king duping them with honeyed words. The final carving at the doors' base had been the true masterpiece; the ravening horde of Ghob's children, crafted true to life, emerging from the fiery depths to bring terror to the isle. To stand before the gate and look upon the forms of the goblins, frozen in bronze, reaching for you with bloody malice was an artistic marvel and a fearful reminder.

Now, only half the goblins rushed forth, as the right door had been removed after the Restoration and melted down to create the one which now hung in its place. When last Deglan was here, the new half remained unfinished but now it hung next to its older mate, the carvings jutting out in pugnacious relief. It portrayed the doings of Goban Blackmud; a different king with a far different legacy. Starting with his crowning and his many years of prosperous rule, the carvings descended into the Rebellion and Goban's fight with the Gaunt Prince and the victory of the Fae. Towards the bottom, the King's abdication and his departure from the city were chronicled, but the base of the door remained unfinished, the craftsmen waiting for Goban's return, so that they might place his triumphant image striding out from the pit.

In life, the events had not been quite so grand. At war's end, Goban Blackmud was a haunted gnome. The death of Aillila Ulvyeh weighed heavily upon him and much of the governance of the city fell to the Burden Bearers. The Gate of the Hated King had remained closed since the day it was constructed, but Goban ordered the doors be thrown wide, removed his crown and handed it to Hob, vowing he would not return until he set things aright.

Now two kings roamed the bowels of the Earth, one in disgrace, the other in self-imposed exile. Whether either would ever be seen again remained a question of faith. Two stone pedestals stood near the doors. Atop one lay a goblet full of wine and on the other a great bronze axe. It was the duty of the Kings' Butlers to suitably greet either of the wayward rulers should they return; Goban with refreshment, Ghob with death.

Standing before the Gate of Lost Kings, Deglan wondered what King Blackmud would say if he returned and found his city in its current state. Maybe it was best he stayed away. Deglan certainly should have. He should have listened to Faabar and gone directly to the Seelie Court, but Durock said the Waywarders had been summoned and not yet answered, adding further proof to Deglan's fear that the strength of the elves had diminished to the point of helplessness. Where else could he turn when his allies appeared as enemies and his enemies appeared as friends? Deglan looked at the fishing pole in his hand.

"At the least, I will figure out which one that pasty bastard is." Toad Holm contained several underground lakes, but Salt Well was the only one fed from the sea. A sharp, tangy smell filled Deglan's nostrils as he came down the long tunnel. The cave was lit from luminous sponges that lived in the water, casting an eerie green light that danced across the stone walls in ghostly waves.

Deglan was not a great lover of the ocean and when he sat down on the edge of the vast water he suppressed a shiver at the thought of some kraken's tentacles or a great toothy whale jumping out to claim him for a meal. A boat labored far out in the middle of the Well, two fishergnomes casting nets into the water; a trade Deglan did not envy.

"*I apologize if this makes you uncomfortable.*"

"Buggery and spit!" Deglan snapped his head from side to side and found the hobgoblin sitting some distance to his right, dangling a pole in the water.

"*A friend came up with this method of secrecy many years ago,*" the hobgoblin sounded almost sad. "*He is more . . . imaginative than I, so I thought it best to use what works.*"

"Why did you want me down here?"

"*It is not necessary for you to speak aloud. Just think it and I will hear.*"

"No need," Deglan said out loud. "I talk to myself all the time. Only one who answers back with any sense."

"*I can certainly see how it would feel so.*" The hobgoblin turned and looked at him for the first time. "Are they biting over there?" he asked aloud with gentle courtesy.

"What? Er . . . yes."

The hobgoblin drew his line in and got to his feet before making his way over to sit next to Deglan. He cast again before looking over. "Burden Curdle Milkthumb, but please, Curdle will do."

"Deglan Loamtoes," he replied. *"But you already knew that."*

"Well done," Curdle laughed in his head. "My honor to meet you. Do you visit Salt Well often?"

"No, I am recently returned to the city," Deglan said flicking his rod absently. *"Why did you stop me from speaking at the Wisemoot?"*

"Oh yes," Curdle said while looking at the water. "You may find the city has changed somewhat. *Because the knowledge of a working Forge Born could prove most dangerous to our cause."*

"I'll say it has," Deglan muttered. *"What damn cause?"*

"To stop Torcan Swinehelm, of course." Curdle looked over.

"Would you take some fishing tips from a stranger?"

Deglan looked back at the hobgoblin's friendly face for a moment. "I would be interested in any help you could give me."

Curdle nodded pleasantly. "First. When you cast, try and disturb the water as little as possible."

"Never my style," Deglan said. *"What do you know about Swinehelm?"*

"A great deal. And now much more, thanks to you. That he was marching on Black Pool was unknown to me. Thankfully I was able to send word to a contact there. The city is forewarned, but I fear it will offer little resistance."

"The Wisemoot was mere hours ago," Deglan scowled at the hobgoblin. *"How could you already ha—?"* Realization struck him.

This hobgoblin knew more than a few seers' tricks.

"But I only know a little about catching fish," Curdle said with cheerful self-deprecation.

"I learn best by observation," Deglan said. "Let us sit here quietly and maybe I will pick up some skill."

"Yes," Curdle agreed. "We will improve our chances of success if we do not frighten the fish with our talk."

"Al right, answers! How did the Flame Binder escape?"

"Torcan broke him out . . . with help."

"From inside Toad Holm!" Deglan knew it. *"All these goblins now living in the city, no wonder. You are taking a risk, my pale friend. Red Cap spies find out you conspire against them . . . nothing they hate worse than a traitor. How many of the hobgoblins on the council does Torcan have?"*

"None."

"None?" Deglan could not help but use his tongue.

"Impossible."

Curdle put a calming hand on his arm. "Have patience. You will catch one."

Deglan glanced around sheepishly, then set his focus back on the water.

"As you say," Curdle's voice was calm. *"Red Caps hate traitors . . . and hobgoblins worst of all. Our lives were forfeit the moment we pledged allegiance to Toad Holm. None of us would dare help Torcan to victory. The Red Caps do not issue pardons, Deglan."*

"Then that would mean . . ." Deglan could not believe it.

"No . . . you lie!"

"I am sorry, my friend."

Deglan stared at the water, as gaped-mouthed as the fish that eluded his hook. All this talk of traitors and they were his own people? That was madness! The Red Caps' hatred for gnomes was two thousand years deep. There could be no common ground, nothing that would unite them in such a plot. They might have turned into spineless lickspittles, but treasonous spies? Deglan looked over at Curdle and shot to his feet.

This was the only spy here! A hobgoblin that could crawl in his head and read his thoughts, turn them against him and play on his already growing doubt. He would hear no more. Deglan threw his rod into the water and backed away, his hand going for his cleaver before realizing he had not taken it to the Moot where weapons were forbidden. He continued to back away, eyes never leaving the hobgoblin who simply stared back at him, face full of serene regret.

"Deglan," he said aloud. "Would you ever set foot in the Ever Dark?"

"So," Deglan replied taking another step, "now you threaten me with death?"

"No," Curdle said. "It was an honest question. Would you ever willingly go down there?"

Deglan thought about that horrible unseen place; a twisting network of narrow tunnels and tight, low chambers where the gnomes housed their dead. No light had ever touched those crypts, the bodies being tended by blind gnomes so ancient they might as well have been walking spirits. Deglan imagined their huge, bleached, unseeing eyes, their lank wisps of white, silk-thin hair, their bony hands handling the corpses, dragging them, laying them in their nooks. He shivered. Deglan did not much fancy going there in death. He would never venture to the Ever Dark in life.

"No gnome would," Curdle said.

"Get out of my head," Deglan warned.

"It was your face I was reading, Master Loamtoes. I am speaking to you aloud, taking a tremendous risk, because I need you to trust me."

"You want me to believe my own people capable of—"

"They are my people too, Deglan." Curdle said. "I was born a goblin, but this is my home. I am not trying to deceive you. I need your help."

Deglan paused. "Why did you ask me about the Ever Dark?"

"Because that is where they imprisoned him," Curdle replied. "The Flame Binder. Surrounded by miles of impenetrable Earth on all sides, with a lake guarded by the undine above. Earth and Water kept him contained and the only way to get to him was through that winding tomb. You would not go there. I would not go there. I doubt any gnome or hobgoblin would willingly.

"So, that leaves the Red Caps. Goblins from outside who have no fear of the Ever Dark. But they would need light to see or they would have no hope of finding their precious Flame Binder. Even a tiny candle would have alerted the grave diggers. For all their age and blindness, those gnomes are wielders of potent Magic. It would take an army to overpower them and no army can operate in those cramped passages, even if it could reach the entrance without alerting the city."

"Then," Deglan said uncertainly. "How did they get him out?"

"It took centuries," Curdle said. "But they tunneled in."

"Impossible," Deglan snorted. "We are the guardians of Earth! It is unthinkable that the Red Caps could accomplish that without our . . . knowledge." He looked into Curdle's knowing face.

"By Earth and Stone!"

"Now you see why the Moot cannot be trusted."

"Dunloe," Deglan was sure. "Who else?"

"Feeney certainly," Curdle replied. "Possibly more."

"Moundbuilder?"

Curdle shook his head. "I do not know."

"How do you not know?" Deglan took a step back towards the hobgoblin. "Crawl into their damn skulls and find out!"

"I have tried," Curdle said sadly. "But I am not the only one with such gifts, Master Loamtoes, and I must tread lightly. This corruption could go as high as the King. If I am discovered, then all my efforts will have been in vain."

Deglan took a deep breath and let it out slowly. *"What does the Forge Born have to do with all of this?"*

Curdle nodded gratefully. *"I believe your prisoner spoke truthfully. Torcan does plan to lead an army of living iron, but to do so he needed a Flame Binder to reawaken them. Now he has one. And only the Gaunt Prince's heir can command them, so if Torcan has indeed found such an heir . . ."*

"He will have an unstoppable army at his disposal."

Curdle nodded gravely.

"And the Forge Born that I saw in Hog's Wallow? What of it?"

"He may be the only one that can stop this."

Deglan's tongue rebelled again. "How? Why?"

"I will explain on the way," Curdle said as he rose, drawing his line out of the water and revealing a plump fish flapping on the hook.

"On the way where?"

"To find your Forge Born, of course," Curdle declared facing him.

"Find it?" Deglan fought the urge to push Curdle into the water. "It could be anywhere! I would not know where to begin. How are we ever going to track that thing down?"

"Oh, do not worry," Curdle said, bending at the waist and extending the fish out past Deglan's leg. "I have some friends that will help us."

"Friends?" Deglan said and then jumped to the side as something suddenly shot past his leg and grabbed the fish from Curdle's hand. He whirled around to find a large, shaggy hound with grey fur settling down to enjoy the fish. Another dog, just as silent, came out from the shadows to share the catch. The two did not fight over the meal.

Sweat and Panic shared every kill.

A tall figure came down the tunnel, the rippling green light reflected in his raptor's eyes.

"Deglan Loamtoes," Curdle said lightly, "I believe you know—"

"Madigan," Deglan finished. "The Sure Finder."

SEVENTEEN

Padric sat on the crags above the harbor, watching as the ship drew closer. Long and low in the water, the men aboard had taken down its sail of red and black stripes, propelling their vessel with uniform sweeps of the oars that seemed to wave effortlessly from either side of the hull. The upward curve of the prow was visible and while the ship was still too far distant to make out the details of the carving, Padric knew it would be fashioned in the likeness of a dragon's head. It was the ninth such ship to sail into the harbor in two days, the earlier arrivals already moored in the choppy, slate grey waters near the shore. Beyond, a fertile flat plain spread away from the sea, nestled between low, boulder-chocked ridges. Padric's perch was atop the highest of these ridges and home to the remnants of a shattered watch castle. Torcan had placed lookouts in what remained of the tower and Padric heard the deep peel of the signal horn sound out above him as the newest arrival came into view.

The harbor was formed by a natural curving of the rocky landscape; the sea almost fully embraced by the jutting swing of dark stones. The green hinterland swept away from the shores, accessible and inviting. Reaver's Meadow, as it was known, had been a popular spot for the seafarers of Middangeard to make land for decades and a small community of longhouses and mead halls now dotted the field. This latest ship would bring another eighty raiders to Swinehelm's growing force, but the amount of Middangearders was nothing compared to the horde of goblins camped in the Meadow. Even the crashing of the surf upon the rocks could not drown out the noise from the teeming swamp of Red Caps that threatened to spill over the human settlement and into the sea. From his vantage point, Padric looked down upon the greasy smoke of hundreds of cook fires, surrounded by countless bodies.

When Padric had arrived with Torcan's retinue of some fifty goblins, only one longship was docked in the harbor. The Middangearders had greeted Swinehelm with drunken smiles and a horn of mead, turning one of the halls over for his immediate use.

Within the day, Red Caps began turning up at the Meadow. They came slowly at first, in raiding parties of no more than fifteen, but as dusk settled and night came on, they arrived in droves. The first morning saw over a thousand armed goblins marshaled, fresh from marauding and eager for battle. Now, a day later, their numbers had more than doubled, with more arriving every hour. Padric did not know where Torcan intended to unleash this force, but he hoped there was a place on the isle strong enough to repel them.

He stood and turned his back on the sea. As always, eight Red Caps waited for him, not a dozen paces removed. Padric snorted. His honor guard. They followed him down from the crags, not gibbering, jesting or whispering to one another. Except for the scraping of their heavy iron boots on the stones, they remained respectfully silent. Clearly, they did not want to disturb the thoughts of their future king.

During the three-day journey from the fort to the coast, Torcan had treated Padric with a strange mix of curiosity and contempt, as if he were a leper that also knew the secret to some wondrous treasure. He felt the goblin leader constantly watching him, but he never approached or spoke directly to him. At night, Swinehelm had Slouch Hat or Kederic brought before him under heavy guard and questioned them for long hours. Often the Thegn's screams would pierce the camp, echoing painfully over the black shrouded fields. During the march, the husk was kept in the front of the column, while Kederic was kept caged in a supply wagon at the rear. Padric was not permitted to speak with either of them and was left to wonder what mysteries of his life they were revealing.

By the time they reached Reaver's Meadow, Padric's mind had become entangled with questions. He worried at the knot of his existence, desperately looking for some memory that could answer this sudden, ill-begotten legacy. That he was different had been made callously apparent to him since boyhood. That he was hated and feared by his neighbors and pitied by his family was something he begrudgingly accepted, until he grew old enough to rebel against such perceptions. But his clumsy attempts at denial only manifested as the feeble acts of a troubled young man, further reinforcing the mantle that he was simply no good. Now, it appeared that mantle had a source, flowing into his veins from the unfathomable past, myth made flesh. How that was possible remained as elusive and distant as the individuals who held the answers.

In the end, his mind was crushed to a numb cloud by the sudden weight of those unsought revelations. He walked down into the coastal settlement with the same detached air he had worn as a cloak these past days, in control of little but his own feet and even their steps were limited. Whatever the truth, Torcan had become convinced of his importance and treated Padric as a royal hostage, seeing to his comfort while simultaneously taking his freedom. He had been moments away from death when Slouch Hat spoke up and now he was being hosted by a thriving camp of fanatics that had been responsible for so much recent pain. Padric wondered if death would not have proven more favorable.

Torcan had commandeered one of the longhouses for Padric's use. He entered, leaving the ocean wind, and his guards, outside. The warmth of the longhouse was layered with the smells of garlic, onion, fennel and hyssop, all undercurrents to the savory aromas of roast bream, baked herring and pike steeped in ginger and galingale.

"Did me bonny prince have hisself a fine turn about the beach?" Heggle asked when he entered.

Padric answered with a meaningless sound, which Heggle took for a grand answer, smiling broadly with her wet gums and lone, brown tooth before going back to her chopping, stirring and mixing. The goblin crone had been sent to him from Swinehelm to act as his personal servant, and she seemed to take great joy in her placement. Padric removed his cloak, damp from the spray, and hung it to dry before sitting on one of the benches to watch Heggle fuss around the fire. She shuffled about the hearth, head covered by a shapeless kirtle dyed the same awful blood-red worn by the soldiers. Her threadbare shawl was likewise dyed, stretched thin over her sizable hunch. Her large, sagging breasts hung past her waist, swinging beneath her filthy smock. Wrinkled and spotted, her grey skin fell loosely, especially at the neck where it dangled freely under a chin ornamented with long, stiff white hairs. She spoke foully and smelled sour, but, for all her loathsomeness, she was a fine cook and had presented Padric with a never-ending torrent of rich meals and delicacies. He did not possess much of an appetite and pushed most of it away untouched. Although Heggle hung at his elbow eagerly awaiting his reaction, she never became discouraged at his lack of enthusiasm or praise.

"Heggle'll find what you fancy, sure as shite," she would say.

"All me lords had their favorite and we'll tickle yours ere long."

She kept up a steady stream of chatter while she worked, often about the many litters of fine goblins she had borne over her long life and once remarked that Torcan might be one of her sons, but she could not clearly recall.

"I'd still be squattin' 'em out, if any o'these gutless wonders had the stones to get on ol'Heggle and grunt. They's all 'fraid I eat their pricks off!"

But her favorite subject was the Goblin Kings. From the legends Padric could remember, it appeared as if she had cooked for all of them, and a wistful glow of pride played across her ugly face whenever she spoke about the long dead tyrants.

"Capon! That was Hogulent's choice, with applemoy I remember, and all the Sweyns loved me mortrews . . . ceptin' that last one. He was more for umbles. Ebraucus, now! His Grace were always too busy ruttin' the wenches to eat proper and his son were worse'n he. Whore masters, the both of 'em! Guess'n you could say they's favorite was suckin' clams!" Heggle had told him this at least half a dozen times, but she cackled louder with every telling.

"Now that slut queen we had for a bit, she ne'er let me serve, slapped Heggle's face and called us a witch, but the Jerrods . . . oh they was princes through and true! The first one, he craved whelks all the time and Jerrod Second, he was apt for bacon collops."

Padric had ignored her for two days, but today his bitter mood got the best of him. "What about the Gaunt Prince?" he asked, pushing away the dishes she set before him. "What was his dish?"

"Roast fawn," Heggle said with a longing smile. "Or kid or lamb. I used to stuff 'em with coney, under a year old. My lord loved his flesh young." She fixed him with a calculating eye and her head nodded with matronly approval. "You favor him."

Padric glared at her, fighting the impulse to throw the steaming platters in her face. "What was he like?" he managed through clenched teeth, furious at his own morbid curiosity.

"My Gaunt Lord," Heggle said, tasting the name and finding it sweet, "He were tall, so tall . . . and graceful. He fought like a song, nought on above his waist, skin like milk, bejeweled red with the blood o'our enemies. And clever! Like a fox . . . he was crafty as I ever saw. And hungry. He were forever hungry."

She looked so happy as she spoke, lost in memory. Padric felt a cruel urge, wanting nothing but to shatter her joy. "And he is dead," he spat at her. "Feeding the worms for nine hundred years."

Heggle opened her eyes and looked at him, but it was confusion, not pain, that filled her face. "So long?" she asked the serving board. "Aye, I would guess it 'tis. Makes no matter. Heggle'll never forget." She went back to her preparations. "And I beg forgiveness for speakin' such, but you are wrong, my Lord. Nine hundred years, his eyes been closed for sure, but nothin' has eaten at him, no. He remains as comely and fine as the day I first see's him."

Padric's brow wrinkled. "Remains? Heggle, you have seen him?"

"Oh aye," a girlish excitement fell over the crone as she leaned in and whispered. "And you'll too, afore long. Torcan will take you, you'll see."

Padric sat in the longhouse, thoughts more troubled than before. A cold, steady rain fell throughout the day and he remained shut in with Heggle, pondering her disturbing words. Could the Red Caps still possess the body of a man almost a thousand years old? In the stories, the Gaunt Prince knew terrible spells, but what malevolence could preserve a corpse centuries beyond when it should rightfully have turned to dust? It was not within Padric's understanding. His father was a farmer, a good, hard-working man of the soil, and his mother, a gentle spirit of deep patience eclipsed only by a silent inner strength. Such people could not be connected to all of this madness.

Torcan sought Kederic's wife, some long-lost heir to the men the goblins had crowned. The thought that Padric's mother had once been wed to a warlord from Sasana was laughable. That she could also be the inheritor of some dread Magic was unthinkable. She was not Kederic's wife. Did that mean she was not Padric's mother?

No! He refused to believe that. Let Slouch Hat and Torcan and this toothless sow say what they want, but he would not dishonor the only family and love he had known in this merciless world. Whatever his origins, he was not a puppet of the past, and he would prove it if it meant his life.

That night, his honor guard came knocking and brought him to the mead hall that Torcan had made his personal quarters.

Padric paused at the entrance, gazing at the crude cage of lashed wood that hung from a pole not far from the hall. Two Red Caps stood nearby, their torches spitting angrily in the wet wind from the sea, granting flickering glimpses of the cage's lone occupant.

Kederic Winetongue huddled against the wet and the cold, his hair and beard drenched and greasy. He hunkered at the bottom of the cage, trying to crawl into himself for warmth, sodden and shivering.

Padric heard him issue a series of damp, choking coughs and stood for a long time watching, but the Thegn never looked up to meet his eyes.

Inside the hall, the thick smells of wet dogs, unwashed men and strong mead filled Padric's nostrils, settling in the back of his throat. Around the central fire, men and goblins drank and laughed with one another, throwing dice and knives with equal recklessness, while the serving women made their way around with heavy jugs, refilling horns and trying to avoid the rough attention of both Fae and mortal. Torcan Swinehelm sat in the high seat on a platform at the rear of the hall, surrounded by the brutish captains of the raider ships. Each of these men was broad and burly, wearing cruelty as easily as the many rings on their fingers, laughter bellowing out from behind beards of yellow, red and black.

At Torcan's beckoning, Padric was led up to the platform where a seat waited for him on the goblin leader's right hand. The Middangeard captains stared at him and issued boisterous comments in their strange tongue, clapping each other on the back and laughing heartily before one of them thrust a sloshing horn into his hand. Padric drained it in four long pulls, the mead filling his mouth with sweetness and his head with silk. The men shouted their approval at this display, but Padric was not interested in impressing them. He just wanted to rid himself of his wits, so that he might endure this raucous gathering. The bear of a man on his left dragged a wench over to refill Padric's horn, beaming broadly and talking to him in the lilting language of the fjordmen.

"Arnheir says kings grow small in Airlann," Torcan translated without looking over, his eyes fixed on the crowded room. "But at least you have a royal thirst."

Padric took another deep drink from his horn. "Tell Arnheir . . . that I am no king."

"No," Torcan said with a strange smile. "Not yet. And it makes no matter to these louts. They follow only the promise of wealth."

"These salt-blooded whoresons have plundered the Tin Isles for years," Padric said while smiling at the captains, raising his horn in salute. "Any wealth we had, they stole long ago."

"The baubles of man," Torcan scoffed, "are nothing compared to the treasures of the dwarves."

"So that was their price," Padric tried not to glower too strongly at the men surrounding him.

Torcan nodded. "For all their boasting, these men have troubles of their own. Their homeland is a frozen and thankless waste, home to giants and trolls. That is why they spend so much of every year raiding these shores. Only the dwarves know how to prosper in Middangeard and these dogs are a jealous bunch."

"So they help you conquer Airlann and you return the favor in Middangeard," Padric scoffed. "They are fools to trust you."

Torcan looked over at him, a knowing gleam in his eye. "It is not me they trust, my lord."

"I am lord of nothing."

"So you were raised to believe," Torcan said mildly. "They hid you well."

"Who?" Padric asked. "Who hid me?"

"The Seelie Court . . . in the beginning," Torcan said with disgust. "Then as the years crawled on and their power dwindled, they passed the burden to lesser beings. It has taken us too long to find the scions of our Lord King and it appears we were ignorant of an entire generation."

"And you might have remained ignorant forever," Padric had to laugh. "Twice you almost killed me, goblin."

"Twice?" Torcan seemed more intrigued than surprised.

Padric nodded. "I stood with the men of Hog's Wallow alongside Faabar of the Brindlebacks against you and that flame-drunk wizard." Padric glanced around the hall. "We do not have the pleasure of his company?"

"He has other duties far from here," Torcan said with a wry smile. "But you are right my Lord, we were careless. We sought a woman. I gave orders to spare the females, but the men . . ." He waved his goblet dismissively.

"Would that I had burned with all the rest," Padric muttered, "and denied you your prize."

"The Magic within your veins may be dormant," Torcan said, leaning over the arm of his chair and growing more passionate with every word. "Unused. Untrained. But it is no less potent in its protection of you. It was not fortune that spared your life. I was destined to find you, my Lord! The days of searching are over! I will restore your birthright and show you from what greatness you issue. Your sons will know dominion over Airlann and lead the goblins back to their deserved station!"

Padric watched as the goblin flushed with anticipation, the frustration giving way to lusts for vengeance and glory. "You are wrong," Padric told him. "Your search has not ended. I am not who you believe me to be."

Swinehelm regarded him for a long uncomfortable moment, then looked past him and spoke rapidly to the man called Arnheir in his own language. The captain nodded, responded simply and then returned to his carousing.

Torcan stood. "Come with me."

The goblin led him through the rear door of the hall and they stepped out into cold, open air. Several Red Caps stood just outside complaining about the rain, but they ceased their muttering when Torcan appeared and fell in behind as he continued walking away from the hall towards a small storehouse squatting in the dark.

Two more goblins were posted near the storehouse door and with a wave of his hand, Torcan ordered them to open it and then stepped aside, indicating that Padric should enter with a nod. The smell of salted fish hung about the room, but Padric could see nothing until Torcan stepped in with a torch he had taken from one the guards. Harsh orange light filled the cramped space and Padric stared grimly at the back wall.

The goblins had nailed Slouch Hat up with iron spikes through his elbows, his body hanging limply. The hat which gave the husk his name lay upon the earthen floor and his stuffed sack head lifted slowly when they entered.

"Tell him," Torcan commanded.

Slouch Hat's laugh was a dry rustle. "Did not believe you, Red Cap?"

"*Tell* him," Torcan repeated.

"Perhaps," Padric suggested, "if you left us, the husk would be more agreeable."

Torcan chewed on this a moment. "I must attend the captains," he said at last, handing the torch to Padric. He thrust a finger at Slouch Hat. "Convince him or you burn!"

When the goblin was gone, Padric tried to pull the spikes from the wall, but they were embedded deep, the broad heads holding the husk's limbs firmly.

"What did you tell him?" Padric asked, doubling his efforts.

"I am not a Goblin King."

"Of course not," Slouch Hat said.

Padric stopped, releasing his grip on the nail. "But you told Torcan—"

"What he wanted to hear," Slouch Hat said. "Fanatics are easily manipulated."

Padric's knees went weak. Relief bent him double and he sucked in air from between his legs. The odor of salted fish did not help his stomach and he fought the need to vomit. At last, his innards settled back in their proper places and he was able to raise his head.

"Why?" he managed.

"Would you rather have a slit throat from one of Acwellen's curs?" Slouch Hat asked. "For me, pinned to a wall is preferred to being a pile of ash."

"You saved our lives." Padric had not meant to say it aloud.

"For now," Slouch Hat responded. "Only as long as the ruse holds."

"Best tell me the ruse then."

The husk nodded and spoke quickly.

"Mostly I told Torcan the truth. I was once in the service of a wandering sage, a goodly man whose intelligence was surpassed only by his near obsession for chronicling the history of the Fae Rebellion. For over forty years, I travelled the reaches of Airlann at his side, helping record the events of that war. At last, we came to Hog's Wallow, so my master might study Bwenyth Tor and the siege that happened there. But he was near seventy and growing feeble. He never reached the top of the Tor. The gnomes had long left the village, but the shepherds and farmers allowed me to bury my master in their barrows. I remained, teaching the children and offering myself in service to the reeve. More than sixty years past and I now served the reeve's grandson."

"Brogan," Padric put in.

"Yes," the husk replied. "And then Kederic Winetongue came with his warriors and built his fort. That the Thegn was a capable man was obvious, but I felt there was something troubled about him . . . something linked to his hatred of the Fae. That he had lost a wife before coming to the Wallow was much whispered, but one night, while drinking with Brogan, I overheard the Thegn mention a child. He was well in his cups and near rambling, but it was there. When I realized Torcan sought the Thegn's wife, I reacted quickly. From my time with my first master, I know much of the Goblin Kings and the Red Caps' crusade to find their heirs, so I gambled that was who Torcan believed the Thegn's wife to be. Why else would the Red Caps seek a human woman?"

"But how did you convince Torcan I was her son?" Padric asked.

"I did not," Slouch Hat said. "Kederic did."

"Kederic?" Padric was puzzled. "But he—"

"Is no fool."

"But why would he lie to protect me?"

"Maybe so they would stop torturing him for answers," Slouch Hat replied. "Or maybe because it is not you he protects."

"No." Padric saw it. "He protects the real heir."

Slouch Hat nodded. "As long as they believe you to be their ruler, they need not hunt any longer. Be it his wife or the child she may have borne, Kederic knows they are safer with a pretender in their place."

"So that is what I have become." Padric was both disgusted and grateful. "A pretender?"

"Until we can find a means of escape . . . yes."

Padric stared at the floor, his thoughts darkening.

"Impossible. There are thousands of goblins out there. We will be discovered and then we will die."

"Yes," Slouch Hat said, his tone forcing Padric to look at him. "But the Red Caps are set on conquest and are ready to declare war on Airlann. However they plan to do it, they must be stopped. The longer we remain in their company, the greater chance we have to thwart them. Would you rather die now, uselessly . . . or wait until you can sell your life dearly at the moment it may matter most?"

Padric looked into the husk's hollow, black eyes and smiled.

"Never thought I would find myself a king."

"Rule wisely," Slouch Hat said with his dry laugh.

"I best go," Padric said bending, picking up the husk's hat and placing it back over his head. He turned to leave, but a thought gave him pause. "Slouch Hat," he said turning back. "What if I had been the true heir?"

The husk stared at him from the deep shadow under his wide brim. "I would have let them kill you."

Outside the storehouse, Padric found his familiar honor guard waiting and they fell into step behind him. He had no intention of going back to the mead hall, he had too much to think on, so he made straight for his longhouse. He might be able to convince Torcan to let him have Slouch Hat as a servant, if he were careful. Husks were greatly prized, and it would only make him appear more formidable to have one at his side. Getting the Thegn free would be trickier and more dangerous, but Padric knew he needed to speak with the man, inform him that he now knew the truth. Three against thousands were better odds, after all.

He dreaded another night with Heggle. The crone slept on a pallet at the foot of the bed, snuffling and snoring, but tonight it would be of little concern. Padric did not expect to rest easy for some time. When he entered the longhouse, he found the old goblin was not the only one waiting for him. Two women knelt on the fur rugs near the fire dressed in short shifts of thin linen.

Heggle rushed forward, almost panting and pressed a goblet of mulled wine into his hand.

"What is this?" he asked, staring at the strangers.

"Milord," she said gesturing to the women. "The raider captains have sent you gifts."

At this both women stood, revealing them to be tall and full-bodied, obviously of Middangearder stock. The raven-haired one regarded him boldly, her sloe-eyed stare twinkling above sensual lips pursed in the slightest secretive smile. The flaxen-haired girl kept her head bowed, hands folded in front of her, trying not to shake and failing pitifully. Padric noticed their feet were bare, but clean. Clearly brought here and then prepared for him. He hoped for their sakes, not by Heggle.

"No," Padric said setting the wine aside. "This is not needed. Send them back."

"Back?" Heggle smiled as if he had jested. "Back where, my king? They was taken in feud and brought for your grace. To warm his bed."

Padric tried not to look at the women. He felt ashamed.

The Middangearders were well known for preying upon each other and taking their neighbor's women for thralls. Likely these two saw their kin put to the sword and their homes burnt on the frozen banks of some far off fjord, just so they could be presented to a false king in tribute. The blonde girl still had not looked up, and while the dark one could not understand his words, she read his demeanor clear enough. Her seductive eyes now held a strange mix of fear and fury, and she held her chin a little higher, daring him to reject her.

"You are tired, my lord," Heggle said soothingly. "Give one a tumble and then sleep. I reckon you could take both afore your strength flees."

He looked down at the hunchback in disgust. "Enough."

Heggle hobbled over to where the women stood. "They's supple and young," she said grabbing the blonde girl's hips in her gnarled hands and squeezing hard, causing the poor girl to whimper. "Give you many strong bairns before they dry up."

Padric took two solid steps and wrenched Heggle away by the wrist. "Leave her be. They are not brood mares!"

Heggle rubbed her wrist and leered up at him. "Likely part o'milord is akin to a horse, so tall and fine he is!"

"Shut your foul mouth," Padric commanded. "I will hear no more from you."

He turned to the quivering girl and went to put his hands on her arms, then thought better of it and looked to the dark-haired woman.

"Could you?" he gestured at the blonde girl and then at the large bed, using broad gestures. "Help her?"

She must have understood, for she took her companion and guided her to the bed, all the while watching Padric, trying to riddle out his very existence. Soon, the fair-haired one was safely enveloped in the furs and, tended by the sultry wench, quieted down into a fitful sleep. Padric paced about, careful not to take a step towards the bed. Heggle skulked off to her stinking nest of blankets and it was not long before Padric heard the off-putting sounds of her slumber. The fire burned low and the night grew old and still Padric stood in thought. The raven girl had drifted to sleep but Padric remained awake, dispossessed in his own cell.

He schemed in silence, eventually sinking down into a chair by the hearth. He stoked the coals and added more turf until the flames kindled once more, dispelling the chill and the dark. He must have drifted off, for when he woke the fire had returned to embers. Something stirred in the dark and Padric sat up, fearing he would find Heggle disturbing the women. But it was not the goblin he saw coming towards him.

The phantom flicker of the dead fire revealed brief, hot glimpses of her face, the outline of cheek, neck and shoulder. Her hair ate the glow, black as the room around her approaching body.

Her hands came up and the shift fell weightless to the floor, the full swells of hip and thigh now carved out of the shadow. She knelt before him, her hands gliding firmly up his legs, the pleasant, torturous weight of her breasts pressing into his lap. He could hear her breathing as she arched up to meet him, eyes reflecting wetly in the meager light. He felt her mouth part, wet heat playing against his ear, moving down to bite exquisitely into the flesh of his neck.

One hand entangled in her hair, the other grabbing at her jaw, Padric pulled her up and tasted her, lost in the rolls of her tongue and the undulations of her body. Half mad with fatigue and desire, Padric felt a sudden rising panic, the wanton dream spiraling into a supine nightmare. He was prisoner and pretender, a condemned man staving off death with only wits and words and now this woman threatened to devour what little mastery he retained over himself.

Padric lurched to his feet, dragging her up with him awkwardly and harder than he intended. She gave a strained hiss of pain and surprise, his sudden aggression causing her to struggle against his clutching hands. They stumbled around the chair and Padric released his hold. The woman barely kept her footing in the dark room and retreated back to the bed, where the commotion had awakened the other girl. Heggle sat up in her pallet, a horrible lump of shapelessness. Padric could not stay in this place any longer and bolted for the door.

He startled his guards when he came stomping out into the depressing haze only worn by the pre-dawn sky. Without waiting for the goblins' reaction to his early rising, he began walking. He had no destination in mind, but his feet took him away from the sea and towards the Red Cap camp. His body and mind limped along in a fog of exhaustion, yearning for only the basest needs of sleep, food, and companionship, everything he had just fled. A quick, near delirious laugh escaped his throat and Padric could not help but shake his head. A witch, a frightened girl and a willing thrall. If only he could add a husk to his royal household of slaves and spies.

Much of the camp still slept, the goblins crammed inside decrepit field tents. A few stirred about, fetching water or relieving themselves, while others sat huddled around the cook fires, staring blankly into the thick, white smoke. Padric picked his way along, shivering without the cloak he had left in the longhouse. He marveled at the sheer number of goblins and remembered the fear he felt when only a fraction had come screaming into Hog's Wallow, thirsty for blood. Wherever this army was pointed, they needed to be warned and Padric plied his brain for a solution, but met with failure.

As he and his escort approached the edge of the camp, the Meadow began to lose the battle with the hills and rocks that invaded most of Airlann. Sentries stood watch, looking away from their sleeping fellows and into the bank of fog running rampant across the world before the sun appeared to chase it away. Padric noticed a sizable group of Red Caps standing ready near something large. As he approached, he saw it was a heavily laden wagon. The shapeless load was covered in sailcloth and tied down with heavy rope. Four sleepy oxen were yoked to the wagon and the two goblins that sat on the driver's bench were impatiently listening to instructions from a Red Cap on the ground.

"We puttin' heel to ground on the morrow," he lectured. "And affer we's thru with Black Pool, we on to you, so no tarryin'! Got to get them with the rest and made ready."

At least fifty Red Caps, all armed with billhooks and poleaxes, stood around the wagon waiting to march, but Padric strode past them without a care, the hopelessness in his heart making him bold.

"Oi there!" the commander shouted, jumping between Padric and the wagon.

Padric took a solid step forward, shooting his arm out to grasp the goblin by the front of his iron studded jerkin. He pulled him roughly forward, until the bulbous nose almost touched his own.

"Stand aside," he growled and watched as the bloodshot eyes widened in fear. The Red Cap tried to stammer something, but Padric shoved him aside, reaching up to pull a span of the sailcloth out from under the ropes. Something heavy dislodged as he did so, and a large metal hand fell out from under the covering, the iron fingers easily large enough to encompass and crush Padric's head.

He wrestled the cloth further away and knelt low, staring up into the wagon bed. A jumble of rusted parts lay heavily upon each other. Among them a great head, face forged with a vaguely human countenance, stared back at him.

"How many?" Padric demanded of the commander, shoving the covering back down.

"F-four complete, my lord," the goblin answered. "And pieces for maybe two others."

"Where," Padric pressed. "Where are they bound?"

The Red Cap hesitated, eyes jerking right and left, feebly searching for aid.

"Where?!"

"C-castle Gaunt, my lord."

Padric straightened, then put on a satisfied smile. "Very well. Best get moving then. Our good Flame Binder will be awaiting these most eagerly."

His statement was rewarded by the relief on the commander's face.

"All right you lot!" the goblin recaptured his authority with vigor. "You heard His Grace, get moving!"

The wagon and its escort turned slowly and made its plodding way out of camp. Padric watched them go. Torcan said the Flame Binder had duties far from here and now he knew where.

The once personal demesne of the sorcerer for which it was named, Castle Gaunt was a cursed ruin, brooding atop its hulking rock somewhere to the west, near the center of the isle. So, Torcan was collecting the lifeless remains of the Forge Born and sending them to the Flame Binder at the hated stronghold. It sounded as if this army would march on Black Pool then head on to Castle Gaunt.

More information he now impotently possessed.

He made his way back to the settlement, hunger gnawing at his gut. Maybe he could get something from one of the fishwives and avoid Heggle completely. No, he must return some time, for sleep if naught else. He did not know what would be required of him in the days ahead and he would need his strength as well as his wits if he had any hope of maintaining this deadly mummery.

Freeing Slouch Hat was of the utmost importance, as was speaking with Kederic. But his encounter at the wagon had taught him something; the goblins feared him. Equal boldness at the Thegn's cage could prove fruitful. If nothing else, he would discover the length of his tether.

The sun had just cleared the choppy waters beyond the harbor when Padric returned to the longhouse. It would accomplish nothing to hide from his vile servant and he had to do something about the slave girls. He found Heggle preparing the morning meal and the blonde girl sweeping out the longhouse, head bent to the broom. Of the other woman there was no sign.

"Heggle," Padric asked, "Where is the other—"

"Not to worry, my lord," she answered, looking up from her stewpot and smiling broadly. "She will no trouble you n'more."

Padric felt ice travel down his spine and land in his gut.

"What did you do?"

"I went straight away to his lord Swinehelm, I did," Heggle said as she worked. "Told him that black-haired hussy had displeased his Grace, and he sent the raiders to fetch her back. You won't have to suffer her again."

"What?" Padric made for the door. "Where did they take her?"

"Down to the water's edge, o'course," Heggle said simply. "Disobedient thralls is always given to the waves."

Padric flew out the door, passing his guards in a bolt and out distancing them with long, pumping strides, their hollers of protest ignored behind him. He made straight for the rocky shore, knocking over a pair of fishermen in his reckless flight. In his bouncing vision he saw a small group of fjordsmen struggling in the surf, their cloaks drenched to black. When he skidded to a halt, breath burning in his ears, they were hauling something out of the water. The men dumped her carelessly, face down on the dark stones, her naked flesh shining white. Her once lustrous locks of jet were a wet mass of tangles and sand. Padric fell to his knees and turned her over as the water crept up the beach, washing over his hands and her drowned face. Her dark eyes looked up at him, unblinking, the luster gone, leaving only the accusing stare of the dead.

One of the men said something in their unintelligible tongue and the others laughed. Padric leapt up snarling and slammed his fist into a smiling mouth. He did not know if it was the one who spoke and he did not care, he simply beat into the man with a fury, following him down as he fell, never ceasing his torrent of blows. The others shouted angrily and Padric felt arms jerking him away from the pulpy face and a hard blow sunk into his gut, churning the air out of his body in a sickening rush. Another set of hard knuckles glanced off his skull above the eye and he fell into the salty grit. Boots kicked savagely at his head, shoulder and hip as he curled up to protect himself. Over the dense sound of strikes to his own body, he heard a blood-curdling series of cries and then screams of fear. The kicks stopped suddenly and Padric felt something rain down upon him in hot droplets. He peeked out from his cradling arms to see one of the men kneeling, gripping at his throat, blood pumping between his fingers and lips. Another lay in the surf, the foam turning an ugly pink as it sloshed over his slashed flesh. Padric rolled to his feet and found his escort swinging their halberds in bloody arcs into the upraised arms and pleading faces of the sailors. The last was on his back, trying to crawl backwards on his hands and feet, a pitifully ludicrous image right up until one of the Red Caps rammed a broad axe into his gut.

Padric stood, dripping blood and salt water, eyes wide to the butchery, trying to find his voice and put a stop to the goblins' savagery, but only a wordless, bestial groan came forth. One of the Red Caps rushed to his side, the blade of his weapon covered in gore.

"Are ye well, my King?" he asked, genuine concern showing in his large, bloodshot eyes. Padric nodded dumbly, and stared at the bodies on the beach. Among the fallen, his eyes again found the woman. Burning bile filled his throat, and anger pulsed through him, fueled by the pains of his bleeding wounds.

He stumbled off the beach, struggling up the rocky embankment and back to the longhouse. He kicked through the door, startling the girl and sending her cowering against the wall. Heggle remained busy at the serving board and smiled at him as he entered, heedless of his grisly appearance. He made straight for her, knocking the board aside and sending vegetables flying. The hunchback tried to dance awkwardly out of his reach, but he caught her fast, kicked her feet out from under her, spilling her to floor.

"You!" he screamed into her repugnant face. "Why?! Why?!"

He shook her roughly, causing her head to thump repeatedly into the boards. Her lips peeled back in a contemptible grimace, purple gums hissing wetly. He heard the heavy boots of his guards slam on the floor as they entered the room. Padric jerked Heggle up roughly and tossed her towards them. She spilled heavily at their feet, her wrinkled face full of hurt and hatred.

"Get out!" he screamed at his guards as they helped the crone stand. "And take that hag with you! Tell the Swinehelm that I wish to see him here. Go now!"

The goblins backed out, leaving Padric to stalk about the broken room. The girl remained curled against the wall, shoulders heaving with muffled sobs. Padric did not approach her, knowing he looked a fearsome maniac, soaked with water and blood. There was a cut above his eye where the sailor had struck him and it seeped steadily down his cheek, dripping off his chin Torcan Swinehelm arrived swiftly and alone. He stepped into the room, not bothering a glance at the wrecked furniture or the weeping girl.

"You summoned me?" he asked, a strange inflection in his voice.

"Yes," Padric replied, knowing he should choose his words carefully, but too incensed for much caution. "I want Heggle removed from my service and replaced with the husk. And no more women! I am well pleased with this girl and she shall not be removed without my consent. If you want me to be king, then let us begin building a proper court. Kederic Winetongue is to be removed from that cage and treated with the respect deserved him. Consider these my first commands. I expect them to be carried out."

A smile played across Torcan's scarred face. "Or what?"

Padric glared down at the goblin warlord, but before he could answer, Torcan continued. "I think you have forgotten who commands here, boy! You may be the descendant of the Gaunt Prince, but you have languished in ignorance, the power within you allowed to lie fallow for centuries. You have no knowledge, no craft and you mistake your place here. If my words offend you, then please, punish my insolence. Unleash the dread Magic known by your ancestors and wreak your vengeance upon my treasonous tongue!"

Torcan paused, waiting, but all Padric could do was stare back at him.

"No?" Torcan asked. "Well until you can do that, you are nothing but a figure-head. A banner for my goblins to rally under. And a source of seed for your formerly glorious line. Prove your worth and get this wench with a swollen belly that we might raise a new king. One which has not been made weak by the molly-coddling of mortals! You say she pleases you well? Show me! Or I will dispose of her and keep looking until I find one that does."

With those words Torcan turned and walked out of the longhouse.

Padric slumped to the floor where he stood, cradling his face in his bruised hands. There was nothing he could do. He had no power, no skill, no allies. All he had was a lie and he wielded it clumsily enough to get innocents killed. Slouch Hat was wrong.

There would be no moment for glory. All there would be was an ugly death after helplessly witnessing days upon days of other ugly deaths.

Something brushed his knuckles. The touch was slight, trembling. He looked up and found the blonde girl crouched in front of him on the floor. Her hand floated reluctantly between them, her face ready to dart back into hiding. He reached up slowly and took her hand, wrapping it in his own, uncertain whether it was comfort she sought or meant to give. Their eyes met and Padric looked at her for the first time. Her eyes were blue and bright and he found compassion beyond the fear; a recognition of despair.

Padric could not save Hog's Wallow. He could do nothing to warn Black Pool. Airlann would need to be saved by greater champions than he. But this woman, this one unfortunate person, her he could save. He took one hand away from hers and touched his chest.

"Padric," he said and then gestured to her.

Her mouth worked slowly, her chin dipping slightly, coaxing the words out. "Svala."

"Svala," he repeated softly and smiled. She smiled back, and he found it beautiful.

EIGHTEEN

Backbone stood patiently while Old Lochlann loaded him down with sacks of provisions. Occasionally, he would twitch an ear or offer a slow blink, but he did not budge one hoof or voice one bay of complaint. Pocket thought he was the best mule in the world.

"Are you coming with us?" he asked Old Lochlann while handing him another bundle.

The old man shook his head. "My place is here."

"But are you not afraid for when the goblins come?"

"Not my first siege," Lochlann shrugged. "And if it's my last, more's the good. Unpleasant is a city under siege."

"Well," Pocket said, "I wish you were coming with us." Just so long as someone else did the cooking.

"Sir said wither you are bound?" Lochlann asked with a grunt, cinching at the load ropes.

"No," Pocket replied. "Only that we are leaving tonight. He wants to go when it is dark. Lady Rosheen is coming with us!"

Lochlann did not respond to that, just creased his wrinkled face further in concentration at his task. Pocket went to stroke Backbone's nose, wishing he had an apple to give him. It was hours before sundown and Pocket was worried the mule would have to stand with his burden for too long, but Sir Corc had instructed that everything be prepared lest they have to leave suddenly. The knight had taken Bantam Flyn into the city so they could visit the foundling houses and warn the matrons of the impending attack.

Flyn had complained about the errand, calling it 'noble and useless', a phrase he had often uttered since being told of their departure.

Actually, the squire was quite happy to leave Black Pool behind until he discovered that their flight was a response to the coming Red Cap attack. Now, he wanted to stay, and constantly urged Sir Corc that they would be of greater service in defense of the walls.

As always, the knight remained immovable.

Pocket felt confused and a little ashamed. Sir Corc was running from a fight. Pocket had never heard of a knight fleeing before. Bantam Flyn was only a squire and he wanted to stay and fight the goblins, defend the people. No one could question *his* bravery. Pocket had seen him fight with his own eyes in the tourney where he had won Coalspur; a tourney that Sir Corc had not even entered. During his long days in the Roost, Pocket used to dream of Sir Corc's visits, awaiting his return with barely contained excitement. Moragh used to tire of his asking when the knight would next appear at the castle. The day he left the Roost was the saddest of his life, until he realized he would be accompanying the knight on grand adventures in Airlann. Then his spirits soared, but thus far, nothing had been so grand. Pocket often found himself wishing he was with Bronze Wattle or Blood Yolk. Surely, they would not be skulking away from Black Pool in the middle of the night.

Lochlann tied the last of the knots and they left Backbone in the little stone stable behind the townhouse, but not before Pocket made sure he had plenty of water. Noon was only an hour old and the day was surprisingly sunny and warm. Back in Albain, the castle servants would be cleaning for the coming spring, but here in Airlann, where autumn never ended, it was windy, wet and cold more often than not. Not wanting to squander the favorable weather and having nothing else to occupy his time until nightfall, Pocket stayed out in the court garden, sitting in his usual spot along the wall to practice changing his skin. Lady Rosheen had insisted it was most important to relax; that a calm mind was more likely to manifest the change, and, of course, she was right. Pocket had discovered more about his changeling abilities in the short time he had known the piskie than in all the years he struggled with them alone in the Roost.

He started slowly, watching the backs of his hands as the skin darkened, ignoring the itching sensation that always followed as the hairs extended, growing into a thicker coat across his flesh.

Rosheen had told him that his skin was not only the surface of his body, but also the surface of his gift. She said that with dedication it would one day be possible to change his muscles, his bones, even his very organs and fully become the object of his mimicry. He was only half gruagach and would be limited by the small stature that would forever mark him as a gurg, but even within the confines of his body the possibilities made Pocket's dreams dance.

He thought of the small, black dog owned by the rat catcher that patrolled the streets around the townhouse. Despite its lack of size, it was no less fierce than the war hounds which often accompanied the city watch, and Pocket had seen it attack a teeming nest of vicious vermin with no hint of fear. It was always outnumbered and suffered the bites from dozens of assailants as the rats defended their home, but the dog stood its ground, dispatching one enemy at a time until it stood alone and victorious.

The courtyard gate swung in hard, banging into the stone wall with a sharp clang that left it shuddering on its hinges. Bantam Flyn strode hotly through, his arm still thrust forward from its assault on the gate. He glowered at the door to the townhouse and did not even glance in Pocket's direction as he pushed it open with the same conviction he had shown the previous portal and vanished inside. The vibrating gate had settled down and swung back into place by the time Sir Corc entered the courtyard. He wore the same exhausted frustration that always settled over him after quarreling with the squire. Pocket watched as the knight stood in the yard, lost in thought and wondered what he was thinking. At last, he came out of his careworn mind and looked over. Pocket perked up. Sir Corc had hardly spoken to him since their arrival in the city. Now maybe, Pocket could ask some of the questions that had troubled him. Where were they going? And why? He saw reluctance in Sir Corc's face, as if the he were struggling over the decision to approach, and Pocket waited patiently. His heart fell when Sir Corc turned and entered the house without a word.

The tight quarters in the townhouse became nigh on suffocating as the smell of the turf fire filled the common room.

The silence and boredom had been tedious throughout the day, but now, as night came on, it was becoming unbearable. Rosheen sat as far from the smoky hearth as she was able, atop an oaken cabinet near the stairs. She could hear the old servant puttering about the kitchen, washing up after the hot, brown, bubbling substance he had served for an evening meal. The knight was secluded behind the door of the solar and had not emerged to sup.

Clever coburn.

Pocket had been sent to his bed in the garret before the sun had set, so that he would have the strength for their over-night journey. Rosheen had expected him to offer up some protest, but the sweet gurg had merely mumbled his goodnights and went up without complaint. At least he was away from the sullen gloom that hung in the close air.

Bantam Flyn sat in a chair by the fire, searching the flames for a culprit to the crimes against his pride. The huge sword that was the young coburn's shadow sat propped next to the hearth, untended by oil or whetstone. This night, it seemed, Flyn was content to simply sit and brood. She did not know how much Corc had told him about the coming invasion, but whatever knowledge Flyn possessed did not sit well with him.

He wants to fight. It is all he knows.

Rosheen had known some coburn in her time, but never long enough to call them familiar. They were not Fae, and thus their years were short, often dying well before what a human would call elderly, but that was mostly due to their warlike ways. The origins of the coburn were murky and not even the elves could say from whence they came. The first of them were not encountered until after the Usurpation, during those awful years when many Fae were forced to live wild in the forests and mountains for fear of the Red Caps and the unjust laws of the Goblin Kings. The first coburn was quite literally stumbled upon by chance. In those days, they were uncouth and barbarous, the males jealously guarding their clutches against outsiders and others of their own kind, wielding nothing but crude clubs and their deadly spurs. But the Seelie Court, even one dispossessed and hiding, was wise and saw much capacity for good within this proud race. They slowly gained the trust of the coburn and taught them language and many of the males took well to the elvish ideals of honorable combat. After many years of tutelage and careful interference, the elves were able to forge the Order of the Valiant Spur, and the coburn that fought under its banner helped win the Rebellion.

The coburn had never known community, as each male individually governed and guarded his mates and their young, an instinct which persisted. Rosheen knew the oaths of the Order forbid coupling, and no female coburn were allowed in its stronghold as it would awaken the warriors' territorial nature and destroy their brotherhood. Many coburn still lived in the old way and, indeed, must for the race to survive. Only the most strong-willed males show up at the Roost, forsaking their drive to breed and covet. Flyn was most certainly an exceptional individual, but that heat remained in his blood and Rosheen saw it well. She only hoped Corc did, too.

Rosheen stifled a yawn and flapped her wings to dispel her weariness. At Sir Corc's request, she had spent the entire day perched on Black Pool's outer wall, watching for some sign of an approaching army. According to that ridiculous hobgoblin, Muckle, they still had at least another day before the Red Caps would reach the city, but the knight was not taking any chances and instructed Rosheen to fly back and report to him at even the slightest inclination of attack. So she had flitted from turret roof to battlement to gatehouse and back again, watching the horizons from west to south. The men and goblins of the city watch also walked the walls in greater numbers and Rosheen was relieved to see the Lord of the Pile had not completely dismissed their warning.

But she was still not convinced the city could hold. It was fortified well enough, with thick walls of stone guarding every landward approach, tall as ten men and interrupted by only two gates, each protected by a portcullis and strong doors banded in iron. In addition to the city watch, Black Pool was home to scores of mercenaries from across the Tin Isles, but rather than add strength to the city they offered only more uncertainty. A sellsword swings to the side of the last coin it was dealt. By its very nature Black Pool was a haven for the itinerant, each resident using the city as a refuge for whatever private ambition they pursued or crime they fled. Could the city's discordant inhabitants rally under the common cause of saving their home? Rosheen dared not hope.

By dusk, she had seen nothing to alert suspicion and returned to the townhouse as instructed to await the fullness of night. Sir Corc wanted to leave when most of the city slept, for reasons he would not share. Rosheen wondered how he planned on exiting the city, as the Lord of the Pile had ordered both gates shut and barred after sundown. Some of her ire for Corc had dwindled since their meeting with Black Pool's disturbing potentate and she no longer questioned his every decision, but the knight's laconic manner continued to annoy her. She trusted him, she would be foolish not to, but that did not mean she was unaware that he kept secrets.

Perhaps that is why the Order chose you, you tight-lipped rooster.

Rosheen was startled out of her revelry by the sudden and strong hammering of a fist beating repeatedly against the door.

Bantam Flyn glanced up from the fire carelessly as Old Lochlann made his creaking way over to answer the violent knocking. By the time the old man opened the door and admitted a sweaty, out of breath man, Sir Corc was already standing in the common room.

The desperate looking visitor wore the doublet of the city watch and he looked hard at the knight as he sucked in air.

"Sir—" the man managed between gasps.

"An attack?" Corc asked pointedly.

The man nodded deeply, his expression as dire as his message. Bantam Flyn shot up out of his chair.

"Do the walls hold?" Sir Corc pressed.

"Not the walls," the man was finding his lungs. "The port. Men attacked the port."

"Men?" Rosheen asked.

The man glanced quickly at her and looked back to Sir Corc before answering. "Aye. Middangearders. They came in ships painted black. Black sails . . . before the moon rose. Some of them were already docked, sir . . . disguised as merchants. All at once they were everywhere!"

"How many ships?" the knight demanded.

The man shook his head in bewilderment, struggling for an answer. "A dozen at least . . . maybe more."

"Did the undine respond?"

Another nod. "They sunk one, maybe two . . . before they could land, but the others made port and raiders hit the docks running . . . took the wharf guard by surprise. They were overrun."

Sir Corc wasted no more time with questions. "Lochlann, get the mule. Lady Rosheen if you would be kind enough to wake Pocket and see that he is ready to leave. Squire Flyn—"

"Is not running," Flyn finished. He looked to the watchman. "You. Lead me to the battle."

"No," Sir Corc took a step towards the squire. "We are going."

"How can you?" Flyn asked, his voice pained. "How can you just run when the city is threatened?"

"I have my duties, squire," the knight answered, his voice taut.

"If that lie holds well with your honor, then go," Flyn said, slinging the greatsword harness over his shoulder. "But I will not so shame myself."

"Do not defy me Bantam Flyn," Corc warned. "Your oath—"

"Is to lend aid wherever I am able! Have you grown so feeble-minded in your dotage that you have forgotten?"

"Flyn, do not . . ." Rosheen began.

"No," the squire said. "Pardons milady, but you had the right of it before. There are no knights in this room."

Rosheen saw the feathers bristle across Sir Corc's arms, shoulders and neck at these words. He radiated fury, but remained silent.

It is his way.

"I am just a squire," Flyn continued, heedless of the elder coburn's anger, "and I may stay one forever, but I will no longer sit idly by while earnestly asked for aid. Your words, lady piskie, remember? I thank you for them." He motioned towards the door.

"Lead on my brave man."

The watchman hesitated, eyes wide and mouth slack at the confrontation, but Flyn sidestepped Sir Corc and clapped the man firmly on the shoulder, turning him towards the door.

"Flyn," Sir Corc said as the squire opened the door. "Leave the sword."

Bantam Flyn paused for a moment, then spoke without turning. "It is a weapon, Corc. Not an heirloom. Coalspur intended it should bear his name and continue to serve the causes of the Valiant Spur. I go to do just that. I would sooner die than see it dishonored with cowardice. I wonder . . . would you die to reclaim it?"

Oh, this could get bloody.

Flyn waited, his back still turned. When no answer or challenge came, he stepped out into the dark courtyard and the door closed behind him. The room was quiet and no one moved.

Sir Corc stood and stared at the door, his fists clenched and then in a heartbeat he shook off his anger.

"Lochlann, the mule," he said and the old man nodded and went to his task.

"Let me go after Flyn," Rosheen offered. "Slap some sense into him."

Sir Corc shook his head. "There is no time. We should have . . . *fled* sooner, and now only good fortune will deliver us."

This sits sore with him. More than with the squire. "I am sorry."

"You need not ever offer apologies to me, my lady piskie."

"Rosheen," she told him. "I have frolicked too many times to be called a lady."

"Rosheen," he conceded, "if you would see to Pocket?"

"Of course," she said and flew up the stairs, but a cold feeling struck her before she reached the first landing. She found the door to the garret room ajar, the window open and no sign of the gurg.

Pocket could not stop shivering. The night was not particularly cold. He had started shaking while still in the garret. He was not afraid, he was certain of that. Sneaking out had taken courage. After all, there was a battle on in the city and he was headed towards it. It was bold of him to leave, and now that he had done it, he found an old feeling returning, the same sneaking anticipation that had ridden between his shoulder blades for years in the Roost. He had spent most of his life alone, avoiding the attention of others in dark places, but lately his days had been filled with open sky, bustling streets, and the gentle, breathing presence of others sleeping nearby. He had just willingly left that behind so he could follow Bantam Flyn to war.

The old habits returned swiftly and Pocket found himself melded into the deep shadows of Black Pool's streets. Flyn and the watchman were ahead of him now and pulling further away with every step. Pocket let them. If he revealed himself too soon he might be sent back and he could not have that. Whether he knew it or not, Flyn needed a squire now that he was acting like a true knight. After they drove the pirates out of the city, there would be a feast, and Pocket would be needed to fill Flyn's cup and care for his weapons. Maybe he would even bear a shield and save his knight from an arrow aimed for his heart in the press of battle.

But the battle still lay in front of them, and the figures Pocket followed were making for it in great haste. Pocket had expected the streets to be alive with fleeing people and shouting watchmen, but word of the attack must have spread quickly, for the streets lay abandoned. Even the beggars and urchins had found some place safe to hide. The houses and storefronts were closed up, barred against danger with nary a candle glowing behind the shutters. It was as if the entire city closed its eyes tight and held its breath, waiting for the danger to pass by. Flyn and his guide were making their way quickly out of Sweynside, heading for the bridge that crossed over the river into Hogulent and beyond to the docks.

The watchmen bore a lantern and soon only a bouncing glimmer marked the pair he pursued.

A dull orange haze began to swell in the sky above the distant buildings. Pocket stopped and watched as the black outlines of rooftops and chimneys stood out meekly in front of the threatening glow. He could not yet see any rising flames, but the light on the horizon was unmistakable.

Black Pool was on fire.

Somewhere beyond the river, the raiders had begun putting the buildings to the torch. He looked back to the street and his stomach lurched. The lantern was gone. Ahead of him, the streets were completely black. The shadowy figures of Bantam Flyn and the watchman had vanished. Pocket broke into a run, pounding down the wet cobblestones as fast as he was able, keeping his eyes forward and hoping to see the little beacon return, but only more empty streets rushed to meet him. He slowed his steps, plodding to a halt as he looked sharply to left and right at the countless narrow alleys and twisting side streets, any one of them a possible path.

Surely, Bantam Flyn had taken one of them . . . or one of the dozen he ran past before stopping. How was he going to choose? He knew the way to the docks, so maybe he should make his way there and hope to find Flyn. He would be where the fighting was thickest, that much was sure. Pocket looked back down the main street where Hogulent lay under an angry, red sky. That was his course.

He had not taken four steps when a sharp hissing sound shot at him from the dark. He stopped and immediately the sound came again, from the left. Looking over, he found a plump young woman staring fearfully out at him from the shadows of an alley.

Her eyes were huge and round in her pale face and she gestured fretfully for him to approach with her free hand.

"Are you all right?" Pocket asked.

"Not so loud," she whispered. "They might hear."

"Who?" Pocket asked in a lower voice and took a step forward.

"Those marauders," she answered, poking her head out of the alley and glancing quickly down either side of the street before ducking back again. "Killers and rapers. You should come off the lane, boy. It is unsafe."

"Do not fear," Pocket told her. "They will be driven off. Why are you out of doors?"

The woman fidgeted nervously with the handle of the bucket she carried, her fear slightly offset by a look of disgust. "My mistress bade me fetch water for her bath. At this hour! She's shot her bolt now, the shrew! Left me out here alone. Come now, come in here with me where it's safer."

"I cannot," he told her. "I must get to the docks and . . . did you see a man of the watch and a coburn come by this way?"

"Yea," she answered brightly. "I did at that."

"Can you tell me which way they went, please?"

"Come," the woman said, extending her hand. "I will take you myself, so neither of us is alone."

Relieved, Pocket stepped forward and went to take the frightened woman's hand, then pulled away as a thought struck him.

"If you saw them," he asked. "Why did you not ask them for help?"

The woman's face scrunched in puzzlement and then was gripped once again with dread. "I thought they might be raiders."

"A member of the city watch?" Pocket asked taking a step back. "And a knight of the Valiant Spur?"

The woman's fear melted and a grin curled her lips. "Clever boy."

Pocket backed away as the woman dropped her bucket and stepped out of the alley. Two men emerged from the shadows behind and followed her out into the street. The first was slight, bald and covered in ashy dirt while the other was thickset, bushy brown hair and beard adorning his large head. Pocket felt more than heard the movement behind him and turned to find four other humans stepping out from another alley. Two of them were women with painted faces, unbound hair and slit skirts. The third was a fat man wearing the stained apron of a butcher and the last a boy, not much older than Pocket, wearing the rags of an urchin.

Pocket's head whirled, struggling to keep them all in sight as they quickly surrounded him.

The old fear grabbed hold of Pocket. This is what returning to creeping through the dark had gained. Malice. Lies. Distrust. He thought Black Pool different from the Roost, but it was not true. A changeling was hated everywhere.

"You need to come with us now," the plump woman's voice was a soothing threat.

"I never did anything to you," Pocket said, his voice near panic. "Leave me alone."

"We cannot."

They were closing in. Pocket spun, looking for an opening, a means of escape. The man with the bushy beard reached for him.

"You found him!" a familiar voice rang out.

The seven strangers paused, turning and Pocket followed their gaze. Bantam Flyn strode down the street, his quarterstaff propped lazily over his shoulders. He made straight for the group, which once again spread themselves out. Flyn did not even glance at them as he walked towards Pocket wagging his finger.

"You know better than to be sneaking off in the middle of the night," the squire chastised him. "What would you have done if these gentles had not come along?" He reached Pocket and clapped a hand behind his neck, before looking at the strangers now surrounding them both. "Truly you must be good folk. Our little page here is rarely so ready to trust."

"You," the serving woman told Flyn, "best move on."

"Yes," Flyn said with a deep sigh. "You are right. We should be on our way. Sir will be most anxious to punish this rascal for his disobedience. Twenty lashes, I'd wager. And not tongue lashes either. Our good knight is not one for words."

Flyn stepped towards the edge of the group, guiding Pocket by the neck, but the dirty man blocked his path. "Boy stays."

Flyn reached over casually and brushed some of the soot from the man's shoulders. "No, good man," he said amiably. "We are quite fond of him despite his recent behavior. So, my thanks again! Please step aside."

The filthy wretch did not move nor reply. He just stared up at the squire, beady eyes locked. Flyn smiled openly, not breaking from the man's gaze.

"Here now!"

Pocket was surprised to see Old Lochlann push his way past the urchin, giving the rest of the ragged group distasteful looks as he did. "What's all this then?"

"Lochlann!" Flyn announced happily. "So glad you are here."

The old man waved a hand at Pocket, a confused expression on his face. "Sir sends me out looking for this one and what do I find? Some rabble . . . and you in the center of it."

"I know," Flyn agreed. "Shameful. Lochlann, if you would see Pocket safely home? I think I will stay and make sure these people get a proper reward."

Lochlann cast squinting eyes at the surrounding group then leaned in, almost reluctantly and took Pocket by the hand. "Come ahead," he said, pulling Pocket out from the middle. The peasants made no move to stop him, their eyes locked on Flyn, all save the serving woman. Her gaze followed Pocket, an odd smile hinting at the corners of her mouth. Pocket held Lochlann's hand as they backed away, watching as Flyn remained surrounded.

"Do you think he will be all right?" Pocket asked.

The old man looked down to answer, but before he could speak two large, feathered hands wrapped around his face, seizing him by the forehead and jaw. The hands twisted sharply, and Pocket winced as Lochlann's head turned unnaturally around, accompanied by the muffled crunching of bone. Mouth slack and eyes staring, the old man fell limply to the cobbles. Pocket found Sir Corc looming over the body, armored in mail.

"Stay behind me," he said, advancing on the peasants.

The seven saw him coming and backed away from Flyn, who stood with staff in hand and confusion across his face. Sir Corc came steadily on. Pocket did as he was told and stayed a pace behind the knight. He saw doubt play across the faces of his assailants and they continued to retreat slowly towards the alleys.

"You cannot keep him from us, coburn," the serving woman spat at Sir Corc.

"Get you gone," the knight replied.

"He belongs with us!"

"He belongs where he is!" Sir Corc declared, tearing his sword from its scabbard. "Under my protection."

The harlots and the urchin had been swallowed by the shadows, the butcher lurking at the mouth of the alley, but he too disappeared when the knight wheeled on him. On the opposite side of the street only the serving woman remained, hovering at the edge of the darkness where Pocket had first spied her.

"You cannot keep him safe enough," she threw at Sir Corc.

"You cannot run forever. One day, you will have no choice but to give him over."

Sir Corc said nothing as he made for her, but before he was within reach the woman fled into the narrow passage and was lost from sight. Sir Corc made a slow turn, looking to all sides, then turned to Pocket.

"Come," he said. "We must away."

They went back up the street where Bantam Flyn stood over the corpse of the creature that had once been Old Lochlann.

In death, it resembled nothing close to human. The limbs had elongated and shriveled to emaciated stalks, the flesh almost black.

The belly was horribly distended, bloating out from beneath the tunic. One hand was a shrunken pig's hoof and the feet had burst the bindings of their shoes, emerging in misshapen lumps covered in scales. But it was the face that Pocket struggled to look upon.

The skin had stretched and split over a protruding snout, lips peeled back over a choking mass of thick teeth. A small antler sprouted from under the lank hair and while one eye retained its human appearance, the other was bulging out of the socket with the slit iris of a predator.

"Gruagach," Flyn said, looking up at Sir Corc. "How did you know?"

"His cooking had improved," Sir Corc said, sheathing his sword and striding past the squire without a glance.

Pocket kept to the knight's heels, his pumping heart competing in a race against his whirling mind. All of those people were changelings? What did they want with him? Pocket had never even met another gurg before, not even in Black Pool, much less a full-blooded gruagach. It seemed he always had questions for Sir Corc, but he was not about to risk speaking when the knight seemed so wroth.

Bantam Flyn also followed, his eyes scanning the alleys.

"How did you find me?" Pocket asked before he could stop himself.

"You shot past like a sparrow," Flyn laughed lightly. "We took a turn and then heard something run down the high street. Something that looked shockingly like you. My watchman friend was not so keen on investigating."

"Enough talk," Sir Corc said without looking back.

He led them back the way Pocket had come, but long before they reached the townhouse, the knight turned down a side street and kept making turns until Pocket lost all sense of direction.

At last, Sir Corc approached a common green; one of the many little islands of flowers and preened trees that dotted the wealthy districts of Sweynside. It might have been pleasant to look upon during the day, but Pocket saw only dark bushes where unseen eyes could stare out at him hungrily, waiting to pounce. He breathed easier when they came around a hedgerow and found Backbone making a meal out of a flowerbed.

"You found him!" Rosheen breathed a sigh of relief and flew over to meet them.

Sir Corc nodded once, then glanced around the green, frowning. "Where is Muckle?"

The piskie cast a disgusted look into a grouping of ferns, just as the ferns said "Right here" and shook slightly.

"Make haste," Sir Corc snapped.

"These processes should not be rushed," the ferns answered.

Sir Corc turned away and looked down at Pocket.

"Backbone is your charge. Need I remind you?"

Pocket shook his head and rushed over to grab the mule's guide rope.

"Good," Sir Corc continued. "We go to the chandler's under Ten Ferries Bridge. Do you remember the place?"

"Yes," Pocket said assuredly.

"If we should become separated that is where you must go. The proprietor will know what to do."

Muckle emerged from the foliage still belting his patchwork breeches under his gut. "The greenskeeper should thank me," he said with a satisfied sigh. "My fertilizer is much prized. Tomorrow those ferns will reach the roofs."

Pocket stifled a laugh as Rosheen wrinkled her nose.

"We move," Sir Corc ordered. "I will lead. Muckle, rear guard."

"I can—" Flyn began, but Sir Corc was already heading out of the green.

Muckle shouldered his huge, garish club and winked at Pocket before urging him out with a wave of his hand. Backbone plodded somberly along, the clopping of his hooves on the cobblestones alarmingly loud in the quiet city. Sir Corc did not waste time with stealth. He made straight for the River Poddle at a quick pace, using the widest lanes. As they drew closer to the river, Pocket saw that the fiery glow in the sky had intensified, covering more of the skyline than before. People began appearing in the street ahead of them, passing them by in their nightclothes or bearing armloads of goods. Mothers dragged children by the hand and men pulled carts, all of them heading away from the river.

Some stopped and urged Sir Corc to turn around and flee, but the knight ignored them, pressing his way forward against the tide of frightened humanity. A watchman came running by and Sir Corc grabbed him by the arm, wrenching him to a halt.

"Have the Middangearders pushed Sweynside?" he demanded.

"No," the watchman answered hurriedly. "We hold the bridges, for now. I am to fetch men from the walls to reinforce us."

"No!" Sir Corc snapped. "This is all a diversion. The Red Caps will assail the walls as soon as they weaken!"

The man struggled against the coburn's grasp. "I have my orders!"

"Do not be a fool!"

But the man wrestled free and shot off once more down the crowded street. Sir Corc turned angrily and pressed on towards the river. They came to the river and found the watch had thrown up a makeshift barricade across the middle of the Goat's Tongue Bridge. Pocket could hear the horrible screams of fighting men as the raiders charged across the bridge to assault the pile of overturned wagons, barrels and planking. The men of the watch held firm, repelling the attacks with spears and arrows. The span was littered with bodies on both sides of the barricade and Pocket could see watchmen running to pull their fallen comrades away from the battle and back to the relative safety of Sweynside where a small contingent of armed men waited in reserve should the barricade be overrun. Across the water, Hogulent was crowned in flames as the roofs of warehouses and foundries burned freely.

Sir Corc wasted no time at the Goat's Tongue, turning to put the river to their right and heading away from the bridge. They traveled along the upper street for several minutes before Sir Corc led them down an uneven boat ramp which dumped onto the riverwalk. Ahead of them, through the gloom Pocket could see the foundations of Ten Ferries Bridge arching above them.

"The chandler's is on the Hogulent side," Bantam Flyn said, hurrying to draw even with Sir Corc. "If the bridge is barricaded, how are we to get across?"

Sir Corc did not answer, but only quickened his pace.

Pocket had to pull sternly on the guide rope to keep Backbone moving swiftly and several times Muckle had to urge the mule on with a few well-placed swats to the haunches. Rosheen flew just ahead, between Pocket and the coburn. She kept glancing back at him, offering a reassuring smile when he met her gaze.

Sir Corc slowed when they approached the bridge. Another boat ramp led up to the street as well as a twisting flight of stone stairs that hugged the support pillar of the bridge. Above them, men fought on the bridge, the ringing of metal and the cries of battles echoing where they stood under the arch. Pocket jumped when something heavy slammed into the water, sending up a violent splash. When the rippling settled, a man floated face down in the river, arrow shafts protruding from his back. Across the river, Pocket could see the door to the chandler's shop nestled under the bridge on the opposite side.

Sir Corc approached and removed his shield from Backbone's loads. Strapping it to his arm, he nodded to Rosheen.

The piskie wasted no time and flew off across the river, keeping directly under the bridge. She was so small Pocket lost sight of her in the darkness, but he thought he saw the distant door of the chandler's shop open slightly. After what seemed an eternity, the piskie returned.

"He is there," she told Sir Corc. "And as yet undiscovered."

Sir Corc motioned Pocket over to the edge of the boat ramp. "Get ready to lead the mule up," he whispered.

"What?" Flyn hissed. "That bridge is crawling with raiders!"

"The watch cannot hold for long," Sir Corc said, keeping his head craned upwards, watching the edge of the bridge. "When the defenses break, the raiders will come rushing across. If we are fortunate they will not leave a guard on their side. Then we cross."

Flyn's face remained dubious, but he said no more.

They stood listening to the sounds of the struggle above, unable to tell which side laid claim to the shrieks of the dying. Then there came a deafening crash of sundered wood, followed by a bloodthirsty roar and the pounding of countless boot heels. Sir Corc waited a handful of breaths then drew his sword and started up the ramp. Bantam Flyn stuck close to the knight and Pocket followed behind, dragging Backbone with him.

Nothing greeted them at the top but the bodies of the slain, most wearing the livery of the watch. Broken weapons and bodies lay strewn next to the toppled barricade. Dropped lanterns and discarded torches accompanied the moonlight, revealing the scene of slaughter in flickering plays of shadow. Some of the bodies still moved, groaning as they crawled away from their severed limbs. Sir Corc made for what was left of the barricade and picked his way over, clearing a path for Pocket and the mule. Beyond the splintered wood, the far side of the bridge beckoned.

A savage, wordless cry cut through the night before them.

Pocket looked, dread seizing him as a mass of large forms came charging out of the darkness towards them. He heard Rosheen curse as at least two dozen Middangearders in mail coats gained the bridge, longaxes swinging over their heads. Sir Corc spun around.

"Back across!" he yelled.

"Damn you!" Bantam Flyn seized the knight by the front of his surcoat. "We can win through if we stand together!"

"This is not the time!" Sir Corc said, shoving the squire away.

"Does your cowardice have no end?" Flyn demanded.

Sir Corc ignored him and turned to Pocket. "You must flee. Leave the mule—"

"No!" Pocket gripped the guide rope tightly. "He is my charge. I won't!"

"Do as I say!" the knight screamed at him and Pocket felt his throat grow thick.

"Wait!" Rosheen yelled over them. "What is he doing?"

They all followed the piskie's outstretched finger and bewildered gaze.

Muckle sat astride his great club, ribbons streaming behind him as he skipped towards the charging raiders in mock gallop. The fat goblin waved one arm ostentatiously in the air as he bounced forward.

"To me my brothers!" they heard him scream. "To me!"

The Middangearders slowed their pace, the queer sight spreading confusion across their faces. They stopped completely when Muckle made a show of reigning up before them, surveying their clustered ranks with a nod. The goblin dismounted and then swung his would-be steed up on his shoulder as he began pacing in front of the confounded raiders.

"'Tis a fine night for reaving, eh my lads?!"

The raiders did not respond, glancing at one another for an answer to the corpulent mystery that addressed them.

Undeterred, Muckle spoke again, but this time it sounded to Pocket like gibberish. Whatever the strange words meant, the raiders appeared to understand for they began smiling, looking at the fat goblin with growing mirth. Muckle said something else in the strange tongue, grandly gesturing back across the bridge, his voice rising with enthusiasm. Pocket marveled as the men cheered.

Muckle said something else, holding up two fingers and clucking like a chicken. The warriors began openly chuckling and looking at one another with approving expressions. Muckle kept up a steady stream of speech, actually going over and thumping one man in the crotch with the back of his hand. The raider flinched back from the goblin's hand which drew hearty laughter from his fellows, and he joined them, louder than the rest.

Muckle began speaking directly to the man and making coaxing gestures with his hands. A gormless grin spread across the raider's face as the others began encouraging him with shouts and pats on the back. They cheered when the man finally removed his helmet and handed it over to Muckle. The goblin said something as he held the head piece up and the men laughed in agreement. Then Muckle placed the helmet over the man's crotch and wrapped on it with his knuckles. This drew guffaws which turned to uncontrolled peals of laughter as Muckle placed the helmet over his own codpiece and began making thrusting gestures with his hips.

Finishing with obscene breathing, Muckle tossed the helmet carelessly over his shoulder, then waved the owner over. The other raiders pushed the man forward companionably, and he plodded over to where the goblin waited. At Muckle's instruction the man knelt on the bridge as his brothers in arms cheered him on. Muckle said something to the crowd, drawing more laughter and brandished his giant club, raising it high above his head. The men began repeating the same word over and over in booming voices, thrusting there weapons into the air.

Pocket heard Rosheen suck air sharply between her teeth.

"Is he—?"

"Yes," Sir Corc said. "He is."

"Pocket!" Rosheen was suddenly hovering directly in his face. "Do not look!"

"What?" Pocket leaned past her. "Why is he—?"

"No," Rosheen darted back into his vision. "Sweetling, avert your eyes!"

The men's cheering reached a fever pitch and Pocket dodged past Rosheen's wings just as Muckle brought his huge club down with all his weight. The knotty wood impacted into the kneeling raider's head with a sharp, wet crunch and he dropped limply to the bridge, his legs twitching.

Pocket giggled.

He did not know why, but the horrible scene filled him with joy, and the other raiders must have felt the same for they too were laughing. Muckle raised the club high again and brought it down on the fallen man's broken skull. A red spray shot into the air on the second hit and the men howled with glee, holding their stomachs, eyes streaming tears. Pocket felt the laughter rising to his cheeks and eagerly awaited the third fall of the club, when Sir Corc's strong hands pulled him around and hugged him close.

No longer a witness to the bloody display, Pocket suddenly felt sick as he continued to hear the club bash into softening bone over and over again accompanied by a chorus of voices lost in hilarity. The sounds of those voices, given over to awful abandon rang painfully in his ears, growing hoarse and breathless with each new rising wave. He heard coughing and gasping begin to mingle with the laughter, quickly supplanting it, and he heard Muckle scream over the din. The goblin's voice rang out, a mix of fury, lust and ecstasy and then . . .

Silence.

Pocket felt himself being guided forward, half lifted over the remainder of the bridge. He kept his face pressed close to Sir Corc, but the corners of his vision still caught harrowing glimpses of sprawled forms with blue faces and black lips, throats raked with the deep gouges of dying fingers and curled hands clinging to thick, pale, ropey entrails spilled upon the cobbles.

Pocket was dimly aware of descending the steps to the riverwalk and entering the chandler's shop. Sir Corc spoke briefly with the candle maker and then Pocket was being ushered into a damp, reeking tunnel. Sir Corc held his hand as they traversed a narrow walkway of slimy bricks, a broad channel of sluggish water only a step to the right.

"Ah the sewers!" Muckle's voice echoed off the close, stone walls. "Do you know what a crocodilisk is, my young cock?"

"No," Bantam Flyn's voice answered.

"Pity," Muckle said. "Neither do I. But I hear they live down here."

The squire seemed to find this amusing and he let out a chuckle.

Pocket winced. It was the worst sound he could imagine.

Curse all cities and their tight, stinking tunnels.

It was morning before they emerged from hours of following Sir Corc through the twisting dark. When Rosheen saw the hazy light of early morning glaring at them from down the passage, she began to breathe easier. They came out well away from the city walls, in a rocky depression choked with scrubby trees. The mouth of the tunnel on this side was well hidden by boulders and weeds, appearing to be no more than a natural fissure in the hillside.

Black Pool loomed in the distance.

Muckle was the last to come out. He stepped forth taking a deep breath, smiling and about to speak some nonsense. Sir Corc silenced him with a hiss and pointed up into the fields bordering the city. Rosheen followed the knight's gesture, squinting across the landscape, but even from their low vantage and across such distance the army assembled before the city was clearly visible.

Rosheen could not guess at their numbers, but if they stormed the walls, she doubted the defenses could repel them.

Sir Corc motioned for them to stay quiet and turned away, picking his way through the dell. Pocket stayed close behind and Bantam Flyn came next. Muckle waited on Rosheen, but she kept her gaze fixed on the walls, wishing no contact with the goblin.

After a long moment, she heard him turn away, plodding heavily into the brush.

Rosheen lingered, not knowing why. She hated the city and was glad to be free of it, but leaving it to so cruel a demise made her heartsick for the people who called it home. At last she began to turn, but something caught her eye, floating on the morning breeze. It drifted down into the dell, settling on the ground where it was snagged by the wild grass. Rosheen flew down and plucked it up; a ribbon, finely woven in patterns of green and gold. She ran it through her fingers, feeling the embroidery and then tied it around her waist before flying off after the others.

NINETEEN

The wind was strong in the pale hours of the morning. The sun had risen some time ago, but remained unseen behind a cloak of cold clouds, stained by the smoke from the city. Padric stood uncomfortably in the chariot, waiting as he had for several hours.

Before him the impressive gates stood closed, the surrounding walls providing mute reinforcement. He did not know what Torcan was waiting for; by all reports the city had been taken before first light, the Middangearders treacherous assault a success. Now the entire Red Cap army stood marshaled at the southern gate, arrayed in a daunting horde, eager to enter their prize. Padric was surprised Black Pool still stood, as the Swinehelm was notorious for leaving nothing of his conquests but ashes. It crossed his mind that the Red Caps would burn the city once admitted; that it had been saved only because the human raiders valued plunder over fire. Once it was plucked clean, robbed of all it had to offer, they would throw the gates wide and let the goblins reduce it to cinders.

Svala stood shivering at his elbow. The raiment the captains had given her was richly made, but covered little, the skirts slit well passed the poor girl's hips. Torcan wished to show off his newfound royalty, and for Svala, that granted little care for modesty.

Or warmth. Padric had given her his cloak as soon as they both mounted the chariot, but the wind tugged cruelly at the black wool and Svala fought to keep it in place. She did not complain. As yet, Padric had not heard her speak since telling him her name.

He looked over and caught her eye, offering what he hoped was a reassuring smile and was struck with how fine she looked.

Arnheir's women had worked her golden hair into fine plaits and braids, adorning it with ribbons and finely wrought silver combs.

The wind had undone much of their labor, giving Svala a regal yet almost savage appearance which somehow suited her well. Padric watched as the wind plucked a ribbon of green and gold from the girl's locks. He tried to catch it, but the wind was swifter and bore the ribbon aloft, tumbling it through the air. Padric marked its journey as it was carried high and away, finally drifting into a dell not far from the city walls where it was lost from sight.

Padric turned to the tramp of metal boots and found Torcan Swinehelm approaching with his personal guard. The Red Cap leader was clad in full armor, his metal bulk dwarfing the goblins surrounding him. He carried his heavy battle-axe and helmet, his head covered only by the blood colored cap that united his brotherhood of fanatics.

"Your Grace," Torcan said as he stopped alongside the chariot. "Are you ready to reclaim the city that was once the seat of your forebears?"

Padric continued to stare at the gates. "This is your mummery, goblin. Pull the strings and let's have done. The lady is chilled to the bone."

"Aye," Torcan leered. "She does look . . . cold."

Padric did not respond, but turned so that he blocked the goblin's appraising view.

"I have a gift for you," Torcan said mildly and gestured.

Slouch Hat came up to the chariot flanked by Red Caps bearing torches. The husk carried a banner before him, a crowned skull wreathed in flame worked upon the rippling cloth.

"A husk is a rare slave," Torcan pronounced.

Padric merely nodded. The Swinehelm could use Slouch Hat for this fraudulent posturing all he wanted. It only served to bring Padric closer to his allies. The proud bearing the husk adopted with the banner in hand made Padric wonder if he had not somehow maneuvered himself into this position. The husk was frightfully clever and displayed a cunning that was nothing short of deadly. Exactly who that cunning would lead to death was still a question.

A man appeared atop the battlements and Torcan waved his axe over his head. The man yelled something down into the city and there came a grinding squeal from behind the gates before they slowly began to swing open. Torcan and his retinue made for the entrance, followed by Slouch Hat. The goblin driving the chariot gave the pair of black horses a snap of the whip, sending the chariot forward in a start. Padric lurched backward and had to quickly grasp the side of the carriage to keep from spilling off the back. Svala's feet remained steady. He laughed bitterly in his throat.

Let the conquered people of Black Pool see what a buffoon Torcan meant to enthrone. The air grew colder as they passed through the yawning stone tunnel of the gatehouse and it was Padric's turn to shiver.

Before them, the dark cobblestones of a wide street ran between rows of aged structures. Padric was relieved to see that no crowd of beleaguered citizens had been assembled to greet them; no blank and desperate faces staring at him with fear and hatred.

Only the Middangearders were present, spaced along every few hundred paces, spears and shields held carelessly. Padric heard the clanging tramp of the Red Caps marching through the gate behind him. It was a force of more than two thousand armed goblins, many of them veterans of countless wars over hundreds of years, and as their foot stomps banged into the cobbles, they announced undeniably that Black Pool now belonged to them.

The section of the city they passed through appeared completely undamaged. Whatever fighting had occurred was over long before it reached the gate. The Middangearders had played their bloody part well. Soon, the sickening victory procession came to where the river flowed through the city, a grand bridge of masterfully cut stone joining the city above the darkly flowing water.

Torcan stopped before crossing the bridge, ordering his army to spread through the city. The Red Caps marched off in well-ordered bands of fifty, taking to the streets and avenues with polearms resting on their shoulders. A sizeable group stayed with the chariot and Torcan led them over the river.

Arnheir and several of the other reaver captains awaited them on the far side where they oversaw a bedraggled group of citizens, hard at work gathering bodies into a heap on the street.

Many of the corpses were raiders and Padric noticed with curious revulsion that they trailed the tubes of their own guts as they were dragged to the charnel pile. The chariot pulled up near the grisly scene and the horses began to snort and stamp in distaste at being so near the dead. Torcan spoke with Arnheir in the raider's tongue and their words grew heated, the Middangearder gesturing several times at the pile of eviscerated warriors. Svala kept her eyes away from the discussion, but Padric could tell she was listening, her face paling. Whatever killed these men had raised Torcan's ire.

"My lord," the goblin captain threw his voice over his shoulder at the chariot. "Perhaps you should see this."

Padric stepped down without a word, catching Slouch Hat's eye as he passed. As usual, the husk's expression was a mystery.

Arnheir stepped to the side as he drew close to the pile of bodies and Torcan gestured towards it with dismissive disgust.

"This," he spat, "is the death you can expect from elf-friends."

Padric did not relish conversing with Torcan, but his curiosity was piqued. "What happened to them?"

"A Jester," Torcan said with a grimace. "It appears this city was home to at least one of the mad bastards."

Padric looked puzzlingly at the corpses.

"This is old Magic," Torcan continued. "Raw and untamed. Deadly to mortals.

Aye, and weak-minded Fae as well. You would be wise to come into your power quick, my lord or you can be certain they'll serve you a like fate."

"They?"

"The Seelie Court," Torcan sneered. "Whatever is left of it! They will have killers like these wherever they can be hid. You are marked."

Padric laughed through his nose. "I thought I was just a figurehead."

"For now," Torcan replied. "But you could become more and they will not wait. Do as I say and I can save you from this . . . you and the wench."

Padric looked back to where Svala stood in the chariot, eyes downcast, flaxen hair and sable cloak blowing in the wind. She was no more a vessel of sorcery than he, even if she were with child.

Fortunately, they had departed Reaver's Meadow in such haste that the question of his bedding Svala had not again been raised. Heggle had been left behind and without her spying eyes, Padric hoped he could keep from dishonoring the girl just to save her life. But for how long?

Torcan wanted a new line, one unblemished by a life among mortals and his patience was thin. The woman would be safer if she carried a child, at least from the Red Caps, but would the Seelie Court pursue the death of an innocent woman and her child just to quell the threat of another sorcerer king? Padric had no answer for that, but the tragic fact remained; Svala's life was forfeit the moment they took her in thrall. His too. Slouch Hat's lie had only granted him time, without it he would have been murdered by Acwellen. He could reveal the truth and they would all burn or hold to the lie and survive another day. Day by day. That was all that was left.

Padric looked at Torcan. "What would you have of me?"

"First," the goblin smiled. "Come and see justice done on our enemies."

Padric spent the day watching others die and fighting the urge to vomit. Torcan had the former leaders of the city held under guard in a large square near the docks. Padric and Svala were given seats on a hastily constructed platform, so they could view the executions unimpeded by the crowd forced to attend by the Red Caps. The humans were tied to stakes and burnt, they're screams echoing off the walls of the surrounding buildings until the smoke stole the air from their lungs and they became nothing but slumped, black figures encased in hungry flames. The Fae were likewise burnt, but instead of tying them to wooden beams, Torcan had them impaled on iron spikes tall as a grown man. Padric had seen a few undine in his life and always found their lithe forms, large eyes and sea-colored skin exotic and queerly beautiful. The four which hung in the air, run threw, writhing and choking were robbed of that beauty as their lives slowly slid down the iron which transfixed their bodies.

Five dwarrow were also held in shackles, and when they were led into the square by their Red Cap guards, Svala leaned forward slightly, mumbling a few words in her own tongue that Padric could not make out. Oddly, Torcan ordered their lives spared, declaring they should be made to labor in the mines beyond the city walls.

Svala seemed relieved as they were led away, continuing to mutter softly, her hands tracing a pattern in the air in front of her chest.

A score of goblins followed, the last of which was dressed in rich robes and heavily bejeweled, thick black hair heavily curled and shining with oil. As his brethren were raised upon the tips of iron pikes, wet shrieks of agony gurgling from their lips, he was led before the Swinehelm and forced to kneel.

"I never would have thought you to be so pretty," Torcan said as he circled slowly. "Should have called yourself the Whore of the Pile! What have you to say, blood traitor?"

The goblin raised his head slowly and his eyes locked on Padric.

"Do not speak to me of blood!" the kneeling goblin said, voice carrying over the crowd. "When it is you who would bend the knee to a mortal. May woe fall upon all who don the Cap! Curse you!"

Torcan laughed as he dragged his axe off his shoulder.

"Curses, eh? Let them see where following a prim and proper fop will lead. Come! Give the Swine's Wife a kiss!"

With that Torcan swung his axe in a vicious arc. The goblin twitched as his body fell forward, the head striking the cobbles with a dull thud and rolling a few paces before Torcan snatched it up by the luxuriant hair, holding it high and showing it dripping to the crowd.

"The Lord of the Pile is dead!" he shouted, then turned towards the dais, looked at Padric and raised his gory axe in salute.

"Long live the King!"

The Red Caps in the square raised their voices in response, and to Padric's dismay, they were joined by the gathered citizens of Black Pool. Poor wretches. They were too afraid to do anything but obey.

"LONG LIVE THE KING!"

Dusk was near by the time Torcan had dispatched all his captives and seen that the Middangearders received their fair share of slaves from among the women of the city. Several men were cut down trying to rescue their sobbing wives and daughters from being dragged to the raider's ships. Padric's blood burned with shame and fury at each act of cruelty, each death, each crying child, his teeth near to breaking as he ground them together in hapless frustration. He dared not venture so much as a glance in Svala's direction for fear of what he might find etched into her face.

At last, near sick with the sorrow and death he had witnessed throughout the day, Padric was ushered back into the chariot. Svala climbed in next to him. They followed one of the rivers towards the heart of the city and finally came to the deep pool that formed where the two rivers met. Here, upon a heavily fortified island at the center of the true Black Pool, the Tower of Vellaunus rose arrogantly into the sky; a twisted old man daring the world to call him weak. The Tower was darkly spoken of across the tales of his boyhood, but Padric could recall none of those tales now. Seeing it with his own eyes, he found it difficult to muster a suitable amount of awe. He was growing weary of legends.

A pair of Red Caps with river poles in their hands waited upon a skiff moored to a rotting jetty.

"Come," Torcan said, motioning towards the skiff. "We will see Your Grace safely lodged for the night."

Padric did not hide his distaste as he looked up at the ancient tower. "There?"

"Oh yes," Torcan said grandly. "Since the day it was first raised, the Tower of Vellaunus has ever been the residence of the Goblin Kings in Black Pool. I assure you, my lord, there is no safer place within the city. And you shall not be without company."

Torcan motioned and one of his Red Caps took the banner from Slouch Hat. The husk looked at the goblins surrounding him and seemed to consider for a moment, then stepped onto the skiff without a word. Padric helped Svala aboard, then stepped down onto the bobbing craft.

"Rest well, my lord," Torcan said from the jetty.

Padric merely nodded as the two goblins began to pole the skiff across the inky water. Only two, and their attention was diverted. There would never be a better chance for escape. He and Slouch Hat could easily overpower the goblins. Padric looked back to the jetty where Torcan and a score of Red Caps continued to watch their crossing. It was no good. They would have a slow, ponderous vessel and nowhere to go.

The skiff bumped roughly into the stones of the island, slime covered steps marching down into the water. Slouch Hat disembarked nimbly, then turned and helped Padric before the pair of them lifted Svala onto land. The girl looked up with fearful wonder at the tower, clutching Padric's cloak tightly under her chin.

Padric craned his neck and followed her gaze. This close, the tower looked as if it would topple at any moment, rising into the sky at such an alarming angle. Padric looked away quickly, and shook off the hackles that played down his spine.

They ascended the stairs to the base of the tower where another pair of Red Caps waited next to a single door of tarnished bronze set deep into the blocks of the tower. The guards at the door were two of the burliest goblins Padric had ever seen, and he noticed a heavy maul and mattock resting against the stones near the door. Discarded in weeds creeping from between cracks in the masonry, lay a great, rusted chain, recently sundered. He was given no time to investigate further as the goblins quickly opened the door and escorted them inside.

Torches burned in the wide gallery within, revealing nothing but dust, webs and the refuse of vermin. The goblins grabbed the torches and immediately made for an arch at the back of the gallery through which the spiral stairs waited. The burly goblins led and Padric followed close behind them. He was several steps up before he realized he held one of Svala's hands in his own, leading her. He glanced back as he continued to climb and she gave him a tremulous smile. Padric squeezed her hand gently and saw that Slouch Hat came next, followed by the skiff pilots bringing up the rear. They passed other arches which led to the increasingly narrow floors of the tower, but the goblins never paused. Padric only had a brief glimpse of rotted wooden flooring and dank stones before the torch light moved on around the curve of the wall, plunging the abandoned rooms back into the darkness they deserved.

Padric's legs burned tightly, and the close, curved walls of cold stone began to steal his breath as they ceaselessly climbed. At last, the stairs ended on a small landing where another heavy bronze door greeted them. One of the burly goblins unlocked it with a key from his belt and opened the door to reveal a circular chamber lit from a fire already burning in the elaborately carved stone hearth. The wooden floor had been hastily swept, the dust of years still lying thick near the walls. A pallet of straw and furs had been placed in the room, a pitcher and a goblet nearby. Otherwise the room was empty.

Padric entered leading Svala, and as soon as Slouch Hat crossed the threshold, the goblins pulled the door shut swiftly, the latch grinding into place and locked. Padric looked around and shook his head. Another archway led out onto a balcony and he stepped out carefully. The wind whipped at his hair as he looked down on the dark, cowering buildings of the city spread out before him. The night sky was devoid of stars, and only the palest glimmer of moonlight shone off the water a dizzying distance below. His knees suddenly buckled and he felt queasy, all but stumbling back into the chamber away from that awful drop.

Svala sat on the floor before the fire, trying not to look at the grotesque faces carved into the hearth. Slouch Hat approached with the goblet in his hands and offered it to Padric.

"It is wine," the husk said, but Padric waved it off, nodding to Svala. Slouch Hat offered her the cup, and she took it from him, but did not drink.

"This is a fine prison," Slouch Hat continued. "Few men have ever stood so high."

"Any who wish to are mad," Padric replied.

"History would agree with you," the husk said dryly.

Padric put his back to the wall and slid down onto the ground, weary to his bones. "I have tried," he said with his eyes closed, "tried to fashion some means of escape, but . . . we are drowning."

"You are becoming a king," he heard Slouch Hat say. "You are referring to yourself as we."

Padric opened his eyes and gave a tired grin. "You know my meaning."

"I do," Slouch Hat said, coming to sit next to him. "I have also failed."

"I left my home," Padric said to his outstretched feet, "looking to be a steel monger's boy. And *that* seemed impossible."

He laughed.

Svala looked over at the sound, a confused look of fearful joy on her face. She seemed so small and alone sitting before that great fire in an ancient chamber at the top of the world.

"Slouch Hat," Padric said, daring to hope. "Do you know the tongue of Middangeard?"

"Crudely," the husk replied, then looked over at the girl.

"Ah . . . yes. What would you like me to ask?"

"If she is hungry?"

The husk's sack face stared at him. "There is no food up here, Padric."

"Oh," Padric looked around. "Right. Grand. Maybe you should tell her your name."

"I think the closest I could manage is Soft Helm."

Padric burst out laughing at that, perhaps longer and louder than was merited but it felt good all the same. When his eyes opened he found Svala still looking over at them, and felt a desperate need to include her.

"Fine," Padric said. "Perfect. Tell her that."

Slouch Hat leaned forward off the wall and spoke a few halting words, gesturing to himself. Svala's teeth appeared when she smiled, but she quickly covered them with her hand and answered.

"She thinks it is a good name," the husk said amiably.

Padric was encouraged. "Ask her if she is warm enough."

Slouch Hat spoke again and Padric was pleased to see Svala nod before answering.

"Yes," Slouch Hat translated. "She thanks you for the cloak."

"Ask her," Padric was searching. "Why she was afraid of the dwarrow?"

Slouch Hat looked over at him. "What?"

"During the executions," Padric felt sheepish. "When they brought out the dwarves, she seemed frightened. I was . . . worried for her."

Slouch Hat nodded slowly, then looked over at Svala and started speaking, his words slow, broken and hesitant. The girl's face fell slightly, and Padric felt guilty for dispelling her smile, hating himself for asking the question, but then she answered and the sound was captivating. It was the most Padric had ever heard her say, and he found he could not imagine her speaking any other language. The words, though a mystery to him, were perfect coming from her lips, folding warmly in the air in tones that pleasantly tickled his ears. Arnheir and his captains spoke brutally, but coming from Svala, the language of the fjordmen was a song that would never tire. Padric was disappointed when she stopped speaking, but relieved to see that the sorrow had fled from her face, replaced with a look of compassion aimed directly at him.

"She says," Slouch Hat relayed, "that she feared the goblins would kill the dwarrow. Something about dwarf-kind growing stronger in death, becoming . . . creatures of death. I am uncertain of her meaning. But she is of Middangeard and her people have dwelt close to the dwarrow for thousands of years."

"Tell her," Padric said, "that I am sorry she is locked up here. That she was given to me because of a lie. That she has had to see so much blood spilled. That I will never be able to free her or save her from all this madness. Tell her . . . just tell her I am sorry for everything."

Slouch Hat spoke briefly and Svala's answer was painfully short.

"She does not blame you," Slouch Hat told him. "And neither should you."

"I don't," Padric said looking over at the husk and smiling.

"I blame you."

The husk gave a derisive creak. "I blame Kederic Winetongue."

"Please, do not," Padric said. "That man is suffering enough. And he lied to save us when he had no cause. We tried to murder him, Slouch Hat. He could have let us die."

"They left him at Reaver's Meadow," the husk said.

"I know," Padric replied. "I was never allowed to speak with him. And there is no telling what will be his fate now."

"Nor ours," Slouch Hat muttered.

"Nor ours," Padric agreed.

They sat in silence for some time and Padric felt his eyelids growing heavy. "Tell Svala to take the bed."

He barely heard the exchange, but felt the husk's lean fingers grip his shoulder. "She says you should share it."

Padric did not bother to open his eyes. "I have no want to move from this spot."

"Come," Slouch Hat shook him. "You are in need of rest."

Padric allowed the husk to help him to his feet and found Svala already huddled under the furs. He looked down at her, nodded and smiled gratefully, then lay down atop the covers, not bothering to pull his boots off. His eyelids settled, blocking out the glow from the fireplace, and he welcomed the release of sleep.

When he awoke, the chamber was dark, the fire out and the air grown cold. He had not slept long, for the full veil of night still covered the sky beyond the arch to the balcony. He rolled off the pallet with the intention of stoking the fire, but Slouch Hat must have guessed his purpose, for the soft light of flame slowly spread through the room. Padric lay back groggily and mumbled a word of thanks, already drifting back to sleep.

A scream split the chamber and Padric bolted upright just in time to see a figure tumble off the balcony. Padric rushed towards the arch as the scream fell away, but skidded to a halt at the sight of something kneeling out on the ledge. Long, dark hair fell across its back and the head turned towards him. It was the face of a girl, her eyes wide, flesh milk-white under the moon. She was so young, barely out of childhood, and she gripped something in her hands.

"My king," she whispered and held out the object. It was a crown, a simple ring of forged iron.

Something grabbed Padric's shoulder and he whirled around in alarm to find Slouch Hat taking a quick step backwards.

"Padric!" the husk said. "Are you well?"

"You!" Padric advanced on him. "Why were you trying to push me?"

"What . . . Padric! I—"

"Trying to throw me off the tower, you murdering husk!"

"No!" Slouch Hat protested his hands raised. "I saw you make for the balcony in the dark. I was worried."

Padric looked back to the balcony and found it empty.

"There was . . . I swore."

He looked over at the concerned face of the husk and shook his head. "I am sorry. Must have been dreaming. Pay me no mind."

Slouch Hat nodded and walked out to the balcony as Padric settled back onto the pallet. Svala rolled over as he stretched out, and he felt a hand caress his manhood. He snatched at her wrist, pulling the hand away and opened his eyes, recoiling at the face of the dark-haired girl from the balcony pressed close to him.

"What do you desire, my lord?" she asked in a hush.

Padric pushed her away, holding fast to her wrist and pinning her to the mattress.

"Who are you?" he demanded, and again he was grabbed from behind, pulled roughly off the girl. He stumbled and fell backwards, but the rich carpet cushioned him.

"What are you doing?" he heard Slouch Hat demand.

Padric looked towards the bed and found Svala staring fearfully at him from beneath the heavy canopy. He jumped to his feet and Svala flinched back further. Slouch Hat clutched at him, but he slapped his hands away, casting frantically about the room.

"Where is she?"

"Padric! Dammit, do want to frighten the woman to death?"

"Not Svala!" Padric said. "Younger. Dark hair. Where?!"

The husk grabbed him by the front of the shirt and shook him. "You are seeing things! You are dreaming, that is all!"

"Am I?" Padric shouted, grabbing a candle from the nearby table and thrusting it at the husk. Slouch Hat jumped away from the flame. "You see this clearly! It was not here before! Neither was this!" He kicked the table over, then reached up and tore the canopy from the bed. "Nor this!"

Slouch Hat paused, slowly turning about the room, seeing the rich furnishings, the mirrored glass, the shelves of scrolls.

Padric tossed the candle roughly on the carpet that had not been there a moment before. The flame went out, the wick smoking pitifully.

"Tell me you do not see it," Padric challenged.

"I see it," Slouch Hat whispered.

Padric turned back to Svala, hoping to make amends for frightening her, but the girl was no longer looking at him. Her eyes stared wide at something behind him and Padric turned. A man stood facing the fire, his back turned. Over his broad, stooped shoulders was draped a fur-lined cloak of deep scarlet. White hair hung thickly down, almost to the pale, long-fingered hands that were clasped behind his back.

"We are betrayed," the man said, his voice quivering and strangely high. He turned, revealing piercing eyes, one completely bereft of color. His face was aquiline, sallow and sunken from care, but retained an unnatural youthfulness. A simple iron band sat upon his brow. The same crown Padric had seen in the hands of the girl.

"Jerrod." Slouch Hat's voice was full of wonder.

The man gave no sign he heard the husk.

"Come," he said holding his hand out, a thin smile playing across his lips. "Comfort your king."

Padric jumped as the girl passed him, taking the king's hand and leading him over to a chair made of animal bones where he sat.

She knelt at his feet, leaning back against his knees as his fingers played across her dark hair, the curve of her cheek, his thumb gliding into her mouth as he brushed her lips. Her eyes looked directly at Padric, watching him as the king caressed her.

"They will come for us now," Jerrod said sleepily, head lolled against the chair back. "Irial and his minions. We cannot stop them. They will sing us to death with their Fae songs, make us swell with honey until we burst, then transform themselves into bees so they may lick us into never being."

"Your son will stop them, my lord," the girl droned, playing her part and no more.

The king smiled at that, his eyes closing in some imagined rapture. "Our dread son. We made him tall and terrible . . . our Gaunt Prince."

The king sat forward, cupping the girl's cheeks in his hands, leaning over her upturned face, his white hair falling around her.

"Do you find him delicious?" he hissed. "Do you wish to be his?"

"If my lord tires of me and commands it," the girl replied, "I would go to him. Had I a choice, I wish to stay here with Your Grace."

"Yes," Jerrod hissed. "And you shall. We will bid Heggle make for us a feast and place it upon the bed where we can devour it in our ravishing! She will serve it raw, that our flesh might press against it and know bliss!"

Padric felt bile rise in his throat. Were she a farmer's daughter, this girl would be a year or three from taking a husband and yet here she sat, the plaything of a lecherous tyrant.

"And what should I tell the Swinehelm, my lord?" the girl asked. "Is he to march?"

Jerrod lurched back, throwing himself against the chair in a fit. His jaw clenched, hissing spit issuing from between his teeth.

His hand clenched into the girl's locks and he sprang to his feet, pulling her up roughly by the hair before flinging her to the ground.

"We are betrayed!" he screamed down at her. "Irial has robbed me of my Forge Born! My glorious warriors of living iron beguiled with charms and sweet words! My goblins will die in droves and it will not be enough!"

The girl did not cower, or whimper or hide herself behind her arms. She simply stared back at the raving king with the resigned expression of long practice, waiting for his tirade to end.

Jerrod straightened, his face flushed with fury, then it suddenly fell as a realization dawned.

"They will come for our crown," he said with quivering lips, removing the iron ring from his head with trembling fingers and gazing at it with covetous wonder. "They will snatch it from our dead skull. We will not allow it!"

He whirled around, his cloak billowing behind him as he strode out onto the balcony. The girl picked herself up, watching her king as he raised his hands towards the night sky squealing with mindless glee.

"We will give them no prize!" Jerrod squealed. "Do you hear me, Irial Elf-king! Airlann is mine! Her people are mine! IT IS ALL MINE!"

The girl's placid countenance did not waver. She rushed forward, her arms outstretched. Jerrod turned at the last moment, his deranged face melting into confusion as she pushed him over the railing. The crown fell from his grasp and hit the stones of the balcony with a toneless clatter. A scream cut pathetically across the sky as he plummeted out of sight. The girl stood a moment, waiting as the sound dwindled to an echo then ceased. She knelt slowly and plucked the crown from the balcony, cradling it in her delicate hands.

Padric released his breath as the candles in the chamber began to dim and as their light faded, so did the opulence of the room. The lush carpets, the chair of bone, the terrible bed, all diminished until only dust remained. Padric looked to Slouch Hat and Svala, finding them stunned yet unharmed. The husk nodded slowly towards the balcony and Padric looked to see the girl still there.

"And so ended the reign of Jerrod, the Second of His Name, last of the Goblin Kings."

Her words hung in the room as she stood and turned to face them, the crown in her hands.

"And you," she said to Padric, "seek to reclaim his crown."

Padric felt his skin grow cold. "No. Never."

"You lie," she said, taking a step into the room.

"Yes," Padric agreed, stepping away from her. "But not about the crown. I was forced to come here by Torcan Swinehelm."

"He seeks to test you," the girl replied simply. "He has sent others to me. All have failed. You too will fail, Padric Piskie-kissed, for you are no heir of Jerrod."

Padric glanced quickly at Slouch Hat, looking for answers but the husk had his gaze set firmly on the girl who continued her slow advance.

"I know," he answered. "But how . . . I do not . . . who are you?"

The girl found the question amusing and she smiled at him.

"You seek a name? I answered to the commands of his voice, the striking of his hand, the lusts of his body, but never once to a name. I was his since I can remember, the most honored and most debased of his servants. And in the end I was his undoing and he was mine.

"With his final breath, he cursed me, binding his crown to me and me to this forsaken tower. Only a legitimate survivor of Jerrod's bloodline can claim the crown. Until that day I am its keeper and its guardian."

She continued to walk towards Padric as she spoke, and he found himself compelled to stay away from her, countering every step with one of his own.

"Why does Torcan want the crown?" Padric felt it was wise to keep her talking. "Let the bastard fashion another!"

His back was to the wall now, forcing him to begin sliding along it as she tracked him across the room.

"The crown is more than a symbol," she told him. "It is a dread artifact from the first days of blood and betrayal. The first warlock, Penda Blood Coin, forged it with sorcery and sacrifice, passing it down the succession. Jerrod put the last of his Magic into the crown as he fell, making it an heirloom that will bestow its rightful bearer with a power terrible to behold."

"You mentioned a test," Padric said, inching away. "That is why Torcan locked me up here? To test me?"

"Only the true heir will leave this tower with the crown," the girl told him. "All others must go the way of Jerrod."

Padric felt the slam of the wind and the back of his legs struck something solid. He fumbled for balance and reached out with his hand, finding a stone balustrade. The night sky was all around and panic seized him as he realized where he had been lured. The girl came through the archway and out onto the balcony.

The crown was in her hands and she held it out to him.

"Take it, Padric," she said. "Take it if you can. Take it . . . or fall."

Padric looked behind him, the horrible yawning darkness of the water so far below, the mind shattering distance of the drop, the long, lonely seconds it would take to reach the unavoidable end.

He looked back to where the girl waited and willed himself to reach for the crown, but his arms would not obey. It was not his to possess. He did not want it.

He wanted to fall.

Padric turned. The balustrade was an insignificant barrier.

He could hop over it with ease and then there would be nothing.

Nothing holding him, nothing between him and death, and once he made the choice there was nothing he could do to stop it. He placed both hands on the balustrade, gripping the stone and gathered himself to jump.

"NO!"

Padric spun and saw Slouch Hat barrel through the archway, slamming into the girl, picking her up, his headlong rush unchecked as they careened over the edge. Padric made a desperate grab and felt the dry crunch of straw fill his palm. Chest pressed into the balustrade, Padric looked over the side and found Slouch Hat's hand in his, the husk dangling over blackness. Gripping the stone with his other hand, Padric hauled Slouch Hat up, grateful he was not a man of heavy muscle and bone. He pulled the husk over the railing and they slumped down together on the balcony.

"The girl?" Padric managed.

Slouch Hat's head snapped up and looked hard at Padric, rage crinkling across his inhuman face. The husk stood quickly and looked down at his hand where the crown lay gripped in his fingers.

Padric rose, staring in confusion.

Slouch Hat began to laugh.

Not the dry creaking Padric had heard before, but a full triumphant sound, almost breaking with emotion.

"Jerrod!" Slouch Hat shouted at the sky. "I found a way! You vile, groping madman, I found a way! You bound my flesh, you bound my spirit and now I am neither! This hollow man shall be my deliverance!"

The laughter rang out once more, then abruptly ceased as the husk suddenly collapsed. Padric caught him as he fell, lowering him gently to the stones. Slouch Hat's sack face was slack for a moment before expression returned and he looked up at Padric.

"She is . . . with me, Padric," the husk's voice was strained, worn thin. "By the Hallowed, she is with me."

"What does that mean?" Padric asked.

Slouch Hat smiled. "It means . . . we are no longer drowning."

Torcan Swinehelm was there to meet them when they emerged from the tower at dawn. The goblin leader's face was a brazen mask of avarice and glee when Padric stepped through the door alive, Svala on his arm and Slouch Hat following, bearing the iron crown. Torcan gazed at it with hungry eyes, lost for a moment in victory.

"I have claimed my birthright, Swinehelm," Padric snapped.

"And passed your test. The crown is mine."

The goblin seemed to remember something, and then went to one knee. The Red Cap guards also knelt.

"Your Grace," Swinehelm said with head bowed low. "We shall arrange a coronation immediately."

"No," Padric said firmly. "Fool, I dare not wear it. I am untutored in the ways of sorcery. Would you see me destroyed and the line ended?!"

Torcan looked up, shaking his head quickly. "No! Of course not. I misspoke. Forgive me, Your Grace."

Padric gave a satisfied nod. "Now, get my lady some proper clothes. If she is to be mother to the one who *will* wear this crown, I will not have her gawked at like a common strumpet."

"At once, Your Grace. What else would you require?"

"What else?" Padric gave the warlord a mocking smile. "My lord Swinehelm, have you so easily forgotten your own schemes?"

Torcan gave a puzzled shake of his head.

"We finish what you started," Padric told him. "We go to Castle Gaunt."

TWENTY

"Foolish chase," Deglan muttered, his words caught and swallowed by the wind. He squinted hard across the rocky expanse of the ridge top, searching for the next of Madigan's damnable piles of stones. The crest of the mountain was a sprawling, windswept march of boulders, interrupted only by ugly, dead moss and ankle-busting cracks. The ascent to the summit had been a grueling scramble up switchbacks littered with loose pebbles and dirt.

Deglan's legs and back ached without reprieve. He had been glad to leave Toad Holm with a fully replenished herb satchel and a pack full of provisions, but now it all seemed like a dragging, painful weight, crushing his joints into meal. He considered pitching his burdens off the mountain, but was forced out of his bitter musings by the sight of the little figure ahead of him, practically skipping across the rocks without a care.

"Blink!" he shouted fruitlessly across the wind. "Do not get too far ahead!"

"*I have reminded her to stick to the cairns,*" Curdle's voice popped into his head.

Deglan turned as the pale hobgoblin approached, pulling himself along by his stout walking staff.

"Tell her not to get out of sight, dammit!" Deglan yelled aloud and turned back to see Blink stop.

"*She is waiting at the next cairn,*" Curdle told him, drawing up alongside.

"I am right damn next to you," Deglan snarled. "No need to buzz about in my brain."

"Apologies," the seer gasped. "But I am finding my breath very precious at the moment."

"Well you can thank your huntsman friend for that," Deglan replied. "Trekking us up this bloody hill."

"Is it only a hill?" Curdle asked, sucking in air. "Pity. I thought I had accomplished something."

"We have accomplished the same wondrous feat today, as yesterday," Deglan waved a hand scornfully at the mountain top.

"And the day before and the day before that! We have walked ourselves sore, following a madman and his dogs in a pointless search for a metal giant that is best avoided!"

Curdle smiled at his rant. "Madigan Sure Finder is no madman."

"So you think."

"He believes we are close," Curdle said. "We will soon find your Forge Born."

Deglan did not much like hearing it referred to as *his* Forge Born, but he said nothing, instead placing his energy in continuing across the ridge. A moment later, he heard the tapping of Curdle's staff as he followed behind.

Their journey had brought them far from Toad Holm; long days of travel that showed no signs of their quarry, at least none that Deglan could see. Madigan and his dogs always stayed well ahead, marking a trail for them to follow, only reappearing at nightfall after they made camp. His mountaintop markers were carefully stacked rocks placed in regular intervals across the ridge, and Deglan found Blink standing near the next such pile as promised.

Bundled against the wind, the girl looked far less starved and pitiful than the day he found her. A light had begun to grow behind her previously abyssal eyes, and she had rediscovered some expressions. She fixed him with one now, a mix of wonder and even a little confused impatience, as if she could not understand why he and Curdle were not in a bigger hurry to see what lay over the next boulder. No sooner had they caught up and she was off again, making for the next cairn with the surefooted steps of youth.

He had never intended to bring her along, but on the day he was to part Toad Holm, Curdle took one look at the child and insisted she go. Deglan had wanted to throttle the pasty-faced mind reader, infuriated that he would contemplate putting the girl at such risk on a dangerous hunt, but before he could voice his anger, the hobgoblin held up a calming hand.

"The danger to her body out in the world is possible," Curdle said gently. "But, the danger to her mind if you abandon her is certain. She will not survive it, Deglan."

Deglan had taken a long look at Blink's lost face, knowing the seer spoke true, and made the only choice he could. As a healer, he could not deny the rejuvenating effects the journey had so quickly bestowed upon his foundling. She marched along with bottomless vigor throughout the days and slept soundly at their nightly camps, disturbed by neither darkness nor dread. The girl had still not spoken a word, despite her reconnection to her surroundings. Curdle was able to discern her basic thoughts and feelings, but Deglan had warned him off mucking around too deep.

He did not truly believe the hobgoblin wished her any harm. He had been nothing but forthcoming since their meeting, but Deglan's sense of distrust was slow to die. He might be an insufferable bastard, but if it meant Blink's safety, Deglan Loamtoes would play his strengths to the hilt.

The day was old before they finally saw the downside of the mountain and the descent was every bit as spiteful as the climb.

Deglan and Curdle arrived on flat ground weary and footsore. Blink awaited them at the bottom, fresh faced and bright-eyed.

Curdle gave a tired chuckle. "We are two old dotards, Master Loamtoes."

"Speak for yourself, Milkthumb," Deglan replied. "I still got my teeth."

The seer smiled broadly at that, showing he still had his as well. "Well, then let us honor our Fae blood," Curdle rallied.

"Onward!"

Deglan shook his head, but could not quite manage the scowl he had intended. They walked on, following a heavily wooded track at the base of the mountain. Sticks had been laid to lead them and Deglan watched with fascination as Blink bent to retrieve each marker, flinging them into the underbrush.

"It appears," Curdle said with amusement. "That our path is only ours to know."

Deglan felt an odd mixture of pride and worry. "Madigan teach her that?"

Curdle shrugged. "I do not know."

As they travelled the sun began to set, throwing the last of its brightness through gaps in the leaves. They found Sweat and Panic waiting for them in a snug clearing off the track, showing where Madigan meant for them to camp. Blink rushed forward and the dogs bounded to meet her, sniffing and licking, circling and nuzzling. Blink patted at them, leaning away from their rough tongues, smiling with delight. She put her arms around Panic's neck, while Sweat lay down, exposing his belly until Blink took notice and went to her knees, hands rubbing freely.

This nightly ritual still made Deglan nervous. The hounds' noses overtopped the child's head and he knew the animals to be tenacious hunters. Madigan's dogs frightened even Kederic's warriors. It was the men of the fort who had named them, claiming that a man would only succeed in two things if he ran from them.

They gossiped that Madigan had freed a barghest matriarch from a hunter's trap and she had gifted him with two of her pups in gratitude. Other versions had him coupling with the animal after freeing her and said the dogs were his own offspring. Whatever the truth, Sweat and Panic were two of the canniest beasts Deglan had encountered, and, like the men of the fort, he was uneasy in their presence. But what bothered him most was how normal they became when Blink was around. They scampered and hopped, their tails wagged and they played with the child with something that could only be called tenderness. A little girl playing with the dogs; a common sight across the farms and feasting halls of the known world, and yet, something remained off. Like their mysterious master, Sweat and Panic had no voice. They were as silent as the death they brought to those they pursued, as silent as the child they now played with.

Deglan set to work gathering fire wood, keeping one eye cocked at Blink and her playmates. Curdle set about digging through their provisions for the evening meal, but most of them would end up being packed right back up. Madigan always returned with fresh game.

He did not arrive until after dark. Deglan had the fire going strongly and after glancing down to shift a log with a stick, he looked up to find the huntsman standing over him, a brace of rabbits hanging from each fist.

"*That* trick," Deglan said casually, "no longer surprises me. But don't worry, Sure Finder, I am still shocked you cook your meat."

Madigan said nothing. He tossed one of the rabbits to Sweat and another to Panic. The dogs caught them cleanly in their jaws and padded away to eat outside the light of the fire.

"Good evening, Madigan," Curdle said pleasantly from his seat on a log.

The hunter gave the hobgoblin the same response he had given Deglan and strode over to a low-hanging branch where he deftly hung the remaining two rabbits. He pulled a long iron knife from his belt and was about to skin the animals when Deglan saw him toss a glance at him and Curdle. Madigan sheathed the iron blade and drew a second, this one of bronze and set to work without further delay.

"Most considerate of you, Madigan," Curdle said. "We thank you."

Deglan frowned. He did not remember thanking anybody.

"He knows iron is poison to us."

Deglan looked over the fire and found Curdle looking at him.

"Not unless he stabs us with it. Which I am still not sure he won't do."

Curdle did not take the bait, merely wrinkling his brow with resignation and going back to his scroll. Damn albino was always reading.

Deglan looked back to Madigan and tensed when he saw Blink standing at the man's leg, looking up intently as he skinned the rabbits. They made a contrasting pair.

Dressed in skins, lean with muscle, every inch of him full of feral strength, Madigan was as savage and hard as Blink was precious and frail. His chin and lip were shaved to rough stubble, but his straw-colored hair hung in long whiskers from his cheeks and in twisted locks from his head. He appeared not to take notice of the child's presence, but Deglan thought he saw the man pause in his task a few times as if giving Blink time to absorb his actions.

She became more reserved when the huntsman was around, her gaze more fixed, but it was not the withdrawn stare of the little girl Deglan had rescued. Rather, she was focused, determined, intently curious. But as encouraged as he was with her recovery, Deglan was concerned about its source. Madigan the Sure Finder was not someone he could ever trust.

When Curdle explained that the man had been hunting him, Deglan could not suppress a shiver. And it was not skill or cunning or even luck that had saved him from Sweat and Panic, no, it was two damn Red Caps. From Madigan's thoughts Curdle had learned that the huntsman was set on Deglan's trail by Acwellen for conspiring with the Red Caps to destroy Hog's Wallow. But then he witnessed Deglan kill Nape and Canker, rescuing Blink in the process, and Madigan began to doubt. He followed all the way to the entrance of Toad Holm where he could not enter, but Curdle sensed him and his dogs.

"Three minds that function as one," Curdle had explained.

"It is a rare and singular sensation. Difficult to ignore."

Deglan had not wanted to explore that notion further and let it lie, still disturbed with the thought that the man had been hunting him. Now, it seemed, Madigan wished to help them, and the seer was all too willing to allow him. It was not a company Deglan relished being among, but he suffered it because he believed the hobgoblin mystic truly wanted to stop Torcan Swinehelm, and that was alliance enough.

After the rabbits were dressed and allowed to roast over the fire, they all ate. Blink fell asleep in Deglan's arms with the grease still on her fingers. Madigan lay down on the bare ground close to the fire, Sweat and Panic curling up around him. Deglan was never certain that they actually slept, but all three lay still enough with their eyes closed to make a good show of it. Curdle continued to read by the light of the fire. The seer was always awake when Deglan closed his own eyes and when he opened them in the morning. Probably why he was so blasted pale.

"That something to help us stop the Flame Binder?"

Deglan asked, pointing at the scroll.

"This?" Curdle said, looking up and smiling shyly. "No. It is treatise on the properties of yarrow root."

Deglan raised his eyebrows. "The bad gnome's plaything? Old noble yarrow!"

"Yes," Curdle said enthusiastically. "It is a fascinating substance. I was just reading that it can help cure even the most grievous of wounds."

"Only if it is harvested at noon on a bright day," Deglan said. "Preferably near the full of the moon. And it works best on bleeding injuries."

"Ah yes," Curdle looked down excitedly at the scroll. "It says here it is a fine cure for nosebleeds."

"If you make a potion of it," Deglan agreed. "Need to be careful though . . . take too much and you will end up flaccid for a fortnight."

The seer blinked at him questioningly.

"You know," Deglan said, raising his fist in the air and then letting it go limp.

"Ah," Curdle nodded in understanding. "Yes. I see."

"Was going to have to brew some myself if I spent another day around a certain piskie," Deglan said almost to himself.

Curdle seemed a bit embarrassed. "They are truly very comely creatures."

"This one," Deglan whistled low and shook his head.

"'Course, that is the tease with piskies. Too small to do right with . . . but the thoughts you have!"

The thoughts seemed to make Curdle uncomfortable, for he smiled, but looked back down at his scroll as if it could save him from wanton winged women. Deglan decided to be merciful, though he enjoyed watching the mystic squirm.

He cleared his throat, returning to a more serious tone.

"You think we can stop Torcan?"

Curdle looked up. "I know that we must try. Same as you."

"I do know," Deglan said. "But, is this Forge Born I saw truly the answer?"

"If he is the last of his kind," Curdle nodded. "Yes."

"How?"

Curdle put his scroll aside, collecting his thoughts. When he began speaking, his words were slow and measured.

"The resurrection of the Forge Born would be a woeful turn for this isle. And we must do all we can to stop that from happening. But of even greater import is not whether they awaken . . . but how they will function if they do. Certainly the Red Caps want them as the mindless drones they were at their creation. An army they can control. But will they wake so? Or will they still possess the mystical heart placed upon them by the Seelie Court? The heart that granted them free will. Or worst of all, will they awaken in that terrible condition so many of them succumbed to in their final years? Bloodthirsty, berserk, unfeeling . . ."

"Unwound," Deglan finished.

"Yes," Curdle nodded.

"Could a Goblin King control them in such a frenzy?"

"No," Curdle answered. "That state of their being was never intended."

Deglan watched something haunting play across the mystic's face. "Intended?"

Curdle looked at him for a moment, choosing his words.

"The Seelie Court was ever of just intention," he said at last. "But they were not infallible. Mistakes were made, especially with the Forge Born."

"Damn right," Deglan said a bit too loudly, and Blink stirred slightly. He waited for her to settle once more before he continued in a quieter voice. "Should have destroyed them all after the war was won. Not forgave and forgot, giving them the run of the isle. Enemies are enemies, and they should be treated as such, not welcomed to the victory banquet with open arms."

Curdle fixed him with a sad expression.

"I think," he said, rolling up his scroll, "that I shall try and sleep. Pleasant night, Master Loamtoes."

Too late, Deglan realized the meaning of his words and felt suddenly ashamed of himself. Why should he? He spoke the truth.

The Seelie Court should have no more forgiven the goblins than they did their creations. He always believed that and still did . . . and yet, here he was, camped out in the wilderness on some desperate quest to save Airlann from further war and degradation, aided by a goblin and a mortal man; the condemned of history.

Deglan remained awake for a long time.

Madigan and the dogs were gone when he awoke in the morning. Blink was helping Curdle pack their camp kit, handing the hobgoblin blankets and cooking implements. The seer always thanked her with a smile. Blink turned and, seeing Deglan awake, tramped over, offering him an apple. He stood, brushed the dirt and leaves from his clothes and took the fruit from her outstretched hand.

"Good morning," he said, brushing her cheek with his thumb. "And thank you."

Holding the apple in his teeth, Deglan walked over and helped Curdle get his pack over his shoulders. The hobgoblin turned and nodded cordially.

"Shall we be off?" he asked, pointing to the first of their daily markers with his stick.

Deglan bit through his apple. "Charge."

Thankfully, their way was flat and even for most of the day, a wandering valley trail shaded darkly by the close trees. Blink stayed ahead as their little forward scout and Deglan was able to walk next to Curdle on the easy path.

"My pardons," Deglan ventured, breaking several hours of silence, "if my words offended last night."

"No need," Curdle replied. "You are welcome to your opinion. I have heard worse, believe me. We hobgoblins are caught between two worlds and must accept the turmoil of our choice. It is you I feel pity for, Master Loamtoes. Your world has been entirely shattered, and for that, you have my sympathy."

Deglan shook the comment off. "I turned my back on Toad Holm centuries ago. I should have listened to wiser words and never returned."

"Perhaps," Curdle said. "But your anger with your own people did not include the betrayal you now feel. That the gnomes would welcome us goblins back is one matter. That they would aid the Red Caps in freeing the Flame Binder is another entirely. And it is in that matter where I share your feelings."

"Why was he ever allowed to live?"

"Many were put to death," Curdle's tone was resigned. "But with each fall of the headsman's axe, the others grew stronger, the Fire leaving the fallen to live in the survivors. We goblins are not like the other elementals, Deglan. We stole Fire. It was not ours by right. And though we are kin to gnomes, the blessings of Earth were denied us when Ghob supplanted the dragons. Magic flows through our veins as it does with all Fae, but we remain mongrels, disinherited from Earth and Stone and illegitimate impostors to Fire.

"Even you, a simple herbalist, can call upon the Earth to aid you. While you do not possess the power of an Earth Shaper, the element will not deny your birth-right. As a goblin, I can no more call upon Earth than I can Fire, both are denied to me. For my kind, the direct use of Magic must be attained through other means and disciplines. Only a very few of us can manipulate the flames and call them to our will, and the path to such craft is a perilous one. The Flame Binders were a dangerous power in the world and their greatest act of madness was giving the spark of life to the constructs of the goblin foundries, making them living iron. That they then granted control of the Forge Born to the Goblin Kings only further proves their deranged devotion to their mortal rulers.

"Earth lives in all gnomes. Water flows through every undine and Air exists in all sylphs. But Fire burns in only a few goblins and must go somewhere when its vessel is destroyed. Toad Holm realized this far too late and the last Flame Binder was swollen with purging Magic before they saw their mistake. If he were to die, what would happen? Would Fire be forever extinguished, destroying the balance of the Elements? That could mean the end of all things. Or would it return to the core of the world, free from goblin bondage and back to its rightful keepers? Not even the wisdom of the elves could answer those questions, for their hold on this world was already dwindling. So the Flame Binder was imprisoned until the riddles could be solved."

"Which is why King Blackmud went underground," Deglan said. "Not just to bring Ghob to justice, but to see if he still held the dragons enslaved."

"Yes," Curdle replied. "Other solutions were sought and—"

Deglan grabbed Curdle's arm, cutting off his words and pointing up the trail. Blink was running forward and coming towards her at a run was the shaggy grey shape of one of Madigan's dogs.

"Only one?" Curdle said, concern etched across his brow.

It was several hours before dusk and the dogs always waited together when it was time to make camp.

Deglan just shook his head and hurried to catch up to Blink.

When they came up, they found it was Panic, panting heavily. Blink tried to pet her, but every time the little girl reached out the dog bounded several paces up the trail before turning back to look at them. Blink turned to Deglan and Curdle, and raising her arm, she pointed down the trail.

"We are to follow the dog," Curdle said.

"Thanks," Deglan wrinkled his face at the hobgoblin. "I needed a mind reader to work that one out."

Panic took off at a swift pace as soon as they stepped towards her, Blink hurrying behind. Deglan's pack jostled around uncomfortably as he ran to keep up. The dog kept pulling well ahead, often vanishing around curves in the trail. Blink was never far behind, and each time the girl was lost from sight, Deglan used the worry to quicken his feet. They would find dog and child waiting, looking back down the trail, but no sooner did Deglan and Curdle come into view and they were off again.

At last, Deglan rounded a bend to find Blink and Panic waiting far up the trail, but they did not look back for him. They were turned towards the forest. Winded and sweating, Deglan plodded to a stop next to the girl and looked where she did. A path a blind man could follow was cut through the trees, snapped limbs lying next to a wide furrow ploughed through the carpet of fallen leaves.

"Oh my," Curdle said when he arrived. But before the hobgoblin could catch his breath, Panic headed into the woods, following the destruction. The dog did not go as quickly as before and they were able to stay right behind her. Soon she peeled off and headed up a gentle rise where Madigan squatted among the trees, spear in hand, Sweat at his side. The huntsman nodded as they approached and then pointed. Deglan followed the man's finger and found a cave nestled into the neighboring hillside below.

The ground became rocky and bare near the cave's mouth, but the trail of disturbed ground led right to it.

Madigan tapped his finger to his ear and then held it towards the sky, his eyes never leaving the cave. They waited, and Deglan felt Blink jump when a sudden tremendous boom issued from the cave, trembling the ground beneath them. Deglan shot Curdle a quizzical look and found the hobgoblin deep in thought.

The ground shook again as the sounds of another concussion pulsed through the air. Without a word, Curdle slipped out of his pack and then started off down the rise, heading straight for the cave.

"Buggery and spit," Deglan groaned, dropping his own pack and then looked at Blink. "Stay here . . . with the dogs."

Madigan looked at him impassively, apparently taking no offense.

Deglan made his way down and caught up to Curdle before the hobgoblin reached the cave entrance. Another boom rumbled forth.

"You need not accompany me," the mystic said.

"Nonsense," Deglan replied. "Who else is going to introduce you?"

The pounding continued, becoming painful to the ears as they stepped into the cavern. It was not deep, barely larger than an outcropping, and the sunlight managed to creep past the threshold.

Deglan winced as the cave roared again, bouncing off the surrounding stone and sending showers of loose dirt to fall from above. At the back of the cavern, Deglan could see a huge, shadowy shape pull back long arms and then slam them into the stones.

"It will bring this whole place down on our heads!" Deglan screamed over the horrible ringing of metal on stone. "We should not be here!"

Curdle pushed determinedly forward, ducked low against the cacophony. Deglan rushed forward and seized him by the arm.

"Do not be a fool! We will die if we stay here!"

Curdle shook him off and continued on.

"Stop!" Deglan heard him scream at the Forge Born's back.

"I beg you, please! Stop! You need not do this!"

But it was no use. The hobgoblin's entreaties were overcome as the Forge Born continued to slam his fists into the cave wall. An anvil sized rock broke away from the ceiling and Deglan watched in horror as it fell towards Curdle. He leapt forward, barreling into the hobgoblin, his arms encircling him, flinging both of them away from a crushing death. They landed hard, but Deglan tried to take the worst of it, shielding the frail mystic from the stone-strewn floor. Pain morphed into anger, and Deglan shoved himself to his feet. The Forge Born kept up its mad destruction, turning the cave into a dreadful bell, tolling itself to pieces.

Deglan marched forward, heedless of the ear-bursting punches and the falling rocks. He had eyes only for this towering machine, this iron brute whose only purpose was death.

He hated it.

He hated hunting it, hated finding it, hated looking at it.

The memory of his first sighting of it pained him. Bulge-Eye had been with him, and Deglan could still feel the panic that rose when he thought it was Unwound. He and Faabar and the piskie and that coal-haired youth had tracked it, hoping to destroy it, but they had found the Red Caps instead; Torcan Swinehelm and his cursed Flame Binder. Hog's Wallow had burned, the villagers had died, Bulge-Eye and Faabar along with them. Deglan's own people had betrayed him, and it had all started with a distant glimpse of this Forge Born. This thing with a name.

"COLTRANE!"

The massive arms pulled high over the thing's head, metal fingers interlaced into a single giant fist, poised for a final, dooming strike. Deglan threw his own arms over his head, preparing for the crushing weight of the cave to fall in on him, but the concussive slams ceased, and suddenly there was only the sound of his ringing ears. Deglan peeked up and found the Forge Born lowering its arms.

"Leave," it said without turning, the deep, slow grind of its voice mixing with the fading echoes of its blows.

"Bugger you!" Deglan spat, and then took an involuntary step backwards as the Forge Born slowly turned. He could barely make it out in the recess of the cave, its towering bulk wrapped in shadow. It said nothing more, seeming to wait. Deglan felt a hand clutch his shoulder and turned to find Curdle standing next to him, gaze locked on Coltrane. The hobgoblin was covered in grit, but appeared unharmed.

"We would speak with you," he said. "We must beg your help."

"I," the ponderous voice answered, "will not go."

"I know you are being drawn," Curdle pressed. "And that you do not wish to go. But destroying yourself is not the answer."

"Go?" Deglan turned to Curdle. "Go where?"

"To Castle Gaunt," Curdle replied in hushed tones before raising his voice again to address the machine. "You have resisted valiantly, but eventually the pull will be too great."

Deglan took a step forward, new understanding dispelling his fear. "The Tor," he declared, thrusting a finger at Coltrane.

"That is why you were there. Because of the Flame Binder."

"Yes," Curdle agreed. "The wizard's reemergence in the world beckons you. He seeks to bring all of your kind back. You can feel it?"

The Forge Born was long in answering. "Yes."

"We would stop him," Curdle said. "But we dare not try without your help."

"I," the halting tones said, "will not fight."

"Why?" Deglan demanded.

"They told us to fight," the Forge Born said, its voice slowing and deepening with every word. "And we fought. Others told us it was wrong to fight. I . . . do not fight."

Deglan's mouth snapped shut.

"Coltrane," Curdle continued, "the choice not to help is yours. But that choice will soon be taken from you, along with every other choice. You will once again be a slave and you will fight whether you wish it or not. And you will kill. Is that what you want?"

"No."

"Then I beg you," Curdle said. "Help us! Together we can ensure your freedom and the peace of the isle."

"I will not fight."

Deglan saw Curdle's face struggle with the finality of the thing's words. The seer's mouth quivered, searching for more words. The hobgoblin hung his head when he found none and turned to go.

Deglan looked up at the Forge Born and found no more anger. He was weary and had been devoid of hope for longer than he could recall, but Curdle had believed, truly believed, that a chance could be found within this living iron. Deglan had just watched that hope die. He did not need to wonder who had been witness the day that light went out of his own eyes.

He knew the answer.

"You were built for war," he told Coltrane, his voice tired even to his own ears. "And war has come again. Our side needs a champion, and the one I would stand with is not here. You helped me bury him, remember? And now you wish to bury yourself." He waved a hand dismissively. "Go ahead. It's a useless gesture. It won't kill you. Won't even stop you for very long. Eventually the goblin's call will be too great and you will go. There are two choices here, Forge Born. Help us now . . . or help them later. There is no middle ground."

They stood in the silence of the cave for a long time.

Deglan stared up into the shadows, wondering if the thing had finally stopped working. He turned to follow Curdle when there came a scraping thud as the Forge Born stepped forward. The weak light from the distant sun revealed its strange face, fashioned with rivets, deep black slits serving as eyes. It still wore the shabby piece of wool over its body and the tip of the scabbard Deglan knew to be empty poked from behind its iron leg.

"I will help."

Curdle bowed his head in relief and his voice was barely above a whisper. "Thank you, Coltrane."

The hobgoblin led the metal brute out of the cave and into the light of day. Deglan stayed behind, watching them.

"I hate this thing," he grumbled at last, shaking his head as he left the cave.

TWENTY-ONE

The old elf road crawled defiantly between the low hills, struggling against the weeds and roots which threatened to consume its once smoothly laid stones. In Ages past, all of Airlann had been connected by such roads, but their caretakers had long since abandoned them, the Magic which sustained them slowly unraveling.

It is all fading.

Rosheen sat inside what was left of one of the intricately carved stone lampposts that stood beside the road. In bygone days, they marked every mile, glowing with Fae light after sunset to offer comfort and safety to travelers. This was the first Rosheen had found still standing after countless miles, and she took shelter against the cold, spitting rain under its crumbling roof. She wondered if it still came to life at night, shining with pale blue fire.

There would be no knowing. Sir Corc had them traveling quickly, and they would be a long way from this spot come nightfall.

Barring the rivers, the derelict roads were still the swiftest way to travel overland, but they were exposed and easy to watch. It was a risk to be on them with unknown numbers of Red Caps loose across the isle, but sticking to the cover of trees and wild hills would be slow going. Too slow for Sir Corc's liking. Wherever their destination, the knight wanted to reach it sooner rather than later.

Rosheen had been asked to scout ahead for signs of goblins or other eyes watching the road. So far they had been fortunate, encountering nothing but a fox slinking across the stones. She had been flying back regularly to report, but her wings were growing tired.

Let them catch up to me.

She plucked idly at the ribbon she now wore as a sash and stared miserably out at the rain. Cold, clinging and constant, that was rain in Airlann. Rosheen recalled the days when it had not been so. Spring rains had been frequent and refreshing, bringing new life to an innocent world. In Summer, the sky did not often open, but when it did the drops were heavy and warm, sliding seductively down the skin, a wet end to hot days. Rosheen still remembered the dances and feasts and lovemaking of those lost Ages, but she no longer yearned for them as she once did. The ache in her loins had been replaced by pain in her heart as the isle slipped further and further towards a frozen death. Autumn had begun the day the warlocks made themselves masters of the goblin race, stealing the throne and sending the elves into hiding. Chill winds arose, sweeping leaves stained red to match the ceaseless bloodshed over the abandoned bastions of Fae-kind.

Word traveled quickly in those days. The dread news of Penda Blood Coin's treachery was spread across the isle by fleet riders, the mind speech of mystics, sewn through ancient ley lines, whispered by the woodwose in the forests, and borne by the undine on the wind. Murder. Treason. War. All of Airlann knew within hours and still it had not been enough. The goblins were too many and their human leaders too powerful, swollen with ill-gotten Magic. Centuries of battle, slavery, injustice, starvation and depravity were to rule the isle.

And now will again.

There was no strength left to prevent it. Airlann had backslid into a pastoral wilderness. The human settlements were few and far between, the Fae driven away or in self-imposed isolation. The roads were ruined, the ley lines dissolved, and the woodwose slept. There was no one left to carry the news of the Red Cap uprising. The goblins would control the isle before any sizable resistance could be raised.

No matter. There are none left to fight.

They had such hope when Irial was returned to kingship, trusting that the bleakness so long remembered would be driven away by sun and warmth and song, but it was not to be. The might of the elves continued to wane, and the isle withered with them.

The clouds did not lighten and green did not return to the forests.

Many said the death of Princess Aillila was to blame. The king's grief for his only child was too much to bear, dooming the isle to these endless days of decline. Whatever the cause, the deterioration permeated the Fae peoples.

The fomori, always so few, had retreated to the coastal crags. The gnomes, divided by their cultural controversy, retired to their underground city, and the ever-fickle sylphs went to play in the winds over other lands. Without the guidance of the elves, the undine had become an unpredictable presence, changeable as the tides in loyalty and temperament. They may fight one day, but stand idly away from danger the next. The gruagach would challenge the goblins and fight as they always had, but theirs would be a personal war, ignoring the well-being of any but their own kind. They would skulk in the darkness and wage their shadow war with trickery and quiet murder, but it would amount to little. There were simply too many goblins in the world to throttle in the night.

Rosheen's own people and the other lesser Fae had never possessed the might needed to wage wars. They were steadfast allies and were much prized where they lent aid, but without a formidable force to rally behind they were of little use.

We watch roads.

Rosheen poked her head out of the lamp house. She found Sir Corc and Pocket, still some distance away, trudging through the rain, the boy leading the mule. Muckle's rotund form was visible just behind them, but Bantam Flyn was nowhere to be seen. The knight had ordered him to walk a fair distance behind so that he could rush forward with warning if anyone tried to overtake them on the road. It was a solid act of caution, but Rosheen was certain that Sir Corc had given him the rear guard for less strategic reasons.

She waited until she could hear Backbone's hooves clomping on the uneven stones before leaving her dry shelter.

"Clear to this point," she said as she flew towards the trio.

Sir Corc only nodded, looking past her to the unexplored road beyond. He still wore mail, despite the rain, the metal rings already beginning to show signs of tarnish from the damp. Rosheen looked down at Pocket. He stood cold and miserable, eyes wide to fight his obvious weariness. The mule's guide rope was clutched almost desperately in his thick-fingered hands, and Rosheen frowned in concern over the shivers he fought to hide.

"We need rest," she told Sir Corc. "Food and warmth."

"Beef and bacon pastie," Muckle licked his lips. "And a horn of hippocras. Go down nicely."

"Not here," Sir Corc said simply.

"When?" Rosheen pressed him. "Pocket cannot handle much more."

"I am fine," the gurg said bravely.

Without taking his eyes from the road, Sir Corc placed an armored hand on the boy's shoulder.

"Soon," he said. "We have put some miles between us and Black Pool, but we are far from outside our enemy's reach."

"Perhaps if you tell us where we are going," Rosheen said.

"Out of Airlann," the knight replied. "To Sasana or the Knucklebones. All the way to Middangeard if we must."

Muckle let loose a mock shiver. "Don't fancy freezing my bollocks off."

Sir Corc ignored him. "Getting off the isle will take some doing. With Black Pool overrun, finding a ship will be difficult. If Seanach's Ford remains unmolested we may have a chance."

"That is on the far side of Airlann," Rosheen pointed out.

Sir Corc started up the road. "Best be on our way."

Pocket rubbed his face before ambling after the knight, Muckle following behind the mule.

"How about the Isle of Mad Women?" she heard the goblin call after Sir Corc. "We could go there! They might be . . . lonely."

Rosheen considered waiting on Flyn, but thought better of it. The squire would not take well to the idea of leaving the isle. To him, everything was a retreat. Besides, he had his job.

And I have mine.

She flew up the road, bypassing the others without a word.

". . . and that is how you tickle a troll with a toothache!"

Pocket nearly lost his footing when Muckle slapped him merrily on the back. He was saved from having to pretend to laugh when Sir Corc shushed the goblin and not for the first time.

Muckle turned to Pocket, teeth clenched past downturned lips as if he were about to be struck on the head. Pocket smiled, hoping it would appease him for a while. He had liked Muckle the day he first met him, with his endless antics and rude humor. The goblin had offered him aid and companionship when he most needed it, and that was something new to Pocket. Now he was fairly certain that Sir Corc had asked Muckle to follow him all along, so the unsought help of a stranger was actually the watchful eye of his keeper. Pocket was not upset about it. Black Pool had been a dangerous place. He understood that now, and he knew why Muckle was an effective protector.

He was dangerous.

Since the night on the bridge, Pocket found it troubling to look at the goblin, afraid that he might find himself entranced. The prospect of laughing at anything he said filled Pocket with a dread that made his stomach turn sour. He had spent his life in constant fear of what harmful intentions lay under the surface of people's every word, every deed, every gesture and expression. The boy who smiled at you was often the first to slap mud in your face, and the man who seemed the most unaware of your presence was watching you closer than any other with violent thoughts in his head. Pocket knew this for truth, and yet he had been drawn in by Muckle, trusting him despite his obvious madness. He had been so confident, so amiable and quick to laugh at others as well as himself.

They had eaten so many sweets that first day in the city, all of them gifts from hawkers who genuinely seemed to like the goblin with the fish in his breeches. But

Pocket could still see the entrails spilling out of the burst flesh of the men on the bridge, their blue faces and black lips. His appetite fled at the slightest thought of that sight.

Still, he was grateful he knew. Maybe if he had seen Muckle's true nature sooner he would not have trusted the woman with the bucket, even for a moment. Pocket had avoided asking Sir Corc about the gruagach, fearing his questions would only lead to a sound reprimand for sneaking away. He deserved one, he knew, but that did not make him want to face it anymore. But he had to know! Sir Corc probably would not tell him anything anyway, and better to get his punishment out of the way. It might even take his mind off the blisters on his feet.

"Sir?" he asked quietly. "Would you tell me, please, why those gruagach wanted to take me?"

"Because they were given a chance," the knight replied without looking at him.

"Thirty lashes for desertion!" Muckle trumpeted, getting a look of warning from Sir Corc in the process. "Sorry."

Sir Corc looked back to Pocket and considered a long moment. "They see you as one of them, Pocket," he said at last.

"But I am only half gruagach." Pocket was confused and it must have shown on his face.

"The Fae-folk," the knight continued, "have always been fascinated by the mortal races. The elves raised my own people out of savagery. The fomori were even granted immortality as a gift, but humans . . . humans intrigued the Fae most of all."

"Can you blame us?" Muckle muttered. "Ever seen a goblin woman?"

Sir Corc's frown deepened and he turned. "Muckle. I have no tongue for stories. Since you seem so keen on wagging yours, please . . . take over."

"Oh!" Muckle seemed genuinely surprised. "Oh! All right . . . um, lemme see. In the beginning . . . No! That is an awful start . . . erm . . ."

"The gruagach were once part of the Seelie Court," Pocket offered.

"Yes!" Muckle snapped his fat fingers. "The gruagach were once par . . . wait, how did you know that?"

"I read it," Pocket replied.

"Ah, books," Muckle winked. "Good lad. Well anyway, they were a part of it. Long before us goblins existed in fact, the arrogant pricks. Now they did not guard an Element, but they were favored and powerful nonetheless, and the elves trusted their council . . . to a point. That point came when humans first came to Airlann from . . ." Muckle waved his hand absently in a random direction, ". . . wherever. The gruagach warned against these mortals, but they were overruled, and humans were allowed to live on the isle. Well, great teachers that they were, after a time the elves decided to tutor mankind in the ways of Magic. The gruagach were not happy with this, and after much yelling and finger pointing, left the Seelie Court in protest."

"And began attacking humans," Pocket said.

"Well, not at first," Muckle replied. "It took a certain group of grey-skinned roustabouts with a fascination with Fire to spark that. Get it? Spark that!"

Pocket just kept walking.

Muckle was undaunted. "So! The goblins returned from the fiery bowels, the warlocks made a deal and give a hop, skip and a jump and you have the reign of the Goblin Kings. We all know how that ended and when it did, suddenly humans started finding themselves giving birth to odd little blighters with horns and tails and what have you."

Pocket knew all this. "Gurgs."

"Righto! War was won, but the gruagach were not in a forgiving mood and they started punishing mankind for their role in ruining the isle."

"But I thought there were gurgs born before the Rebellion," Pocket put in.

"Well, there were," Muckle agreed. "A gurg is just what happens when gruagach fu . . . I mean, couple with humans. Like the dusk elves, they are the result of Fae and mortal relations. Irial Ulvyeh's own cupbearer was a gurg . . . still is, if they are both alive. Anyway, Fae and man were having litters long before the Usurpation, but it was rare. Not until after the war did the gruagach think to use you little bastards as weapons."

"Weapons?" Pocket glanced dubiously down at his stunted body. "How?"

"To make mankind distrust," Sir Corc answered. "Their own neighbors, husbands, wives . . . children."

"It is working," Pocket mumbled. "Humans hate gurgs. Maybe the gruagach would be kinder."

Sir Corc stopped and turned, kneeling down to look him square in the face. "You must not think that. Ever." The knight placed both of his gauntlet-clad hands on Pocket's shoulders and clutched him tightly. "Pocket, the elves have known several kings and more than a few gnomes have ruled in Toad Holm, but the gruagach have only ever followed one lord. One, in tens of thousands of years."

"Festus Lambkiller." Pocket had read about him, too.

Sir Corc's eyes suddenly turned sad. "Yes. He is one of the most powerful and dangerous beings alive, and the gruagach are completely loyal to his every command. He wants all gurgs returned to him, and his subjects will stop at nothing to please him. We do not know his intentions, but they can only be designs of evil. You have to stay away from him at all costs."

Pocket nodded quickly. "Well then, can I stay with you?"

"Only if you do not go running off again."

It was strange having Sir Corc so close. "I promise."

"Good." The knight released him and stood, turning back to the road. "We should be . . ."

He trailed off, and Pocket followed his gaze up the road to find Rosheen speeding back towards them, her wings a furious blur.

"Red Caps," she said when she reached them. Despite the urgency of her movement her voice remained calm. "A mile ahead. Four of them guarding a large wagon."

"A road block?"

Rosheen shook her head. "The horses are still attached and traveling the same direction we are. It looks like they just stopped . . . waiting."

Sir Corc took only a moment's time to think. "If you would go and get Flyn. Bring him here. We will await you off the road . . ." the knight scanned the landscape and pointed, ". . . there, in that copse of trees."

Rosheen left without hesitation. Pocket wrapped Backbone's guide rope tightly around his hand and led the mule off the road, following Sir Corc into the dense thicket nestled in the low hills. They did not have to wait long before the piskie returned, the squire close behind her at the run.

"Only four?" the squire asked as he slid to a halt. "What are we waiting for?"

"You," Sir Corc told him. "I need you to stay here with Pocket. Muckle and I need to go ahead for a better look. Rosheen, I want you to go with us. As soon as we find a way around, I will need you to come back here and fetch these two."

"You mean not to take the wagon?" Bantam Flyn asked.

"No," the knight replied flatly.

"But there could be prisoners inside!" Flyn declared.

"Slaves!"

"It could be barrels of headcheese," Muckle told the squire dryly.

Flyn remained resolute. "So . . . supplies. Those should be denied an enemy during war! It is worth a look!"

"Yes," Sir Corc agreed. "And it is a look I am going to take."

He motioned at Muckle and Rosheen. "Come."

Flyn scowled at the knight's back as the trio made their way through the copse. They stuck to the trees where they could, keeping the road a good distance to their left. Pocket had a good view of them as they entered the hills, but they were soon lost to sight over the rolling landscape.

"Left with the baggage." Flyn gave a self-mocking laugh and pulled lightly on one of Backbone's ears.

"They will be back soon," Pocket told him. He did not know what else to say.

Rosheen led Sir Corc and Muckle to a heavily wooded ridge from which they could view the wagon unnoticed by the four guards. The knight stared at it for a moment, watching intently.

"There are more somewhere nearby," he whispered. "A wagon that size would need a sizable escort."

"Red Caps do value their headcheese," Muckle said, nodding sagely.

"There are no barrels in there," Rosheen said. "Look at the covering . . . too irregular to be barrels."

"And heavy," Sir Corc agreed. "That is why they are stopped. The road grows worse ahead, look."

Rosheen saw large patches of muddy ground between the thinning stonework. *Might get stuck.*

"The others may be out looking for stones to bridge the gaps," Sir Corc said, almost to himself. "This is good. They will be slow moving. If we can get around them without being seen and put some distance between us, then we run no risk of them overtaking us further on."

"Should I go back and get our wayward babes?" Rosheen asked.

Sir Corc shook his head. "Not until I know where the main body is. If they are ahead, we may stumble right into them."

"Well," Muckle said lightly. "You could always just walk up and ask those four."

Rosheen shot the goblin a venomous glare. "Only you would be fool enough to think of that."

"Oh," Muckle gave an exasperated sigh, "I doubt I am the only one." He pointed. *Damn strutting bravo!*

Bantam Flyn came striding casually down the road, heading towards the wagon. The two Red Caps at the rear saw him coming and alerted the other pair. The four leveled their polearms and began converging on the squire. Flyn waved at them cordially and kept walking.

Sir Corc stared balefully for a moment, then turned and began making his way down from the ridge. Muckle shrugged and followed.

By the time they reached the road, it was all over. Bantam Flyn was perched up on one of the wheels, working to pull the covering away. The four Red Caps lay in broken heaps near the wagon.

He is good. Empty-headed, but good.

"Where is Pocket?" Sir Corc demanded, coming around the wagon.

"Back in the trees where you left us," Flyn said dismissively, not pausing in his efforts to uncover the wagon.

"You left him alone?" Sir Corc reached up and grabbed the squire by the belt, yanking him off the wheel and spinning him around so that they were almost beak to beak.

Bantam Flyn remained nonchalant. "Do not worry. He will stay there until we get back."

Rosheen watched as the coburn faced off, one pair of eyes burning with repressed fury, the other twinkling with naked challenge.

"Corc!" Muckle's voice barreled between them. "You should see this."

Rosheen flew over to where the goblin stood atop the driver's bench. He held the sailcloth covering in one hand, exposing a corner of the wagon bed.

The Hallowed save us!

The massive forms of several Forge Born lay in the wagon, as menacing in silent stillness as they were in violent motion. There were separated arms and heads, but Rosheen could see that at least two were whole, their heavy iron bodies reclined in this rolling casket.

But they do not intend to bury them.

Sir Corc came and looked, Bantam Flyn marveling over his shoulder.

"Are those Unwound?" the squire asked, voice full of awe.

"If they were, we would all be dead," Muckle replied without a trace of mirth.

"Come," Sir Corc said. "We must get back to Pocket."

Flyn was at his heels. "What about the wagon?"

"Leave it," the knight said brusquely, avoiding secrecy and heading back down the road.

Rosheen went to follow him and stopped short. A mass of goblins was marching down the road directly for them. Sir Corc turned on his heel.

"Off the road," he commanded.

A horrible, cackling cry wiggled in the air as the Red Caps caught sight of them and Rosheen saw them break into a run.

"Go!" Sir Corc yelled.

Bantam Flyn ran up to him. "We could take the horses!"

"No," Sir Corc barked, shoving the squire towards the roadside. "They will not abandon this cargo! If we take the horses, they have no choice but to follow. Now do as I say! Go!"

They all slipped off down the side opposite from the ridge and fled over the downs.

Rosheen flew even with the knight, yelling next to his head.

"They came from behind us! They might have seen Pocket!"

Sir Corc quickened his pace. "We will go back for him! But we must be sure we are not pursued!"

"I can go!" Rosheen said. "Make sure he is safe!"

The knight looked over at her. "Do it! We will lead these vermin a chase!"

Rosheen nodded and peeled away, flying high. She risked a glance back. Below, the Red Caps had circled the wagon, thirty at least, while a smaller detachment broke away in an attempt to run down her companions. She was surprised to see Muckle well ahead of the two coburn, sprinting nimbly despite his bulk.

Pocket went over to Backbone and stroked his nose while the mule sniffed at his other hand.

"Sorry, friend," Pocket told him. "I don't have an apple for you."

He giggled when the mule gave him a gentle push, glad that he was not totally alone. He had tried to tell the squire not to go, but Flyn would not listen, making for the road when his impatience got the better of him.

"Wait!" Pocket had called after him. "Sir Corc told us to stay here!"

"And this will make him angry!" Flyn said over his shoulder.

"He will grouse and do nothing! Like he always does!"

Pocket opened his mouth to protest further, but the squire had already reached the road, tail feathers bouncing jauntily as he quickened his pace. Pocket frowned after him, but made no move to follow. He had learned his lesson, even if Bantam Flyn had not.

So he waited, and he watched.

It was not long before movement in the hills caught his eye and he looked, expecting to see Sir Corc returning with the others.

He hoped Flyn would be with them. He did not want to have to explain to the knight that the squire had run off again, but at least this time he would not have to make excuses for his own behavior.

But it was not Sir Corc.

Pocket crept to the edge of the copse, heart beginning to quicken as he watched a large group crest one of the hills and he got a good view of some forty goblins, each wearing that unmistakable hat. They were heading for the road. Rosheen said the four Red Caps at the wagon looked as if they were waiting, waiting on the main group to return! They might catch Sir Corc unawares or spot them as they returned. They would be caught out in the open, Pocket had to warn them!

Even if he ran down the road, he might not make it in time and he did not know where the others had hid themselves. Besides, the Red Caps would see him coming. But he could not just stand here and do nothing while his friends were unknowingly trapped.

He had to move fast. Leading Backbone would be slow, but he would not leave him behind. The mule was Pocket's charge and he would not disappoint Sir Corc again. They would have to go together.

His decision made, Pocket snatched a good stick off the ground and led the mule out of the copse and back out onto the road. The Red Caps were still some distance away and had not yet gained the road themselves. Hoping they had not yet seen him, Pocket took Backbone's guide rope in his teeth and grabbed hold of the lines securing their supplies to the mule's back. He jumped, using his arms to haul himself and clambered up to settle among the loads. Backbone whined in complaint and took several awkward sidling steps in response to the new weight. Pocket took the rope from his teeth and bent low over the mule's neck, before reaching back with his stick and giving him a solid swat.

Backbone lurched forward, away from the snapping stick. It took several more hits before he gained a decent speed, finally picking up into a steady trot. Pocket jostled along, their supplies bouncing beneath him, and struggled to keep the animal following the road and himself firmly seated. He scanned to the left of the road for the goblins, his racing heart leaping to his throat when he saw them. Backbone was not going fast enough. They were going to reach the goblins right as they gained the road! Pocket laid into Backbone's flank with the stick, driving him to greater speeds.

There came a cry of alarm as the Red Caps saw them coming, a few rushing up and spreading out to intercept them. Pocket urged the mule to barrel right over them, but Backbone spooked at the last moment, turning away from the nearest goblin and running off the road. Pocket felt a sudden impact behind him and Backbone screamed in protest as they shot down the grassy embankment off the roadside. Pocket looked over his shoulder and cried out when he saw the goblin clinging to the load ropes near the mule's rump.

He swung at the wickedly grinning face with his stick, but the goblin merely flinched away and struggled towards him. He risked a look ahead and was almost thrown off as Backbone flew headlong across the sloping fields. A hand seized the back of his tunic and yanked him backwards, causing him to pull up hard on the guide rope. The sharp, ornery cry of an angry mule filled his ears, and Pocket was flung off the lurching bundles, sky and ground trading places dizzyingly in his field of vision.

He did not remember landing, only picking himself up painfully from the wet grass, right knee and both wrists throbbing.

He stood in a grassy depression, gently sloping hills on all sides.

Relief flooded over him when he saw Backbone standing some yards away, looking winded and annoyed. His loads were loose and dangling, several of the bundles spilled upon the ground. Pocket approached slowly, hands outstretched. As he drew nearer, he saw the Red Cap's leg had become caught in the load ropes and the body lay awkwardly, head dashed against some nearby rocks.

Pocket felt his own head, grateful for his luck. Backbone shied away from him, dragging the limp goblin a few yards further. With many soothing words, Pocket managed to get close enough to grab the guide rope and calm the mule down. Face wrinkled in disgust, Pocket untangled the Red Cap and was about to begin gathering the fallen supplies, when he heard harsh voices coming towards him from beyond the rise. Hails and calls drew closer and it would not be long before the Red Caps found him at the bottom of the bowl. There was nowhere to hide and he could not run anymore.

They would see him soon. There was no way to avoid it.

Working frantically, Pocket stripped the goblin of his leather jerkin and iron plated boots. The blood colored cap was nowhere to be seen, and he had no time to search for it. Pulling his own tunic over his head, Pocket quickly dressed the body in it, hoping Sir Corc would forgive him for putting the colors of the Valiant Spur on a Red Cap. Lifting the twisted leg, Pocket again tied it to the mule.

"Sorry Backbone," he whispered and slapped the animal as hard as he could on the rump, sending him bolting up the easiest slope and out of sight.

Pocket fought to stay calm and clear his mind as he put the goblin's armor on. The voices were almost on him, the sight of the running mule bringing them swiftly in his direction. Pocket closed his eyes and took a deep breath, remembering everything Rosheen had told him.

"Oi!" a voice shouted down at him.

Pocket opened his eyes and looked up to find a half dozen Red Caps staring down at him, weapons in hand.

"Daft bugger!" one of them said. "What were you on about, leapin' on that critter?"

Another of them laughed. "Even he don't rightly know! Lookit!" he pointed. "His hands are still shakin', the crazy bastard!"

The others found this equally funny, and all had a good chuckle.

Pocket looked down at his hands. They *were* shaking; every knobby-knuckled, grey-skinned finger.

It was ugly afternoon by the time Sir Corc returned to the copse. Rosheen was glad to see Muckle and Flyn with him, the goblin looking as if he were about to vomit at any moment. The knight hurried into the trees, concern overpowering the weariness on his face.

This will not be easy.

Rosheen fluttered down from her perch on the branch of the tree where she had tethered Backbone. The charm she had woven to make the animal follow her was still strong, and he only blinked sleepily as the others approached.

Sir Corc came up to her, his entire being asking the question before he gave it voice.

"Pocket?"

Rosheen willed herself to look at him, then slowly shook her head.

Defeat settled on the coburn's shoulders, dragging them down as loss spread across his countenance.

"I left him," the knight's voice was a whisper. He turned and raised his head, looking at Bantam Flyn. "You. You left him."

Rosheen watched as guilt and pride wrestled across the young coburn's face, knowing which would win.

"Had the boy come with us he would still be safe," Flyn threw at the knight. "If you had not been too afraid of four goblins, we would be well on our way! Together!"

Sir Corc took a step forward. "You have called me liar." He stepped again. "You have called me craven." Another step. "And I have suffered it. You have impugned my honor at every turn. You, who could not stoop to safeguard the life of one little boy!"

Sir Corc darted forward, grabbing for the squire. Bantam Flyn sidestepped quickly, his staff moving faster than Rosheen could follow. She shut her eyes tight at the sound of the impact and opened them with sorrow. But Sir Corc still stood, the staff caught deftly in his fist. The knight jerked the staff from the squire's grip and split it over his leg, casting the splintered pieces aside as he advanced. Flyn danced agilely backward, hand going to the haft of the greatsword poking over his shoulder. Sir Corc kept coming, his own hand going nowhere near the blade at his side. Flyn pulled up, the blade shining as it rose from its scabbard about two feet before stopping. Confused panic fell across the squire's face, his fully extended arm unable to draw the long blade completely free from across his back. Sir Corc took a final step, then slammed his fist into the squire's gut, bending him double before felling him with an elbow to the back of the head.

Flyn sprawled face down in the dirt, but recovered quickly, rolling into a crouch and shrugging the harness off his shoulder. Sir Corc stood over him, waiting as Flyn drew the greatsword. The squire stood, naked steel in hand, pain on his face. He swung. Corc stepped into the blow, allowing only Flyn's swinging arms to strike him, grappling them quickly then ducking low, tossing the squire bodily over his shoulder. Rosheen heard the wind rush from Flyn's body as his back slammed into the ground. Sir Corc now held the greatsword but tossed it aside, wasting no time in hooking his hands under Flyn's beak, dragging him across the rotting leaves.

The squire kicked and struggled feebly as the knight hauled him up, locking his thick arms around Flyn's neck and head. He buffeted weakly at the hold, struggling to breathe, but Corc did not release him.

"Enough," Flyn choked. "Yield . . . I yield."

There was a horrible moment when Rosheen feared she would hear the young coburn's neck snap.

This needs to end.

"Corc," she said firmly. "I know where Pocket is."

The knight looked up at her, the feral ferocity of his race running rampant across his features. She stared him down, willing him back to reason, but the coburn only looked back at his captive.

"You," Sir Corc hissed, "have a lot to learn."

He pushed Flyn away contemptuously and snatched the greatsword from the ground while the squire coughed and wheezed.

"Tell me," he said, looking up at Rosheen.

She gestured at the body of the goblin, still dangling from the mule's harness.

"Look at his tunic," she said.

Corc bent and ran the heavily soiled garment between his fingers.

"Pocket's," he said.

"I think he is trying to tell us something," Rosheen said.

"That he is with them . . . as one of them."

"Clever lad," Muckle muttered.

Sir Corc stood, facing her. "Can he hold the change?"

He needs hope.

"Yes," Rosheen answered. "I believe he can."

"Then we go after him."

"I . . . do not wish to duel," Muckle offered carefully. "But we cannot defeat that many Red Caps on our own."

"We have no choice," Sir Corc said.

"Yes we do," Muckle countered. "I know where the Red Caps are going. You said it yourself, they are moving slowly. We still have time. With help, we can get the boy back."

Rosheen looked at the goblin dubiously. "What help?"

"Oh, the best kind," Muckle smiled broadly, showing every tooth. "The desperate kind!"

TWENTY-TWO

Castle Gaunt.

Padric stood on the ramparts looking into the night, the glare from the dancing brazier blinding him to all that lay beyond and below the walls. The great fortress spread out around him, behind him, but he kept his gaze fixed on the familiar, star-filled sky, ignoring the ancient menace of stones. He could still feel it; a huge, blind, predatory weight ready to swallow him.

The steady strike of wood upon stone drew near, passed behind him, then faded as one of the sentries made his rounds, but Padric did not turn. There was only one person in the castle who could wrest his eyes from the freedom of the moon-bathed clouds, and she would come when she was ready. He fought the urge to seek her out, impatient for the solace she brought just by standing near, breathing.

The goblins thought him a king, and, having no tradition of courtship or betrothal, she was his queen. She held no power in their eyes, just a bedmate, a plaything, no more regal than a whore.

To Padric she was neither queen nor harlot. She was a woman, gentle and soft; a smile, a smell, tangible and strong. He looked at her and saw the plough, the hearth, the stacks of cut turf, the simple aspects of mortal life once so reviled and now more desired than the embrace of her body. Padric was a farmer's son. Svala's father had been a fisherman.

They did not belong here.

The sounds of ringing metal resumed, bouncing off the stones of the great keep behind him, a chorus of screaming hammers. Padric clenched his teeth, but still did not turn. The goblins' labors were as sickening to him as the source of their fire.

Let them sweat over searing iron, shaping with hammer and tongs.

They could not smelt the night nor shape the truth over the anvil.

They could break their backs with work. It would not change who he was and who he was not. For now, in this moment, he was a king who could not sleep, standing a silent vigil on the walls waiting for his living lullaby.

His mind relaxed when she finally arrived, but he could feel a gentle nervousness running through his body. She was tall, so much taller than he had realized those first days. Torcan had heeded his command and provided her with clothing more suitable to Airlann's climes. Padric knew her homeland was far colder, and he was more likely to die from chill than she, but the woolen dresses had given her something more than warmth. No longer was her head bowed, her eyes downcast. Like him, she was still afraid.

They would be mad not to be. But at least now she could face the threats surrounding them with dignity. Padric had seen her supple flesh exposed in strumpet's clothes, but he found her far more beautiful now.

In the harsh flicker of the brazier, it was difficult to see how blue her eyes were, but her smile was plainly visible as she drew up next to him, placing her hands upon the walls and following his previous gaze. Padric no longer looked out. Her long tumble of golden hair was bound against the wind in several thick braids and he stared for a lingering moment over the curve of her jaw. She must have been the envy of her village before it was burnt and she stolen away. Padric had never seen an Airlann-born girl that was her equal. Mayhaps she was even wed. He hoped that her phantom husband had defended her to the death, spilling raider blood until his own spilled from him, making the slavers pay a heavy price for thrusting her into this life of fear, servitude and the ravings of monsters.

"Kederic?" he asked at last, hating to break the silence.

Svala looked over at him. "Svefn," she said.

"Svefn," Padric said, and she smiled a little, watching him puzzle through the few words Slouch Hat had been teaching him.

"Ah, svefn. Sleeping . . . sleep?"

"Ja," she said, nodding with approval. "Sleep."

He smiled back, delighting in the accent of her people. She spoke again, maybe four words, but he only caught one of them.

"Kvila? Um . . . illness? Sick? He is sick."

She nodded, her face veiled slightly with a resigned sadness.

"Ja."

Padric turned away, not wanting his grimace of anger to fall upon her. At his insistence, Torcan had the Thegn brought to the castle from Reaver's Meadow. He had arrived only a day behind their own party and was in a wretched condition.

Since obtaining Jerrod's crown, Padric had found Torcan all too willing to please. The Thegn's lies had never truly convinced the goblin warlord, Padric saw that now. The deadly test in the Tower of Vellaunus had always been part of his plan. Any previous courtesy had been nothing but a precaution, a show of respect, lest he actually prove to be the Gaunt Prince's heir. And now he was, at least to Torcan's mind, and the goblin's uncontrollable hunger to give his devotion to that perverted lineage consumed him.

The clamor of the hammers in the yard below drove the peace away and Padric took Svala's hand so that they might walk the walls together. For all their lies, the fortress was still a prison, and the only way to escape it was to get out under the night sky, and see that even Castle Gaunt sat dwarfed under the heavens.

The ancestral bastion of the Goblin Kings was a hulking citadel of towers and barbicans, linked by a chaotic web of walls, all atop the dominating hill known as Penda's Rock. Even growing up in the shadow of Stone Fort, Padric found the construction of the castle mind-boggling. Each of its rulers had built atop the Rock, adding a keep or tower or gatehouse at their whimsy until the compound beyond the walls was a hideous, disjointed mating of the minds of madmen. The oldest structures had been raised with knowledge now lost to time. The sharply pointed conical roofs of thin, round towers soaring up and away from the central keep made Padric's skin crawl. Much of the castle had been shattered during the Rebellion and several of the inner buildings were nothing but rubble. The Red

Caps had repaired most of the outer wall, but some of the watchtowers lay broken, their stones still scattered down the slope of the Rock.

He felt Svala squeeze his hand, and he turned to her. She looked at him, all trepidation and worry gone from her face. She knew him now, and he knew her, neither of them afraid to meet the gaze of the other.

"Hvila," she said simply. There was no coaxing in her voice, no shyness nor boldness, she just spoke the word.

"Yes," he agreed, suddenly exhausted. "Bed."

There was no passion in their coupling, no lusty cries of relief or surrenders to animal abandon. They had been forced together by terror, driven to companionship by their shared nightmare. She had not seduced him, and he had not taken her as the goblins wanted. They had laid together in comfort, merely holding onto each other in the blackness of strange bedchambers, each trying and failing to find peaceful sleep, listening to the other draw in and breathe out the air that would one day no longer fill their mortal bodies. Ghosts and goblins tormented their days with only a straw-stuffed mockery of a man to call friend. But at night they were alone, clinging to their weak humanity, and finding in their union a reminder of the strength such weakness required. It was a ritual of comfort, always slow, deliberate and necessary. They did not take from the other, nor did they give. They clung to each other and became one, breathing together in the darkness, forgetting it was all around.

But, before they were allowed their succor, they had to cross through the Cog Yard.

Descending the stairs from the walls, they made quickly for the keep, the ancient stonework suddenly looming around them.

The stars no longer held dominion. If Padric and Svala dared glance up, they would find the night sky held fast between the jaws of battlements and drum towers, gnashed by the teeth of spires before being swallowed down into a bubbling gullet of steam where motionless metal giants stood waiting.

They wound their way between the dead iron; the slumped bodies serving as their own gravestones. A sudden blast from the furnaces lit the yard, unveiling the towering silhouettes for what they were; the Forge Born covered in burial shrouds of rust, standing in irregular rows, crowding the inner bailey.

Slouch Hat kept a daily count.

One hundred and nine currently stood and the Red Caps never stopped working, hauling a newly reconstructed warrior to its feet every few hours. According to the husk, only six hundred were ever made, and they almost destroyed all life on the isle.

The foundry sat in the center of the Cog Yard, belching flames and smoke from its chimneys and furnaces. Through the steam, the goblin ironmongers smote the anvils and pumped the bellows, reworking the separated limbs and bodies with heat and pressure, molding them whole. Padric and Svala flinched away from the blistering heat as they passed, the sharp hiss of cooling metal adding a painful note to the cacophony of hammers. One goblin emerged from the press of workers, staggering and coughing.

He made it a few steps, then fell against the leg of a completed Forge Born, heedless as his skin began to sizzle against the iron.

Wracked with spasms and choking, the wretch vomited blood on the Forge Born's foot before slumping lifeless to the ground.

Padric kept walking, his jaw clenched disdainfully.

For all their belief, Red Caps were still goblins, and goblins were Fae. Iron killed them, quickly if it pierced the flesh, slowly with exposure. The Red Caps defied this weakness with maniacal delusion, wielding iron weapons to better slaughter their kindred and wearing their heavy iron boots over layers of wrapping to keep the metal from their flesh. But the crafting of living iron was a taxing, noxious labor, and the smiths quickly weakened, collapsing into shriveled, blind, wheezing shells before they were dragged away and given to the Fire, feeding the flames of unnatural life to their last measure. New workers came to replace the fallen, and the labor continued uninterrupted, day and night, an ugly unending cycle of death and creation. The Red Caps gave their lives to birth the Forge Born, that they might bathe in the blood of the isle.

The Cog Yard was a horrifying garden, growing thick with metal monstrosities and its center was a hot, stinking, suffocating heart of industry and sacrifice. Padric defied his fear and looked, willing himself to witness the source of all this insanity, the creature he would risk everything to destroy.

The Flame Binder.

He sat in the center of the foundry, his body surrounded by a nimbus of near-white flames flowing through stone channels and feeding the furnaces. The Red Caps needed no wood, nor coal to fuel their fires, not when they harnessed Fire itself. The wizard's eyes looked up as Padric passed, his crazed smile distorted by waves of heat. The goblin's flesh may have been untouched by flames, but his mind was completely consumed. He was less frail, less stooped than when Padric had last seen him that dreadful night in Hog's Wallow. The night Faabar had died. He did not know how he would succeed where the fomori failed, but for the memory of their brief friendship, he knew to his soul that he must try.

Padric had been given a bedchamber high in the central keep, its window far from the noise of the Cog Yard. Two guards stood by the door, but they were no longer posted to keep Padric and Svala in. They stepped inside and Padric tossed the bolt on the heavy oaken door, closing off their shared sanctuary.

He awoke before dawn, dressing quickly in the dark chamber and leaving Svala to sleep. Passing his guards without a word, he made his way down the vaulted hall to another door. It was also guarded, and Padric had to wait for one of the Red Caps to unlock it before he slipped in quietly, making for the bed wrapped in deep shadows.

As he reached for the blankets, he was grabbed from behind, arms encircling him. Padric struggled, and his assailant fought to hold him. A wet, wheezing cough filled Padric's ear, and he broke free of the quivering arms, spinning just in time to catch the thin, naked form of the man who had once been Thegn Kederic Winetongue. Padric laid him gently on the bed as he continued to cough violently. Lighting a candle, he grabbed a rag from the bedside stool and began wiping away the feverish sweat covering the man's flesh. The goblins must have barely fed him, for the sinewy torso now looked shrunken, a patchwork of rib bones and raised scars. Svala had been forced to shave away the Thegn's lice-ridden hair and beard, leaving him a pitiful, bald invalid, more corpse than man.

"This is an ill-luck reversal, my lord," Padric said gently. "I do not have your gift for healing."

Kederic's eyes fluttered open at his words, clouded and slow to focus.

"Then send the girl back," he replied weakly.

Padric grinned. "Tell me what to do."

"Supplies?" Kederic asked.

"We have . . ." Padric looked to the bedside stool, ". . . a basin of water."

Kederic let out a congested chuckle. "Good news is often a balm," he said wryly. "Tell me some."

"You are alive," Padric offered.

The Thegn accepted that with an approving nod. Kederic was not a man to wallow.

"And," Padric continued, "clearly your strength is returning if you can attack your nurse. Fortunate it was not Svala. She would have hurt you."

"Need to escape," Kederic mumbled.

Padric reached again for the wet rag. There was no escape, but he could not say that to this man.

"Who is she?" Kederic managed as Padric placed the rag on his brow.

"Svala?" Padric shook his head ruefully. "The royal consort, thanks to you. Though I think that title is yours by rights if the true heir is your wife."

Kederic's hand darted from the bed, grabbing Padric by the front of his shirt. "Do not say that."

Padric removed the man's hold. "Where is she, my lord?"

Kederic looked away, closing his eyes. "Better if you do not know."

Padric could not let this rest. The knowledge would not help him, but he wanted to know. "You told Torcan I was your son. Did you have a child?"

The answer came quickly. "No."

"Then we are stuck with your lie."

Padric did not know why he was growing angry. Even if he knew who the heir was and where, he would not reveal it to Torcan, not even for his own life. He just wanted answers, some truth before the end.

"Do they still believe?" Kederic asked.

Padric thought of the crown and unease settled firmly over him. "Now more than before. But the truth will come out and when it does . . ."

"We are dead," the Thegn finished.

Padric nodded, though the man's eyes were still closed.

"Is there a plan?"

"Slouch Hat is working on something," Padric replied, knowing better than to say anymore.

Kederic tried to take a deep breath, but his lungs rattled wetly and he succumbed to a fit of coughing.

"That husk," he said after recovering, "was always too clever."

"I should leave you to rest," Padric said rising.

"No," the Thegn's eyes opened. "Help me stand. I need to be out of this bed. Are there garments?"

Choosing not to argue, Padric went back to his own chamber and fetched some of his spare clothes. Svala was awake and she accompanied him back to the Thegn's room, finding the man already sitting up, his legs swung over the bedside. Svala said something to Padric and then to the Thegn, her face none too happy.

"We are being chastised," Kederic told Padric, then spoke to Svala in her own tongue. She calmed a little, but still wore a concerned frown as she and Padric helped the Thegn dress. He was unsteady on his feet, his breathing labored, but the fever appeared to have broken. Together, Padric and Svala helped Kederic walk to their bedchamber, where the morning sun was beginning to come through the window. They sat Kederic in a chair by the fire and Padric told one of the guards to send for food.

Torcan Swinehelm arrived before their breakfast. The goblin bowed low to Padric as he entered the chamber.

"Your Grace," he said solemnly. "I trust you slept well."

Padric merely nodded. Torcan's eyes scanned the room, ignoring Svala completely before fixing on the Thegn.

"I see your lord father is somewhat recovered," he said courteously.

"And in no mood for company, goblin," Kederic spat.

Torcan smiled thinly. "Then I must offer pardons, for I am afraid His Grace has a visitor."

Padric could not keep the frown from his face. "Visitor? Who?"

"One who wishes to pledge his allegiance," Torcan replied and opened the door.

Kederic cursed and Padric's mouth went sour as Acwellen stepped into the room, travel-stained and smiling. When he reached the center of the chamber, he knelt, bowing his great shaggy head.

"Hail Padric Goblin King," his deep voice filled the room.

"I offer my service to you and bring two hundred armed riders to your cause. Please accept this gift as a token of my loyalty."

Acwellen held out his hand. Padric looked down at the seax for a moment, its scabbard more worn than last he looked upon it.

"A worthy gift," Padric said, reaching down and taking the weapon from

Acwellen before looking to Torcan. "My lord Swinehelm, see that Acwellen's men are well looked after. I would speak with my huscarl alone."

"Your Grace," Torcan bowed and left.

Acwellen waited for the door to close before rising swiftly, fixing Padric with a mocking grin. The big man turned slowly, looking appraisingly at the chamber, his smile widening when he saw Svala.

"Kingship has its privileges," he said laughing.

"What do you want here?" Padric asked through clenched teeth.

"Why to pay tribute, of course," Acwellen replied pointing to the knife in Padric's hand.

Padric scoffed at him. "You would give me what was already mine?"

"'Tis no mean gift," Acwellen said with mock exasperation.

"Drefan was loath to give it up. Forgive me, Winetongue," he continued cheerfully, turning to where Kederic sat by the fire. "I would have brought a gift for you, but I did not expect to find you alive."

Kederic rose, his hatred giving him strength, and took a step towards his former huscarl.

"You bring me what is mine as well, dog," he said. "Those two hundred riders. I will have them back."

Acwellen grinned down at him. "But will they have you?"

"I am their Thegn," Kederic growled.

Acwellen snorted. "You are a beardless, bald babe. A wasted old man. They will see no lord in you."

"My men will never fight for a goblin," Kederic said, quivering.

"Your men," Acwellen returned, "are ten years living in peace! They have grown comfortable, Winetongue. You gave them a fort, livestock, good drink and wives. They do not wish to return to war! So they will guard an ancient rock, while these Fae bastards dance about their flames. Then we go home, and they leave us in peace. Far better than the battles you would have them wage."

Kederic stared at him, his body unable to exact the vengeance his heart desired.

"Traitor," he said at last.

Acwellen shrugged the accusation off. "It was either stand loyal and die, or betray you and prosper. Simple choice."

Padric stepped between them. "You were a fool to come here, Acwellen. One word from me and the Swinehelm will spit you over a fire."

Acwellen shrugged carelessly, turning away to swagger about the room.

"Will he? I very much doubt it. He needs me too much, me and my men. Look at this place," Acwellen spread his arms, going to the window and nodding out. "A huge, crumbling ruin. That rodent cannot hope to defend it all, even with all his damn Red Caps. He has us camped below, outside the walls to patrol the approaches. I do not think he will give that up for you, boy."

Padric stepped up, right in the lout's bearded face. "Are you blind? Did you not see the work that is being done . . . the living iron?"

"You are the blind one, whelp," Acwellen said. "There is nothing living about those rusted toys."

"As soon as those Fae bastards dance about their flames," Padric said, throwing the man's own words back at him, "you will see how wrong you are. And it will be your last mistake."

The big man looked at him for a moment, his eyes twinkling with private glee. He looked over Padric to where Kederic stood. "The memory is a tricky bugger," he said. "See . . . I remember all those years we fought together. All them strange lands. Bloody bad times, I recall." Acwellen stepped around Padric and approached the Thegn. "I also remember your wife, Kederic. Pretty lass. No, that is not worthy of her. She was beautiful. What was her name?"

"Do not," Kederic warned through his teeth.

"Beladore," Acwellen breathed the name and Padric watched Kederic's fists clench.

"Found her in Sasana," the big man continued. "Quite a prize. Quite a bride. You were so happy, and she must have squirmed like a weasel in bed, for you had her with a swollen belly right quick. And then, the babe was born and something just . . . changed."

Kederic was not even looking at the man now. His eyes were downcast and far away, lost in some bitter memory. Acwellen turned and looked at Svala, continuing his story with relish, though the girl looked at him quizzically, his words lost on her.

"The babe was sickly and they kept it confined . . . until it died, only days old. Tragic. Beladore, she was hardly recovered herself when she vanished in the night. None saw her leave. None but me, that is! So, I tells the Thegn, and he goes after her. But he did not want me along, nor anyone else."

Acwellen turned to Padric then.

"It was weeks before he returned," he said. "And with the most grievous wounds I ever saw on a living man, hole through his shoulder wide as any spear could do. And he's alone. No Beladore."

Acwellen knocked pretend dust from his hands. "Told me the Fae enchanted her, led her away and murdered her, and nearly him, too. Never spoke of it again. We leave Sasana, settle in Airlann, and some years later, imagine my surprise when that sheep-stinking Brogan starts asking me all secret-like about our Thegn's dead wife. Says he read in some dusty book that husk kept about the descendants of the Goblin Kings, and has a thousand questions about Beladore that I cannot answer. Then Brogan, he goes and offers me the fort and all the land if I help him deliver Kederic to some goblins he's been talking with."

Padric had never known the man in life, but he found it difficult to believe.

"Brogan?"

"Liar," Kederic said.

"He betrayed you first, Winetongue," Acwellen said. "Said the Red Caps would reward us handsomely for you."

"And you murdered him for it," Padric accused.

Acwellen looked genuinely offended, casting an angry look at Padric. "Damn husk did that! Must have found out Brogan was reading his books and consorting with Red Caps. I never touched the man. We had an accord."

Padric's mind was racing. Lies came easy to Slouch Hat.

The Thegn was right, he was too clever.

"So, I managed without him," Acwellen went on, "and upheld my end . . . gave you over, Kederic." The big man reached up and made a show of scratching his temple. "But here is where the memory plays tricks. That business with your wife, see I recall that being just after we came to the isle, some what . . . ten years ago now? Red Caps wanted your wife, and they get your long-lost son instead." Acwellen fixed a bemused face on Padric, teeth showing through his beard. "Passing queer that he's twice too old."

Padric raised a hand and glanced worriedly at the closed door.

"Acwellen," he said quietly. "You mention word of this and we are all dead. You as well."

The man shook his head. "Oh no. I intend on coming out of this alive. Always did. So you keep your secret . . . long as you can. I got no ken for spells and wizardry, but I know you are not who they need to bring those metal buggers to life. I am guessing they kill you all when they find out."

"They will kill you, too," Padric pointed out.

"They might try," Acwellen agreed. "Me and my men are gonna be ready to put heel to horse when they do."

Acwellen smiled, bowed, and left the room.

Kederic sank back into his chair, face haunted by the past.

Padric had no time for him. He tried to give Svala a comforting look, failed, and walked out of the chamber. He made quickly for the end of the hall to the spiral stairs and took them two at a time, passing several galleries before finally coming to the uppermost floor of the keep. Coming into a great antechamber, Padric approached a set of double doors flanked by half a dozen guards.

"See that we are not disturbed," he told the goblins as they dragged the doors open to admit him. Within was a vast solar, tall, narrow windows set high on every wall. Torcan had told him this room once housed countless tomes, scrolls and other relics of the warlocks' collected knowledge. All destroyed after the Rebellion.

The room housed nothing now but dust and its new steward.

The husk stood in the center of the room, his head bowed, face hidden under the floppy brim of his hat, staring down at the iron crown grasped in his thin hands. As the doors closed behind him, Padric approached and the sound of his footsteps raised the husk's head.

"Secrets," Slouch Hat whispered. "She shares such secrets."

"Time you shared some of your own," Padric said.

Slouch Hat seemed to blink, the wrinkles of his sack face smoothing into awareness.

"Padric," he said tonelessly.

"You killed Brogan."

"What?" the husk said. "No."

"No more lies, Slouch Hat. He betrayed Hog's Wallow to the Red Caps and you killed him."

"No," the husk continued to protest. "I was not even there. Why is this suddenly important?"

"Acwellen is here," Padric had to remember to keep his voice low. "He knows I am not the heir. He claims Brogan betrayed Kederic, and that you killed him."

The husk held up a hand. "Padric, listen to me. Had I known this, I would not have killed him, I would have exposed him to the village, taken him to the fort, warned them of the goblins. I would not have slain him and fled, leaving the village to its fate. Why would you listen to a man like Acwellen?"

"Because he could not have known about the heir! The man is a fool! But Brogan did know! He read your first master's work . . . reasoned it out, somehow discovered the truth about Kederic's wife."

Slouch Hat looked away, thinking. "The histories were buried with my master in the barrows near Hog's Wallow. I was away looking for them when Brogan was killed."

"Looking for them? In the barrow . . . why?"

"Jileen," Slouch Hat said. "Jileen said she had found my dead master's tomb open while visiting her parents' barrow. I went to look, and the works were gone. When I returned, she told me about Brogan and told me to flee, as I was suspected. I did not kill him, Padric."

Padric spun on his heel, pacing in frustration, stifling a scream. "Enough," he said, turning back. "It does not matter now.I should not have bothered with it. We are here now, whoever betrayed Kederic. Acwellen is a lout and a liar, but he does know I am false. He says the goblins cannot bring the Forge Born to life without the rightful heir. Is that true?"

Slouch Hat shook his head. "No. The Flame Binder will awaken them, but the Goblin King must command them."

Padric thought furiously. "You possess the crown. Can you not command them? Turn them against the Red Caps?"

"The crown is only an artifact, Padric," Slouch Hat told him gravely. "There is Magic within it, but the power to control the Forge Born lies within the bloodline of Jerrod the Second. Whatever sorcery he poured into this crown, it is not his seed."

"Then what will happen?"

Slouch Hat's face went slack, his hollow eyes stretching into long pits. Padric grabbed the husk by the shoulders.

"Slouch Hat," he said, shaking him. "What can we do?"

The husk regained himself, pulling away from Padric's grip.

He raised a hand to his face, the other holding the crown limply by his side.

"She whispers to me," Slouch Hat's voice was tired. "She wants her freedom. But more than that, she wants revenge. Such hatred . . ."

"What does she intend?" Padric asked, fearing the response.

Slouch Hat looked up at him. "I know not. But . . . we will not survive it."

"No," Padric said. "But this is the moment that dying will matter most."

Among fifty Red Caps there was no place to hide.

Pocket wore his fear as he wore the goblin face. It was on his shoulders, calling out, pointing at him, encouraging the goblins to come look at the impostor in their midst. Every moment became the last moment before he would be discovered. One of them would look at him and see him, *really* see him and those eyes would fill with hatred and cruel intent before he brought the others running with his shouts, so they might descend upon him with their brutal weapons. Pocket had a weapon, too; an ugly iron blade atop a long wooden pole, thrust into his hands the moment he reached the wagon. It was heavy, but not as heavy as the boots on his feet.

They marched and the boots bit, bashing his toes.

The wagon creaked along ahead and sometimes Pocket had to help push, straining with the others, coaxing the large wheels out of a hole or over a rock. The goblins complained and cursed, spitting on the ground and cuffing each other more and more as the march drew on. They never stopped. Not for rest, not for food, and not for sleep. They crawled atop the moving wagon in small groups, allowed to catch what sleep they could for an hour. Pocket never took his turn, fearing he would lose the change if he nodded off. So he marched. He marched and he pushed, feet and hands beaten into broken blisters and raw, open flesh.

Panic grabbed hold of him the first time he was spoken to.

He found himself staring dumbly, looking into the increasingly annoyed face of the goblin waiting for a response to something Pocket had not heard. He shrugged, hoping that would be enough.

Pain shot dully into his shoulder as the speaker struck him with a hard knuckled fist.

"Don' be a closed tight cunny!" the Red Cap complained.

"What were on that ass you jumped like a hoppin' looney?"

The repeated question drew jeers of approval and Pocket looked around, horribly aware that now some dozen faces were peering at him expectantly, clustering around him as they walked.

He swallowed hard, his throat tight and painful.

"Ehrm," he stalled and nearly choked at the deeper, rougher sound that emerged. Another hard shove rocked him. "Come on, out with it!"

"Bloody gnome!" Pocket said quickly in a voice that was not his own.

The Red Caps made noises of disgust. Cursing with bitter ardor.

"Did you gut him?" the original inquirer pressed as the others pushed in eagerly, some struggling to walk fast enough to hear.

"Fell offa the mule," Pocket griped. "Dashed his filthy skull on a rock!"

The laughter and back slaps went on for some time, and Pocket forced a smile. The talk died as they bent their backs to the wagon once more, each saving their breath.

Pocket grunted and groaned with his false brothers, wondering how he had saved himself. Rosheen had told him that he would be able to do such things with practice, but Pocket had not been able to practice, and the piskie had said it would take time.

Surely the span of days was not enough! How had he managed it?

How long could he keep it up?

Night fell, and still the goblins pressed on, using torches to light their way. Pocket tried to find a moment to sneak away, slip off the road and into the darkness, but the fear hissed in his ear, telling him he would be seen. Why would a loyal Red Cap slip away? Even if they did not see, where would he go? Which way?

No. No escape. He wore his shadows now. The best hiding place was in the crowd, just another foot soldier grinding ragged behind the wagon.

The journey was endless. Body past the point of pain, mind near broken with constant worry, Pocket struggled on in a cloud of numb torment. Each step in those torturous metal boots threatened to drop him, each jarring bang of the wagon on the brutal road made him wince. He had to keep the whimpers from escaping his lips, fighting back tears of exhaustion and despair. The second day was the start of some long, unending punishment, and Pocket knew that he would march behind that wagon forever, unable to ever stop walking. Neither rest nor death would give him ease. There was only the fear, and it existed in every-thing.

The sun was setting when the castle came into view, and the goblins began to complain even more bitterly, as if the end of the road was more terrible than treading upon it until the end of time. The castle sat atop a great, rocky hill, wider and shorter than the perch of the Roost. A long, ascending bridge supported by arches of stone led up to the gatehouse, a lolling tongue into the mouth of some bloated beast. There were men on horses near the base of the bridge. Pocket saw them staring, each man fighting to hide the confusion, hatred and doubt on their bearded faces. The wheels hit the stonework and the horses' hooves scraped sharply as they pulled steadily up the incline. It was not too steep, so there was no cause to push. Pocket walked wearily along with the rest, but where their heads looked to their boots, his was held up high, staring at the gate.

The walls of the castle were thick and in poor repair.

Towers peeked up over the ramparts, wall-walks and covered bridges linking them to the dominating bulk of the central keep.

Inside there would be narrow passageways and turret rooms.

Cellars and garrets, lost stairways and forgotten depths. Chambers would be ruled by spiders and the dust of years. Shadows held sway here.

Pocket smiled as he crossed under the gate. This was his new playground.

TWENTY-THREE

Panic was her pillow. Deglan reached down carefully, adjusting the blanket so it covered the girl's shoulders. The dog was awake and raised her head slowly, fixing him with a look that seemed insulted, as if doubting the child's wellbeing was a personal affront. Blink slept on, her head resting in the crook between Panic's belly and back leg.

"Sorry to disturb," Deglan muttered at the dog. Panic simply lay her head back down. He turned and left the room, though with no roof it hardly qualified. He used the doorway, though there were half a dozen other holes in the three remaining walls just as large. Coltrane stood at the edge of the ruins, his back to Deglan, looking off at Castle Gaunt. Over a mile in the distance, the great fortress was nothing but a jagged black hole in the purple-hued curtain of stars.

"Might be better if you didn't look at it," Deglan told the Forge Born. "I don't fancy trying to stop you if you start marching that way."

"Over eight centuries," Coltrane tolled, "since last I was there."

A bad taste filled Deglan's mouth. "Home sweet home."

"You mock me," Coltrane replied in a voice devoid of pride.

"Your kind was always a mockery," Deglan returned, enjoying the barb far more than was warranted.

"They were as they were made," Curdle stated, stepping out of the darkness. The hobgoblin came to stand beside Deglan and looked out across the black expanse of fields towards the object of the Forge Born's temptation.

"Such a dreadful, impressive sight," he said with quiet regret.

"The exact qualities I wanted for my tombstone," Deglan said dryly.

Curdle hummed a laugh, then reached into his robe, producing a small flask. He pulled the cork free and offered it to Deglan.

"Root whiskey?" Deglan said after sniffing the contents.

"The best in Toad Holm," Curdle said wistfully.

Deglan took a pull, enjoying the smooth heat spreading down his throat and into his chest. He passed the flask back with a nod of gratitude, not trusting his voice. Curdle took a sip, looking down at the flask and nodding appreciatively as he swallowed.

Deglan cleared his throat. "What was the occasion?"

Curdle shrugged. "Might be the only funeral we get."

Deglan nodded darkly, glancing around at the sprawl of depressing ruins surrounding them.

All that was left of the Kings' Stables.

Established by the fourth man to rule the goblins, the Stables began as little more than a camp where the king kept his living entertainments. Ebraucus the Unspent was one of the most perverse of the warlocks, his carnal tastes varied and numerous.

The Stables became his personal retreat, a place where he could indulge in his decadent pleasures in comfort, only a short ride from the castle. Here he housed a menagerie of beasts to fight before his eyes, while his collection of women from every race serviced his unspeakable desires. It was said that Ebraucus grew easily bored, and soon the animals became his lovers while the women fought to the death at his command. The Stables grew more lavish as arenas, feasting halls and living quarters were constructed. It became a veritable village, a community of wranglers, slaves, whores and pit fighters, all living in service to the Goblin King. Ebraucus the Unspent was greedy, licentious and cruel, and a lamb compared to the son that followed him.

Prasugut Daughtersbane expanded his father's retreat, bringing the orgies of flesh and death to a pinnacle of unimaginable debauchery. He had the Red Caps searching the known world for the most comely children, wanting to possess them early so that they might know a life that was meant only to please him. But the Stables and Prasugut's reign came crashing down not long after he stole the twin daughters of a fomori widow.

Neavain was a celebrated beauty among the fomori clans.

Her husband had been a blacksmith and was executed by the Red Caps for providing weapons to the Fae rebels. Faabar often spoke of him with respect, and his wife with something near to reverence.

If she was anything like the female fomori Deglan had seen, she must have been magnificent. Tall and statuesque, with manes of thick curls, fomori women were an impressive sight. They have few children, and Neavain's twin girls were a rare treasure. When they were stolen away to become Prasugut's unwilling consorts, Neavain flew into a frenzy, taking up her husband's smithing hammer and tracking the Red Caps to the Kings' Stables. She slaughtered the goblin garrison, freeing her daughters and all the other slaves, who rose up, tearing the Stables down in a fury of liberation.

None of the following Goblin Kings ever rebuilt them.

Deglan now stood in the ruins, looking at the distant silhouette of Castle Gaunt, wishing he could reduce it to rubble.

How they hoped to storm that cursed citadel, even with the help of a Forge Born, was something Deglan had pestered Curdle about for days. The seer had only told him to remain patient, which, of course, had the opposite effect.

"So if we are having our funeral," Deglan said, reaching over to take the flask again, "we must be ready to make a move."

"Nearly," Curdle replied. "We must do something soon or the Swinehelm will act unimpeded and we shall miss our chance."

"To do. . . ?" Deglan fished.

"Anything we can," the mystic replied vaguely. "But for now, we are waiting."

Deglan was getting tired of his own questions, but he asked anyway. "For what?"

"For them," Curdle replied, turning towards the dark just as Sweat came padding silently forward. Madigan was close behind, and following him was the fattest goblin Deglan had ever seen. He smiled broadly over his chins when he saw Curdle and, dropping the huge club in his hands, he bounded forward, gut bouncing and wrapped the seer in a hug.

"Milkthumb, you candle-colored flirt," the sack of lard said, hoisting Curdle off the ground. "Give us a kiss."

Curdle suffered the embrace stiffly, adjusting his robes primly after being set back on his feet. "A greeting as enthusiastic as it is dignity-robbing. As always." The mystic gave a resigned sigh then looked up at Deglan. "Master Loamtoes, may I present Burden Dughan."

"Yelch!" the fat goblin grimaced, before extending his hand.

"Please, call me Muckle . . . or Mule or Dandy Breeches or Fishfucker.. . . call me anything but *that*!"

"*You* sit on King Hob's council?" Deglan asked incredulously.

"Not often," Fishfucker replied cheerfully. "That damn Moot chamber makes my ass itch."

Deglan was saved from a response by the pair of coburn approaching. One older and stern, the other young and brooding, but both armed and wearing surcoats of crimson and grey. Curdle introduced them as well, but Deglan did not hear their names. His attention was entirely devoted to the last newcomer, flying up to greet him.

"I'll be buggered."

Rosheen planted a kiss on his cheek. "I should have known you were too stubborn to die."

"I'll be buggered," he said again, slack-jawed.

Rosheen wasted no time once she pulled the gnome aside.

"Padric?" she asked and watched as the surprise on Deglan's face was chased away by pain.

Do not say it.

"The Wallow," Deglan began slowly, "was ash. The bodies burnt—"

"He might have escaped," Rosheen cut in.

The gnome opened his mouth, lost his words, struggled to find them.

No. "No."

"Faabar," Deglan managed.

Yes, he was with the fomori.

"Rosheen, even he did not make it."

And it fell over her, the fear made solid, becoming knowledge. Spoken on the lips of another, it became real and terrible. She had held onto him in her heart, a vision of hope, healthy and whole. Now he was gone, nothing but a memory of the last time she saw him in a night-covered forest. A face, a known and loved face, gone forever, nothing now but a skull lying in a pile of indistinguishable bones. Why had she left? She could have gone back, been with him at the last, burned away at his side never having to wonder whether he was alive or dead, never having to imagine searching in vain for some semblance of him in a sooty pile of fleshless, faceless corpses.

"I should have stayed with him. Deglan, he was so young."

The gnome looked at her, eyes trying to pull her sorrow away. "I am sorry."

She nodded once. "We have to get him out of there."

"He is dead, Rosheen."

"No, not Padric. Pocket. Pocket is in the castle."

Deglan shook his head. "Who is Pocket?"

"He is just a boy. Ten years old. He doesn't belong in that place."

"Well," Deglan said, looking over her shoulder at the others, "if you want to assault Castle Gaunt, this is the lot to be with."

Rosheen turned, her eyes settling on the Forge Born standing silently off to the side.

"You have fallen in with some unlikely allies," she told the gnome.

Deglan shot a scowl at Muckle and the coburn. "Like you haven't. That damn goblin looks right touched."

Better to get it over with. "He's a Jester, Deglan."

"Buggery and spit! Well, mine is a damn seer, so be mindful of what you think."

"Do you trust him?" Rosheen asked.

Deglan thought about it for a moment. "Curdle, yes. Haven't quite gotten used to the Sure Finder."

Rosheen could not help but laugh. "I about had a fit when he and that dog of his found us."

But the gnome was not listening. Rosheen watched as he took a step forward, concern spreading across his face. A little girl emerged from one of the ruined buildings, wiping sleep from her eyes. Madigan's other dog was at her side and the child kept a hand on it as she looked doubtfully at all the new faces. The coburn seemed to scare her the most, but Sir Corc held his hand out to the dog who sniffed it carefully. Seeing this, the girl relaxed. Muckle tried to greet her, but Panic nipped at him, sending the fat goblin dancing backwards. Deglan's relief was palpable and Rosheen saw on his face an expression she had often worn.

"What is her name?" she asked gently.

Deglan looked over at her, still distracted and cast a few more glances back at the girl before answering. "Never told me her given name. Red Caps did for her family. I think she saw it happen. I call her Blink."

"She is adorable."

A self-conscious smile split the gnome's face and they both turned back to watch as Blink chased Muckle around the ruins with the dogs. Sir Corc was deep in conversation with the other goblin, the one Deglan called Curdle. Bantam Flyn sat upon some rubble, completely detached.

"Those coburn," Deglan pointed with his chin. "Knights?"

"The older one is," Rosheen replied. "Sir Corc. Order of the Valiant Spur. The other is his squire."

"Bad blood between them," Deglan stated.

"Flyn is learning the sobering effects of shame," Rosheen said sadly.

Deglan squinted at the group and clicked his tongue. "A seer. A Jester. Two trained coburn. Madigan Sure Finder."

"Formidable company."

Deglan nodded. "And they are all kittens compared to *that*."

Rosheen did not bother looking at the Forge Born. Its very presence was already making her head ache. Deglan must have noticed her wince.

"I have a remedy for the pains," he said, starting for the ruined building. "Let me fetch my satchel."

Ever the healer.

The goblin seer pulled Deglan aside when he reappeared and the two spoke briefly. Nodding, Deglan looked up and waved her over.

Time to talk.

They all gathered inside the ruin so that the tumbled walls might mask the fire that Madigan had kindled before drawing off to a far corner with his dogs. Rosheen saw the little girl Blink was also with them and watched as Deglan went to pull her away, leading her closer to the fire before sitting down with the child in his lap.

Sweat and Panic watched her go, noses sniffing, but Madigan's eyes were cocked in the opposite direction.

Indifferent, Sure Finder?

Rosheen was relieved to see the Forge Born had not moved from his silent vigil. Muckle flopped down heavily by the fire, while Flyn leaned against the wall near the hole that was once the entrance. Sir Corc stood further in, arms crossed. Rosheen fluttered over to Deglan and kissed Blink lightly on the nose.

"Hello, sweet one," she said, and the chubby cheeks creased with delight. "May I sit with you?"

Blink nodded, eyes wide, and Rosheen settled down in her lap, smiling to herself as she felt a finger slide gently, curiously down her wing. The pale goblin approached the fire, the shadows settling deeply in his wrinkled face.

"We have come together in defiance," he began, looking to each of them and nodding respectfully. "Defiance of a past that must not darken our future. As I speak, Torcan Swinehelm and his followers are preparing to awaken the Forge Born. We have little time, so I will be brief. The Flame Binder allied with the Red Caps will soon ignite the fires of life within the most dangerous foes this land has ever known. The Seelie Court remains silent. Toad Holm lies corrupted, and the race of man is divided, unprepared. All that stands between Airlann and cruel domination are we few, brought together by roads of fortune, retribution, desperation and design. We can stop this. We *can* stop this, if we are willing to risk all."

It was Sir Corc who spoke. "What do you propose?"

"Kill the Flame Binder," Deglan said gruffly.

"Impossible," Curdle said sadly. "He very well may be the last vessel of the purging element. The sole wielder of Fire. The power within him is more than any of us can contend. I doubt even Muckle could stand against him."

"You never know," the fat goblin said, his face considering.

"No," Curdle defeated the notion with a cut of his hand.

"Alone the Flame Binder is dangerous, and within the castle he will be surrounded by Red Caps. We are not an army. Were it possible to slay him, it remains unwise. We do not know what will happen to the Elements if his life ends. It could very well spell the end of all things." The seer squinted into the oblivion. He shook his head with finality. "No. The chances of preventing him from completing his ritual are near to nothing. I do not think we can stop him in time."

"Then those towering bastards will awaken," Deglan said.

"And we are doomed."

"They will awaken," Curdle agreed, "but we have a chance to affect how."

"Explain," Sir Corc said.

"Coltrane is the key," Curdle said, nodding at the tall form of the Forge Born visible over the crumbling wall. "The Magic within him is still strong. Though he is drawn to the Flame Binder like a moth to a candle, he is not yet a slave. The Red Caps have the Gaunt Prince's heir secured within the castle. If the other Forge Born return to life they will be servants to his will . . . unless we can restore their own will to them."

"How?" Rosheen asked.

Curdle took a deep breath. "By redirecting the Fire that grants them life and channeling it through Coltrane, allowing his heart to flow into them."

"And who is going to do that?" Deglan demanded.

"That would be me," Muckle said, standing up next to Curdle.

"You?" Deglan laughed in disbelief.

"Us, actually," Curdle said, shrugging off Muckle's attempts to place an arm around him. "It will require both of us to succeed."

The gnome was still not convinced. "What by Earth and Stone makes you two think you are capable of something like that?"

"Well," Muckle said haughtily, "we did it once, didn't we?"

Rosheen frowned up at the goblin. *Bag of lard and lies.*

"My friend, astonishingly, speaks the truth," Curdle spoke directly to her. "It was we who first crafted the spell that freed the Forge Born."

"Toad shit!" Deglan barked. "The elves wove that spell!"

Curdle nodded. "We needed their considerable power to magnify it, push it past the defenses of the warlocks, but Muckle and I created the spell. Only we had the knowledge of the Forge Born required to change them."

Rosheen did not like the sound of that. "Knowledge?"

A deep sorrow filled the white goblin's face, and Rosheen saw Muckle set his jaw, his normally dancing eyes growing hard.

"Yes," Curdle said. "Knowledge we gained while in service to the Goblin Kings."

There was a long silence. All eyes locked on the two goblins standing by the fire, their shadows cast on the ruined stones behind them; black, distorted, flickering imitations. It was Deglan who finally spoke.

"You are Red Caps," he said, his voice hushed.

"Not my color," Muckle said, trying and failing to put levity in his voice. "Besides, I look awful in hats."

"The Red Caps were . . . are just soldiers," Curdle told them gravely. "We were more than that. We were councilors . . . spies, each of us wielders of unique Magic. Muckle began his service with Vellaunus the Cackler, and I with Jerrod the First."

"Evil bastards," Muckle said without humor.

"But not so evil as Jerrod the Second," Curdle's shoulders slumped with shame. "We knew the isle, maybe the world, would be destroyed the day he took command of the Forge Born."

"So you betrayed him," Deglan said.

"No," Curdle replied. "We stopped betraying the Fae. We went to Irial and placed ourselves in his custody, begging him to listen. It took years before he trusted us for more than spies, but finally, with no other course, he heard our council and agreed to help us cast our spell."

"And gave the Forge Born a conscience," Rosheen said.

"It was the only way to defeat them," Curdle said. "I knew the secrets of the mind. Muckle, for all his buffoonery, is a master of emotion. What is a conscience but the meeting of mind and heart?"

"And now you want to cast your spell again," Deglan said.

Curdle looked hopeful. "With the elves all but vanished from the world, we lack the power to enchant the Forge Born ourselves unless we use the spell still residing in Coltrane and infuse it directly into the others as they regain their lives."

"How can we trust you?" Rosheen asked, watching her words sting the mystic.

The goblin only looked at her, knowing nothing he could say would help.

"I have known Muckle Gutbuster for more than twenty years," Sir Corc said. "He could have betrayed me many times. I will vouch for him."

Rosheen felt herself and Blink being shifted as Deglan stood. He approached the hobgoblins, looking Curdle square in the face.

"You have always told me the truth," the gnome told him.

"Even when it was difficult to hear." Deglan turned to face the rest of them. "I say we trust this damn albino."

"And I think you are all mad for following us anywhere," Muckle chuckled, "which makes you my kind of crazy."

"To do this," Rosheen said. "Cast your spell . . . you will need to be close?"

"Yes," Curdle confirmed. "Coltrane, Muckle and I will need to be inside the castle and in the path of the Flame Binder's spell."

"How are we going to accomplish that?" Deglan griped.

"You two might be able to sneak in, what are two more ugly goblins in a castle full of Red Caps."

"Oi!" Muckle threw in.

"But Coltrane?" Deglan continued. "He cannot just go striding in!"

"Not a problem," a voice said from the back. They all turned towards Bantam Flyn. "Now what about Pocket?"

"Half a moment," Muckle looked intrigued. "Did you just say, not a problem?"

"Yes," the squire returned. "I know how to get you two and the walking anvil inside. Now what about Pocket?"

Curdle gazed for a moment at the young coburn, his face a mask of concentration.

Reading his cocky mind.

"Yes," the seer said hopefully. "I do believe that will work!"

"I know," Flyn said impatiently. "Now answer my question about Pocket."

"I am going in to get him," Sir Corc said simply.

Bantam Flyn looked at the knight for a moment. "Good enough for me."

"There is something else," Deglan said. "Curdle said we have to be willing to risk all . . . and we are, but there is still a great chance this will fail. Whatever happens there is an opportunity here that we cannot miss. The Flame Binder is strong, and should our hobgoblins' spell falter, the Forge Born are worse. There is nothing any of us can do against them, but there is somewhere we can strike . . . a weak and vital link in the Red Caps' plan. No matter what happens, one of us must make sure it is severed."

Of course.

"What are you saying?" Sir Corc asked.

"He is saying," Rosheen announced, "for the sake of the isle, the Gaunt Prince's heir must die."

TWENTY-FOUR

Padric's thoughts were of home. He wished he were back there, helping his father and the other men, coming home sore and soiled to find a warm meal waiting, his mother's easy smile and quiet acceptance filling their small house. The cider-house would be up in the fort and the warriors as well; other men to do the fighting, the killing, the dying. He would learn all the things he had ignored or been too downtrodden to pay any mind. His father would help him build his own house, and he would take Svala inside each night and feel no guilt or shame or fear. They would not seek comfort in each other, it would simply exist between them, and he could allow himself to love her. He would walk into the still woods alone and hear that bright laugh, her laugh, and he would look up to see his friend smiling down from the branches, eternally playful.

Like him, the thoughts were a lie. He could no more be a contented farmer than he could a king. Stone Fort may have suffered the same fate as so many other villages; burned by the very maniacal immortals that now sought to serve him. It was a maddening thought, and he pushed it away, willing his family's survival by stripping it of the sweet dream he drizzled upon it. His father did not need his help. Padric had been nothing but a breathing misery to his mother, a burden she had been too kind to put down. He hated the fort and the ciderhouse and the warriors.

The day he turned his back on them had been a cause for rejoicing.

Svala would never be his wife and Rosheen was gone. Even if she lived, he would never hear her laugh again. That chance had ended the night he first saw Torcan Swinehelm and the Flame Binder.

Both goblins waited on him now. The wizard was outside in the Cog Yard among his sleeping children while Torcan stood in Padric's chamber, watching as Svala helped him don the raiment provided for the ritual. No fur-trimmed robes of soft cloth for him.

Torcan wanted the king to greet his army as a warrior. Boiled leather, studded with iron over blackened mail. Gauntlets covered his hands and a heavy cloak of crimson hung from silver brooches.

His seax hung from his belt and Torcan had given him a heavy iron mace to carry as both weapon and scepter. Svala tied his hair back with a simple strip of leather, brushing the cloak smooth across his shoulders when she was done. Padric turned and looked at her, receiving a smile and an appraising look from her blue eyes. He had ordered she stay in the keep to attend to Kederic Winetongue. The man had not spoken nor hardly moved since Acwellen's visit, and Padric had leapt upon his infirmity to ensure Svala was well away from the ritual. Padric worried that Torcan would require her presence, but thankfully he did not raise any objections. The goblin thought his plans were finally coming to fruition and he stood in full bronze armor, eagerly waiting to escort Padric down to the Cog Yard.

Slouch Hat also stood by. The goblins had not seen fit to offer him fresh garments, so he still wore the stained, threadbare shirt and breeches and his rumpled, filthy hat. The husk held Jerrod's crown steadily in his hands, holding it before him with solemn respect. Padric tried to read some hint in the pits of Slouch Hat's eyes, but there was nothing. No spark of hope nor sign of the phantom servant girl now residing within his stuffed body. Padric suppressed a shiver, grateful that Svala would be nowhere near them during whatever end was fast approaching.

Pocket awoke with a start, the sudden presence of sun and silence startling him. Remaining on his belly, he shuffled forward and peered down at the castle yard from the edge of the shattered tower. It was a good vantage point and he had chosen it carefully.

The stone stairs leading to the turret room were mostly smashed, and anyone wishing to reach his hiding place would be forced to make the difficult climb from the middle landing level with the ramparts. This castle was larger than the Roost, and he had not yet explored it all, but his first discovery was by necessity a seemingly inaccessible hideaway.

The Red Caps did not have the numbers to cover the entire fortification, and in the hours between coming to the castle and sneaking to this tower, Pocket had learned that they kept their attention directed on patrolling the curtain wall and guarding the central keep. He did not know how he managed the climb, but weary as he was he hauled himself up and collapsed at the top.

Sleep came, only to be driven away by the work being done in the forges below. He fell in and out of troubled dreams, aggravated by hunger, thirst and the possibility of being discovered. At some point the hammers must have ceased, for he finally slept, unaware of the rising sun.

Now, the activity in the yard was growing again. The forges were cold and silent, but the goblins still crawled over them, taking down the canvas coverings, hauling tools and anvils away. When he had come through the gate at dusk, the sight of the metal giants standing motionless around the burning goblin unnerved him greatly, making his skin tingle. That same goblin now stood upon the steps of the keep, no longer bathed in flames, watching the preparations and gazing lovingly over the ranks of those hulking suits of armor. Pocket had seen drawings, paintings, and woodcuts of the Forge Born. But those did not come close to capturing the cold lethality that radiated from them even after centuries of repose.

Some of the most famous knights of the Valiant Spur had fought and defeated Forge Born, but seeing these monstrous killers with his own eyes, Pocket could not help but doubt the tales. How could anyone of mere flesh and bone stand a chance against living iron?

A stir of activity caught his eye and Pocket looked down to see another Forge Born being dragged into the yard. Even from a distance it was clear that this one was less rusted than the others and appeared in no need of repair. It lay upon a stout wooden litter attached to a single mule. A mule Pocket knew immediately.

"Backbone," he worried to himself.

His beloved companion struggled forward, aided by half a dozen goblins pushing at the litter or straining to pull with ropes.

Two Red Caps followed the litter, talking with one of the smiths.

One of them, Pocket noticed, was quite fat.

"They are inside," Rosheen announced when she returned.

"Bloody wonder," Deglan said, still not ready to believe it had worked. The young coburn's idea had been simple and bold, traits the squire fully embodied. Deglan had expressed his doubt that the mule could drag Coltrane at all, but Flyn said the beast need only make it to the castle gate. The Red Caps would help after that, so long as Curdle and Muckle played their parts convincingly.

Deglan had doubted that, too, and said as much. Neither of their singular-looking hobgoblins fit the muster for the typical foot soldier. He looked to Rosheen for support, but the piskie merely smiled slyly and nodded back to where the goblins stood with the mule. Where once a pale, wrinkled goblin and his bawdily clad, corpulent companion stood, there were now two average-looking goblins wearing filthy armor, iron boots and blood stained hats.

"Damn albino mind-twiddler," Deglan scowled at the smaller of the two Red Caps.

"The mind sees what it wants to see," Curdle replied.

"He's still fat," Deglan said, pointing at Muckle.

"Even Magic has its limits," Curdle said wryly.

Muckle laughed the loudest but slipped in, "Both your mothers were whores," between guffaws.

Curdle looked up at Coltrane, who stood waiting near the mule. "Are you ready?"

"Yes," the Forge Born answered. He lay down on the litter and Deglan was struck by how agile the thing was despite its size.

The litter Sir Corc had constructed held firm, its inclined design helping distribute Coltrane's weight. Both the coburn helped push from the back while the mule pulled forward, and the litter got moving. It was a mile to Castle Gaunt and Deglan waited with the coburn until Rosheen came back with the good news.

"Now for our part," Sir Corc said.

Deglan nodded and went inside the ruined building. Blink was playing with the dogs while Madigan sat off against the wall, sharpening his spear.

"It is time," Deglan told him, and the Sure Finder pierced him with his raptor's eyes for a moment before rising smoothly.

They crossed the plain together, making no attempt to hide among the scrub and boulders. The coburn had donned their full arms. Bantam Flyn wore brigandine and mail, his greatsword unsheathed and propped on his shoulder. Sir Corc wore mail with steel plates covering his arms and torso, a shield across his back, sword, mace and dagger hanging from his belts. Deglan held Blink's hand as they walked and Rosheen flew next to them.

Madigan led the group, with Sweat and Panic loping on either side.

The Sure Finder's stride was fluid, almost careless. Deglan wished he felt as confident.

The mile passed quickly and Castle Gaunt loomed ahead of them, the pale morning light staining the thick clouds above it an ugly yellow. Madigan turned before reaching the bridge and made for the horsemen's camp. Tents and makeshift paddocks covered a large swath of ground in the shadow of Penda's Rock. Deglan saw warriors, grooms, errand boys and serving wenches going about their morning chores while the warriors milled about. Fully half their number was mounted, ready to begin their first patrol around the Rock. A challenge went up from the sentries when they saw Deglan's little group approaching, and he tightened his grip on Blink's hand.

"Earth and Stone," he swore under his breath. "What are we doing?"

Madigan walked past the slack-jawed sentries and directly into the camp. Deglan and the others followed close behind with Sweat and Panic running a circular patrol around them. The warriors surrounded them now, some on foot and others mounted, but hesitance on every face. Deglan saw more curiosity than aggression, and something else. The men cast only furtive glances at him, the coburn, Rosheen and the child. Mostly they looked at Madigan. They knew him. They knew his dogs. And they feared all three. The Sure Finder stood, returning the men's stares with placid savagery, his spear held loosely at his side. He waited. Deglan held his breath.

An angry voice moved through the men and they shuffled aside, parting at the edge to reveal Acwellen pushing his way through. His loyal curs followed him and Deglan knew them all.

Aglaeca. Drefan. Banan. Big Cunny. Seon. Fat Donall and Poncey Swan. He remembered the last night he had seen these murderers, and his reluctance was burned away by the painful recollection.

Acwellen took the scene in quickly, for a lout, his darting eyes lingering on Deglan for a moment before finally coming to rest on Madigan.

"Sure Finder," Acwellen said welcomingly. "I see you have finally brought me the treacherous gnome! Boys, bring that stunted leech here so that we may have off his ugly head."

Drefan and Big Cunny stepped forward. Sir Corc and Bantam Flyn did, too. The men eyed the coburn warily for a moment, then glanced back to Acwellen.

Deglan found his voice. "It is not my head that needs to be taken, Acwellen! It was not I who betrayed Hog's Wallow. Where is Kederic Winetongue? Bring him out here that he may answer for the crime you place at my feet."

"He is dead," Acwellen pitched his voice so all could hear.

"As you say, he was a traitorous coward, and I killed him for it."

Deglan looked into the big man's eyes and found the lie.

"If that is so," Deglan said, "why are you here now? Far from home, serving the goblins?"

"The price of our safety," Acwellen lied easily.

"Winetongue brought this upon us. I am merely trying to see to it we survive his skullduggery. Our fort remains standing because of me!"

"I believe that," Deglan shot back. "Because of you . . . the Red Caps came! Because of you, Hog's Wallow had no warning!"

He turned as he spoke, addressing the men that surrounded him.

"You all know me. Seen more than a few of you through a fever, brought some of your children into the world with my own hands. I was riding to the fort with news of the attack when this man," he thrust a finger at Acwellen, "ambushed me! Tried to kill me. And when he failed, sent the Sure Finder to hunt me down!"

"I did!" Acwellen returned. "But on Kederic's orders! It was he who lied to us, not I!"

"You are the goblins' pet, Acwellen! Always were. Kederic Winetongue hated the Fae. I do not believe he would have made such a pact."

"So you say," Acwellen said slowly. "But we have no cause to trust you, immortal."

Deglan nodded at that, then drew Blink slowly forward by the hand. The men looked at her, many of them unknowingly exchanging their warriors' faces for those they wore as fathers. Sir Corc produced a spare buckle from his armor and handed it gently to the girl. Blink took it in her chubby fist, looking down at it with the pointed curiosity of youth.

Deglan swept the men and pointed at the buckle. "Iron. The bane of my kind . . . and nothing but a new plaything to this girl. She is no changeling. There is no cause to distrust her. No hidden evil. She is a human child, born with no special gifts save the innocent ability to inspire feelings of protection and love to any who look upon her. You mortals are frail, and in your children that frailty is beautiful. This one . . . her parents were butchered by Red Caps. I found her and cared for her, but that is my way. I am a healer and I swore to care for all life, mortal and immortal. If you can discount that because I am Fae, so be it. But you stand here, guarding the fanatics that tried to kill this little one. And the man who leads you? He allowed it to happen. You may believe you are saving your own daughters by being here. You are not. Acwellen's treachery bought your children some time, but it robbed this girl of everything."

"Enough of your bewitching words!" Acwellen screamed, turning to the assembled men. "Kill them now! Before he can further enchant you!"

No one moved.

Acwellen stood, red-faced and breathing hard, daring the men to defy him. They did. The big man smiled, regaining his composure. "Very well. If you choose to believe this gnome! But I will not be condemned on his word alone. If you no longer want my leadership, I will go. And you can figure how best to survive what Kederic brought down on our heads." He motioned to his own men. "We ride."

Acwellen turned and found Sweat and Panic blocking his path.

"I think," Deglan said, backing away with Blink in tow, "Madigan has unfinished business with you lot. He does not take kindly to being sent after the wrong prey."

The warriors backed away, widening the space and leaving Acwellen and his loyal henchmen alone. Aglaeca wasted no time and drew his sword. Big Cunny's dim-witted face searched for answers and Fat Donall began laughing, pulling a dirk from his belt.

Acwellen turned slowly, trying to keep both Madigan and the dogs in sight.

It was Drefan who ran, darting towards a mounted warrior and knocking him from the saddle. The sour old man had one foot in the stirrup when Panic dragged him down. There was a wet thud and Fat Donall stopped laughing, Madigan's spear sticking through his blubbery neck. Acwellen snarled, ripping his sword free and slashing furiously. The hunter ducked smoothly and leapt to the side, rolling to come up next to Big Cunny, his arm arcing upwards as he stood. Red spurted forcefully from the unfortunate man's groin, and Deglan recognized the sure sign of a severed artery. Big Cunny dropped with the confused look still on his face. Madigan flipped his bloody dagger deftly, catching it blade down. Aglaeca was at his back, sword raised to strike, but Madigan ignored him as Sweat barreled into the man, taking him down and ripping out his throat.

Acwellen surged back in, sword swiping to keep the advancing hunter at bay. Panic had finished with Drefan and joined her mate to converge on Poncey Swan, who pissed himself and fell to his knees, weeping and begging the advancing dogs for mercy.

They showed none.

Madigan avoided Acwellen's attacks with preternatural grace, his sinewy body snapping away from the big man's sword.

He ducked a stroke, then darted in, grabbing Acwellen's sword arm by the wrist and punching his dagger down into the elbow joint.

Acwellen screamed as the dagger was pulled free, dripping. He slammed his head into Madigan's face and the hunter retreated a few paces backwards. He looked at his opponent for a moment, seemingly unfazed, then shook his head quickly, shrugging off the blow. Acwellen's sword arm hung limply at his side, bleeding freely.

He choked on the pain and spit, the drops landing in his beard. His own dagger was now in his good hand and he brandished it at Madigan, screaming a wordless challenge. The hunter just stared back at him, standing up straight as if the fight was over.

It was.

The dogs struck from opposite sides, Sweat hitting Acwellen low, while Panic slammed into his midriff, knocking him spinning to the ground. The man squealed as he was savaged and Madigan pounced, burying his dagger to the hilt. Sweat and Panic released their jaws, leaving split flesh and torn muscle behind.

Madigan stood, pulling his dagger free from Acwellen's stomach.

Of Acwellen's men, only Seon and Banan still lived. Neither had drawn their weapons or even moved during the slaughter.

Banan remained calm, his hand gripping Seon's wrist down at his side, willing the younger, shaking man to neither fight nor flee.

Sweat and Panic circled the pair, sniffing. Seon let a whimper escape his lips and the dogs bared their teeth, hackles rising. The onlookers were still, breathless, waiting for the final kill. Madigan came up, pulling his spear from the ruin of Fat Donall's throat as he approached. Seon's eyes were clenched tight, but Banan met the hunter's gaze.

"Kederic Winetongue is guiltless," the grim-faced warrior said. "We betrayed him to the goblins. They have him in that castle. Judge me as you will."

Madigan leaned forward, and Deglan fancied he sniffed the other man. Then he turned and walked away, his dogs at his heels.

Banan released his hold on Seon and the young man's legs buckled, spilling him to the ground.

"Place those two in irons!"

Deglan recognized the speaker as Orvin, one of Kederic's other huscarls.

"Best pardon them," Sir Corc told the man. "You will need every sword for what you intend."

"And how do you know my intentions, coburn?" Orvin asked with a hard smile.

"I know the look of a man about to do the right thing."

Orvin's smile broadened and he nodded slowly, watching the knight.

"Mount up!" he yelled over his shoulder, and the warriors scrambled to action.

As the men marshaled, Deglan led Blink by the hand, walking over to where Madigan squatted, his dogs licking the blood from his hands. Deglan cleared his throat, but the man did not look up.

"Madigan," Deglan began feebly, silently asking the Earth to give him strength for what he was about to do. "I would ask a boon of you." The dogs looked up at him, but the man's eyes were on his knife, cleaning it on the grass. Deglan swallowed hard, willing his voice to remain steady and failing. "Take Blink away from here."

Madigan's head snapped up, his predatory eyes searching Deglan's face. There was a twist to the man's mouth Deglan had never seen before.

"I . . . do not know what will happen here," he told him.

"And I would see her safe. I cannot protect her, not like you can . . . and . . ." His words broke off, his resolve failing. He faltered, looking down at the ground, vision drowning with pain. He could not do this. He could not give her up.

A hand touched him gently. Deglan looked up and found Madigan's strong fingers pressing into his shoulder. The raptor's eyes were no longer there, the animal was gone. Madigan Sure Finder nodded, and in that slight motion Deglan saw a promise. He turned, going to his knees, and took Blink's hands in his own.

"Will you be happy?" he asked her gently, trying to hide his sorrow, but betrayed by his tears. "Tell me you will be happy. I need to know."

Blink looked at him with her large, round eyes. She nodded.

Another promise.

He wanted to embrace her, but promised himself he would not, for fear if he did he would never let her go. Of the three of them, he broke his promise, pulling her close and smelling her hair for the last time.

"Take her," he said without moving his eyes off the face he loved. "Please. Take her now."

Madigan lifted Blink up, and Deglan felt her fingers slide away. He knelt on the ground a long time before finally turning.

Madigan had already walked a fair distance across the plain. Blink rode on his shoulders, reaching down to tease Sweat and Panic as they followed, jumping excitedly. She did not look back.

All two hundred warriors were ahorse and assembled in formation by the time Deglan got to his feet. Rosheen and the two coburn waited nearby, watching as the huscarls inspected their battle lines.

"They are going to fight?" he asked Rosheen when he drew near.

"They are," the piskie replied. She looked at him for a moment. "You made the right choice."

He shooed her words away with his hand. "Don't nursemaid me."

She allowed him his gruffness, and he was grateful. They all watched as Orvin addressed the men.

"They have our Thegn!" he cried over the ranks, gesturing to Castle Gaunt with his spear. "I mean to ride in there! And I will not ride out unless it is with Kederic Winetongue! Follow me if you be men!" He spurred his horse forward and the ground thundered as every man followed, screaming their war cry and galloping for the bridge.

"We best get moving," Sir Corc said, and began making his way swiftly towards Penda's Rock. Bantam Flyn followed.

Rosheen looked at Deglan. "You coming?"

"No," he replied, nodding at the column of warriors. "I will be of more use here when the blood spills." He looked at the piskie.

"Good luck."

She winked at him and flew off after the coburn.

Deglan barked some orders at the camp followers, making sure they had a field tent ready to receive the wounded. Checking his satchel, he ambled over to where Acwellen lay in the mud. The man's eyes rolled in his head, his breath coming in choking gasps, his tongue pushing blood from his mouth in gobs. Deglan squatted down next to him, looking impassively at the damage the dogs had done, and then at the knife wounds in his elbow and gut.

"These are grave," Deglan said, and Acwellen's head lolled over at the sound of his voice, his eyes trying to focus. "Grave, but not necessarily mortal. With the right care, you might live. I could certainly save you." Deglan nodded slowly. "Think I will give your injuries the same time you allowed me to tend to Bulge-Eye. That seems only right." Deglan reached into his satchel and removed a roll of linen and some herbs. He held them in his hands for a moment then looked at Acwellen and stood.

"Time's up."

Rosheen flew carefully upwards, staying close to the wall.

She reached the edge and crept between two of the merlons, listening. She peered around the stone, first left then right, searching the length of the ramparts for patrolling goblins. She saw none. A watchtower lay not far to the left, its yawning doorway straddling the wall, hiding a span of it in deep shadows. She could see the wall march back into the sunlight on the other side of the tower and nothing approached from that direction. To her right the rampart ended in the solid bulk of a barbican, stairs leading from the wall to its roof. The ruined corpse of a broken drum tower blocked her view of the inner bailey.

A forgotten, crumbling corner of the vast castle.

Sir Corc chose his spot well.

Rosheen dropped off the wall, gliding down past the stonework and then past the natural stones of the crag. The coburn waited for her at the base of the hill.

"It is clear," she told them.

The knight nodded and immediately set off, scrambling up the rocks, hauling his armored body over the boulders, making for the wall. Bantam Flyn watched for a moment, then shrugged out of his harness so that he could sheath his massive blade.

"I would have thought you would have gone with the horsemen," Rosheen said to him. "Charge the front gate."

Flyn slipped the harness over his shoulder, adjusting the sword comfortably across his back. "Pocket is one of us," he said.

"He is of the Valiant Spur. This is my place."

We all find it sometime. Maybe too late.

"Tell me, piskie," Bantam Flyn said, his head lifted. "Have you any gift with poetry?"

Rosheen wrinkled her face. "No."

"Pity," Flyn said, eyes still upraised. "This is a deed worthy of remembrance."

Rosheen followed his gaze. Above them, already past where the crag met the foundation, she could see an armored figure, shield across his back, reaching for another handhold.

"Sir Corc the Constant," the squire said with awe, "is scaling the walls of Castle Gaunt."

TWENTY-FIVE

Pocket found Backbone tucked away in what was left of the castle stables. The goblins had hung a filthy canvas over the remnants of the walls, providing some shelter for the draft animals they kept inside. Pocket had slipped out of his tower and into his goblin face the moment the alarm was raised. The Red Caps were marshaling to defend the main gate, and in the chaos of shouted orders and pounding boots, Pocket simply ran through the castle yard, looking purposeful. He stole a look at the group on the steps of the keep as he passed. The armored goblin was shouting at the soldiers, while the brooding man with black hair watched impassively. The scarecrow holding the crown stood next to the man, and Pocket felt for a moment that the stuffed man was watching him, but he put it out of his mind, hurrying on. The stables hugged the curtain wall, almost directly across from the keep. Thankfully, the forest of Forge Born stood between, providing plenty of concealment, and Pocket checked to make sure he was not seen before ducking inside.

Backbone looked a little tired, but otherwise was unharmed.

The goblins had not bothered to unhook him from the litter or give him water or fodder. Pocket searched the stinking stalls for anything suitable. He was rummaging through a pile of filthy straw when a hand clapped firmly on his shoulder, wheeling him around.

Pocket stared into the broad face of the Red Cap who held him.

Pocket smiled.

"Nice disguise," he said.

"And yours," Muckle replied with a grin, releasing his hold.

"I am glad to see you have discovered the doors that will open for you simply by becoming that most handsome of creatures, the goblin."

Pocket shifted back to himself. Holding another skin was still difficult and gave him a throbbing pain behind the eyes. He took a step back when the other Red Cap emerged from the neighboring stall.

"It is all right," Muckle said. "He is a friend."

Pocket looked back to find the Red Cap was still a goblin, but dressed in robes and possessing very white skin.

"Greetings, Pocket," the pale goblin said. "My name is Curdle Milkthumb. I am honored to meet you."

"Hello," was all Pocket said in reply before turning back to Muckle. "What are you doing here? And why did you bring my mule?"

Muckle crept toward the front of the stables and took a cautious look out into the yard as he spoke. "It is all a part of a very intricate plan to get ourselves killed."

Pocket joined him. Leaning carefully, he could just make out the top of the keep stairs through the ranks of Forge Born.

"Who is that?" he asked, pointing to the black-haired man.

Muckle shrugged. "The once and never king."

"Muckle," the other goblin said from the back of the stables. "We must make ready."

Muckle gave the stairs one more searching look and nodded his agreement.

"Looks like they are about to begin."

Padric suppressed a smile as Torcan heard the news of the attack. They had no sooner emerged from the keep than a Red Cap came running, reporting to Swinehelm of the horsemen's charge up the bridge. The gate to Castle Gaunt no longer held doors or portcullis, and the men had almost reached the walls by the time the goblins could respond, throwing themselves into the breach to repel the riders.

"We hold for now, my lord," the runner said, "but the bridge is too narrow to bring our numbers to bear."

Torcan slammed a bronze-clad fist into the messenger's face, sending him tumbling down the steps.

"Push them back!" the warlord screamed. "Drive them into the fields and devour them! They must not interrupt us now . . . Go!"

His bulbous nose broken and bleeding, the Red Cap picked himself up and bowed before running back to the fray. Padric could not see the main gate from where he stood, but the sounds of battle echoed through the inner bailey, and he watched as goblins hurried from their posts, rushing through the yard and across the ramparts to lend aid. Torcan commanded Padric's honor guard to remain, but ordered the rest to the defense of the bridge.

There were more than a thousand Red Caps in the castle, and Padric wondered what could possibly encourage two hundred men to assault such a garrison. It seemed Acwellen was a treacherous bastard no matter which way the wind blew.

The Flame Binder waited in the center of the Cog Yard, where the foundry once stood. He raised his head, looking up the steps, a smile beneath his mad eyes.

"Let them come," he said and Padric watched as smoke billowed from his mouth with the words. "They will find only death."

Fire came to life in the wizard's eyes, licking up from the sockets. The Flame Binder spread his arms, hands splayed, fingers curling stiffly and lifted his head, filling the sky with black smoke and dark words.

"Hear me, my children. Hear my words and remember. In a molten cradle did you quicken. Wrought at the core of the world and fashioned in the likeness of war. The anvil was your mother. The hammer your father. Remember their ringing voices and let them call you from slumber. Awake! Awake and walk the world! Receive the Fire as your breath! Let it fill you, and once more become living iron! You are destruction! You are death! You are Forge Born!"

A blast of flame and rushing air burst from the goblin with his final words. Padric raised his arms against the heat, turning his head away and clenching his eyes tight as the wind slammed into him. A terrible, crackling wail filled his ears, and he squinted back, eyes watering in the suffocating wind. The Flame Binder slowly rose into the air, his robes snapping around him. The flames poured from his eyes in radiant torrents, caught in the maelstrom which lifted his body, encasing it in Fire. Laughter sparked from the wizard's mouth as he continued to float within his twisting cloud of smoke. Flames shot from his hands, rending Padric's ears with an angry roar, and the Fire lanced into the nearest Forge Born, their metal bodies quickly beginning to glow with heat.

As the first statues of iron grew white hot, the Fire spread, jumping from one body to the next. Sweat ran freely down Padric's face as the Cog Yard turned into the heart of a forge. Next to him, Torcan basked in the stifling heat, his face suffused with triumphal ecstasy. Slouch Hat stood motionless, his brim curled downward in the blistering wind, hiding his face.

A cry of rage snapped Padric's head back to the yard. The flames had stopped spreading. The Flame Binder struggled, convulsing in the air, cursing in wordless fury. The tongues of Fire coming from his hands had joined into one and flowed directly into a single Forge Born far to the rear of the yard. Unlike his slumped counterparts, this one stood braced against the Fire, almost crouching, metal arms flung back wide. Another cry issued from the Flame Binder and he strained against his own flames, pulling away, but they held fast to the single Forge Born as if drawn to it.

"What is this?" Torcan hissed.

The Fire radiated from the lone Forge Born, now jumping to the two on either side, then forward, passing from one still body to the next, but it did not engulf them. As the flames reached each one, the Fire diminished, slowly kindling into a single burning point in the chests of the iron warriors. Padric watched as those flames began to pulse, began to beat, and he felt his own heart pounding.

"The elves' spell," Slouch Hat said with hushed reverence.

Torcan looked wildly from the husk to the Forge Born, recognition and fury twisting his face. The warlord growled in hatred, slamming his helm down over his head.

"Stay with the king," he told the eight Red Caps on the steps before rushing down the stairs, battle-axe in hand. When he reached the bottom he stopped and looked up at the Flame Binder, who still fought for control of his spell.

"Where?!" Torcan's voice rang over the howling wind.

"Show me!"

Padric saw the Flame Binder turn his head with great effort, the muscles in his neck straining. Thin gouts of Fire shot from his eyes, striking the makeshift canvas roof of the crumbling stables across the yard. The covering began to burn, and Padric's brow wrinkled in confusion. The Forge Born drawing the wizard's Magic was nowhere near there, but Torcan wasted no time, his armored form weaving through the ranks of iron. Padric looked to Slouch Hat, a question on his lips, but there was no time. Something was thwarting the Flame Binder, and the Swinehelm was going to stop it. He could not let that happen. He did not know who was hiding in the stables, but he was not going to stand idly by while they were butchered. Padric wrenched the cape from his shoulders, the wind catching it as it fell from his fingers. He tested the weight of the mace in his left hand, then drew his seax with the right.

"Come on," he told Slouch Hat and his guards, but the husk did not even look at him.

"Slouch Hat!" he persisted, "Are you coming?"

Slouch Hat continued to stare blankly. With a curse Padric ran down the steps with his guards following close behind. He suddenly found himself wondering where these goblins' allegiance would lie once he tried to kill Torcan Swinehelm. He pushed the thought aside and headed into the Cog Yard.

"It is working!" Rosheen yelled over the wind, pointing to Coltrane on the far side of the yard.

Sir Corc and Bantam Flyn crouched on the ramparts next to her, looking down into the chaos of swirling flame and blowing dust. The Flame Binder hovered in the center of it all, desperately trying to regain the energies that now poured into Coltrane.

Movement at the keep to their right caught Rosheen's eye. Through the smoke she could just make out Torcan Swinehelm approaching the Flame Binder, yelling something lost on the wind. Fire leapt from the wizard's eyes and something under the wall to their left began to burn.

"Curdle and Muckle," Sir Corc shouted. "They have been discovered!"

"Look!" Bantam Flyn exclaimed, pointing. Torcan was hurrying through the yard, making for the burning structure, and he was being followed. Rosheen could just make out a man, pressing through the tumult, guarded closely by eight Red Caps.

"It must be the heir!" she declared, looking at the coburn.

"Can you do it?" Sir Corc asked, his voice directed at the squire.

Bantam Flyn nodded. "Leave it to me."

"Go," Sir Corc replied. "I will help the hobgoblins."

The knight turned and ran across the wall, making for the rising flames. Flyn headed for the nearby stairs, descending quickly into the yard. Rosheen watched him slip the harness over his head and pull the greatsword free as he ran, heading directly into the whirlwind. Through the choking cloud, she could just make out the heir, weaving his way between the sleeping Forge Born. She watched him, wondering if he possessed any of the dread powers of his forebears. Even against the wind, his stride was strong, purposeful. There was a forward bend to his shoulders that seemed to challenge everything in front of him. His walk was determined.

Familiar.

Rosheen went cold.

"By the Hallowed! No!"

She flew straight for him, but the swirling winds were too strong, tossing her about, forcing her to retreat. She tried again, screaming in fury as she was denied by the gale. Helpless anger boiled inside her and she screamed for Flyn, begging for him to stop. She could not see the squire, but she knew he was down there somewhere, sword in hand, stalking. She screamed and screamed, knowing it useless. Her voice was swallowed by the wind.

The wind surrounding the Flame Binder almost swept Padric off his feet. Grit and cinders stung the flesh of his face, his eyes flowing with hot, painful tears. The air buffeted him in terrible gusts, first one way, and then another. Each step was a fight for balance. He worked his way through, dimly aware that the fiery hearts were manifesting in the Forge Born all around him. They were near twice his height, and Padric tried not to imagine one of them springing to life next to him. The whirlwind of smoke grew thick and Torcan was nowhere to be seen, but Padric continued to head in what he hoped was the direction of the stables.

"Spread out!" he yelled back at his guards, waving his arm.

"Find the lord Swinehelm!"

The goblins looked at each other, wordlessly trying to decide whether to follow his orders or Torcan's.

They died before the decision was made.

The thing that attacked the goblins was fast, darting out of the smoke and striking down three of them before the others could respond. Padric saw a long blade strike and the guards' desperate attempts to interpose their own weapons. They were too slow.

Their killer was armored, feathers covering its body where steel did not. The last goblin fell in an attempt to flee and was finished off by the dagger-long spurs sprouting from the thing's feet. It looked at him then, eyes piercing. When it spoke, Padric heard laughter in its voice.

"I would have your name before I slay you, Goblin King."

Pocket coughed as the burning canvas poured choking smoke into the stables. The draft horses whinnied and bucked, spooked by the flames. Backbone stomped and complained. Pocket grabbed a bucket of rancid water and tossed it high, hoping to slow the flames.

"We have to get out of here!" he yelled, but Muckle and his friend were not listening. Both goblins had fallen to their knees, their eyes rolled back to sightless eggs, faces contorted with tormented concentration. Burning bits of canvas floated down into the straw around them and Pocket ran back to stomp them out.

The fiery whirlwind continued to rage outside, and through the flying dust and smoke, a figure approached; squat and thickly armored, bearing an axe.

"He's coming!" Pocket told the goblins, but they did not come out of their feverish trance. He looked around desperately for some way to stop the advancing warrior, and his eyes fell upon the horses. Pocket ran to the paddocks, throwing aside the crude logs the Red Caps used to contain the animals. The horses wasted no time, rearing as they turned, charging away from the fire above them. They bolted outside, the unnatural churning forces further spooking them as they ran, but they all darted away from the armored goblin, and he only paused a moment before continuing forward. He reached the entrance and pushed inside, his hideous helmet catching the light from the fire. A snarl echoed from the bronze boar's face.

"You two!" the voice rang dully. "Scheming blood traitors!"

He stomped towards Muckle, his axe raised. Pocket grabbed for the armored arm as it swung, trying to stop it, but only succeeded in turning the blow. The blade struck Muckle between his neck and shoulder, the iron hissing as it cleaved his flesh.

Muckle screamed in pain and his cry was echoed by the pale goblin next to him and in the air outside as the burning goblin added his voice to the anguish.

The Flame Binder's cry split through the howl of the wind, sharp and horrible. Rosheen heard another voice join the goblin's, this one a deep lowing of inhuman pain. She looked and saw it was coming from Coltrane. The Fire no longer linked him to the Flame Binder and his head flew back, no mouth giving release to that sound of perfect agony. He fell to his knees. Rosheen watched as the fiery hearts of the Forge Born all across the yard began to gutter out, and as each one was extinguished, its possessor lifted its head, adding its own cry to the suffering chorus. Soon every heart was gone and every iron head lifted skyward in a deafening song.

It was the death toll of the world.

She saw the Flame Binder falling, the twisting column of elements that held him aloft dwindling. The dust began to settle, even as the shrieks of the Forge Born grew. Rosheen looked into the yard and saw Bantam Flyn staggering forward, the end of her life heralded on the edge of his great blade.

Padric was on his knees, hands clutching his ears in a futile effort to block out the bone-rattling din. He could feel his skull being battered to dust by the noise leaping from the iron warriors surrounding him. Fighting to stay conscious he looked up and saw the bird creature struggling towards him, unbalanced by the noise but still on its feet. He heard the steel scrape across the stones as the thing dragged its sword upwards, taking a last step before bringing it down in a flashing, final arc.

Death was silent. The wail of the Forge Born ceased. Padric felt something lightly brushing his face, steady and rhythmic. He opened his eyes, not realizing they had clenched shut.

Wings.

Wings flapped in front of him, each one brushing a cheek.

Between them hung a dense auburn tangle choked with braids and bones.

"Rosheen?"

He slid out from under her and found the edge of the sword a hair's breadth from her nose, held firm by the thing that tried to kill him.

"Flyn," Rosheen said slowly, not taking her eyes from the blade. "Would you be so kind as to get that thing out of my face?"

The thing she had called Flyn blinked hard and closed its beak, pulling the sword back gently.

Rosheen straightened herself in the air, nonplussed, and turned on Padric.

"You," she said pointedly, "are in so much trouble."

He could only stand and stare.

She flew right at his face, pressing her lips into his cheek over and over.

"Piskie-kissed," she whispered in his ear. "In case you forgot." She turned on the sword-wielder. "And *not* a Goblin King!"

The thing, the coburn, Padric realized as his wits returned, laughed and directed a bow at him. "Bantam Flyn at your service."

Even when not trying to kill him, the coburn was intimidating.

Padric nodded back curtly, cleared his throat. "Padric the Black."

Rosheen laughed at him and sat on his shoulder.

There came a sudden, grating squeal from above them and Padric looked at the surrounding Forge Born. The thrown-back heads were jerking down, the slumped shoulders straightening in fits. Rust split and fell away from long-fused joints while metal fingers closed creakingly into massive fists. They twitched, moving in stops and starts, struggling against the torpor of centuries.

"They are awakening," Padric said. His mouth was dry.

A screech of perverse delight split the Cog Yard. Through the ranks of reviving metal, Padric could see the Flame Binder picking himself off the ground, face contorted with mad glee. The goblin raised his arms over his head, laughing maniacally, practically dancing in his triumph. He pranced and cavorted as the Forge Born nearest him took a first, crushing step forward. Then it raised the hulking iron sword in its hand and the Flame Binder stopped laughing. The goblin backed away only to find another metal giant behind him. His head shot to left and right, eyes full of confusion and fury as four of his children began to converge on him.

The Flame Binder raised his hands and Fire shot forth, the flames breaking harmlessly upon the iron bodies closing in around him. With a snarl the goblin gnashed his teeth, and conjured Fire flew from his trembling fingers once more, this time punching into the metal torso of the nearest Forge Born, before spewing from its back through a hole of warped metal. The life went out of the unnatural warrior and it fell heavily forward, but the others continued to draw near the panicked wizard. He threw arcs of tearing flame, ripping the heads and limbs from the monsters he had just given life. Padric watched with grim satisfaction as the goblin spun desperately, trying to cut them down before he was overcome. He may well have tried holding back the tide.

On his shoulder, Rosheen hissed. "They are going to kill him!"

Padric felt a surge of dark joy. "Good."

"No, Padric! You do not understand." He craned his head to look at her. "If he dies . . ."

The coburn warrior took a step forward.

"Flyn!" Rosheen stopped him. "There is nothing you can do."

Padric did not understand why they would want to save the wizard and he did not care. He was through with riddles. It was enough that they could not save him. Nothing could.

"Padric," Rosheen's voice was in his ear. "We need to move!"

But he only smiled and watched as the Flame Binder was eclipsed by a dozen Forge Born. A moment later he was raised back into view, caught in the powerful clutches of his children. The wizard screamed in feeble protest as he was held aloft, his flesh boiling where the iron gripped him at wrist and ankle. He choked out one final cry before the Forge Born ripped him effortlessly in two.

His blood flew from the rent flesh, thick and molten. It bathed the Forge Born beneath, glowing and alive with wisps of blue flame. The metal warriors stood dumbly as the burning blood ate through their bodies, digging mercilessly through them as it dripped toward the ground. There it coalesced, swelling as it consumed. The warriors caught in its churning mass melted with the speed of wax, feeding the raw, infernal essence. White-hot, angry torrents leapt, sending blazing droplets into the air as the bubbling pool began to spin, slowly at first, but quickly gaining speed, sinking as it whirled its way downward, eating the flagstones, devouring rock and soil.

"The Fire," Rosheen breathed. "It is free."

The three of them were forced to back away from the heat and the ever-spreading edge of the pit. They watched as the element burned its way down to the unfathomable depths of the world, leaving a yawning, smoking fissure in the center of the Cog Yard as evidence of its passing.

"It's over," Padric said, staring into the chasm.

"No," he heard Flyn reply, "I do not believe it is."

Padric turned and found the coburn slowly pivoting, sword at the ready. All around them the remaining Forge Born were coming alive, brandishing their weapons.

Flyn gave a cry of warning and he dashed forward, slamming into Padric and knocking him off his feet. A massive, pitted blade smacked into the stones where he had just stood, sending sparks flying. Rosheen had taken to the air and Padric rolled to his feet. The Forge Born turned its head and looked at them, pulling its sword away from the split stones and raising it for another strike. Bantam Flyn leapt to his feet, swinging his blade in a sweeping upward cut. The hand fell from the Forge Born, dropping to the stones with a clangor, the ancient sword still clutched within its metal grip.

Another awoke next to them, immediately swinging its blade savagely at the coburn. He ducked, and the Forge Born's weapon slammed into the first, knocking it to the ground with ear-splitting force. Flyn slashed at the standing Forge Born's leg, his blow failing to cut through. It sent Flyn sprawling with a heavy kick, and Padric rushed to his side, helping him stand.

"They are all Unwound!" Rosheen shouted, her face a dawning realization of horror.

"You have doomed us all," Muckle told Torcan weakly from the ground.

"Your doom was sealed the day you betrayed His Grace, Jester!" Torcan's voice dripped with disdain.

Pocket jumped in front of his fallen friend.

"Stay away from him!"

His vision burst with light and pain as the armored goblin backhanded him across the face, spilling him into the straw. He rolled over, head swimming, and saw the bronze tusks of the boar staring down at him, raising the axe over its head. Pocket threw his arms up, knowing it would not save him.

A figure dropped heavily through the burning hole in the roof. There was the sharp snap of shearing metal, and the swine-faced helm landed in the straw next to Pocket. The bronze armor stood unsteadily for a moment, looking odd without a head, then fell over.

Sir Corc stood to his full height, sword in hand.

"Are you all right?" the knight asked.

Pocket nodded, picking himself up.

Sir Corc looked at him for a moment, then seemed satisfied.

"See to Curdle."

Pocket came around to find the pale goblin conscious but very weak. He smiled thinly as Pocket helped him to his feet and remained by his side, supporting him. Sir Corc sheathed his sword and lifted Muckle onto the litter.

"I am far too near the nether regions of this ass for comfort," the goblin pronounced in a quivering voice.

Sir Corc motioned for Pocket to bring the other goblin over and they lowered him down next to Muckle.

"Pocket," Muckle said. "I wonder if you would be so kind as to dump Torcan's head out of that helmet and bring it here."

Pocket wrinkled his face. "Bring the head or the helmet?" he asked, not really wanting to do either.

"Well, I'm too weak to juggle, so just the helmet," Muckle clarified. "Make a nice chamber pot."

"No time," Sir Corc said, looking out into the yard and pulling his shield from his back. "Pocket, lead Backbone and stay close."

The knight pulled the heavy mace from his belt and ducked out of the stables. Pocket clicked at Backbone and they followed him into the chaos.

A crazed Forge Born leapt at them and Sir Corc charged forward to meet it, turning its first vicious slash aside with his shield then hammering twice into the side of its knee with his mace.

The joint buckled and the Forge Born fell. Sir Corc stove in its head with a swift stroke. Another of the metal monsters barreled towards the knight, its huge blade coming down to split him in two.

Sir Corc rolled away, and the falling sword sundered the stones. It recovered quickly, slashing as it turned, but the knight ducked under the stroke, coming up inside its reach to slam his shield into its body, his mace striking downward to knock the sword from its grip. The Forge Born toppled backwards, and Sir Corc wasted no time smashing in its face.

Pocket marveled at how fast he moved. The Forge Born were broader and taller, their crushing blows capable of breaking stone and crushing metal, but Sir Corc did not try to overcome their strength. He avoided it, or turned it aside, using it to throw the berserk iron off balance. His mace fell on the exposed joints, crippling their movements before landing a killing blow to the head.

Four now had come, and four lay in heaps of bent metal.

It would not be enough.

All across the yard the Forge Born were awakening, searching for prey.

"There!" Rosheen pointed to the mule.

Bantam Flyn rushed forward, clapping Pocket heartily on the shoulder. His smile fell when he looked into the litter.

Rosheen breathed a curse. She did not know how Muckle was still breathing. Sir Corc nodded to her, giving Padric only the most cursory of glances.

Never one for questions.

Besides, their deaths were not far off.

The Unwound were coming from all sides.

Some still stood dormant, and they were the greatest threat.

One sprang to life next to them, its fist slamming forward. Sir Corc barely raised his shield in time and the wood splintered under the force of the blow, sending the knight stumbling backwards. He threw the ruined shield at the charging killer, sending it shattering against the iron body. Sir Corc tried to leap back as it swung, but the blade caught him in the side and he grunted hard. Rosheen saw a great dent in his breastplate. The knight sprang back into the fight, pounding at his opponent, the mace a blur. Bantam Flyn came to his aid and soon the Unwound fell.

Sir Corc staggered away, clutching his side, his breathing labored. Rosheen saw blood dripping from underneath his armor, running down his mail skirt in dark rivulets. But there was no time for wounds. Another Unwound was upon them. The coburn met its ferocious charge, Flyn parrying its swinging sword while Sir Corc struck it with his mace. The Unwound ignored the blow, swatting the knight aside and swinging wildly at Flyn. The squire was swift and managed to turn the attacks, but the furious onslaught pushed him back.

A shadow fell over Rosheen and she looked up to see another of the metal beasts looming over her.

There was nowhere to go.

Padric scooped her into his arms, cradling her into his body as the massive iron blade came down. Rosheen's ears burst with the sound of ringing metal and she heard Padric cry out. She looked up to see the Unwound's wrist caught and held firm by another metal hand.

Coltrane.

He grappled the Unwound and threw it, sending it crashing into the one attacking Flyn. Half a dozen more were coming and Coltrane stepped forward to meet them.

"Brothers," he said, "control yourselves."

The Unwound charged.

"Very well."

He rushed into their midst, unarmed, catching the first sword stroke and sending his fist through the attacker's head. Metal screeched as he pulled his hand free, flinging the limp body aside.

He sidestepped another slash, clasped his hands together and brought them down, hammering the Unwound into the ground.

They surrounded him, their blades whirling, but Coltrane was indomitable. Rosheen could feel the concussion of his fists in her chest as he beat his opponents back. Iron struck iron, again and again with reverberating force. The Unwound were fierce, wild, thoughtless, their swords striking each other. Coltrane laid punishing blows with fist, shoulder and elbow, ripping heads and limbs off with calculated prowess. The six he fought were soon destroyed and others came. A dozen at least. Coltrane fought them all. Rosheen saw Flyn helping Sir Corc to his feet. She detached herself from Padric's protective embrace.

"We have to get out of here!" she screamed over the clamor of combat.

"Head for the gate!" Flyn shouted.

"The goblins hold it," Sir Corc wheezed.

"Not anymore," Flyn pointed.

The Red Caps came fleeing back into the yard, trying to escape the swinging swords of the horsemen who pursued them. It was a rout, and men and goblins poured into the inner bailey, but the victory cries of the horsemen died in their throats as the Unwound set upon them. The Red Caps rallied themselves, ready to stand beside the Forge Born and slaughter their enemies, but the cheers turned to screams of panic as the living iron tore into them with equal bloodlust.

"We will never make it through that," Rosheen said.

Coltrane approached, victorious. "I will lead you."

"Then what are we waiting for?" Bantam Flyn asked.

"You go," Padric told them. "I must go back to the keep."

Rosheen whirled on him. "What? Are you mad?"

"Rosh, I have to. Svala and Kederic are there. I cannot leave them."

"Then I am going with you."

Padric shook his head. "Go with them. I will follow."

"Stubborn boy! I am going with you—"

"Wait," Sir Corc cut in.

Rosheen ignored him. "If you think I am going to let you run off again—"

"WAIT!"

The knight's growl silenced her. They all turned to Sir Corc.

"Where is Pocket?" he asked, his wound forgotten.

Rosheen looked around. She was startled to find Muckle on his feet. He looked ghastly, leaning on Curdle for support.

"We tried to stop him," the pale goblin's voice was full of sorrow.

Backbone stood patiently by, his guide rope dragging the ground.

It called to him. It called to him and he came. The voice was sweet, coaxing and Pocket trusted it. The girl whispered to him, promising all he had been denied. He deserved his prize. It was time he claimed what was his by rights.

He walked through the yard. Past the Forge Born who still slept, past those that thirsted for the blood of history. They did not harm him. Her voice led him, and he came to the steps of the keep, climbing them slowly.

The husk waited at the top, holding the crown. Pocket stood before him and looked up into the sack face beneath the wide brim of the rumpled hat. The husk spoke, but the voice was that of the girl. And she laughed.

"A half breed! The irony is rare and sweet after nine hundred years. Your ancestors broke the most sacred oaths, sacrificed the most precious gifts in life, all to try and gain dominance over immortals. Now here you stand, the blood of Fae and sorcerer mixed inside of you."

Pocket heard cries behind him. Familiar voices calling his name. He turned and saw them running, fear on every face. But they were more than faces. He could see all of them now.

The piskie was made of sprouting seeds, drops of dew, gentle puffs of air and brief, tiny sparks; all the hopeful promises of the Elements. The tall, metal man had a heart that still burned and the flames flowed upwards into the iron cavern of his head, a gift given and one not taken away. In the coburn, he saw chained aggression, the links newly forged in the younger, and, in the older, they snapped before his eyes. Such raw emotions, held back with pride and vows. Mirth danced in the dying goblin; the joy of laughter, the pain of ridicule. In the other he saw the crushing burden of truth, made all the more heavy by the kindness that floated deep within the vast pool of knowledge. The black-haired man carried a withering belief, a fraying thread between mortals and Faekind. They reached the steps, this group of frail beings. The husk raised the crown above his head, and the girl laughed again.

By the Hallowed! What is wrong with him?

"Pocket!"

She screamed his name as she flew towards the steps of the keep. Her voice was a feeble thing and the boy did not heed it. He stared down at her, the life gone from his face. Next to her, Padric also screamed as he ran, but his entreaties were cast at the husk.

The gangly arms held a simple, terrible crown above its head, the featureless face an icon of contempt.

"Fight her!" Padric yelled. "Slouch Hat, damn you, fight her!"

Rosheen could hear the burden in his ragged shouts, rage and impotent guilt. *He knew there was a danger here.*

There came the tickling of a girl's laughter in the air, cruel and tainted with madness. It issued from the husk's mouth, ringing off the stones of the ancient keep, but Rosheen did not slow her pace. And neither did the others. Even Muckle, bleeding and wan, leaning his bulk on Curdle for support, did not falter.

Coltrane was the first to reach the steps, his iron foot shattering the stonework as he surged upward. The phantom girl found this most amusing and her giggling accompanied the squeal of swiftly bending metal. Coltrane stumbled, catching himself on his powerful hands midway up the stairs. He tried to rise, but his knee joint was twisted and useless. Rosheen heard the sound of a hammer on metal and saw Coltrane racked with spasms as huge dents punched into his body, the violent work of some great, unseen hand. The Forge Born strained against an invisible pressure, his arms shaking as they fought to keep the force at bay. Rosheen winced when the metal warrior's limbs collapsed and his torso buckled, the iron folding as if cloth. The body tumbled down the stairs, clattering, bent and lifeless. She did stop then and Padric halted next to her, staring wide-eyed at what had been, moments before, an unstoppable being of living iron.

But the coburn did not break stride. Bantam Flyn leapt over Coltrane's ruined remains, taking the steps two at a time. Sir Corc, injured and snarling, was only a stride behind.

"Witch!" the knight cursed. "Release him!"

"Such bravery," the girl mocked him. "Such nobility! From little more than an up-jumped animal!"

There was a clangor as Flyn's sword hit the stairs. He spun on Sir Corc, his feathers bristling, head bent and craning forward.

A hiss escaped from behind his dripping tongue. Sir Corc had no words to reach the squire, for he too dropped his weapons, descending into brutishness. The coburn circled each other, their movements feral, their faces ugly and reptilian. Flyn pounced first, driving his long spurs into Corc's body, beating at him with fists and head. They rolled down the stairs in vicious, mindless violence, stabbing with their beaks, leaving a trail of crimson on the stones.

Rosheen felt more Magic flood the air as the hobgoblins reached out to the coburn, trying to release them from their barbarity.

"You think to deny me with your hedge-craft?" the girl demanded.

Curdle and Muckle screamed as one, the pale seer grabbing at his skull while the Jester's wound began spewing smoke and pumping black fluid.

The husk raised the iron circlet higher.

"Hear the voices of the thousands whose lives were claimed by the crown of your former king, Curdle Milkthumb!"

The mystic dropped to his knees, gibbering as blood pumped from his nose, ears and mouth. Muckle had already fallen, the poison in his blood quickened by the crown's sorcery. He was perfectly still. At the base of the stairs, the thing that had once been Sir Corc rose from the broken form of Bantam Flyn, pulling a foot of dripping spur from the squire's throat. The triumphant coburn issued a savage cry of dominance to the sky and then sank down atop his slain foe, his life leaving him from a hundred flowing wounds.

Rosheen turned away from all the death and found herself looking into Padric's eyes. Ages ago, she had known a life devoid of hardship, bereft of sorrow. Each day was a dance and a song and she, like all her kind, was content to laugh as they feasted. Even after the wars, she found it easy to put the bloodshed behind her, and for centuries she gave not a passing thought to the hatred of those days. And then this boy had been born, grown to a man in a moment, and with no power or Magic, he had enthralled her. Now, she would rather struggle on with him, in toil and misery until the last day of his short life than live herself, immortal and carefree, through the final Age of the world. She knew that now, just as she knew the life of the changeling boy threatened every life on the isle.

But there was no evil in Pocket. And she could not give him up to this murderous spirit.

She wished there was another choice.

Padric met her gaze and nodded, crushing her with the choice he had already made.

"I will save him, Rosh."

He charged up the stairs, over the blood and bodies of their fallen comrades, through the maniacal laughter of the possessed scarecrow. Rosheen flew after him, making for the crown. The iron would destroy her, but she did not care. She would give her beloved boys every chance.

The husk turned as she sped towards him.

A horrible constriction suddenly seized her wings and she fell roughly to the stairs. Straining back she found she was wrapped in spiders' silk. The strands snapped and slithered over her body, winding themselves around her wrists, pinning her arms behind her.

Padric continued to barrel forward and was only a few steps away from the entranced form of Pocket when he lurched, stopping short and grunting with pain. He snapped his hand to his leg and blood welled between his fingers.

"We freed you," he growled at the air, taking a limping step upwards. "This is how you would thank us?"

"Boy," the girl's voice was biting, "there is only one way to be free of my prison!"

Rosheen struggled uselessly against her bonds and let out a wordless protest as Padric once again stumbled with pain, his shirt and skin splitting from another incorporeal blade. He bled freely, but he continued to climb.

"Then Jerrod masters you still," Padric proclaimed. "You remain his puppet."

Slouch Hat's jaw gaped wide as the girl screamed with fury.

Padric's cry of agony overpowered her rage as his skin erupted with dozens of red cuts. He fell to his knees, his clothes sodden with his own blood, but still he reached for Pocket.

"I pitied you," Padric said with a quivering voice, but Rosheen could see the set of his jaw and knew his grin remained steady, defiant. "But now I see your place will forever be his servant. His plaything."

The girl did not answer. She had ceased laughing. There was silence.

Padric took Pocket's hand in his own.

Rosheen recoiled as something sprayed heavily across her face, forcing her eyes shut. The liquid was hot and she tasted copper as it dripped into her mouth. She shook her head roughly, clearing her vision. Her mouth dropped open at what she saw, but no sound came forth. Padric clutched desperately at his ruptured throat, his fingers grasping feebly at the thick life's blood pumping between them. He fell forward, choking, and his head came to rest on the stair where Rosheen lay bound by webs and frozen by horror. They looked at each other and her world shrunk to his face, struggling in an ever-deepening pool of red. The apology stayed in his eyes even after the life fled them.

The blood spread across the stair towards her. She let it come, waiting for her own death. But the grief would not kill her.

No matter how much she wished it.

He watched them all die. All except the piskie, who now lay trapped and forgotten. He had known her. Her, and the rest. But they were nothing. They were not his purpose. He turned back towards the husk and once again it spoke with the voice of a girl.

"Kneel."

He did as she commanded.

"How fitting that I may have my freedom as I take my vengeance. Receive your birthright, seed of Jerrod. Receive it and die!"

The husk lowered the crown on his head.

Excruciating pain lanced hotly through his skull. He felt his brain begin to boil. The girl shrieked with the rapture of liberation and was gone, her voice fleeing his head and replaced with perfect agony.

Pocket reached up and tried to remove the crown, finding it fused to his sizzling flesh. His fingers blistered as they touched the iron, desperate to pry it free, teeth clenched so tightly he felt them cracking. Visions assailed him. Dead kings and their atrocities; the line from which he was descended. Blood and Fire. Rapine and slavery. Degradation and death.

Blood and bile rose in his throat, and he retched, spilling his guts on the stones as the crown poisoned him. He looked and saw his friends lying on the steps, dead and dying, tormented by madness. They had come to save him! He who was the product of a deceitful union. The issue of tyrants. A changeling! A gurg! An unwanted curse on the mortal world and with no place in the realm of the Fae.

Weak, thin fingers grabbed at him.

"I am sorry," an odd, reedy voice said. "I am sorry."

He caught a glimpse of the husk through seeping eyes and felt the fingers move to his head, prying at the crown. Pocket jerked away, causing a bolt of fell energy to slam into the husk. It flew away and crashed into the door of the keep. Pocket had not wanted to harm him, but he could not allow the crown to be removed. Through the pain there was power and while his Fae blood burned, his mortal blood fused with the legacy of lost domination. His will would be absolute, even as his body fell to ruin.

He could feel them dying. His friends. The men in the yard and the goblins too. The Unwound crushing them into pulp. It was not what he wanted. It must stop!

And at his command the Forge Born slept. He led them back to the oblivion of mindlessness. No will, no bloodlust.

Nothing. And they obeyed.

The crown fought his desires, screaming voices chastised him, and he felt the hot flow of blood spilling out his ears. He screamed, silencing the voices, forcing them to listen.

He mended Flyn's body, his first true friend. The squire's chest rose and fell, his breath restored. Pocket then returned the life of the one who had given him his; the knight that he worshiped and loved. He chased the voices from Curdle's mind, restoring his peace and purged the venom from Muckle's veins. Next, he repaired the form of the last true Forge Born, recognizing the necessity of his existence. He closed the throat of the man he did not know, for Rosheen loved him, and she had given Pocket so much.

They were his friends.

They had smiled with him, laughed with him, shared meals and stories. It was more than he ever thought he would have, and if he must give his own life to save theirs, he would give it.

He would give it gladly.

Padric sucked in air. He coughed and sputtered. The memory of choking on his own blood, unable to breathe, the feeling of his severed windpipe in his fingers, both still hung in his mind. He tried to rise, but his legs were quivering and useless. He looked over and saw Rosheen flying in weak sputters up the stairs, her eyes wide and staring.

"Pocket?" her voice broke.

Padric crawled up and saw Slouch Hat lying slack and motionless. Next to him was the small, crumpled form of the boy.

The older coburn limped up the stairs, his eyes lost, searching for any other sight. He fell to his knees next to the boy and gathered him up in his arms, rocking back and forth. With a shaking hand he removed the iron crown from the small, scorched head and dropped it to the stones, brushing at the boy's hair and looking into his still face. They all came up and surrounded the fallen child. The child who had saved them all. The knight clutched the limp body to his chest and threw his head back, shattering their hearts with his lament.

TWENTY-SIX

Deglan washed his hands in the bronze basin, drying them on a well-used cloth as he stepped out of the field tent. The morning was wet and grey, the air refreshing after the close smells of wounded men. Barely thirty of Orvin's warriors had survived Castle Gaunt, and most of those were men lucky enough to take their wounds on the bridge battling the Red Caps. Of the riders who entered the castle, only two still lived, and Deglan could not say what injuries their minds had sustained.

The cairns for those who fell on the bridge were just outside the camp, raised with stones brought from the fields. The poor fools who died in the castle yard would molder where they lay.

No one was willing to reenter that cursed place to retrieve them.

Deglan rubbed wearily at his eyes, grateful he had saved the ones he could. He ambled through the camp. There were more horses and grooms now than fighting men. A yawn snuck out, and Deglan considered doing the sensible thing and resting for a while, but ended up walking out of camp towards the castle bridge. He found Coltrane standing sentry as he knew he would. The Forge Born had not moved from the base of the bridge since emerging from the castle the day before. This morning, Curdle stood with him. "You are very tired," the mystic said as he approached.

"Keen observation," Deglan grumbled back.

Curdle's wrinkled face tried to smile.

It was Deglan's turn to be observant. "You are leaving."

"As soon as Muckle joins me, yes."

"What will you do?"

"Go back to Toad Holm," Curdle replied. "Search out the corruption and put an end to it, if we can."

"We?" Deglan rolled his eyes. "That fat bastard going to be much use?"

This time the smile held. "In the Wisemoot, no. But in other tasks, our Jester is unequivocal."

Deglan raised his eyebrows in dubious acceptance.

"And you?" Curdle asked.

"You already know."

The seer said nothing for a long while.

"The coburn need me to . . . preserve the body," Deglan finally said. "They wish to see the boy cremated at their stronghold, in their fashion. And it has been a long while since I've been to Albain."

"I think the child is in the best hands," Curdle told him.

"And what is this thing going to do?" Deglan said, changing the subject and pointing at Coltrane.

"Wait," Coltrane's deep voice answered. "And watch. Ensure that no more of my brothers awake."

"And once you are sure?" Deglan pressed.

Coltrane continued to face the castle. "I will find another purpose."

Deglan turned back to Curdle and regarded him for a long time. The hobgoblin looked back comfortably.

"Do not give up on them," Deglan said at last. "Not like I did. Our people are not beyond hope."

"Our people?"

"Stay out of my head!"

"Pardon me," Curdle said. "It slipped out."

Deglan stuck out his hand. Curdle took it, and they nodded their farewells.

Padric had not slept. Torcan was dead. Rosheen was alive.

And he was finally free. None of it brought his mind peace. He had passed the night in solitude, pacing the edge of the camp, trying not to look at the castle. It stood empty and condemning, and he fought the insane urge to return to it, to be swallowed by its walls.

He wanted to walk within without fear, see the failure of the goblins and somehow convince himself that the place and the events he survived no longer ruled him. Grimly, he imagined Slouch Hat's lifeless shell still lying below the keep, nothing now but tattered clothes and straw to be slowly separated by rats and wind. He wanted to see that and not be afraid.

He had gone back for Svala. And Kederic. Led them out of their mutual prison, but Padric still felt confined, trapped by the things he knew and the lie he had used to survive.

Dawn was slow in coming, but when the first servant stirred in the camp, Padric went searching. He found Kederic Winetongue at the camp paddock, watching the horses with eyes that, like his, had not closed during the night. Padric stood next to him, looking at him, waiting. The man did not acknowledge him.

"Beladore," Padric said through clenched teeth. "Your wife, Kederic, where is she?"

He saw the man swallow hard, the hatred in his eyes wet and brimming.

"It wore my face," Kederic choked out. "The . . . thing that lay with her. She said she never knew. How could . . . how could she have not? The creature that came out of her," he gave a snarl of bitter disgust, "it was unnatural, covered in fur. Hideous."

The man finally turned and looked at him, and Padric saw the pain of the memory flood his mouth as he spoke. "It changed. The skin would split, grow scales and then . . . turn back into the son that should have been mine. I wanted it dead, but Bel . . . but *she* ran. She knew I would follow. I caught her. Caught her giving the changeling monster to that coburn. I fought him and should have died, but she begged for my life and begged him to take her child. She called it *her* child. And he took it away, leaving us alone."

"And you killed her," Padric accused.

Kederic shook his head. "Worse. I exiled her. Put her on a boat. To the Isle of Mad Women."

Padric wanted to strike the man. He saw in Kederic's face no regret for what he had done, only a festering remorse for the life he felt was stolen from him. But Padric knew he could not judge him. His own village had sentenced women to that same isle, and more than once he had voiced his approval of such acts. In truth, he was fortunate his own mother had not been sent there. The enmity of the village was directed at him, and, for the first time, he was grateful for it.

"Did you know?" he asked Kederic. "Who she was, did you know?"

Anger flashed in Kederic's eyes, clearing them. "What? A witch, a sorceress! How could I?"

Padric leveled a harsh stare at him. "How could you have not?" he asked, throwing the words back.

Kederic returned his gaze, quivering with fury.

"You are still taken in by them!" He pointed up at Castle Gaunt. "Even as they try to destroy us! Had I known what she was I would have slain her, for the good of us all. Do you not see? They used her, these immortals. Through her they created that boy! The power of the warlocks *and* the Fae! He was the most dangerous thing alive in this world. And the most evil!"

The seax was suddenly in Padric's hand, and he had hold of Kederic, pressing him roughly against the paddock beam, the blade at his throat.

"And if I feel the same of you?" Padric demanded, his breath mixing with that of the struggling Thegn. "Should I deal with you now, for the good of us all? Ask yourself this question, Winetongue. Did Beladore know? Did your wife know what she was? That boy didn't!"

He released his hold, pulling the knife away.

"I am not a warrior," he said. "I am not a Thegn or a sorcerer or a king. But I know something about your wife and her son. I share something with them. None of us should be blamed for our birth."

His words spoken, he turned and walked away.

Bantam Flyn was tying the last of the loads to the mule's back.

A page's work. And he does it with honor.

"You are soon away?" Rosheen asked as she approached.

The squire looked at her and nodded as he continued with the ropes.

"You will enjoy the gnome's company," she told him. "He is easy to rile."

"Sounds like merry sport," Flyn replied, his tone not matching his words.

I only remind him.

"Well," she said. "I will leave you to it."

She turned to fly away.

"My lady," Flyn's words stopped her, and she looked back.

The squire bowed low. "It was my privilege."

She gave him a wink.

Sir Corc knelt inside the tent, holding his naked sword in front of him.

Keeping the vigil.

Rosheen slipped past the closed flap and into the dark space. The body lay covered, wrapped in crimson and silver, the colors of the Valiant Spur. She waited patiently. Sir Corc stood at last and turned to face her.

"Did you know?" she asked bluntly.

The knight did not hesitate. "No."

Rosheen let out her breath. She had not known she was holding it.

"All his life, I fought to keep him free of the gruagach," Sir Corc said. "And eventually they succeeded in penetrating even the Roost. It was no longer safe, so I thought it was best if he stayed close to me. Having the most skilled fighter among the squires accompany us only increased his protection. Festus Lambkiller wanted him, of that I was certain. And now I know why.

"His mother," the knight said sadly, "was just a woman that needed my help. She asked me to save her babe."

He struggled and looked to say more, but remained silent.

Now for the gamble.

"Might I have a moment alone with him?" she asked.

"Certainly," Sir Corc replied stoutly. "I will help Flyn with the last of the preparations."

He bowed and stepped outside.

Rosheen flew to the top of the tent where the shadows were darkest. She did not have to wait long. The flap opened and the blond head poked inside, carefully looking before stepping inside. Rosheen did not let her take two steps towards the body.

"I thought you might come."

Svala looked shocked, her big blue eyes wide and demure.

All harmless innocence.

The girl held up her hands apologetically, speaking quickly and softly in her foreign tongue. She began to back towards the flap.

"You are good," Rosheen told her. "I do not know how I missed it in Hog's Wallow." She looked at her sharply. "Jileen."

Svala's meek expression fell and slowly turned into a knowing smile. The straight flaxen locks thickened into dark waves, the long legs giving way to the full hips of the alewife.

"Sharp-eyed piskie," Jileen complemented her, still smiling.

"You killed Brogan."

The gruagach's now sultry eyes rolled casually. "He discovered Kederic's secret. And troublingly, told it to Swinehelm before I was aware. His death was sloppy and a bit too late."

"You were keeping the heir from the goblins."

"The boy, yes," Jileen said, enjoying her role. "The mother we care nothing for, but if they found her then she might reveal to whom she entrusted her son. Kederic needed to die before he told where he had dumped her, but the husk and your mortal pet failed."

Rosheen bristled. "You used Padric." It was not a question.

"The husk did," Jileen admitted. "And I was using the husk. Neither of them realized it, of course. Once they were captured, I needed a way to get close so . . ."

Svala was once again standing in the tent.

"He cares for her." Rosheen let the venom flow into her voice.

"And why should he not?" Svala asked. "The dear girl was every bit the sweet, beautiful creature in life. I merely took her place."

"But you failed," Rosheen said. "Kederic lives. And any words he might speak are useless. Pocket is dead."

Something settled on Svala's face.

Fear. And not an act.

"I wanted to see for myself," Svala said gravely. "My lord will be displeased. If I return to him with this news, I will die. But I have no intention of returning."

"Stay here and you suffer the same end," Rosheen promised. "The knight is just outside."

"You won't summon him," Svala said, "for two reasons."

"Don't tempt me, skinchanger."

"First," Svala went on, "if you slay me, Padric will know the truth and you would spare him that pain. Svala kept him alive, and knowing that the woman he swore to save was already dead . . ."

"Damn you."

"Second," the gruagach paused. "You know the truth."

"And that is?"

Svala's face showed true sorrow. "If the boy had been with us . . . he would still be alive."

Rosheen looked down at the small, covered form lying on the ground. Seeing she had no response, Svala turned to go.

"Your life has a price," Rosheen called her back. Svala turned, waited. "Answer me this question, and if you lie, I will know." She took a breath. "Are you carrying a child?"

Svala's gaze did not falter, her lips remained steady. "No."

Rosheen remained in the tent a long while after she was gone.

When she emerged she found the coburn making their final preparations. She passed without a word, catching Sir Corc's eye as she went. The knight gave her the slightest nod.

Padric was saddling a horse on the edge of camp, the saddlebags resting in the grass, bulging with provisions.

"Kederic gifted you with a mount?" she asked, flying over to stroke the animal.

Padric cinched the girth strap tight.

He has learned so much.

"No," he said earnestly. "I just took it. Plenty of them to spare."

She laughed. "So, now you're a horse thief?"

"Been a good deal worse," he grunted.

"Svala not coming?" she asked innocently.

Padric shot a glance at her then went back to the horse.

"She is going home. Back to Middangeard. At least that's the word I understood."

"I see."

"For the best," he said. "I was never going to be anything but the man she was given to as a slave."

He straightened and let out a deep breath.

He is relieved.

"So what about us?" she asked, giving the horse an appraising look. "Home, too?"

Padric thought about it, nodding more deeply as he did.

"For a time."

She smiled, wondering what that would be like and looking forward to finding out. Padric reached down and hefted the saddlebags up onto the horse's back, securing them deftly.

Rosheen heard whistling and looked to see Muckle walking by, the ribbons of his huge club caught on the wind. The goblin saw them, and with an enthusiastic wave, came over to greet them.

"The road beckons?" he asked cheerfully.

If it leads away from you.

"Yes," Rosheen said simply.

"Very good, very good," Muckle said, grinning broadly. He turned to Padric, whose back was turned, extending his task as long as possible. "And you, sire?" Muckle asked. "Will the life of a lowly vagabond, of which I am very personally fond, not seem dim after the trappings of royalty?"

Padric turned slowly, giving the Jester his darkest glower.

Muckle shrugged. "Perhaps not." He turned to go then snapped his fingers in a show of discovered remembrance and turned back. "Just remember, lad," he said pointing. "It is not what you are, it is what you would have been if it had not been for what you were."

Padric tried to puzzle that out for a moment, then turned to Rosheen for help.

She threw up her hands.

Muckle gave them a satisfied grunt and a final stab of his finger, daring them to forget his words before turning away.

"It is not foolishness," they could hear him telling his fish as he crossed the fields. "Those are wise words. I should know. I am a member of the Wisemoot. I was *not* ousted! How dare you! Broke wind? Me? Never! I will have you know . . ."

Rosheen found Padric staring at the grass.

There's the brood I was waiting on.

"Shall we go?" she asked.

His eyes found her. "Why do you stay with me, Rosheen?"

She wrinkled her face at him. "What kind of question is that?"

"I never thought to ask," he said pensively. "Why are you with me? Who am I?"

"You," she said slowly, "are the same as you were before we left. A stubborn, brooding, mildly handsome youth . . . with the worst luck in the known world."

She beamed at him.

He grinned in spite of himself, shaking his head ruefully as he swung himself into the saddle. Rosheen took her place on his shoulder.

"That still does not answer," he said, cocking his eyes at her, "why you are with me?"

Rosheen thought about it a moment, making him wait.

"You were a cute babe," she said simply. "And *bald*. The black head did not come until later, so do not place that at my feet. And," she added, cutting him off when she saw his mouth open, "do not ask me why they think you are cursed. I have never understood the fears you mortals place upon yourselves. Nonsense!"

Padric closed his mouth and urged the horse forward, his frown increasing over the first mile.

They were traveling an hour before his mood finally broke.

She saw the crease between his eyes relax and the clouds pass from his countenance. The corner of his mouth turned up just a little.

"What are you thinking on?" she asked, giggling at him.

"Cider," he said lightly.

She gave a coo of delight. "That sounds lovely."

"It will be in season," he said. "Always is in Airlann. That is the one thing about this isle and Autumn. It never changes. The sun rises, it sets and it is always the same."

Rosheen smiled, humoring him. He was wrong, of course.

She looked up at the sun, just now beginning to shine through the grey clouds. No, it was not the same.

There is a change in the light.

EPILOGUE

There was pain. Floating and dull, rising with the light. Not light, at least not seen. But the absence of dark. There was something else too. Half smells, half sounds. Salt. A knocking. All of it hurt. There was warmth. All around, but heavier in places. It moved, soft pressures approaching. A soft fluttering sound, tickling, pleasant. A nudge. Then another, firmer, insistent. The light grew away from black. Blurred orange. Spots of black, no green.

Something pink, sniffing. Whiskers.

Napper?

The nose touched him and it was cold. It searched him and the paw came up, almost hesitant, and touched his face, making sure he was real.

He reached up, his arm feeling heavy, his fingers numb, and felt soft fur, the gentle rhythm of purring. His fingers came awake as he scratched the cat and his vision cleared. He was really there.

"Napper!"

Pocket sat up in the bed, ignoring the pain that dropped into his skull and hugged the cat to him, getting a small yowl of complaint, but refusing to let go. He kissed the furry head, again and again, looking around him as he did.

It was a cottage. Stone walls and a large hearth, sunlight and blue sky showing through the windows. A large figure moved in front of the fire, tending to a pot.

She turned, her face glancing at him out of habit and then away before realization struck.

"Child," Moragh said softly with a breath of relief. "You are awake."

Half of her face lit up, and even the drooping side seemed to smile.

She hurried over and lowered herself down on the bedside, her weight causing him to slide towards her. He felt her hands on his face, inspecting him lovingly with her thumbs.

"You gave us such a fright," she said, her voice breaking, and he pulled himself into her.

She released him reluctantly, a set task pulling her away.

"Master Loamtoes," she said, rising from the bed.

Pocket looked past her and saw a gnome, slumped in a chair, fast asleep.

"Master Loamtoes," Moragh repeated again, hovering over the chair. "He's awake."

The gnome's eyes opened and he looked at Moragh for a moment, frowning, then her words registered and he jumped to his feet. He came over and looked Pocket over, gave a grunt of approval and something near to a smile almost made it across his cheeks.

"Broth," he told Moragh a little gruffly. "And water."

Moragh continued to smile despite the gnome's manner and returned to the hearth. The gnome gave Pocket's eyes a final inspection, then withdrew. Pocket heard the door to the cottage open, the sound of gulls slipping through before it closed again. He felt suddenly tired and scooped Napper, displaced after Moragh's embrace, back into his lap before falling back onto the pillows.

His eyes closed and he slipped back into black throbs of pain. When he opened his eyes again he found Sir Corc looking down at him.

"You're alive," Pocket said, his voice weaker than he expected.

"Yes," the knight said. "I have you to thank for that."

"And . . . the others?" it was becoming difficult to speak.

"Can you not hear it?" Sir Corc asked gently.

Pocket listened, and somewhere outside he made out the distinct sound of wood striking something over and over.

Pocket smiled. "Flyn."

"Damn racket!" the gnome complained, coming to the bedside and handing Pocket a bowl of steaming liquid. "Drink this down. All of it, now!"

Pocket did as he was told.

His eyes were feeling heavy by the time the bowl was half empty, and the pain was lessening.

"I thought I was dead," he said.

"So did we," Sir Corc replied, laying his hand gently on Pocket's shoulder. "And many still do. It is better that way. Sleep now. Rest."

Pocket did not think he could do anything else. His lids dropped, but he fought them open one last time.

"Are you going to be here when I wake up?" he asked, his own voice sounding distant.

He felt Sir Corc squeeze his shoulder and heard him say, "I swear it."

ACKNOWLEDGMENTS

Books are akin to blades. They take a great deal of heat, pressure and time to produce. And once forged, require more exhaustive labor to hone before they are ready to wield. That may be a trite analogy for a fantasy novelist, but it remains true for me. The following are the people that, knowingly or unknowingly, helped me work the bellows, swing the hammer, grip the tongs and mop the sweat. To all, I am grateful.

James MacMurray, for providing the very first AF artwork, and Christopher West for carrying that banner even further. Drew Staton, for letting me talk . . . a lot. Michael French, the original Coltrane. Graddy and Gamaw, for being Norman Rockwell grandparents. Matthias Weeks, for inviting me to the Basements & Drakes gaming crew and becoming my GM, my friend and my web master. Matt Gale, for his boundless friendship and shenanigans. Jake Burt, for being less a cousin, more a kid brother, and entirely a Best Man. My father, for instilling a love of the outdoors and showing me the qualities of true strength. The city of Chicago, for being my anvil. Saadi Mazjoub, because I left him out the night I became an Eagle Scout. To my fallen Hero, a sorcerer-cat and writing companion that is deeply missed. Cameron McClure, for working so hard to find this book a new home. Betsy Mitchell, for her keen eye and enthusiasm. To the two men who are more than fans, more than friends, more than brothers: Vas and Rob, thanks for sharing the battlefield with me. And finally, to my son Wyatt, for the bike rides, the dice rolls, the vermin tides, and for always finding the secret passages.

ABOUT THE AUTHOR

Jonathan French is the author of the Autumn's Fall Saga and *The Grey Bastards*. His debut novel, *The Exiled Heir*, was nominated for Best First Novel at the Georgia Author of the Year Awards in 2012. His second book, *The Errantry of Bantam Flyn*, was a top ten contender on the Kindle Norse/Viking Fantasy bestseller list. French has also served as consultant on the cultural impact of the Dungeons & Dragons franchise. He currently resides in Atlanta with his wife, son, and two cats.

THE AUTUMN'S FALL SAGA

FROM OPEN ROAD MEDIA

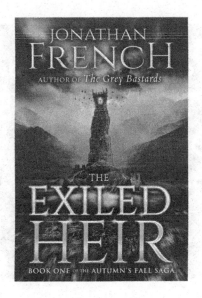

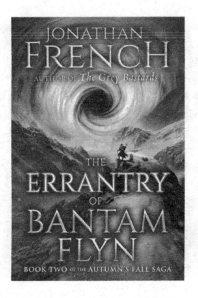

OPEN ROAD

INTEGRATED MEDIA

Find a full list of our authors and
titles at www.openroadmedia.com

FOLLOW US
@OpenRoadMedia

EARLY BIRD BOOKS

FRESH DEALS, DELIVERED DAILY

Love to read?
Love great sales?

Get fantastic deals on
bestselling ebooks delivered
to your inbox every day!

Sign up today at
earlybirdbooks.com/book